RESCUE RUN

CAPT. JAKE ROGERS' DARING
RETURN TO OCCUPIED EUROPE

The Peggy C. Saga, Volume 2

bancroft
press

JOHN WINN MILLER

PRAISE FOR *THE HUNT FOR THE PEGGY C*

AWARDS

Editor's Pick: Booklife by Publisher's Weekly
Finalist and Gold Medal: Military Writers Society of America
Finalist and Gold Medal: Literary Titan Book Award
Finalist: Page Turner Awards
Finalist: The IAN Book of the Year Award
Semi-Finalist: Clive Cussler Adventure Writers Competition
Five Stars: Readers' Favorite
Must Read and Five Stars: Reedsy Discovery

REVIEWS

"The action—and there is no shortage of it—is electrifying. Further, the author's knowledge of the relevant historical material—in particular, the naval aspects—is extraordinary. A captivating, action-packed thriller that's historically astute." — *Kirkus Reviews*

"John Winn Miller keeps his eye on the history surrounding this era, but translates it into action-packed scenarios that will delight readers looking for a backdrop of nonfiction spiced by the intrigue and psychological depth of fiction." — *Midwest Book Review*

"Moving through unpredictable, dramatic twists, its tension is resolved via gripping action scenes and moments of sacrifice, helping to make *The Hunt for Peggy C* a riveting thriller about the risk that a steamer captain takes at sea for the sake of duty and love." — *Forward Reviews*

"Miller's scenes are so vivid readers will wonder if they are reading a novel or watching a movie." — *Independent Book Review*

"Diving into an intriguing plot with complex characters and urgent human stakes, this maritime World War II thriller from Miller immediately captivates." — *Booklife by Publishers Weekly*

"This is a brilliantly researched and superbly plotted adventure story." — *Reedsy Discovery*

"A fantastic story that is highly recommended to all adults, young and old." — *Readers' Favorite*

OTHER AUTHORS

"A rare book indeed! A very well-researched and informative tale about an often-overlooked place and period in history, yet the story never gets lost in the details. Instead, this is a tense, fast-moving and stirring account of men called upon to overcome about the most daunting situations imaginable."
—**DON KEITH,** *AUTHOR, WARSHOT*

"The Hunt for the Peggy C delivers action, excitement, and romance from the very first page! Amazing in-depth research buttresses this exciting tale of believable people facing unbelievable odds. Occurring during a period of history that few know about, the story both thrills AND educates! Recommended—this is a good one!"
—**ROGER MAXIM, AUTHOR,** *THE LONG GRAY TARGET SERIES*

"Kudos to John Miller for this riveting and suspenseful tale. I was on the edge of my seat reading it! Impeccably researched, this intense sea chase has at its heart a wonderful love story that will keep you riveted until the very end! I could not put it down until I found out how it was resolved. I highly recommend this book!"
—**ROBIN HUTTON,** *AUTHOR, THE NY TIMES BESTSELLER, SGT RECKLESS: AMERICA'S WAR HORSE*

"The Hunt for the Peggy C is a *tour de force* of historical research that has pace, clarity, suspense...and perhaps most importantly, heart."
—**CHRIS EVANS,** *FORMER RANDOM HOUSE EDITOR, AUTHOR, OF BONE AND THUNDER*

"The *Peggy C* shows us the Battle of the Atlantic from an unusual perspective, that of the ordinary sailors who faced death by the guns and torpedoes of Hitler's U-boats. Miller takes us on an adventure from the Channel to the Eastern Mediterranean, as an obsessed U-boat commander pursues the equally obsessed captain of a tramp steamer. It's a story Bogart and Bacall would have been proud to star in."
—**ROBERT FARLEY,** *AUTHOR, THE BATTLESHIP BOOK*

"Pack your seabag and prepare for adventure! John Winn Miller leads the reader on a swashbuckling wartime tale of the tramp steamship *Peggy C* and its captain, Jake Rogers. This exciting tale is a page-turner from page one and will leave the reader breathless with all the action. This is a must read for historical naval fiction lovers!"
—**MATT ZULLO,** *AUTHOR, "THE US NAVY'S ON-THE-ROOF GANG" SERIES*

Cover Design: Christine Van Bree Design

Interior Design: TracyCopesCreative.com

Author Photo: Bill Roughen

978-1-61088-643-7 HC

978-1-61088-644-4 PB

978-1-61088-645-1 Ebook

978-1-61088-646-8 PDF-Ebook

978-1-61088-647-5 Audiobook

Bancroft Press

A Top-Ten Indie Since 1992

4527 Glenwood Ave.

La Crescenta, CA 91214

818-275-3061 (office)

410-764-1967 (fax)

Bruce L. Bortz, *Founder & Publisher*

Printed in the United States of America

To the brave heroes and heroines

who gave their all, and often

their lives, to defeat fascism's

heinous ideology of intoler-

ance, racism, nationalism, and

anti-Semitism.

Never again!

AUTHOR'S NOTE

Many characters in this novel are actual historical figures. In some cases, I placed them in fictional locations or situations; in other cases, I paraphrased their own words or incorporated their wartime actions into the plot. In all cases, I tried to remain true to who they were, what they would say, and what they would do, for good or evil.

At the end of this novel, you'll find a summary of what happened to them after this story ends, as well as additional background on some of the people and subjects mentioned. There is also a summary of the prequel, *The Hunt for the Peggy C*, for those who haven't read it and for others who might want a refresher.

A bibliography at the end of this book provides my sources, including memoirs, history books, biographies, government files, archives, blogs by historical societies, academic papers, museum and foundation websites, films, and documentaries.

My goal in including so much detail is to portray the time's history and technology as accurately as possible in a work of fiction that educates and engages (and often appalls) the reader. I hope I succeeded.

John Winn Miller (www.johnwinnmiller.com)
Lexington, KY
March 2024

CHAPTER 1

The torpedo shot out of the darkness through a raging sea and slammed into the steel hull amidships with the ominous clank of a death knell. At the awful sound and the steel hull's violent shudder, Capt. Jake Rogers bolted to the three small windows at the front of the wheelhouse of his newly minted American Liberty ship, the 7,100-ton SS *Charles C. Walcutt,* but couldn't see any flames or smoke. Swirling fog banks and torrential rain driven by gale-force winds shrouded the heaving North Atlantic, making it difficult to see any of the other 40-odd ships in the convoy.

"Helm, hard left!" Rogers yelled, his windburned face and hazel eyes impassive, his tall, gaunt frame rock steady, projecting a calmness for the benefit of his men that he did not feel.

"Hard left. Aye, Captain," said the young helmsman at the small wooden wheel in front of him.

Rogers slammed the General Alarm on the aft wall, setting off a loud bell, signaling the forty Merchant Marines and twenty-eight US Navy Armed Guards to man their stations. He lifted the sound-powered Hose-McCann telephone receiver on the wall, set it for Number One, the engine room, and cranked the handle. "Chief, what's the status?"

"No serious damage to the engine room, Captain. A few gauges broke, and asbestos flakes came down. We're checking the hull. Bosun's sending men to the holds."

"So, did we hit something, or did something hit us?" Rogers asked. Out of the corner of his eye, through the front windows, he glimpsed another ship ahead. "Helm, hard right," he shouted.

"Hard right. Aye, Captain," the helmsman said, spinning the wheel just in time to avoid the approaching ship. Another deafening bang rattled the ship as it slammed down from the crest of a thirty-foot wave.

"Report to me as soon as you know anything," Rogers said, slamming down the phone.

First Mate Ali Nidal rushed in from the starboard door, shaking the rain off his sou'wester hat and oilskin raincoat. "It does not appear to have been a torpedo, Captain," Nidal said, his swarthy, pockmarked visage grim as usual.

"A dud?" Rogers asked. German torpedoes sometimes failed because they struck at the wrong angle.

Stroking his black goatee, Nidal shook his head. "I do not believe so. If it was, we should have been struck by other torpedoes by now. Must be something else," said the Tunisian, one of the few men aboard with whom Rogers had sailed before and trusted completely. They had barely survived their last voyage together on the ancient tramp steamer the *Peggy C*, one-third the size of their current ship.

Steel scraping across steel caused a dreadful shriek—something that meant serious trouble. "Take the watch. Keep the men at their stations until I find out what's going on," Rogers said, pointing at Nidal with a crooked right arm that he couldn't straighten out all the way. Gunfire from a German Armed Raider had shattered it during a surprise attack on the *Peggy C*. "And continue evasive action." He threw on his rain gear, including rubber boots and gloves, grabbed a large flashlight, and ducked out into the driving rain, slipping in his haste down the ladder almost to the main deck three stories below. He leaned over the starboard bulwark and searched the hull with short flashlight bursts. Trying to avoid detection by any nearby U-boat, he inched his way toward the stern. Relentless waves rammed him back against the main deckhouse.

To continue his inspection, Rogers had to tug his way along the bulwark, head down and leaning at almost a forty-five-degree angle against the wind. He anchored his feet from one metal stanchion on the side to another like rungs on a ladder.

"Come see this, Captain," a voice called out behind him. The nearby sailor clicked a flashlight on and off his face in a short burst so Rogers could see he was the ship's bosun. Able Seaman Thomas Vimont, who oversaw the deck crew, was one of the older crew members, having "come up through the hawse pipes," what sailors said of someone who had risen in the ranks without much formal education.

Vimont led Rogers forward toward the bow and pointed his flashlight down from where the superstructure met the hatch for Hold Number Three.

In front of them was a horrifying sight: a long, jagged tear stretched up the hull where two prefabricated sections of the Liberty ship had been welded together. The tear seemed to grow with each bounce of the ship on the turbulent waters. The bosun clicked off the flashlight.

"Station two men here to monitor the damage!" Rogers shouted over the howling wind. "Have one of them run up to the wheelhouse every five minutes and report to me. Send two others down below to check inside Hold Number Three and report back to me in the wheelhouse on the phone. Is that clear?"

"Aye, aye, Captain," Vimont said.

"And tell Chief to organize a damage control team with Chips to see if we can do anything to patch it up from inside!" Rogers yelled, using the nickname for the ship's carpenter.

The bosun motioned over an immense black sailor named Obasi, who always hovered about whenever the captain was on deck or in dangerous situations. Rogers smiled at his old friend before running to the officers' mess. There, Chief Steward Cookie, another old friend and cook from the *Peggy C*, and the other stewards had laid out bandages, yellow sulfa powder, and other medical supplies on tables in preparation for treating the wounded. "All set, Cap'n," said the portly Brit. With molted jowls and thin white tufts of hair on his bald head, he was easy to spot.

Rogers saluted and struggled back up the ladder to the wheelhouse. "She's coming apart, Mr. Nidal," Rogers said, brushing back his wavy brown hair as rain streamed off him.

"How is that possible?" Nidal asked. "Were we hit?"

"I have no idea. Didn't look like damage from a torpedo. But sections are splitting apart. Bosun and the Chief are checking it out," Rogers said, scanning the ocean through the windows with large binoculars. Visibility was less than the length of a football field. "Helmsman, hard right. All ahead slow."

"Hard right. All ahead slow. Aye, aye, Captain."

"We will lose the convoy," Nidal said.

"No choice," Rogers said. "We have to slow down and get out of the way." U-boats were always lurking about, waiting for a lame duck like his ship to fall behind and become easy prey. It was a terrible dilemma. But Rogers couldn't risk endangering the other ships in the east-bound convoy.

HX-229 ships were trying to maintain a rectangular formation with five columns 1,000 yards apart and 600 yards from the stern of one ship to the bow of the trailing vessel.

It didn't take Rogers long to do the math. The convoy was moving at seven knots, the slowest ship's speed in rough seas. If his ship slowed down to even three knots to do repairs, it would take less than five minutes for the trailing ship to ram his ship. With the *Charles C. Walcutt* blacked-out except for a low-voltage, shielded blue light on its stern—a light that couldn't be seen in such low visibility in time to prevent a disaster—she would be all but invisible. And that assumed the ships could maintain any semblance of a convoy formation in the violent seas. That near-impossibility made the situation even more dangerous and unpredictable.

They were on their own. No rescue ships were assigned to this convoy. And it was too dark to get protection from covering aircraft, even if the convoy wasn't in the dreaded "Black Pit." The 300-mile-wide gap from east to west in the middle of the North Atlantic was out of range for almost all land-based planes from either America or England. It was a hell of a way for Rogers to celebrate his fortieth birthday, an hour away on St. Patrick's Day, 1943.

A burst of light flooded the wheelhouse before the sound caught up, rattling the windows and sending shock waves through the ship. Tentacles of yellow and orange flames ripped through the sky. A second blast followed within seconds. Given the proximity, Rogers guessed it was the Norwegian motor ship *Elin K*, carrying a load of manganese, an essential ingredient for stainless steel used to make helmets and other military equipment.

"Those were definitely torpedoes," Rogers said. But he could do nothing about it as his ship fell farther behind its assigned position in the convoy. He could only hope any survivors would be picked up by one of the four destroyers in their escort or by the lone corvette, a lightly armed warship smaller than a destroyer that could match the speed and range of U-boats.

At the whining squeal of the sound-powered phone, Rogers hustled to the back of the wheelhouse to answer it. "Chief here, Captain. We've got a real problem. Hold Number Three is flooded, and we can't get to the crack for repairs. We'll have to try to weld it from the outside."

"Using a blow torch would attract every U-boat for miles, even if we could get someone safely over the side in this weather," Rogers said. "Can you pump out the hold enough to lower a welder inside?"

"Possibly. But we'd have to come to almost a full stop." A full stop would kill any hope of catching up with the convoy, even at his ship's top speed of 11.5 knots, which wasn't possible anyway. She was loaded down with 8,000 tons of steel, cotton, and food and had a deck crammed with aircraft, tractors, and trucks.

The proud stevedores in New York had bragged that the *Charles C. Walcutt* was "full and down," meaning they had accomplished the rare feat of filling all her cargo space so that she was loaded down to her white-painted Plimsoll lines, marking how low the hull was in the water. That wasn't true. The Plimsoll line was *below* the waterline, and his ship was clearly overloaded. It didn't matter for Rogers' ship. It was wartime, and being beyond capacity was a necessity, even if it meant his ship was slower and more unwieldy than usual.

"Helm, all ahead slow," Rogers said.

"All ahead slow. Aye, Captain," the helmsman said, pulling the handle to his right back and forth on the brass engine order telegraph, which was connected to the engine room's telegraph by a chain. He halted the arrow on "ahead slow," which the engine room acknowledged by repeating the steps with a loud clanging of the telegraph's bell.

"Chief," Rogers said into the telephone, "you've got less than five hours until sunrise to make repairs. After that, we've got to make a run for Liverpool as best we can."

"Aye, aye, Captain."

"And send someone to find Bosun and tell him to deploy the torpedo nets." The nets were interlocking steel rings attached to cargo booms lowered to ninety degrees port and starboard. They only protected about three-quarters of the hulls, but that was better than nothing.

Rogers returned to the windows and searched the turbulent sea with his binoculars. In the distance, a cargo ship passed through the fog to his port, its blue taillight fading like a dying ember. The passing of what sailors called the "coffin corner"—the last ship on the starboard column of a convoy—meant they were now utterly alone and at the mercy of luck and the weather.

Urgent ship alarms wailed in the distance. Rapid explosions shot flames and billowing smoke sky high, illuminating dreaded silhouettes: conical towers atop low-slung hulls of U-boats. The German subs blasted away with their 8.8cm deck guns and launched torpedoes as they wove in and out of the columns like steel sharks in a savage frenzy among lumbering whales. More torpedoes found their mark, turning the whole area into a horrible scene of shooting flames and burning metal.

Rogers pivoted to US Navy Ensign Johnny Mitchell standing at his battle station in the wheelhouse. "We have reduced speed," Rogers said. "So, I'd advise you to hold your fire unless you're 100 percent certain you see a target."

"That is my decision, sir," Mitchell said. Rogers had no authority over the Armed Guards, and relations were not always the best between the naval personnel and the unionized Merchant Marines, who were employed by private companies and paid higher salaries, including combat bonuses, than the Navy. The Armed Guards, most of whom had never been to sea before, were bitter about being the "Navy's stepchildren" and often derided by sailors as "fish food" on suicide missions.

"Of course, Ensign," said Rogers, who always went out of his way to be deferential to the sensitive young officer. "But if you open fire while we can't maneuver, you'll be sending a signal flare to all the U-boats to come pick off an easy trophy. Better to let them keep moving away with the convoy."

There was a long pause. "OK, Captain. I understand. We'll keep our powder dry as long as we can."

"Thanks. And you should know that we have developed a serious crack in the starboard hull amidships. If it gets worse, I'll recommend you pull your men on the bow back to the stern."

"Aye, aye, Captain." Using his helmet phone, Mitchell told the chief gunner's mate in the stern gun tub, who commanded the ship's primary weapon—a 4-inch 50-caliber gun that required at least seven men to operate—to hold his fire. He repeated the commands to crews manning the 3-inch 50-caliber gun in the bow, the 20mm Oerlikon anti-aircraft machine guns on the four corners of the main deckhouse, and the two 20mm Oerlikon guns atop the poop deck at the stern.

They all huddled in the driving rain in their semi-circular gun tubs made of "plastic armor," a made-up name to confuse the Germans. It was actually a thin steel plate covered with a layer of stones mixed with asphalt that would deflect bullets and not shatter as concrete barriers would.

Although there were many weapons on the *Charles C. Walcutt*, they were primarily defensive. In the event of an enemy attack, the recommended course of action was to flee and use the stern gun for cover. That was another source of bitterness among the Armed Guards. They had joined the Navy to *attack* the enemy, not run away, a frustration reflected in a derisive sign at one training center: "Ready—Aim—Abandon Ship!"

A speeding British corvette hurtled past Rogers' ship, churning up a foamy wake as it chased the U-boats into the flaming convoy, its spotlight swirling around. As it roared away, the corvette launched a flurry of barrel-shaped depth charges over both sides of the ship. They exploded with bone-jarring thumps in rapid succession, triggering geysers of water and sound waves that rocked the *Charles C. Walcutt*.

Long-tailed snowflake flares, tracer bullets, and bursts of star shells lit up the sky over another exploding cargo ship. Rogers never understood the use of flares because, in his opinion, they simply made the Allied ships easier targets. He couldn't be sure what ship had been attacked because Liberty ships painted over their names after launching so the Germans couldn't track them. But based on its position in the convoy, it appeared to be the SS *James Oglethorpe*. It, too, was on its maiden Atlantic crossing, aflame and listing to its starboard.

Desperate sailors scrambled over the decks, some fighting to lower two lifeboats. One boat flipped over when someone prematurely cut the fall—the rope and blocks used to lower the boats from davits—and dumped more than a dozen men into the icy sea. Death for them was mere minutes away.

Rogers let out a silent curse as he lowered his binoculars, unable to watch any longer. He had repeatedly drilled everyone on his ship to lower the lifeboats slowly and safely. Now, there was nothing he could do to help as the wounded ship circled out of control to port.

One of the rain-drenched sailors who had been monitoring the crack in the hull darted in the starboard door. "Come quick, Captain! You gotta see this!"

Rogers followed the sailor down the ladders to another sailor, holding a large flashlight. He handed it to the captain with a shaking hand. When Rogers pointed the flashlight down onto the hull, a chill shot up and down his spine. The crack was still growing.

CHAPTER 2

Rogers raced back into the wheelhouse, headed straight for the telephone, and cranked it. As he waited for the chief to respond, he shouted to Mitchell, "Ensign, get your gunners to the stern! Now. And tell them to wait for further instructions. I repeat, await further instructions."

"Aye, aye, Captain."

"Mr. Nidal, get the men to their boat stations." In frustration, Rogers hung up the phone and rushed back to the starboard door, stopping and calling out. "And get the lifeboats overboard and rigged for quick launching. Drop over the Jacob ladders and the scrambling nets. But nobody moves to abandon ship. We do not want to create a panic."

Rogers was gone before Nidal could verbally acknowledge the command. At the bottom of the ladder on the main deck, he bumped into Obasi. "Where's the Chief?" Rogers said.

The Nigerian sailor motioned the captain forward to the cracked-open hatch of Hold Number Three, one of five cargo holds in the ship. Inside, the chief and a welder, wearing metal face shields, hung halfway down the flooded compartment on bosun chairs of wooden planks between two ropes. They struggled to weld a metal sheet over the gushing crack in the hull.

When he succeeded in reducing the flow of seawater to a trickle, the welder killed his blowtorch and signaled for Obasi and other sailors standing above to haul him and the chief up. As soon as his feet hit the deck, the chief flipped up the face cover and sucked in the frigid air. "That'll only last for a short while, I'm afraid, Captain," he said. "The damage is right at the engine room bulkhead."

"And the engines?"

"Fine for now. But I'm not sure what's going to give first, the bulkhead or the hull. I've never seen or heard of anything like this. Not on a Liberty ship.

Not on any ship, for that matter."

"All right," Rogers said. "Let's get back underway and hope the patch holds." Distant flashes filled the sky ahead, followed by the rumblings of explosions and the rat-tat-tat of gunfire. Smoke redolent of cordite rolled by. Rogers got the attention of Obasi and the bosun. "Set up tag teams to keep watch inside the hatch and tell them to do their best to shade their flashlights."

"Aye, aye, Captain," the bosun said, waving over sailors from their boat stations and giving them their assignments.

Ensign Mitchell skidded down from the wheelhouse ladder and tapped Rogers on the shoulder. "What about my men?"

"Bow's still not safe. But they can return to their gun positions aft and atop the wheelhouse. We're far enough away from the fighting that you might consider securing from General Quarters to a modified Battle Stations Condition One. Let them get some food and rest where they are."

"I appreciate your concern for my men, Captain," Mitchell said, apparently doing his best to follow naval training and not irritate the much older ship master. "But I think it best to continue with General Quarters. Including in the bow."

Rogers paused for a moment, considering how to respond. "I'll have Cookie send some stewards with food and hot coffee for your men."

"Thank you, Captain. Very kind of you," Mitchell said, appearing taken aback by Rogers' generosity.

"Listen, son. I know being in command's hard," Rogers said, putting his hand on Mitchell's shoulder. "You're doing what you believe is right. I respect that. Just always take care of your men." With that, Rogers headed back to the wheelhouse. "All ahead half," he said to the helmsman, who acknowledged the order and rang the engine order telegraph.

When the engine kicked in, the ship rumbled. As he scanned the darkness outside with his binoculars, Rogers worried about a surprise attack and wondered what the hell had damaged the brand new "ugly duckling" he commanded.

Three years before, Liberty ships didn't even exist. Newspapers called the boxy ship—the length of a forty-story building and six stories wide—an "ugly duckling" because it had been designed to eliminate as many time-intensive, manufactured curves as possible; President Franklin D. Roosevelt dubbed it a "Liberty ship." Like so many other things in the war, they were invented out of necessity and produced on a scale and speed never seen before.

Each ship was a Herculean task involving 250,000 parts, forty-three miles of welding, five miles of wiring, and seven miles of piping. But the new method of building the ships in sections all over the country and welding them together in one port created unforeseen problems. Welding the hulls was faster and required less steel and used fewer workers than traditional riveting. As Rogers was learning, the welds sometimes cracked in cold water or rough seas.

Rogers got a few hours of sleep in "full rig," not even taking off his boots, before returning to the wheelhouse at dawn. The rain had stopped, but intermittent fog still limited visibility, and the swells had dissipated to a more manageable ten to twenty feet.

"Nothing to report, Captain," Nidal said. "We are proceeding at 3 knots but not making much headway. Chief says the patch appears to be holding well enough."

"Good. Go get some rest and—"

"Torpedo trail sighted three points to port!" yelled Mitchell as he ran back out to the flying bridge in front of the wheelhouse.

"Hard right, Helmsman. Full speed ahead," Rogers commanded, sounding the alarm throughout the ship for General Quarters.

As soon as the helmsman acknowledged the order and rang the engine room, Nidal said to Rogers, "Captain, are you sure that is wise? Even in these seas, the hull might not be able to take it."

"No choice. The greater danger is staying a sitting duck. Have Sparks send an S-O-S," Rogers said, referring to the radio operator. "And S-S-S, so the Brits know we're being attacked by a submarine, for whatever good that'll do us."

Grabbing his helmet and life jacket, Rogers raced outside to join Mitchell at the far end of the flying bridge. The ship rocked to starboard when the rudder shifted and to port as the engines revved up to full speed.

Together, the two men searched the turbulent waters with their binoculars for the tell-tale phosphorescent trail of a torpedo, a cigar-shaped canister the length of a truck that carried 617 pounds of explosives at 30 knots.

"There!" Mitchell said, pointing to port. The torpedo raced toward the fo'c'sle outside the torpedo net, where the bow gun crew gawked, helpless. Rogers followed the trail backward until he spotted a U-boat bouncing in and out of sight on the waves a mile or two away. The Germans often fired torpedoes in groups of two or three and would close fast on a target to finish the job using the 8.8cm gun on their forward decks.

Rogers could see no other trails, but that was little comfort; some torpedoes with magnetic triggers traveled deep below the surface to explode under ships and couldn't always be spotted in time for evasive action.

He searched the clearing skies in a futile hope some plane could miraculously penetrate the Black Pit and save his ship. As he lowered his binoculars, the torpedo passed a few yards ahead of the prow. The gunners jumped and cheered. Mitchell exhaled sharply in relief until Rogers pointed out the U-boat closing in for the kill. A U-boat could travel at 17 knots, which meant Rogers had little hope of outrunning it.

"Ah, hell," Mitchell said, raising his binoculars and fighting to appear calm. "Any chance you could ask the helmsman to keep us stern on so my crew can get a clean shot?"

Rogers said he would do so and returned to the wheelhouse. "Helm, set a course for 150 degrees and zigzag at thirty-second intervals. Give me flank speed." As the helmsman repeated the instructions and rang the engine order telegraph, a whistle sounded over his head from the brass speaking tube. Rogers popped out the rubber stopper. "Captain here."

"Captain, flank speed on these waves could put too much stress on the crack."

"We just dodged one torpedo, Chief, and the U-boat is on our tail."

"Flank speed it is, Captain. And the torpedo nets?"

Rogers thought the matter over. "They only cut our speed by a knot or so. Better to have the protection."

The entire ship shook and banged as cresting waves lifted the racing propellor out of the water and smashed the hull into a trough. Rogers jogged outside to the far port wing of the flying bridge to see what was happening. Mitchell, using his telephone headset, directed the gun crew on the stern's

4-inch 50-caliber gun.

One gunner's mate lugged a thirty-three-pound shell from the ready magazine and shoved it into the breach. Other sweaty Armed Guards and Merchant Marines relayed shells up into the gun tub from the magazines below deck. Another gunner called out the distance, "3,500 yards," well within the gun's 9,000-yard range, but the fast-approaching U-boat was still a difficult target. Mitchell ordered the gun elevated to aim at its conning tower.

"Fire!"

The gun cracked with a violent recoil. The Armed Guards didn't wait to see the results before cleaning the barrel and reloading. In theory, they could fire eight or nine shots a minute. They would be lucky to get off a couple a minute in wartime, under fire, on a rolling sea and a weaving ship. The first shot landed short of the U-boat. The Germans returned fire with their deck gun, using similar-sized shells as the Americans' but with a longer range.

Shells exploded all around the *Charles C. Walcutt*. Water domes shot up, rattling the lifeboats dangling over the bulwarks like trinkets on a baby's mobile. Mitchell's crew matched the U-boat shot for shot, but it was clear the Germans were gaining ground and would soon give up the useless deck gun and return to using torpedoes.

"Launch three smoke floats!" Mitchell yelled. His crew fired off the 165-pound canisters full of a toxic mixture of hexachloroethane, zinc oxide, and aluminum that could produce thick clouds of smoke lasting twenty minutes or so. Mitchell phoned the bridge, where Mr. Nidal stood watch. "I'll try to give us some cover from the torpedoes, Mr. Nidal. But I don't think it will fool them for long."

"Do what you think best, Ensign Mitchell," Nidal replied. He stepped outside onto the flying bridge to consult with Rogers. "We might want to prepare to abandon ship once they run out of smoke floats, Captain."

"They've only fired three. They have seven more. So, let's wait and see."

"It is hopeless, Captain. No one will come to our rescue."

"Such a pessimist, Mr. Nidal," Rogers said with a thin smile. It wasn't the first time they had found themselves in an impossible position.

Their last ship, the tramp steamer *Peggy C*, had outrun a pursuing U-boat for thousands of miles in a desperate rescue of Miriam Maduro and her Jewish relatives. It ended up at the bottom of the Mediterranean but took the chasing U-boat with it. Leaving Miriam, the love of his life, safe in Palestine so he could return to America was the hardest thing Rogers had ever done. Nidal had initially called that escape attempt "hopeless." Rogers was betting he would be wrong again.

For several tense hours, neither ship could make much headway or aim with any accuracy in the rough seas. From time to time, the Armed Guards launched a smoke float, obscuring their position and giving Rogers time to maneuver away from any torpedo's path. By 4:30 p.m., the sun had almost set, and Mitchell was down to his last smoke float.

Once night came, all hope would be lost. The moon would be close to full, making the *Charles C. Walcutt* as brightly outlined as a slow-moving duck cutout at a shooting gallery.

Rogers stood on the port wing of the flying bridge, kneading his lower lip between his thumb and forefinger. He estimated the U-boat had made up half the distance between them. Now he had a decision to make: abandon ship or risk being blown to smithereens with all hands on board.

He hated to quit. He couldn't help but recall a quote from one of his favorite characters in one of the books he so loved. "Once you eliminate the impossible, whatever remains, no matter how improbable, must be the truth." Sherlock Holmes' advice had always served him well.

Outrunning the U-boat was impossible. Outgunning it was impossible. Letting all these men die for a futile effort was impossible. The remaining answer was an orderly abandonment of the ship. Mitchell and the Armed Guards would resist because they were under orders never to let a Liberty ship fall into the enemy's hands. Rogers would try to give them enough time to set detonation charges and safely join him in the last lifeboat.

As he headed into the wheelhouse to announce his decision, a noise made him twist around and cock his head to listen, searching the sky for what sounded like the faintest whine of engines. *Impossible? Wishful thinking?* Tapping on the door's window, he motioned Nidal outside to the windy flying bridge. "Do you hear something?"

Nidal shook his head and headed back inside. Then a blinding circle of light flooded the bridge, freezing both men in their tracks. It moved aft over the stern and out to sea, heading straight for the U-boat. The two men exchanged looks and followed the dancing light with their binoculars.

High above, Rogers found the light's source: an airplane with a glass cone on its long nose, four engines on longer-than-normal wings, and a flat tail with what appeared to be upright cafeteria trays at the tips. A giant spotlight hanging on its front held the U-boat captive as the plane descended and dropped depth charges. "I don't believe it," Rogers said. "A Liberator. Must be one of the long-range ones."

"Are they not all bombing Germany?"

"I guess not."

The U-boat raced forward to submerge in a crash dive, but not fast enough. On its second pass, the bomber hit home, buckling the U-boat in an arc of flames and smoke. Cheers erupted all around the *Charles C. Walcutt*. Rogers winked at Nidal, "Never bet against my luck. Now, let's get out of here and find the convoy."

Mitchell skipped up the ladder and slapped Rogers and Nidal on their backs, making even the taciturn Nidal crack a smile. They laughed, inhaling deeply, invigorated at being alive and still aboard their ship.

The celebration came to an abrupt halt when the bridge rumbled as if the ship had driven over an old country road lined with lots and lots of potholes, each bigger and deeper than the one before. To keep from falling, the three men grabbed tight to the rails.

A massive pop rang out as loud as an explosion, followed by an earsplitting screech of tearing metal. Rogers covered his ears as the ship's bow lurched up, knocking him and the other two men off their feet. Struggling to pull himself up on the rail, Rogers had to blink repeatedly and shake his head, not believing his eyes:

The entire front half of the ship, from the tip of the prow to the wheelhouse amidships, had broken loose and was floating away, the ocean's ferocious waves clawing it down to a watery grave.

The *Charles C. Walcutt* had split in half.

CHAPTER 3

The aft end of the ship slowly settled down, but forward, planes, tractors, and trucks slid off the deck into the sea. Frantic Armed Guards scurried from the gun tubs and hurled themselves into the frigid waters rushing over the bow, their helmeted heads bobbing as they floated away into the darkness with the safety lights pinned on their life jackets blinking red.

"My men!" Mitchell shouted at Rogers.

"We'll swing around and grab them as soon as we get the lifeboats launched," Rogers said, amazed his portion of the ship was still afloat. He hurried into the wheelhouse, pulled the whistle chord for three long blasts to signal "abandon ship," and called out to the helmsman, "Ring Finished with Engines."

The terrified young sailor didn't move, holding on tight to the wheel. "I said, 'Ring Finished with Engines.'" When the helmsman didn't move fast enough, Rogers rang the engine order telegraph himself and pried the sailor's shaking hands off the wheel. "Head to your boat station," he said without anger or disapproval. *The boy was upset enough.*

The sailor gazed at his captain with terror in his eyes and mumbled something before taking off through the starboard door.

Rogers snatched the weighted box containing the codebook and the ship's confidential papers and followed him out and down the ladder to his boat station. There were two twenty-six-foot-long metal lifeboats on either side of the deckhouse. The Maritime Commission designed the eight-foot-wide vessels to hold twenty men each, although they could, in a pinch, accommodate up to thirty-one. Crew members had raised the cargo booms with the torpedo nets and were already lowering the lifeboats as sailors and Armed Guards crawled over the bulwarks and down scramble nets and Jacob's ladders.

As soon as the keels splashed into the water, boat crews released the falls and struggled to hold the boats steady for the men to jump aboard. Some missed and had to be fished out of the water while the boat crews used eight-foot-long wooden boathooks to keep the lifeboats from being smashed against the ship's tilting hull.

Despite Rogers' best efforts at training, everything was chaotic. Panicked men shouted, running around, scrambling in vain for their proper boat station. Others flung themselves into the freezing water. Still others jerked out the pins to release two ten-foot-square balsawood life rafts over the side and tried to leap on them. Most missed and had to pull themselves to the rafts with the "painter," a long, thick tow rope connected to the raft.

After tossing the weighted box over the bulwark, Rogers stumbled around the deckhouse to the port side to ensure the two boats there had gotten away. Instead, he found men fighting and shoving Nidal and the second mate, desperate to crowd aboard the half-lowered boats. Shaking with anger, Rogers grabbed and shoved sailors, yelling at them to calm down, but most couldn't hear him, and those who could paid no attention to him.

One of the boats flipped over, dumping a half-dozen men into the heaving sea. Nidal was able to right it and lower it with him in it. After watching the other boat safely descend into the water, Rogers returned to his station.

Seeing no more men on the decks, he scampered down the side of the hull and hopped into his crowded boat, almost falling. "Free the falls!" he shouted, indicating the men should unhook the ropes that lowered the boat from the davits. "Now, ship the oars and push her away!" Rogers shouted at the four-man lifeboat crew.

They didn't have to be asked twice to insert the oars into the oarlocks and pull, but the towering waves slammed them back no matter how hard they rowed.

"Pull, damn it, pull!" Rogers screamed, holding tight to the tiller.

The men redoubled their efforts, straining every muscle they had, but couldn't escape the steel sword of Damocles looming over them. The curling waves continued to threaten to overturn them.

In frustration, Rogers tried to lend a hand. But something was out of place. The metal cradles used to lower the lifeboats were still attached to the bottom of the boat. "Release the damn cradles!" Rogers shouted. As soon as that was done, the lifeboat sprang away from the ship.

Steering the lifeboat in a wide arc toward the bow, Rogers hoped to pluck some of the Armed Guards out of the water before they froze to death, despite their thick life jackets. They were stuffed with kapok, a fiber from kapok tree pods that weighed one-eighth as much as cotton and could support thirty times its weight in water.

Their emergency whistles shrilled all around, but no blinking lights were visible except the ones casting eerie red shadows on the faces of the fourteen frightened men in Rogers' own boat. As they rode up a mountainous wave, flashlights from the other three lifeboats illuminated the waters around the almost immersed bow and the thrashing Armed Guards being reeled into safety. That was a relief until ...

"Captain, we're leaking everywhere!" someone shouted over the wind, swirling with the beginnings of a snow squall.

"Start bailing with the bucket. Use your boots, your hands—anything you can find!" Rogers shouted, handing off the tiller to another sailor so he could work his way forward to deal with the leaks. Frigid water gushed in from several gashes, probably caused by the earlier explosion of U-boat shells, and had filled the boat up to the thwarts. "Cookie, use whatever you can find to plug the holes."

"Aye, aye, Captain," said the Brit. Because he knew everything about ships, Cookie didn't panic.

"Bloody hell. Too many holes!" Cookie shouted after repeated attempts to stuff the gashes with blankets and spare life jackets.

"Keep bailing. We gotta make it to the other lifeboats," Rogers said, fighting to keep the small craft on course to the flashing lights ahead.

The four sailors strained at their oars, their hands almost frozen to the wood, their faces determined but making little headway over the furious waves.

Rogers fired a flare from a snub-nosed Very pistol in hopes the others would spot the distress signal and row in their direction. The flare's bright glare illuminated the boats, but only one was nearby, piloted by the second mate. The other two had been driven apart by the storm and were fading behind sheets of snow.

Rogers' lifeboat inched nearer the other lifeboat, only to be tossed farther away by foaming waves and wind. Before long, the two vessels steered close enough for the sailors to throw ropes to each other and pull their boats together with a grinding crunch. Cookie and Rogers helped the sailors and Armed Guards across and hurriedly handed over all the emergency supplies they could gather before joining the others in the second mate's now seriously overcrowded lifeboat.

The extra weight lowered its freeboard, similar to the Plimsoll line designating overloading, to within inches of the water's surface. The drenched men squeezed into any space left in the boat, but some were forced to stand while straining to keep their balance. As the rowers pulled away from the *Charles C. Walcutt*, the bow pointed to the sky and slid under the waves in a gurgle of bubbles; the stern section remained eerily afloat, a chicken with its head cut off and refusing to fall.

The second mate kept the lifeboat headed into the ever-growing swells to prevent it from being swamped or flipped. Through the jam-packed men, Rogers made his way with difficulty to the bow, and streamed a sea anchor, a cone-shaped canvas bag attached to a thick rope tossed in front of a lifeboat to keep it heading into the waves. With Obasi's help, Rogers dumped a bucket of bunker oil over the bow with the wind to their backs—what sailors call windward—to break the heavy seas.

There was no sense using a compass or trying to set a course. All they could do was ride out the storm and wait for daylight. As the lifeboat ascended the crest of one whitecap, Rogers spotted blinking red lights around a lifeboat but lost sight of them until the next crest. The lights appeared to be around the boat, not in it. He focused the flashlight on a wallowing hull, where men were clinging to steel grab rails attached to the lifeboat's underside.

One of the men appeared to have a goatee. A wide-eyed Rogers fought his way through the mass of men to the stern, waving his arm toward the upturned boat and shouting at the second mate, "Port! Steer to port!"

"I'm trying, Captain. But she's not responding. And if I make too sharp a turn, we'll be swamped," the second mate said.

"I don't care. We have to save them!" He shoved aside one of the exhausted rowers and began pulling himself. "Pull, men! Pull!"

The second mate fought the tiller, and the sailors made a mighty effort, but to no avail; the sea wouldn't loosen its grip. A powerful comber swept over the lifeboat, tossing it back and almost flipping it.

Rogers stopped rowing and instructed another sailor to take his place. "You're not trying hard enough!" he yelled. "Pull, pull! And you," he said, pointing at the second mate, "you're a worthless son of—"

"Captain!" Cookie yelled, grabbing Rogers by the shoulders and shaking him. "They're doing the best they can."

"But Nidal." Rogers waved his hands. "He's there. I saw him. We have to save him."

Cookie clutched Rogers' arms and tried to calm him down, speaking in low tones so no one else could hear. "If you keep making them try, our boat will be swamped, and we will all die." Rogers stopped squirming and focused his watery eyes on Cookie. "These men are counting on you to do—what do you always say?—the right thing. Now sit down and help row."

With the realization sinking in that there was no way to save his friend and the rest of the crew, Rogers grabbed one of the oars and pulled mechanically, staring straight ahead, the glow of red flashes from his safety light casting shadows on the sullen men. "Kill the damn emergency lights. You want a U-boat to machine gun us?!" Rogers shouted, unplugging his own light with an angry jerk and returning to his mindless rowing.

By daybreak, the other lifeboats had disappeared, and the ghostly hulk of the *Charles C. Walcutt's* stern, hovering behind them on the horizon, was somehow still afloat. The sea had calmed enough for Rogers to steer the lifeboat east toward Ireland.

With the sun hidden behind black and gray clouds, the sextant was of no use to Rogers, who focused all his attention on a compass and his charts—fortunately, part of the emergency kit on all lifeboats. He tried not to let the men see how distraught he was.

Cookie distributed the rations of one spoonful of pemmican—a mixture of tallow, dried meat, and berries in round tin cans—one Horlick's malted milk tablet, one piece of chocolate, and half a dipper of water.

Around midday, the second mate stepped the mast and raised the small red sail used by most Liberty ships' lifeboats. Rogers maneuvered the tiller while Obasi kneeled in front of him, holding the compass. "Cookie, try to inventory the food and water."

"Aye, aye, Captain." The chore was easier said than done. Cookie had to twist and wiggle through the overcrowded lifeboat carrying thirty-nine shivering men, well over its capacity. Men grumbled as Cookie made them move out of his way so he could inspect the lockers under the thwarts.

Rogers estimated they were around 500 nautical miles from land. Still, it was hard to project how many days the journey would take because of the wind-driven waves breaking over the gunwales from all sides, drenching the men, and knocking the lifeboat around like a cork. The wind had freshened, the seas were getting higher, and conditions were ripe for a worse storm to blow up without warning.

To be safe, Rogers rationed the provisions based on twenty days at sea, a bare subsistence amount of food and water. The sailors took turns bailing and rowing, standing and sitting, and passing around a bucket to use as a toilet. Every one of them kept a weathered eye on the horizon in the slim hope of spotting a ship, but shifting fog banks and sheets of rain squalls cut visibility to almost nil.

As the day grew darker, Cookie handed out reduced rations, drawing loud murmurs of discontent from men facing another wretched and terrifying night adrift at sea. Rogers leaned against the stern planking, staring blankly ahead, paying no attention to the sailor at the tiller and brooding about his lost friend Nidal.

☆☆☆

For two awful, blustery days of bitter cold, pounding rain, and swirling snow, they tacked over monstrous White Horses—what sailors called cresting waves—and rotated men on the four oars. With no sun or stars, Rogers couldn't know how far they had traveled or how far they had to go.

Out of desperation, the sailors crafted a small fire from pieces of a spare oar they stacked into a bucket. Matches were kept in a Mason jar, so there was no trouble finding dry ones to light the fire. The men took turns huddling under a tarp to keep out the waves and warming themselves, a temporary but welcome respite from the bone-chilling cold.

Several men became too sick to move. Obasi and the others covered them with blankets and rubbed their hands and feet. On the third night, fewer men were fit to row, and there was no need for the toilet bucket. The sailors were dehydrated and starving.

The monotony of leaden skies, shifting fog banks, and the rhythmic grating of the oarlocks cast most of the men into a kind of trance, mumbling their daydreams of home and warm food. Some had to be restrained from drinking seawater while others babbled to themselves.

"What's that?!" someone shouted.

Rogers snapped out of his reverie and searched the darkened sea.

"Off the starboard bow! See it?" another voice called out.

Rogers couldn't see anything because the lifeboat was in a deep trough, but when it crested on a wave, a distant outline of what might be a ship appeared in the mist. As the lifeboat plunged into a deep trough and then rode another crest, the men screamed and jumped up, waving shirts, blankets, and oars. Rogers focused his binoculars on the silhouette. *It must be a ship.* He pulled out his Very pistol and fired a distress flare.

All the men plugged in the emergency lights on the collars of their life jackets, hoping the flashing red lights would draw the ship's attention.

On the next crest, they were disappointed. The ship—if it had been a ship—had vanished into the mist and fog. As the cheering and waving sputtered out, the glum sailors looked to their captain for guidance. Rogers lit the boat's lantern and waved it while keeping the binoculars pressed to his eyes. He held his breath as the lifeboat soared to the top of the next wave.

There it was: a merchant ship, all lit up, heading their way from out of a fog bank. Cheers erupted among the huddled sailors; they staggered to their feet and waved.

"Sit down, men!" Rogers shouted. "Strike sail and row with all your might for the lee side." The ship should shield them enough from the wind so everyone could climb aboard without the steel hull smashing their tiny lifeboat to pieces. Rogers plucked the tiller from the second mate and directed their bobbing and weaving craft as close as he dared to the ship's hull. There, spotlights shined on "EIRE" amidships in giant letters and the green, white, and orange flag of Ireland at the bow and stern.

White letters on the bow said, *Irish Palm*. The Irish crew unfurled a Jacob's ladder and tossed long ropes to the sailors below, who lashed them to their swaying and pitching lifeboat. One by one, the trembling survivors leaped for the ladder and scurried up to safety.

After the last sailor was aboard, Rogers waited for the crest of a wave and vaulted to the ladder's wooden planks. The frozen hand on his crooked right arm couldn't get a good enough grip, and his feet slipped off the rungs, leaving him dangling by one hand in the bitter wind and waves, banging hard against the steel hull like a bell clapper. His left hand slipped.

In desperation, he slapped his right hand on the ladder, hoping against hope it would awaken his frozen hand enough to close his fingers on the rope. It didn't work. Down below, his own black pit loomed.

Pain shot through his neck as his collar jerked against his Adam's apple, abruptly stopping his fall and giving him enough time to lodge his boots on the rungs. Obasi, holding on tight, helped him claw his way up and over the bulwark. "Thank you, Obasi," he said, hugging the massive African. "This time, we truly are even."

Obasi smiled and shook his head. "You never stay out of trouble."

Someone wrapped Rogers in a blanket and handed him a cup of steaming hot coffee. "Here you go, Captain."

Rogers downed the coffee with shaky hands before raising his head to thank the sailor. "Vimont?" he whisper-screamed in a hoarse, dry voice. "You're alive. Thank God. Who else made it?"

"My lifeboat only had fifteen mates and guards, sir. They included the chief and Chips," the bosun said, referring to the ship's chief engineer and carpenter.

"What about Nidal's lifeboat?"

"We lost sight of it after it capsized. Sorry, Captain. But we couldn't fight our way through the storm to help them," Vimont said, his voice drifting off.

"Ensign Mitchell?"

"Must've been in Mr. Nidal's boat," Vimont said as he helped the shivering captain make his way to the warmth of the crew's mess. "He's not here. By my count, that leaves fourteen men unaccounted for. God rest their souls."

"We don't know for sure that they're dead, Bosun," Rogers said. As they stepped inside the mess, Rogers shook hands with all his remaining crew and with the Armed Guards, addressing them by name and smiling and joking. He stripped off his wet clothes, dried himself with a towel near the stove in the galley, and donned a borrowed work shirt and dungarees.

With the blanket wrapped tight around his shoulders, Rogers headed up the ladders to the wheelhouse, where he found the white-capped captain sitting in a tall chair behind the helmsman at the wheel. "Captain," Rogers said, extending his hand. "I want to thank you for saving me and my men."

"Padraig O'Sullivan, Captain," he said, stepping over to shake hands.

"Rogers. Jake Rogers."

"You're a very lucky man, Capt. Rogers. We were about to abandon the search, but your bosun wouldn't have it," he said with a toothy smile.

"Thanks. But there's one more lifeboat missing."

"I'm sorry, but we can't linger," O'Sullivan said, shaking his head. "There was a massive U-boat attack against your convoy and a larger convoy not far ahead of it. Lots of ships were hit and sunk."

"We weren't hit. At least, I don't believe so. The old girl split apart on us in rough seas."

"Jaysus." O'Sullivan handed Rogers a cup of hot coffee and returned to his chair with a cup for himself. "Anyway, as I was saying, can't take the chance of a ship—from either side, mind you—shooting first and asking questions later."

"But nobody fires on Irish ships. You're neutral."

"Aye. 'Tis true what they say—Hitler's afraid Ireland will let British ships use our port. And Churchill's afraid of the IRA using Germany to gain independence. So, both sides are supposed to leave us be. But the attacks still happen. Did to my company's *Irish Pine* last November. U-boat must have sunk it because all thirty-three souls have never been seen again." He paused to cross himself and mouth a silent prayer. "It's a sad fact of 'The Long Watch,' unfortunately."

"Long watch?" Rogers said as he took a seat on a stool at the chart table.

"That's what we Mercantile Marines call the state of things during 'the Emergency.' Danger's always about, and we never know for sure who's friend or foe." He took a sip of coffee. "Even though we're well-lit and clearly marked as neutral, we must be ever vigilant, especially in low visibility conditions like this."

"But my men," Roger said, jumping up to pace. "Surely you can search a little longer. Please."

"Sorry, Captain. I truly am. And I'll pray for your crew to Saint Brénaind," O'Sullivan said, referring to the sixth-century Irish priest considered one of seven patron saints of sailors. "But there be too many U-boats swarming about, smelling blood in the water. We can't take the chance."

Rogers tried again to argue with O'Sullivan about searching for the last lifeboat, but the captain wouldn't change his mind. They were in a war, and Rogers knew in his heart that commanders had to make hard decisions. He thanked O'Sullivan, made his way back down to the crew's mess to be with his men, and tried not to blame himself for the ones he had lost at sea.

CHAPTER 4

It required three days to reach the *Irish Palm's* home port of Limerick, some sixty miles up the River Shannon from the Atlantic. Once past the stubby Kilcredaun Head lighthouse and the fifteenth-century Carrigaholt Castle's thin tower, they tied up on the Limerick docks in front of the six-story limestone Rank's Bannatyne Mills, part of one of the largest flour milling complexes in Ireland and England. A concrete silo in the shape of a shoebox towered over it. Michael Gleeson, an agent for the Limerick Shipping Co., greeted Rogers and his crew at the quay.

"Which one of you chaps is Capt. Rogers?" Gleeson said, doffing his bowler. When Rogers stepped forward, Gleeson shook the captain's hand with both of his. "My, my, awfully good to meet the famous Capt. Jake Rogers. If you and your men would be so kind as to follow me, we'll get you situated," he said in a heavy brogue.

Feeling his face flushing in embarrassment, Rogers waved his men on behind the fast-walking Gleeson, who guided them down the bustling Dock Street to a Romanesque, two-story brick house with a bay stone facade and arched windows with "Limerick Shipping Company" written in large letters on the brick gable. Once inside, Gleeson lined the men up in front of his cluttered walnut desk. "Capt. Rogers, you'll be first."

When Rogers approached, Gleeson wrote his name down in a ledger and handed him a £1 Irish banknote. "This should keep you fed while you're lodging at Hanratty's Hotel down the way on Glentworth Street. Your company and the US Consulate have arranged for all of you to catch the first train to Belfast in the morning," he said, holding out a ticket as he checked Rogers' name off his list.

"I can't leave tomorrow," Rogers said. "I need to wait to see whether a ship rescued the rest of my men."

"Sorry, Captain, but we haven't heard of any other survivors from our captains," Gleeson said, waving the ticket at Rogers, who swatted it away.

"What about other ships? There was at least one steamer trailing us on the river."

Gleeson curled his lip. "That'd be the *Erin Go Bragh*. Her captain is, well, he doesn't report to us."

"Maybe he'll talk to me," Rogers said, turning on his heels, followed by Obasi. He shouted over his shoulder to Cookie that they'd meet at the hotel later. Obasi struggled to keep up with Rogers as he hustled down Dock Road to the quay. The three-island steamer *Erin Go Bragh* had just arrived, and Rogers walked over to two sailors looping the ends of thick hawsers over metal bollards.

"This your ship?" Rogers asked. The older man had a full gray beard and stooped shoulders.

He muttered something to his companion in what sounded like German but might have been Dutch. One of Rogers' past bosuns hailed from Amsterdam and never stopped jabbering to other Dutch sailors in their native language.

"*Ik spreek geen Nederlands,*" Rogers said, mangling the phrase for "I don't speak Dutch."

"*Nee*, no, you do not, mate. What's your business with this ship?" the sailor said, eyeing Rogers and Obasi suspiciously.

Rogers stuck out his hand with a smile. "I'm Capt. Jake Rogers, and this is Able Seaman Obasi. We're survivors of the Liberty ship *Charles C. Walcutt.* We're hoping you picked up some of our mates."

The sailor shook Rogers' hand and patted him on the shoulder, shaking his head in sympathy. "*Het spijt me, nee,* Captain."

"His English is not so good," the younger sailor said. "He says, 'He's sorry but no.' I'm Able Seaman Pieter Coolen. We passed some burning ships but didn't see no lifeboats or rafts." He pointed at Rogers' chai pendant on his necklace. "You a Jew?"

"What? Oh, this," Rogers said, touching the pendant. "No. It's a gift from a friend. Someone I knew in Amsterdam."

The two sailors exchanged knowing looks. "If your friend is Jewish, he is no longer there," Coolen said with a long sigh.

"She," Rogers said. "She's in Palestine, but some of her relatives are still

38

in Amsterdam."

"I'm afraid the *Moffen* rounded up almost all the Jews they could find and sent them to camps for labor," Coolen said, using the Dutch nickname for Germans.

"All of them?"

"A few remain. Many are in hiding, but there is a bounty on them now."

"Have you heard of a ship owner named Maduro?"

"Solomon Maduro? Of course. Everyone has. He owns many of the warehouses along Keizersgracht. The Dutch fascist NSB made a big noise last month about sending him to Kamp Westerbork. They said he volunteered and that other Jews should do like him and come out of hiding."

"Where is Kamp Westerbork?" Rogers' chest tightened.

"In northern Holland. They say it is not so bad for Jews there," Coolen said. "They work hard, but they have schools, a synagogue and restaurants, and an orchestra. Some are even allowed to leave temporarily, or so they say."

Stunned into silence, Rogers lowered his head and drifted back toward Dock Street, Obasi following next to him with his arm over his shoulder. Without warning, Rogers stopped in his tracks and spun around. "Wait a minute. How could they know about Maduro?"

Before he could ask them, the Dutch sailors scurried up their ship's gangway and disappeared out of sight. Determined to get an answer, Rogers jogged after them and hopped onto the steel deck with a thud. Obasi waited at the top of the gangway.

"Well, well, well. Aren't you the chancer? On my ship. Uninvited."

When Rogers turned to apologize, he was surprised to come face to face with a grizzled sailor wearing a white captain's hat, a sly grin under his red and gray walrus mustache.

"Even if you be the legendary captain of the *Peggy C*," the man said, laughing and shaking Rogers' hand. "It's been donkey's years, my friend. *Fáilte*."

"Gerald Griffin, you old sea dog. This your ship? How is it you're not already in prison?"

"Luck of the Irish, Jake," Griffin said with a short laugh. "Care for a spot of tea?"

"Sure."

"You, too, mate," Griffin said to Obasi, who shook his head and stayed behind on the gangway. Griffin led Rogers to the officers' mess, poured them both a cup of tea, and settled down at a wooden table. He offered Rogers an unmarked bottle of 140-proof *poteen*—Irish moonshine—but Rogers waved it off. "Oh, I forgot. You don't imbibe." Griffin added a splash to his own cup. "Now, what are you doing in Limerick? Smuggling out potatoes?"

"Shipwrecked. My Liberty ship split in half, and we were brought here on the *Irish Palm*."

"That was your ship? Heard about it. We spent the better part of a day looking for survivors, but the weather wasn't cooperating. Your crew?"

"All but fourteen accounted for," Rogers said, savoring a long, comforting sip of the steaming tea. "I'm hoping some other ship picked them up."

"I know there were others out there searching. Maybe..."

Rogers blew on his tea and cleared his throat before looking up at Griffin's bright green eyes. They had been competitors for years, landing in the same ports, hunting for cargo for their tramp steamers, and trading in the same contraband. Their rivalry wasn't always friendly. Smuggling is a cutthroat business, and sometimes not everyone played fair. But over the years, they developed a grudging admiration for one another and came to enjoy the competition. "So, Gerald, how'd you get in and out of Amsterdam?"

Griffin's head jerked back. He removed his hat, rubbed down his reddish-brown, gray-streaked hair, and seemed to be mulling over how to respond. "Don't know what you're talking about, Jake."

"Don't worry. I'm not interested in your cargo. I only need to know whether you can take me there with you."

"Jesus, Mary, and Joseph. Why would you want to do something foolish like that?"

"I have a friend I need to get out. A Jewish friend. And I'm figuring you know how to help me do it."

"What you're asking is impossible. You got lucky getting that Jewish family out on the *Peggy C*."

"Not all of them. I left the father behind. Solomon Maduro. I'm sure he'd pay you a handsome reward. In fact, you could probably name your price."

Griffin arched his eyebrows at the name, downed his cup, and poured another, this time more whiskey than tea. "Even if I were to go to Amsterdam—and I'm not saying I would—the Germans would kill us all for smuggling Jews, especially a prominent Jew like Maduro. Sorry, Jake, I can't have any part of that."

Seeing the futility of pleading any further, Rogers finished his tea, thanked his old friend, and headed down the gangway with Obasi to the quay. They passed a tall, middle-aged man in a suit and bow tie who tipped his fedora and headed onto the docks.

A small ship's horn echoed across the water, a sound so familiar that neither Rogers nor Obasi paid it any mind. A prolonged blast made them pause and squint into the setting sun over the River Shannon. A rusty commercial trawler with two masts and a funnel belching black smoke chugged toward the docks, her Irish flag snapping in the stiff wind.

A little more than a third of the length of a football field, the coal-powered trawler kicked up a bigger wake than usual for ships in the harbor and blew its horn over and over. Shading their eyes with their hands, Rogers and Obasi studied the fishing boat.

"Some kind of celebration?" Rogers asked Obasi, who shrugged. As the trawler drew closer, it appeared that men on the deck were waving hats and coats in the air, and a helmet.

"It's them, Captain!" Obasi shouted, startling Rogers. The Nigerian had rarely raised his voice before. They waved and screamed until the boat bumped into the dock. A sailor in torn dungarees and a watch cap vaulted out even before the boat stopped. With a rope in hand, he tied it to the metal bollards like a pro, and looked up. Mr. Nidal flashed what appeared to be a smile.

There was a big celebration that night at the Hanratty Hotel's small pub, nicknamed "The Glue Pot" by locals, tinged with sadness at the loss of two of the Armed Guards who had flung themselves at the life rafts but missed.

"We could not reach them," Nidal said between bites of steamy colcannon—mashed potatoes with kale and onions swimming in butter. "After we got the lifeboat righted, we were left with two oars and no sail, so we drifted. Luckily for us, the trawler picked us up two days ago west of Tory Island. We were out of food and nearly out of water."

"Mr. Nidal is quite the sailor," Ensign Mitchell said, taking a long gulp from a pint glass of Guinness before slamming it down on the table. "We never would've made it without him." Nidal bowed his head modestly in acknowledgment.

"Here's to your men," Rogers said, raising his glass of water in a toast and quoting from Nathaniel Hawthorne's poem *The Ocean*: "The earth has guilt, the earth has care, / Unquiet are its graves; / But peaceful sleep is ever there, / Beneath the dark blue waves."

"Begging your pardon, Captain," the bartender said after the sailors and Armed Guards clinked their glasses. He pulled Rogers aside and said, "A TD would like a word outside."

"A TD?"

"*Teachta Dála*. A member of Ireland's parliament, the Dáil Éireann. He's an important man," the bartender said. Outside, they found the same man, still dressed in a bow tie and fedora, whom Rogers and Obasi had passed earlier in the day on the quay. He was hard to miss with his lantern jaw, large ears, and mostly aquiline nose. Its slight slant to the left, Rogers guessed, was the result of a sporting accident or a fight. "Capt. Rogers, may I introduce Deputy Robert Briscoe?"

"Bob, please," Briscoe said, clasping Rogers' hand and pumping it vigorously. "Take a walk with me, will ye?"

As they wandered along, Briscoe locked arms with Rogers. "You know, my brother Wolfe Tone served in the American Merchant Marines in the last war," Briscoe said. "We were quite proud of him. It takes a strong and dedicated man to work for such a cause." He steered them around the corner onto O'Connell Street. Once past the bustling White House Bar, the oldest drinking establishment in Limerick, Briscoe stopped and made sure they were out of anyone's earshot. Two men wearing broad-brimmed slouch hats and trench coats hovered nearby, but Briscoe didn't seem to care about them. "Our friend Capt. Griffin says you want to rescue Solomon Maduro from Amsterdam."

"That's right. Only he won't take me there. So that's out."

"You have a plan?"

"Excuse me, Bob, if that is your name, but why do you want to know?"

Briscoe chuckled and resumed walking. The two men in trench coats followed at a distance. "Smart to be cautious these days. I'll tell you why I'm interested, and then maybe I can help with your plan if, indeed, you have one. Deal?"

"Deal." Rogers spotted Obasi, ever the protector, hiding in the shadows.

"Solomon is important to us. After the Great War, when I was smuggling weapons from Germany for the IRA, I rented some warehouses from him in Amsterdam. And, when I went to Europe before this war to convince Jews to leave for Palestine, he helped fund my travels," Briscoe said, stopping to face Rogers. "Believe it or not, we planned to evacuate 750,000 Jews from Hungary, Poland, and Romania. Even got approval from all three governments. But the plan was vetoed by the British and foolishly dismissed by Chaim Weizmann, the chairman of the Zionist Organization, and others. They worried it'd cause more anti-Semitism."

"Who is 'we'?" Rogers asked, still suspicious.

"Ze'ev Jabotinsky, founder of Hatzohar, the Union of Revisionist Zionists. Unlike the Zionist Organization, we do not believe in appeasing the British," Briscoe said, his voice rising as he resumed walking. "Over and over, Jabotinsky warned the Jews of Poland that they were 'sitting on the edge of a volcano.' But no one listened until it was too late. But Solomon, though he was a friend of Weizmann, took us seriously. Wouldn't have the beginnings of a navy without him."

"He bought ships for Ireland?" Rogers said as he kneeled to tie his boot.

"Palestine, not Ireland." Briscoe waited for a crowd of rowdy sailors to pass before continuing. "Mussolini believed a strong Jewish state would be a good counterbalance to the British and his other enemies in the Middle East. A sort of 'the enemy of my enemy is my friend' situation."

"But Mussolini hates Jews," Rogers said as he rose to continue the stroll.

"Not like Hitler, at least not before the war. He admired Zionists. So, he let us set up the Betar Naval Academy at Civitavecchia outside Rome to train young Jews to be sailors," Briscoe said. "Solomon helped a philanthropist named Kirschner from Belgium raise funds to purchase our training schooner, *Sara I*. You can see why he is important to us."

"Wait, are you Irish or Palestinian?"

"One can be Irish and Jewish and be passionate about both, Capt. Rogers.

Although I was born in Dublin to Jewish immigrants from Lithuania, they named me after Robert Emmet, the eighteenth-century Irish rebel leader hanged by the British." His breath made small puffs of condensation as he blew on his clasped hands to warm them. "Now you know my reason. What's your plan?"

Rogers raked his hands through his hair. "I know Amsterdam pretty well. If I can sneak in and have a ship in which to escape, I know certain people who can help me. For a price, of course."

"That's your plan?" Briscoe said with a scoff. "And you have money for this plan?"

"Well, no, but—"

"I am sorry to have wasted your time, Captain. I'll be taking my leave. Good night and good luck." Briscoe stormed away in a huff.

Rogers chased after him. "Wait, I have to save him," he said, grabbing Briscoe's arm and pulling him to a stop. "I love his daughter Miriam. I managed to save her but not him. And I was the cause of his brother's murder by the Germans on my ship. Please, if you can get me in, give me that chance. I owe him."

Briscoe tugged free from Rogers and glared at him. "Captain, you don't know me, but, like you, I'm an old gunrunner and smuggler. I know you're a resourceful man, and I know what you did on the *Peggy C*. That is the one reason I decided to meet with you. But I can tell you that your plan is not a plan." He jammed both hands into his coat pockets and resumed walking away.

"Oom Piet," Rogers blurted out.

Briscoe stopped and turned around. "How do you know about Uncle Pete?"

"Miriam told me about him when I was recuperating in Haifa. She said Oom Piet had worked with her father to hide some of his companies' assets. Said he's some kind of banker or bank robber who helps fund Dutch resistance groups. So, I'm betting the people I know—given the type of people they are—will be able to put me in touch with Oom Piet. He can connect me to the funds and people I need."

Briscoe studied Rogers. "You are indeed a very resourceful man, Capt.

Rogers. We will again talk in the morning."

"Does that mean you'll help?"

"It means we'll talk," Briscoe said, disappearing into the night.

"But I have a train to Belfast I'm supposed to catch tomorrow morning," Rogers shouted after him.

As his footsteps echoed around the deserted street, Briscoe shouted back. "Don't board it."

CHAPTER 5

"I'll catch up with you later," Rogers said to the other survivors not long after dawn as they gathered in front of the hotel for the trek to the train station.

"Why can't you come with us?" Cookie said.

"I have something to take care of here. I can't leave."

Cookie leaned over to Nidal and Obasi, who waited nearby, patting themselves to stay warm in the cold morning air. "He's up to somethin', mates. I know that look, and it always means trouble."

"Does this involve the man you met last night?" Nidal said in his usual voice. That unemotional tone, combined with his stern, pockmarked face and piercing black eyes, often confused and terrified sailors under his command.

"It doesn't involve you. I can take care of it on my own," Rogers said. "You should get on the train and find yourself another ship."

"We signed up for *your* ship, Captain, not *a* ship. And we ain't leaving without you," Cookie said, drawing grunts of approval from Obasi and Nidal. Merchant Marines, unlike Armed Guards, were contracted for one roundtrip voyage at a time and were under no obligation to work for a particular ship or company.

Ensign Mitchell worked his way through the crowd of men to join Rogers. "What's this I hear about you not going with us, Captain?"

"I have business to attend to, Ensign. Farewell," he said, shaking Mitchell's hand.

Gleeson, the shipping agent, urged the group forward. "This way, gents. Limerick Colbert Station's less than ten minutes away."

"Thanks for everything, Captain," Mitchell said. "Good luck with your next ship."

"I'm zero-for-two in this war, so you're probably lucky not to be on it," Rogers said with a grin.

Mitchell laughed. "We'd sail with you any day. It's been a real honor to serve with you," he said and marched away with his men.

Cookie, Nidal, and Obasi didn't move. Gleeson spotted them and gestured for the sailors and Armed Guards to wait. He hustled over to Rogers. "Captain, you and your men must hurry along."

"We're staying here for a few days," Rogers said.

"But your company only paid for one day at the hotel," Gleeson said.

Rogers shrugged.

"I can tell you that the *Irish Palm* don't need any more crew," Gleeson said. "And...Oh, I see. You couldn't possibly be thinking of sailing on the *Erin Go Bragh*. It's not a...a regular ship, if you know what I mean."

Rogers raised an eyebrow.

"We heard the Jewman Briscoe was in town looking for crew. Don't see many of his kind around here anymore, not since the 1904 Boycott," Gleeson said.

"And what kind is that?" Rogers said in a cold voice, squinting his eyes.

Gleeson took a step back and cleared his throat with a nervous cough. "Got no problems with Jews, mind you," Gleeson said, speaking as fast as he could, his ears turning red. "Got no problem with Catholics either. I'm what you call ecumenical. No, Deputy Briscoe is a fine man, a longtime friend of *Taoiseach* de Valera, he is," Gleeson said a little too loudly, referring to Irish Prime Minister Éamon de Valera, a founder of *Sinn Féin*. Gleeson leaned in to whisper to Rogers. "But he's also a dangerous man, Captain." He mouthed the letters "I-R-A." Seeing that Rogers was unmoved, Gleeson added, "Likes to call himself 'Chair of Subversive Activity against England,' or so I hear." Still getting no response, Gleeson tipped his bowler and waved the group of men to follow. "Righty-o, gents, this way."

"Now what, Captain?" Nidal said.

"We wait."

It didn't take long for Briscoe to arrange a meeting that afternoon with Rogers at The People's Park, a short distance from Hanratty's Hotel. Rogers found him sitting there on a bench along a pathway that circled a towering limestone Doric column. The column itself was anchored on an octagonal base and topped by a small statue of a man. Nearby, two men in slouch hats with their hands in their trench coat pockets appeared to be surveilling the park.

After Rogers took a seat, Briscoe pointed to the top of the seventy-nine-foot-tall monument. "Do you know who that is up there?"

Rogers shook his head.

"Neither does anyone else in this conflicted town, I wager. Thomas Spring Rice is his name. The question is, why is there a statue in Limerick honoring a nineteenth-century Anglican landlord who fought against independence and wanted to rename Ireland "West Britain?"

"Does seem strange. Why?"

"Because he was also a member of Parliament and a cabinet minister who fought for the rights of Ireland's majority Roman Catholics to be able to practice their religion and hold political office—so-called emancipation," Briscoe said, pulling out a handkerchief to blow his nose. "And when the Great Famine struck in the 1840s, he was one of the few wealthy landowners to take care of his tenants and to rail against government policies that killed more than a million people. Sent millions more fleeing to the Americas. Most of the damn British landlords drove them out of their miserable cottages so they could enclose the fields and raise cattle. More profitable than growing crops, they were. See what I mean about contradictions? We're a conflicted people. No better place to illustrate that than right here in Limerick."

"What's special about here? Seems like a nice little town," Rogers said, kicking himself for asking a question that would further delay getting to the point of the meeting.

"Ireland's a wonderful place full of lovely people, and I have rarely seen anti-Semitism raise its ugly head here. But it did in the worst possible way nigh on forty years ago."

"Mr. Gleeson said something about Jews and a boycott in 1904."

"Some called it a pogrom. But nobody died. A crazy priest, for whatever reason, delivered a sermon attacking Jews. Called them leeches and murderers. Triggered violence and a boycott of Jewish businesses that lasted for two years. A lot of Jews, some of them from Lithuania, like my parents, fled. Now, only a handful remain in town."

Rogers sat upright and sighed. "I'm sorry, Mr. Briscoe, but is there a point to all of this? Will you help me or not?"

Briscoe hopped to his feet and began not just to pace but to repeatedly pound his palm with his fist. "What it means, my friend, is that this is why we need people like Solomon Maduro. Not because he's a rich Jew or well-connected or smart. He's the very antithesis of all these contradictions. He's a man of principle. He believes in *Eretz Yisrael*. And he fights for it in his own way. Such an audacious rescue of a prize Jew will provide hope to others that one day we will help them—even if I couldn't save my own Aunt Hedwig and my niece. So, yes, I will help."

"Thank you," Rogers said, letting out a long breath.

Briscoe plopped down on the bench, pulled out his handkerchief, and wiped his brow. "Of course, you realize the chances of you succeeding are almost nil."

"Us."

"What'd you mean *us*?"

"Three members of my crew are going with me."

Briscoe shut his eyes, squeezed the bridge of his nose, and shook his head before returning his gaze to Rogers. "Then ye'll be three times more likely to get caught."

"They'll stay on the ship most of the time. But I don't want to meet the type of people I have to see in Amsterdam without men I trust completely to cover my back."

"Very well. I'll arrange for four Irish passports and four licenses."

"One of my men is Tunisian, and another is Nigerian. I doubt they could pass for Irish—even black Irish," Rogers said, knowing his joke was feeble.

"The Tunisian won't have any problems since he comes from a French colony. Your African mate could be from Senegal. I have a man who can take care of all that tonight. In the meantime, you can bunk on the *Erin Go Bragh*." Briscoe pulled a wad of Irish pounds from his coat pocket. "Go buy clothes and boots that don't look too new. Wear nothing and carry nothing American, right down to your pants. Got it?"

Rogers didn't respond.

"You know, knickers. What you Yanks call underpants."

"OK. I got it."

"Good. And take off the necklace."

"Sorry, I forgot," he said, handing it to Briscoe.

"I'll keep it for you in Dublin until you return. We'll meet again tomorrow before you depart. I have an appointment with a friend who might be able to help with your so-called plan."

Later that afternoon, Rogers explained the rough outlines of his plan to his crew, who, despite the danger, agreed without hesitation to join him. Afterward, they went shopping at second-hand shops for clothes, rain gear, and kit bags, and Rogers treated them to another hearty meal at a local pub.

After dinner, they shopped at Power & Mangan's Chemist on O'Connell Street for toothpaste and toiletries and then ducked into O'Mahony's Booksellers a block away, where they were led to a back room where a photographer took their pictures for their identity papers.

When they boarded the *Erin Go Bragh*, Capt. Griffin assigned them cabins in the petty officer quarters of the main deckhouse. He explained their duties and what watches they would work. Griffin was quite happy to have them aboard because it was always challenging to find qualified seamen.

When he learned Cookie was an actual, experienced cook, he thanked Rogers profusely. "Had to fire my last one two days out of port. I don't have to tell you that the quickest way to spark a mutiny is to feed lousy food to grumpy, overworked sailors."

At daybreak, a young boy came for Rogers and led him down Dock Street, weaving back and forth through alleyways, sometimes the same one more than once, making sure they weren't being followed. As they meandered along Upper Hartstonge Street, the boy grabbed Rogers' hand and yanked him around the corner of a five-story brick townhouse with an Adamesque cast-iron balcony. The words "St. Vincent du Paul Society" were etched on the fanlight above the three-centered arched wooden front door. They ducked into a back entrance to a basement, where Briscoe paced. He tossed the boy a coin and told him to wait outside.

"Your plan will never work," Briscoe said.

"But—"

"Sit and listen."

Rogers scooted over a vegetable crate to sit on.

"My friend at the SOE said there is a bounty for Jews now, and no one knows for sure who is collaborating," Briscoe said, "However, there might be a way to connect you to *Groep 2000* and Van Tuyll."

"Wait," Rogers said, holding up his hand. "I understood about half of what you said. SOE? Group something-or-other? Van who?"

"SOE is the British Special Operations Executive. It is known in some circles as the Ministry of Ungentlemanly Warfare because it operates agents and saboteurs in Europe with the help of resistance groups. One of the Dutch resistance organizations they help is known as Group 2000. They receive some of their funding from someone known as Van Tuyll and sometimes as Uncle Pete. With their help, your chances improve to slightly better than zero."

"So, how am I supposed to find these people?"

"Your passports and other papers will be delivered to you on the ship before you sail tomorrow." Briscoe handed Rogers a crumpled piece of paper. "Here are your instructions. Memorize them and throw the paper away before you arrive in Amsterdam. Have your Dutch crewmen teach you how to say these phrases exactly. Do not, under any circumstances, speak English in public. Capt. Griffin will see to it that you have passes to go to Dam Square for supplies on a Tuesday or Thursday at noon." Briscoe reached into his coat pocket and pulled out a torn half of a calling card with "Herr Johann von—" on it. "Ye'll be needing this, too. After the person you meet in the square takes you to members of Group 2000, show them this to prove you're a friend."

"Why will British Intelligence help us?" Rogers said as he studied his instructions and stuffed the calling card into his shirt pocket.

"They won't. My friend will, for reasons of his own. He only asks one thing: If you are captured, tell the Nazis that all you know about your contact is that he was a large man with a prominent birthmark on his right cheek whom you met in Dam Square." Briscoe paused and locked eyes with Rogers. "That is when you can no longer endure the torture, and you be beggin' to hear the wings of Azreal," he said, referring to the winged Angel of Death.

Struck by the grim reality of what he was getting himself into, Rogers rose to leave, then asked one last question, but one he didn't expect to be answered. "Why are the Germans letting the *Erin Go Bragh* into Amsterdam?"

"Who are we neutral against?"

"I don't understand."

"That's how one Irish wit summed up our neutrality dilemma. We can't have the IRA antagonizing the British because we depend on them for our country's overseas supplies. Yet we hate the British, Churchill in particular, for what they've done and continue to do to our beloved land, which the IRA are fighting to stop." Briscoe crossed his arms and lowered his head, taking his time before raising it again. "Remember how I talked yesterday about the Irish and all our contradictions?"

"Yes."

"That's all you need to know."

As a one-time professional smuggler who had made a living from sneaking ships in and out of dangerous places, Rogers had to respect that answer. Still, he hated riddles and, as he returned to the ship, this one triggered a wave of shivering alarm bells throughout his body.

☆☆☆

The following day, not long after the sun rose behind fast-moving gray clouds, the same young messenger brought Rogers a package containing all the forged documents. Rogers handed them out to his crew with a warning. "Memorize the information and never, I mean never, use each other's real names in Amsterdam."

Rogers and his crew did what they could to help finish loading the four holds on the ship, a 2,500-ton coal-fired steamer similar in size and design to the *Peggy C*. First, they filled three storage areas with grain and potatoes. Next, they lowered pigs, famous for producing Limerick's cured ham, one by one into the fourth hold lined with stalls. To do this, they used a crane and the small "donkey" engine on the deck.

Obasi had been the "donkeyman"—a kind of utility man—on the *Peggy C,* so he took over the operation for the short-handed Capt. Griffin. Nidal, holding his nose against the smell, worked with the deck crew to prepare to sail.

On the third level of the deckhouse, in the chartroom behind the wheelhouse, Rogers and Griffin leaned over a table studying a map. Griffin drew a line with his finger north through the Atlantic. "We be sailing due north and then around Scotland through the Pentland Firth."

"The tides in the strait are vicious this time of year," Rogers said.

"Nothing to be done about it. From there, we head to Leith to deliver our load and pick up coal for the return," Griffin said, tapping on the port area north of Edinburgh on the Firth of Forth. "At least, that's what our papers say. Right before we get there, we'll take a detour and make a quick downhill run to Amsterdam on the North Sea."

"Why not head south and around? It's a couple of days shorter. Don't you have to stop anyway at Fishguard for a Navicert?" Rogers said. The Welsh port was where Irish ships were required to stop for inspection to obtain a Navigation Certificate, which they needed to sail through the British blockade of Europe. They were supposed to be going only to neutral countries' ports.

Griffin pulled an official-looking document from his pocket and handed it to Rogers for inspection. "Don't you worry. Capt. Swift was kind enough to provide the Navicerts for going and coming."

"Who?"

"Our friend," Griffin said, raising an eyebrow.

"Briscoe?"

"Aye, mate. That was his cover name when we were running guns from Germany," Griffin said, turning his attention back to the map. "The Channel's too dangerous. 'Tis crawling with mines and U-boats and warplanes that might not notice or care we're neutral," Griffin said as he plotted their course. "Our route is a wee bit safer. But you know what they say: 'The minute you leave port, you're in enemy territory.'"

CHAPTER 6

Occasional squalls in heavy seas cut visibility down to less than three nautical miles as the *Erin Go Bragh* puttered along at 8 knots up the coast of Ireland; Griffin didn't seem concerned. When they approached the flashing lighthouse on Eagle Island in County Mayo, about 110 nautical miles north of the River Shannon, the weather deteriorated with stunning suddenness. Though the daylight was fading fast, it was impossible to miss the towering waves crashing against the island's soaring cliffs. The foamy spumes shot up almost to the base of the squat lighthouse on top.

"Used to be two of 'em up there," said Griffin, sitting like a serene Buddha behind the helmsman in the wheelhouse.

"What?" Rogers said, staring out the front windows in amazement.

"Fifty years ago, a storm whipped up the waves more than 200 feet high. Knocked out the lantern and swamped the East Tower."

"Shouldn't we be giving it a wider berth?" Rogers said. With its two coal-fired Scotch boilers and overworked triple-expansion engine, he was concerned Griffin's ship might not have enough power to resist the powerful currents crashing into the jagged rocks.

Griffin laughed. "You heard him, Helmsman. Can't have the good captain all shook. "Right 5 degrees rudder. Make your course 25 degrees. All ahead full."

"Right 5 degrees rudder. All ahead full. Aye, Captain," the helmsman said.

Rogers wasn't amused. Griffin clearly had planned all along to head north-by-northeast and, once he spotted the lighthouse on the farthest western point of Ireland, move from hugging the Irish coast into open waters. From there, it was around 480 nautical miles to circumvent northern Scotland to the North Sea.

It should have taken three days. It took almost six. The turbulent sea proved almost too much for the ship's engine, which had to be repaired repeatedly as the ship spent hours anchored in protected bays.

During one stop, they were inspected by the crew of a British "Dog Boat"—a Fairmile D motor torpedo boat—within sight of Cape Wrath at the northwestern tip of Scotland, a navigation point thought to have been used by Vikings for steering south. Atop the cape's ninety-story-high sandstone and gneiss cliffs, a white granite lighthouse flashed its paraffin beam with white and red reflectors.

The motor torpedo boat, similar to an American PT boat, could travel three times as fast as Griffin's ship. And it was armed to the teeth with 6-pounder guns, Oerlikon 20mm cannons, and Vickers K machine guns. So, Griffin was quick to comply when the warship flashed "stop" with an Aldis lamp. The grumpy boarding party was also quick. After checking the Navicert, they did a cursory inspection of the cargo. When they came to the pig pens, the stench sent them fleeing back to their motorboat, holding their noses and gagging.

After another hour of fighting to make the mammoth pistons churn again, the *Erin Go Bragh* sailed into the treacherous Pentland Firth between the Orkney Islands and mainland Scotland. The strait was twelve nautical miles of hell. Violent eddies, tides known as races surging up to twenty miles an hour, and random overfalls like a series of jagged speed bumps—all combined to knock the decrepit ship about for three hours. Even seasoned sailors became seasick and threw up into buckets for fear of venturing outside onto decks battered by thundering white horses.

Unable to rest in his assigned bunk, Rogers stumbled to a tiny desk in his cabin to practice the Dutch phrases Briscoe had told him to memorize. Growing frustrated, he set those aside and opened a copy of Sir Walter Scott's *The Pirate* he had purchased at O'Mahony's Booksellers. He found it amusing that the novel, set around the Oakley Islands and Shetland, was the inspiration—some would say the irritation—for his hero James Fenimore Cooper to write the first American sea novel, *The Pilot*. Cooper, a merchant sailor and Navy midshipman like Rogers, was disturbed by the naval descriptions in Scott's fourteenth Waverly novel, which he described in the introduction to *The Pilot* as "not true in the details."

Rogers had always identified with America's first best-selling author, who had become a merchant sailor after being expelled from Yale. Similarly,

Rogers had fled the US Naval Academy under a cloud. Some said Cooper had blown up a fellow student's door and taught a donkey to sit in a professor's chair. Some said Rogers had killed someone before fleeing America as a young man.

As the book skittered across the desk and the ship rolled precariously from side to side, Rogers distracted himself by playing in his head the thrilling end of the first movement of Felix Mendelssohn's *Scottish Symphony*, which was inspired by the composer's rough sailing to Scotland. With its desperate violins and cellos, thundering kettle drums, and ominous, swirling horns, the music soared and crashed in melodious torment like the rhythm of the monstrous waves. The torture didn't end until the ship swept past the sixteenth-century Barrogill Castle and sailed into the North Sea.

In the relative calm, Rogers grabbed two cups of hot coffee and some biscuits from the galley. He had Cookie help him carry them up the heaving ladder to the wheelhouse, where they found Nidal at the helm and Griffin in the captain's chair. The captain puffed a Peterson Calabash pipe. With its curved stem and large conical bowl, it was the pipe favored by Sherlock Holmes.

"Thought you could use some coffee, Captain," Rogers said, handing one cup to Griffin and the other, with a grin, to his former first mate. "And you too, Helmsman."

Nidal grabbed the coffee without taking his eyes off the sea ahead and without cracking a smile.

Rogers was never sure: Did Nidal not understand his jokes or simply choose to ignore them? Rogers glanced at the gyrocompass in front of the wheel and was surprised they were heading east by northeast and not south to Edinburg or even Amsterdam. "Heading to Sweden?" Rogers said in a jovial tone so as not to appear presumptuous. He might be an experienced sailor, but this wasn't his ship.

"I'll do it now in a minute," Griffin said, using Irish slang meaning something like "when I feel like it." He used the stem of his pipe to illustrate his point. "Taking a wide swing before heading toward Amsterdam. Not as many Royal Navy ships around here."

"But plenty of U-boats," Cookie said, giving Rogers a worried glance.

Griffin puffed on his pipe and slowly blew a stream of smoke rings before mumbling a response. "Aye, that's a fact," he said, studying the rings floating over his head.

Cookie looked at Rogers for an explanation, but the captain shrugged.

The following day, the ship did turn south. And so did their luck. The dense clouds were too low for planes to spot her, and the sea was too rough for U-boats to take aggressive action. Still, for any hostile ship, the long black smoke plume trailing behind the tramp steamer marked it with a lethal bulls-eye from miles away.

It didn't take long before a German *Schnellboot,* called an S-boot for short, appeared on the horizon. The 114-foot-long fast attack craft was armed with torpedoes, flak guns, machine guns, and a 40mm cannon. Its three Daimler Benz diesel engines could drive the S-boot up to 43 knots, almost four times the top speed of the *Erin Go Bragh* on its best day. There was no escaping it.

Griffin, standing outside with Rogers on the flying bridge in front of the wheelhouse, did nothing to alter his ship's speed or direction. The German ship flashed a message on an Aldis lamp. Griffin grunted, picked up a hand-held Aldis lamp, and signaled something back.

"What did you signal?" Rogers said.

"That I will."

"Will what?"

"Follow the Germans. We're caught, mate. We are now a prize ship."

The ruse provided Griffin with an excuse if stopped by a British warship for being in the middle of the North Sea. Rogers figured Griffin would argue that he had engine trouble and drifted until his ship became a prize captured by the Germans. So, he had no choice but to follow them after completing the repairs. The S-boot was more guide than guard.

Additional S-boots swarmed around the ship as it approached Holland's Port of Ijmuiden. Concrete bunkers brimming with weapons lined the entrance of the North Sea Canal to Amsterdam. They sailed with some trepidation past the half-submerged remains of the SS *Jan Pieterszoon Coen.* Stuck in the sandy, shallow harbor, its two gold and black funnels towered over its exposed upper decks. To block the harbor entrance, the fleeing Royal Netherlands Navy had scuttled the passenger ship and several smaller ones between the piers in May 1940. It remained closed until the following year, when the Germans removed the ship's stern and opened a fifty-meter-wide gap.

Rogers was astounded at how many new concrete pillboxes and bunkers were being constructed along the sixteen-mile waterway since his previous visit, not quite two years ago on the *Peggy C's* last fateful voyage. German soldiers guarded the construction workers, many of whom were black or dark-skinned foreigners in kufi caps and turbans.

Although it was rare for a non-Axis ship even to try to enter, the *Erin Go Bragh* passed unmolested through the canal under the watchful eyes of armed guards on the banks and at the Eastern Docklands, the deep-water harbor in Amsterdam lined with cranes, warehouses, and railroad tracks.

As soon as the gangplank was lowered, sailors scurried down to hook the thick hawsers to the metal bullocks; machine gun-toting German soldiers and police scampered aboard. A Dutch inspector, long past retirement age by the looks of his gray, thinning hair and uneasy steps, puttered along behind them and greeted Griffin.

In faded dungarees, a blue work shirt, and a dirty Irish Tweed newsboy cap low on his brow, Rogers joined the rest of the crew, like a common sailor, to unload the cargo. The inspector locked eyes with him. Rogers ducked his head and moved on, avoiding eye contact. He knew the inspector well; they had met many times before, and from the surprise on his face, there was no question that he recognized Rogers.

"O'Rourke!" Griffin called out.

Rogers continued on his way, forgetting the new name on his passport, one he knew that the inspector knew was a lie.

"I said, Ordinary Seaman James O'Rourke. Belay whatever it is you're about and c'mere to me," Griffin said.

"Don't you know your own name, *imbécile?*" Nidal said, blocking Rogers' path and roughly turning him around. "Sorry, Captain. This one is a bit slow." He shoved Rogers forward. "Move it. He is talking to you."

With a tug on the cap as if saluting, Rogers shuffled over to the captain and the inspector and stared at his feet.

"Chief Inspector De Klerk here will give passes for you, Nidal, and what-ever the African's name is to pick up some supplies at Dam Square," Griffin said. "Can you do that?"

"That I will, Cap'n."

The inspector scribbled a note on a pad with an official seal and handed it to Rogers. "Have you ever been to Amsterdam before, Seaman O'Rourke?" he asked in perfect English.

Rogers shook his lowered head.

"Well then, I'll have one of my men show you the way. It's not far, so you should be able to find your own way back," the inspector said.

"*Go raibh maith agat*," Rogers said, using the Irish phrase the crew had taught him for "thank you," which literally means "may good be at you." Rogers rejoined Nidal and winked, thankful his luck had held out.

Perhaps all those years of bribes to De Klerk had been worth it. He had looked the other way when Rogers smuggled Miriam, her younger sister Truus, and her uncle Rabbi Levy, along with his three young boys—Wim, Julius, and Arie—aboard the *Peggy C* in a large shipping crate. This favor must have been on the house.

De Klerk spoke to a young inspector, who hurried off the ship and headed down the quay toward the city center, turning to wait for the others. Nidal signaled Obasi to follow and shoved Rogers along. "Imbécile," he said, shaking his head in disgust.

Rogers knew perfectly well how to get to Dam Square; in better days, it was one of his favorite haunts with its magnificent Royal Palace, the nearby Gothic New Church, and, of course, "The Beehive"—De Bijenkorf's six-story department store, where he used to roam as a young sailor admiring the luxury items he would never buy even if he had any money. Rogers had memorized his instructions, so he knew where to go and what to say. The scene shocked Rogers when they arrived a few minutes later and said goodbye to their Dutch guide.

The once-bustling square was almost empty. A few men in caps and baggy Volendam worker pants smoking clay pipes wandered past horse-drawn wagons and closed shops. Vehicles were scarce except for German military trucks and Zündapp KS 750 motorcycles with sidecars. Most bicycles, which used to fill the square, had been confiscated by the Nazis, and German soldiers rode the ones that still had real rubber tires; civilians, for the most part, rode on wooden or worn-out rubber wheels stuffed with straw or, if they had no alternative, the metal rims themselves.

In the adjacent alleys, men in time-worn dark suits and heavy coats, fedoras on their bowed heads, engaged in hushed conversations. German soldiers and officers laughed nearby and ogled women strolling arm-in-arm, the clicking of their heels echoing across the square. Trash swirled in the fresh, cool sea breeze, smelling of spring.

An SS officer deliberately bumped into Obasi. "*Affen*," he said with a sneer, brushing imaginary dirt off his uniform.

Obasi, his eyes downcast, didn't react. Nor did Rogers, who was appalled but couldn't say anything. He waited for the officer to move out of earshot and instructed Obasi and Nidal to separate so they could watch over him from different parts of the square while he found the address where he was supposed to meet a boy kicking a soccer ball by himself.

When Rogers reached the corner of Nieuwendijk and Dam, he stopped mid-stride, finding it hard to believe this was the correct address. He was positive he had memorized it correctly. Then he laughed to himself; it was the perfect location. No one would expect to find a spy or downed Allied pilot or prison camp escapee here. No, no one would expect to find them standing in front of the *Waffen-SS* headquarters with *Ersatzkommando Niederlande* in one of the wide arched second-floor windows. Below was an enormous black banner with the runic insignia, ancient Germanic runes, or letters resembling double lightning bolts.

Also below was a row of poster-sized pictures of Dutchmen in German military caps, resolute and proud. A painted banner in capital letters wrapped around the building said in Dutch, "United in the struggle to save Europe from the Bolsheviks."

Thousands of young Dutchmen had joined the Wiking Division to fight the Russians as part of the elite military branch of the German SS—the Nazi Party's *Schutzstaffel* or "Protective Echelon." Its insignia was not only the organization's initials but symbolized the rallying cry of "Sige, Sige" ("Victory, Victory"). From blaring megaphones above the building's entrance, martial tunes echoed throughout the square.

Several boys in shorts and knee socks studied the recruitment propaganda and patriotic pictures of smiling Dutch soldiers in battle plastered over the ground-floor windows. But there was no boy with a soccer ball. It was Tuesday, and it was noon, so a boy should have been there.

Refusing to give up, Rogers ambled past the building's corner entrance and checked out the shady Nieuwendijk. A boy in a cap with a soccer ball was playing by himself. With a glance over his shoulder to ensure Obasi and Nidal could see where he was going, Rogers turned into the side street, stopped near the boy, and pretended to read the bulletins in the window.

"Hoe kom ik bij het treinstation?" Rogers said, asking for directions to the train station.

"Waar ga je naar toe?" the boy said, asking about his destination without taking his eyes off the ball.

"Utrecht."

The boy doffed his cap and wiped his brow with his sleeve. *"Volg me,"* he said, picking up the ball and flicking his fingers for Rogers to follow him down the street toward the central station. Without warning, the boy ducked around the first corner, waited for Rogers to make the turn, then hurried him into an unlocked, abandoned store and out a back door into an alley. A horse-drawn cart full of hay blocked their way.

From behind, someone shoved a burlap sack over Rogers' head and lifted him into the cart, forcing him to lie down as he was covered in hay. "Don't move or say a word," someone whispered into Rogers' ear in English. The cart rolled away, the horse's hooves clop-clop-clopped at an unhurried pace, and the sound of the boy kicking the ball faded.

Blinded and suffocating in the stifling heat inside the burlap sack and choking on the musty hay, Rogers lost all sense of time and direction as the horse plodded along, making several turns and passing murmuring passersby. He did the best he could to stifle any sneezes.

At last, the cart rocked to an abrupt stop. Hands lifted him from the cart and guided him inside a building and up a flight of creaky stairs. They emptied his pockets and forced him down into a straight-back wooden chair, tying his hands behind his back and through the spindles.

Light blinded him as someone ripped the sack off his head. Blinking to adjust his eyes, Rogers gulped in breaths of fresh air mixed with perfume and tobacco smoke and spat out bits of hay. In front of him sat a man with the square jaw, high forehead, and the penetrating eyes of a movie star, an image enhanced by a dapper coat and tie and studded tie pin.

The man, who appeared to be in his late thirties, tapped out a Dutch cigarette from a red and gold Amateurs Sigaretten pack and offered it to Rogers, who shook his head and examined the stuffy room.

A young blond man with a Luger in his hand hovered behind him. On a couch to the side sat a woman in a simple dress, maybe in her 40s, with a strong, dimpled chin, and graying short hair parted in the middle and brushed back over her ears like a helmet. With a notepad and pen at the ready, she waited.

Silently, the man at the desk examined Rogers' papers. As he flipped through the passport, the torn calling card fell out. The man picked it up, examined it with interest, and pulled another calling card half from his desk. When he pieced the two halves together, their edges fit exactly, as did the letters in the name on the card. He showed the woman the card and passport.

"So, Mr. O'Rourke, is it? How did you come into possession of these?" he asked in English.

"The name's Rogers. O'Rourke is my cover name, and I need your help," Rogers said, making no effort to fake an Irish accent.

"What unit are you with?" the man said, exchanging glances with the woman, scribbling in her notebook.

"None. I'm a merchant marine."

"So, how did you escape from a prisoner of war camp?"

"I didn't. I told you. I came here on an Irish ship."

The man sat up straight. "Do you expect us to believe that an American sailor walked off a ship into Amsterdam and just happened to have this?" He held up the torn card. "Who sent you?"

"I came on my own. But I had help from somebody at the Special Operations Executive. He gave me the calling card and said I should hand it over when I met with Group 2000."

"What do you know about Group 2000?" The man spoke in low, ominous tones.

"Nothing except that I was told the group helps Jews and downed Allied airmen escape."

"Who at SOE-N told you this?" the man said, referring to the SOE branch that handled agents in The Netherlands.

"I don't know his name. Never met him."

"What was his code name?" the man said, veins popping out on his forehead.

Rogers shrugged his shoulders and, with his eyes, pleaded to the woman for help. Instead, he was met with a stare of cold fury.

"You realize we can radio London and find out in a few hours who you really are," the man said.

"No one knows I'm here. Look, I came unarmed, seeking help to bust out a prisoner from Kamp Westerbork."

The man slumped back in his chair, glancing from the woman to the man with the gun behind Rogers. "Are you a Jew?"

"No. My friend is. Solomon Maduro. You heard of him?"

"Of course."

"I was told that Group 2000 could put me in touch with someone named Oom Piet, and he would finance the escape."

"Mr. O'Rourke, or Rogers, or whoever you are, I don't believe you," the man said, standing up to lean over his desk with his hands flat on the top. "I admit, you sound like an American. I even saw you walk like an American in Dam Square. But what you are saying is so detailed that you must be a German spy trying to uncover all our identities."

"But the torn card," Rogers said. "And the passwords with the kid in the square. How would a Nazi know about all that? And who in his right mind would invent such a crazy-sounding story as mine? I'm telling you the truth."

The woman rose from the couch and bent over in front of Rogers, searching his face with her intense brown eyes. "We have no idea how you did all of this. And we will certainly change our procedures," she said in English, motioning to the gunman with her head. "Mr. 400, take this spy out to the woods and shoot him. Make sure no one finds his body."

"Yes, Miss 2000," he said, pressing his Luger against Rogers' head. He snapped back the slide to chamber a round.

CHAPTER 7

With his hands still bound to the chair, Rogers sprang up, fighting against the rope cutting into his wrists. Twisting and turning, he tried to swing the chair as a battering ram, but then a gun cracked down hard on the back of his head, knocking him to the floor, half-conscious. Stars danced in his eyes, and muffled voices swirled around him, as hands picked him up and positioned him upright in the chair again. When the woman came into focus, she showed no emotion. Rogers mumbled the first thing that popped into his scrambled mind.

"What did you say?" the woman said, leaning in.

"Capt. Swift sent me," Rogers said in a hoarse whisper.

With her head tilted in surprise, the woman recoiled, glancing at the man at the desk and then at the gunman pressing his bloody Luger against Rogers' head. Then, like a balloon losing all its air, she collapsed onto the couch, and shooed the gunman away. "How do you know Bob?"

"I met him in Limerick after my Liberty ship sank. When I told him what I wanted to do, he contacted someone at the SOE, who arranged for me and my men to sail here on the *Erin Go Bragh*."

"Tell me more about him. What does he look like?"

"I don't know—a tall guy, maybe six feet, with, uh, with big ears."

"Anything else?

"Oh, yeah. His nose. Tilts to port like he'd been in a fight or something."

A faint hint of a smile crossed Miss 2000's face. "That's our Briscoe. Untie him." The gunman cut the ropes. "And get some bandages for his head."

Taking a handkerchief offered by the man behind the desk, Rogers wiped the blood off his head and rubbed his wrists. "Do you believe me now?"

"So sorry," she said, glaring at the young gunman. "He wasn't supposed to strike you like that, Mr. Rogers—"

"Capt. Rogers."

"Oh, yes. Capt. Rogers. My apologies. We never intended to shoot you. We only wanted to scare you to make sure you were telling the truth. I do not advocate violence. But we must be even more careful now because resistance groups have lost many members recently. And that means they have traitors within or have been betrayed by phony downed pilots. That is why my organization never uses names, only numbers, to identify our members. Would you like some coffee?"

"Yes, thank you," Rogers said. It struck him that the woman said, "My organization," and the kid had called her "Miss 2000" as in "Group 2000." The man who had been sitting at the desk walked out of the room without contradicting her. Who would have guessed that a woman would be leading resistance fighters?

"How do you know Briscoe?" Rogers asked Miss 2000.

"Guns," she said, pouring into a porcelain cup what was called "surrogate coffee"—a weak concoction of ground grains that included chicory or acorns. She handed a cup to Rogers and poured one for herself before returning to the couch. "He stored some of them in warehouses here for years, probably even in some of Mr. Maduro's warehouses. My father pointed him out to me once on the street and said, 'There goes the famous Capt. Swift.' He is a legendary Jew who made fools of the English and the Germans. No German spy would know to use his name. And it makes sense that Briscoe would support your mission."

"And will you?"

After taking a long sip of coffee, she set the cup on a side table and leaned back, eyes narrowed. "First, tell me your plan."

"I need money and counterfeit papers so I can travel to the camp. I heard they let some of the prisoners out from time to time to shop or to visit relatives. If you can help me get word to him to meet me outside the gates somewhere, we'll smuggle him back here in a stolen truck or wagon and sneak him onto my ship."

"Do you know why the prisoners always return to Kamp Westerbork?" she said with a frown.

Rogers shook his head.

"The Dutch guards will kill their relatives or friends if they fail to return to camp," she said. "If Maduro escapes, they will execute dozens in retaliation, as I'm sure he knows."

"But there must be a way to make him disappear."

"Perhaps." She rose as the man from behind the desk returned with a camera and a towel for Rogers' bloody head. "Mr. 2200 is head of our Personal Identity Center. He will take your picture and prepare all the documents you will need if—and I emphasize if—we can devise an escape plan."

"How will you do that? I don't have much time before my ship sets sail." Rogers backed up against a blank wall so Mr. 2200 could take several pictures of him from the front and in profile with a small 35mm Tenax camera.

"We can only go so fast, Capt. Rogers," she said. "First, we will visit someone I know who has been in Kamp Westerbork and might have some ideas."

When Mr. 2200 finished shooting the pictures, he retrieved a blank piece of paper from the desk and told Rogers to sign it. "What is your real name?" he said, handing Rogers a pen.

"Jake Rogers."

"You are now Joop Roosa." He spelled it out so Rogers could practice signing his new name and provide a template for his fake identity card.

Once satisfied with the signature, Mr. 2200 motioned to the woman, who led Rogers down a hall, stopping at the front door. "I'm sorry, but we can't take any chances."

Before he could ask what she meant, the young gunman slipped the burlap sack back over his head, led him outside, and helped him into the cart. When he was covered by hay, the horse trotted off at a leisurely pace. This time, the ride was much longer, traversing several bridges from the sound of it and making multiple turns.

When the cart rolled to a stop, someone whispered to Rogers, "Wait. When I say 'come,' remove the bag and follow me quickly." Footsteps and heated conversations faded down the street, followed by several minutes of silence. "Come, now."

Sitting up and ripping off the bag in one motion, Rogers leaped to the ground. Down the street was a palatial nineteenth-century building he recognized as the Royal Concertgebouw, or concert hall, in South Amsterdam. A man he didn't recognize lurked in a nearby doorway marked No. 6, waving him in.

Rogers scurried into the four-story red brick building to join Miss 2000, waiting by the stairs. She pressed a finger to her lips and led him to a bedroom on the third floor. "My friend is quite ill," she said. "Although she is a lawyer and language teacher, she is not always coherent in her current condition. She sometimes—what's the word?—meanders. But do not interrupt her, and let me do all the talking."

"Sure."

"And no names." She opened the door into the small, unlit room. A sliver of light was shining on a woman in bed, wrapped in blankets, rivulets of sweat flowing down her half-hidden face. "Hello, dear. This is the gentleman I was telling you about. He only understands English," Miss 2000 said, opening the thick blackout curtains and bathing the stuffy room in sunlight.

With Miss 2000's help, the woman scooted up and backward to prop herself up on a pillow and fiddled with her tangled hair as if to make herself more presentable. She could have been in her twenties or her sixties. Her smooth cheeks, pointed chin, and thin eyebrows said she was younger; her ashen complexion and sunken eyes, so full of sadness, made her seem ancient. "You want to know about the camp?" she said in a shaky voice.

"Yes, I have a friend named—"

"He has a friend he would like to help," Miss 2000 said, her eyes flashing as she pointed for Rogers to sit down at a desk covered with exercise books, Russian grammar books and dictionaries, a small Bible, and a dog-eared copy of Austrian poet Rainer Maria Rilke's collection of poems *Über Gott (About God)*. Next to the young woman's bed, a bookcase overflowed with an eclectic collection of classics: Russian novels, Shakespeare, Kierkegaard, and St. Augustine. This was a woman after Rogers' own heart. He had read most of the books here and would have loved nothing better than to discuss them with her—if there wasn't a war going on. He tugged his cap off and set it near an ancient typewriter.

In the corner next to a cracked armoire, an overcoat with a prominent yellow Star of David about the size of a hand hung from a coat rack. On the star was the word *Jood* in large letters. Rogers had heard Jews were required to wear the star since his last visit in 1941. He recalled with horror that no one in Dam Square wore one. The tens of thousands of Jews of Amsterdam were vanishing without a trace.

Miss 2000 handed the woman a glass of water from her bedside table, but she nudged it aside.

"Mud," the woman said.

"What, dear?" Miss 2000 asked.

"Everywhere there is mud and barbed wire and drafty wooden barracks filled with iron bunk beds stacked in triple decks that they say came from the Maginot Line. People living in them like so many rats in a sewer. Not enough mattresses. Babies screaming all the time. Thousands of Jews of jammed into a square half-kilometer." She coughed and seemed to lose her train of thought before resuming. "There is a lovely field in the middle of yellow lupins every spring, stretching as far as the delousing barracks. A little bit of sunshine to warm the heart," she said, reaching for the glass and sipping some water, her wan face briefly lighting up.

Taking the glass from her, Miss 2000 stroked the woman's unruly mass of curls. "My dear friend gave up a safe job with the Jewish Council here to work in Social Welfare for People in Transit at Westerbork," she said to Rogers. "That is why she is allowed to travel back and forth to Amsterdam to pick up medical supplies and deliver letters. Now, dear, if you don't mind, please tell us about the guards and how some people are allowed to leave."

"Those are the worst, the OD, the Service to Maintain Order, they call it, the absolute worst. German Jews are our guards. They wear green coveralls. Some call them the Jewish Gestapo." She coughed up phlegm that Miss 2000 wiped away with a handkerchief. "I think of their oafish, jeering faces. Not the slightest trace of warmth. I'm amazed at God's work. But they cannot rob me of anything that matters,"

"Can they be bribed?" Rogers said, unable to contain himself despite Miss 2000's glare.

The woman blinked at him, surprised, as if she'd forgotten he was there. She raised her hand to her mouth, ruminating. "I don't know. They say the camp commander is a proper gentleman. And he cannot be bribed," she said, pausing again, deep in thought. "Maybe *Oberdienstleiter* Schlesinger. He is the German Jew who is the camp's chief administrator. The Germans let him decide who to load onto the trains to the east, who gets what job, and who gets sent to the Punishment Barracks. They say he accepts money or sex for favors." The woman laughed to herself, "You know I am an accomplished lover—not with him, of course."

"Dear!" Miss 2000 gasped, blushing and changing the subject. "How do we get to this Schlesinger?"

"Oh, he leaves camp often to shop in Westerbork for things he can sell on the camp's black market. You can't miss him. Dresses like a Prussian in fawn riding breeches and boots, a black leather coat, and an officer's hat. He even has a toothbrush mustache like Hitler's. Imagine, a Jew doing that." The woman tried to throw off her covers. "I must return to my journals...must write," she said, rising, but Miss 2000 gently lowered her back down.

"No, dear, you must rest."

"Yes, yes, you're right. I must build up my strength so I can return to help my people. Can't give in to despair. I must not let the fire inside go out," she said with a fragile smile. "Even there, we find joy in our little cabaret shows and weddings and synagogue services. The children have school and play soccer, and I can visit many people in the hospital there. Life is still glorious."

"Is there any other way people have escaped?" Miss 2000 said, trying to steer the conversation back on point.

"Maybe, but—"

Several car doors slammed in the street below, followed by a sharp rapping on the front door. Rogers and Miss 2000 sprang up together and peeped out the window. Below, submachine gun-toting German soldiers stood guard on the sidewalk while an SS officer pounded on the woman's front door with a gloved hand.

"Is there another way out of here besides the front door?" Rogers asked the woman.

"No, except the back door on the first floor," she said, squinting her watery eyes. "Who are you?"

"Come on." Rogers grabbed Miss 2000 by the hand and led her into the hallway. He could hear the sound of German jackboots banging on the stairs. Unable to find a way to an attic, Rogers flew down the hall to a dormer, but the window wouldn't budge. All the other doors on the floor were locked. Shaking his head, he bolted back to Miss 2000, pulled her into the woman's bedroom, and hid them both among the few clothes in the armoire. The moment Rogers closed them in, he heard footsteps tramp into the room. Rogers watched through a crack.

The SS officer removed his gloves and retrieved something resembling a red leather cigar tube from a black bag. He slid off the lid, removed a five-inch-long fever thermometer, and stuck it in the woman's mouth. As he studied his watch, the officer felt the woman's pulse and asked her questions, to which she made short replies out of the side of her mouth.

Rogers yanked his head back when one of the armed soldiers stared at the armoire before turning his attention to the nearby desk. Holding his breath, Rogers pressed his eye to the crack. The guard was moving toward the desk. *Oh, hell*! Rogers reached up to feel the top of his head. *The cap!* He'd left it on the desk. The guard said something over his shoulder and turned his back to the armoire, holding his hand toward the SS officer. Rogers couldn't tell what it was.

Eyes wide with delight, the officer removed the thermometer from the woman's mouth, took the object from the soldier, and handed it to the woman: Rilke's *Über Gott*. She flipped through pages and recited passages from it while he pressed a rubber and brass stethoscope to her chest and back. He seemed to enjoy the reading and piped in from time to time with what must have been memorized verses. When he was done, the officer packed his bag, shook hands with the woman, slipped on his leather gloves, and marched out with his guards.

Miss 2000 held Rogers back until the front door banged shut and the vehicles squealed away. Once sure the coast was clear, they crawled out of the stifling wardrobe, gulping in the fresh air.

"He said I was too sick to return, but I said I was feeling stronger," the woman said.

"I'm sorry you're not well," Rogers said. "But I need to know, is there anyone, anyone at all you know who could help us at the camp? Trying to bribe a guy like Schlesinger is too risky. He's as likely to take the money and turn us in as he is to help."

Miss 2000 tugged on his arm to back off.

"Please," Roger said. "Anything you can think of."

"Werner, maybe," the woman whispered, drifting off.

"Werner who? How do we get to him?" Rogers said.

"Stertzenbach—Werner Stertzenbach. You know him, Jacoba, don't you?" she said, using Miss 2000's real name by mistake. "He's the communist who once offered to help me escape. I didn't ask how. Anyway, I said no. Maybe he has a way to help you, mister. He's easy to find. Works almost every day outside the barbed wire on the sewage system and, I hear, a new crematorium. He's good with his hands. Does that help?"

"Yes, yes, thank you so much," Rogers said, letting out a huge breath.

"Rest, dear. You look exhausted, and we must leave. Now," she said, nudging Rogers toward the door. "You should listen to Werner. Let us hide you."

The woman shook her head. "They need me, and I must share my people's fate. My life must have meaning." She laid back on the pillow and appeared to fall into a fitful sleep.

With tears in her eyes, Miss 2000 kissed her on the forehead. "Get well, my sweet Etty." Turning her attention to Rogers, she said, "It doesn't matter anymore if you know her name. You know mine, and you must forget it. If you are captured, I am Miss 2000."

Rogers nodded in agreement, flipping on his cap and pulling it low on his brow. She led Rogers down the stairs, opened the front door, and gasped.

The cart to transport Rogers into hiding was gone.

CHAPTER 8

"Will it come back?" Rogers said.

"No. They know never to pass the same way twice," Miss 2000 said. "The Germans must have scared them off."

"What do we do now?"

"Dam Square is a thirty-minute walk from here. Follow me at a distance. And don't walk like an American, marching in a hurry and gawking. Keep your head forward, take confident but slow steps, and for goodness' sake, do not whistle or jingle the change in your pockets."

"Yes, ma'am," he said, giving a stiff military salute.

They headed past the concert hall and the nineteenth-century Rijksmuseum, with Renaissance and Gothic features on its twin towers and ornate facade. Much to Rogers' disgust, Nazi soldiers were hauling crates of artwork from the museum to a long, covered truck.

When Rogers followed Miss 2000 over the Singel Canal, the last one before Dam Square, a pair of *Grüne Polizei*, German police in green uniforms, blocked his path. Miss 2000 glanced over her shoulder and froze. After composing herself, she strode back toward him as if on a mission to somewhere else that happened to be in that direction.

Rogers couldn't understand a thing the Germans said, provoking them to raise their voices and keep repeating the same thing with their hands held out. He pulled out his pass from Inspector De Klerk, pointed to it, and waved his hand around. "Dam Square. *Wo ist*?" One of the soldiers snatched the paper and read it to his companion, then shouted something in German.

As if startled, Miss 2000 stopped abruptly and spoke to the police. "*Ich glaube, er ist verloren*," she said about the poor man being lost. "*Ich spreche Englisch.*" She scrutinized Rogers. "Where are you trying to go, mister?"

"I'm to go to Dam Square for supplies for me ship," he said in an exaggerated Irish accent, pointing at the pass in the German's hand.

She told the Germans what Rogers had said and offered to show him the way. Muttering between themselves, the policemen checked the pass before shoving it back at Rogers and motioning him away. Arm-in-arm, Rogers and Miss 2000 traveled north along the Rotkin Canal to Dam Square. "I will talk to Oom Piet about funds," she whispered to Rogers when she was sure no one could hear her. "Be prepared to leave in the morning if you see Mr. 400 on the quay at daybreak."

"And my crew?"

"You travel alone. Now, I must leave," she said and hurried away, leaving Rogers to find his way back to the ship.

☆☆☆

As soon as Rogers stepped on the quay, Nidal and Obasi sprinted down the *Erin Go Bragh's* gangplank to greet him, relief on their faces. "Sorry, Captain," Nidal said. "We lost you, and we couldn't linger too long in the square. We were already getting suspicious looks."

"I understand," Rogers said as they climbed aboard the ship. "They moved me pretty quickly."

"Where've you been, Cap'n?" Cookie asked, out of breath from running over. "You scared the life out of us."

"I found the group we were looking for, and they've agreed to help," Rogers said. "They may come for me tomorrow."

"What about us?" Cookie said. "You'll be needing our help."

"They only agreed to take me. Sorry. I guess it's too complicated with more than one of us," Rogers said. He put his hand on Cookie's shoulder, who was bent over to catch his breath. "Any idea how much longer we have in port?"

"A few days, I guess," Nidal said. "They are still unloading some of the holds. And Capt. Griffin said that before we can sail, the ship has to dock at the Amsterdam Dock Company for repairs once the backlog clears up. But there is something you should see."

They led Rogers to Hold Number Four in the ship's stern. Pinching his nose, Rogers leaned over and was surprised to see the pigs gone, replaced by stacks of wooden crates of all sizes. He took several steps back upwind. "Pretty fast work."

"They unloaded the pigs first thing, and German soldiers carried on those crates," Nidal said. "They forced us to help. We got some sweat rags from the black gang and wrapped them around our faces, but the smell down in the hold was still almost overwhelming," he said, using the nickname for crew members who shoveled coal into the boilers down below and were always covered in black coal dust.

"Why didn't they clean it out first and get rid of at least some of the smell?" Rogers asked.

"Capt. Griffin wouldn't allow it. Said he liked the smell," Nidal said, shaking his head in disbelief. "We figured out why when one of the young soldiers gagged at the smell and dropped the box he was carrying on deck into the hold and—"

"It burst open," Cookie interrupted, still wheezing. "Lugers spilled out everywhere. A German officer made the poor lad come down and pick them all up. He thought it was funny to watch him speaking Welsh." The three men waited for translation from Cookie, who straightened up with a chuckle. "Vomiting. The boy lost breakfast, dinner, and supper."

"Smart," said Rogers, beating a hasty retreat to the port bulkhead for some fresh air, followed by his companions. "They'll probably cover the crates with coal or grain, knowing that no inspector will ever go down there with that odor."

"Who do you reckon the guns are for?" Cookie said.

"Let us see," Nidal said, his voice dripping with sarcasm. "We came from Ireland on an Irish ship with fake papers, and we're taking guns back to Ireland. Who could possibly want guns there?" He crossed his arms with a blank expression, waiting for Cookie to catch on.

"The bloody IRA, that's who," Cookie said in disgust. "Cap'n, we can't arm those bastards. They'll be killing me mates and helping the Germans."

Having suspected as much before they sailed from Ireland, Rogers wasn't sure how to respond. Briscoe was connected to the IRA, and he was followed by men in slouch hats and trench coats, the traditional IRA uniform. Rogers had hoped he was wrong, that Griffin was picking up some other contraband or taking cargo to the highest bidder, which Rogers had done for a living on the *Peggy C.* But he ignored his fears because he was so desperate to travel to Amsterdam. Now, the hard, cold reality was sinking in. "I'll have a word with Capt. Griffin," he said and trotted up the ladders to the captain's quarters. He knocked on the half-open door and stepped inside without waiting for an invitation.

"Ah, Captain, you gave us a fright," Griffin said, glancing up from a small desk, where he was writing in his log. "Did your visit go well?"

"I need to talk to you about the cargo."

With a dour expression, Griffin scooted his chair back and reached for the bottle of poteen, poured himself a stiff drink, gulped it down, and slammed the glass on his desk. "Don't be askin' me that."

"Look, Gerald," Rogers said, taking a seat on a chair in the corner. "I'm not going to be a hypocrite. I've smuggled worse things in my time. But this is different. There's a war on now."

"A war on who and for what? And why should I give a tinker's damn?" Griffin said, pouring himself another drink.

"I know you Irish have your problems with the English," Rogers said, "but do you truly want them to lose to the Germans? Do you want more bloodshed in Ireland?"

"Bloodshed?" Griffin scoffed. "I'm a Griffin from County Kerry, and I can tell you plenty about the bloodshed brought on Ireland by the British for centuries—for centuries, I tell you. And do ye know who's the worst of them all?"

Rogers shook his head.

"Churchill," Griffin said. "And who is England now? Churchill. He may not have killed my cousin at Ballyseedy, but he was still the cause of it. So, if I can contribute to Churchill's pain, even a wee bit, I'll be doing it with pleasure." Griffin started slurring his words. "His whole family has been a curse on Ireland since the day the first Duke of Marlborough got his first independent command there. His grandfather was Lord Lieutenant, ye know, and his father, Lord Randolph, was the viceroy's private secretary."

Rogers tried to take away the bottle of poteen, but Griffin wouldn't let go of it. "But to help the IRA—"

"He continued the family tradition of tormenting us in every new cabinet post, he did. He's the one who sent in the Black and Tans, those murderous thugs. He armed the Free Staters and pressured Michael Collins and our Provisional Government to crush the Easter Rebellion. And it's because of him that the cursed Anglo-Irish Treaty ended our independence and split Eire apart. Aye, the blame for that night twenty years ago, this very month, rests squarely on Churchill's head."

"That was a long time ago," Rogers said, moving his chair closer to lock eyes with Griffin.

"'Tisn't to my mind. My poor cousin was nigh on eighteen when the Free Staters dragged him and eight others out of the prison and hospital at Tralee. They all had broken bones from being tortured and beaten by hammers, but they had to ride in bumpy lorries and walk to the Ballyseedy crossroads late at night." He waved the bottle at Rogers. "The Free Staters' blood was up on account of five of theirs being killed by a booby trap. So, they told the prisoners they'd have to clear mines from the road under the moonlight in freezing cold." He coughed and paused for a moment, taking one more sip of poteen.

"You've had enough, old timer," Rogers said, reaching again for the bottle, and failing again to wrest it from Griffin's grasp.

"They took 'em to what looked like a log or tree trunk in the middle of the road and tied 'em up, together, around it, hands behind their backs, ankles and knees bound together with rope. They gave each man a cigarette and knocked off his cap. They taunted them about saying their prayers and called them Irish bastards. When the last officer backed away, our lads knew what was about to happen."

Rogers handed Griffin a handkerchief, and he paused and wiped a tear from the corner of his eye.

"They shouted their goodbyes to one another. And tugged at the ropes. But weren't no getting away from that tree trunk." Griffin slammed the bottle down on his desk. "It exploded in an awful blast. Body parts and blood flew everywhere. That trunk...that cursed log...weren't no piece of wood. 'Twas a mine..." His voice trailed off.

"I'm awfully sorry, Gerald," Rogers said, patting his arm and sliding the bottle away.

"They blew my poor cousin and all of 'em to pieces and stuffed 'em into nine coffins and told everyone they had stepped on the mine while clearing the roads. Only, they didn't realize—because body parts was all they had—that they hadn't killed them all." He blew his nose in the handkerchief and tried to hand it back to Rogers, who waved him off. "Stephen Fuller had been blasted clear across the road and survived to tell the tale. He heard grenades and machine guns finish off his moaning and crying friends. So don't tell me times are different. Churchill has to pay, one way or the other."

Rogers slipped the glass out of Griffin's hand and helped him into his bed, where he cried himself to sleep.

CHAPTER 9

Alone with his thoughts, Rogers paced the flying bridge in front of the wheelhouse, a dusting of snow swirling over the quay in the brisk dawn of what promised to be a sunny day. In the distance, two armed soldiers climbed out of a gray Volkswagen Kübelwagen, a Jeep-like convertible with a spare tire on the hood, and marched toward Rogers' ship.

The closer they got, the more uncomfortable Rogers felt. One carried a stubby MP-40 submachine gun, and the other had a *Karabiner* 98k bolt-action rifle slung over his shoulder— standard issue for the German military. The orange, white, and blue shield on the left sleeve of their gray four-pocket uniforms and the SS lightning bolts on their collars indicated they were Dutch Waffen-SS members.

Rogers leaned on the bridge railing, pretending not to notice the soldiers in the dim morning light, and wishing they would pass by his ship's gangplank. He checked the nearby streets to ensure Mr. 400 wasn't falling into a trap. They hadn't arranged any kind of signals, so there wasn't much Rogers could do to warn him without drawing unwanted attention from the soldiers.

Abruptly, the soldiers stopped and stared up at Rogers. The one with the submachine gun pointed a finger at Rogers, gesturing for him to come down to the dock; his companion unshouldered his rifle and cocked it with a loud click, holding it at his waist.

"What are you going to do, Captain?" Nidal said, stepping onto the bridge with a cup of coffee in his hands.

"Not much I can do. There're only two of them, so I doubt it's a raid. I'll have to find out what they want." He flipped on his cap and shuffled down the gangplank to the soldiers.

The one with the submachine gun seemed to be in charge. He had a black patch with a white V on his sleeve and a single stripe on his left gorget patch, or collar tab, indicating he was an *SS-Sturmmann,* a corporal. His companion was an *SS-Schütze*, a private with no insignia.

Not bothering to ask for his papers, the soldiers led Rogers at gunpoint to the waiting Kübelwagen and shoved him into the back seat next to another soldier wearing a gray-green M40 wool cap with a grinning *Totenkopf* skull on the front. On the hat and above his right breast pocket perched a *Wehrmachtsadler,* the national emblem of a silver eagle with outstretched wings clutching an oak wreath surrounding a swastika. He had a single pip and stripe on his collar tab. After everyone climbed in, the private drove them away.

Rogers did a double take at the smiling soldier beside him: Mr. 400.

"Sorry for the dramatic pickup," Mr. 400 said. "We can't be sure if you're being watched or not. Soldiers arresting civilians is such a common sight that we're almost invisible. Plus, we need you to put these on." He tossed Rogers a Waffen-SS uniform and knee-high black leather jackboots with hobnails.

Changing clothes in the back of a moving vehicle required quite a bit of twisting and turning and grunting. But Rogers managed to strip off his work clothes and don the four-pocket tunic, riding breeches, and boots, which were a little big for him. "Nice tailoring job," he said, inspecting the field-gray tunic with the Dutch shield and a black band on the left sleeve that read *"Frw. Legion Niederlande"* in white letters. The SS lightning bolts were on one collar tab and three diamond-shaped pips above two stripes on the other. "What do these mean?"

"You are an officer, an *Oberstrumführer*, what you Americans would call a lieutenant. And you are a doctor," Mr. 400 said, tapping on the shoulder boards decorated with a gold Rod of Asclepius, a single serpent entwined on a staff like the one carried by the Greek god Asclepius, who was associated with healing and medicine. "This way, you don't have to carry a gun, Herr Doctor Roosa."

The Kübelwagen slowed to a stop at a curb in front of Amsterdam Centraal, the palatial nineteenth-century Dutch neo-Renaissance train station. "I don't speak a word of German or even much Dutch," Rogers said.

"That will not be a problem," Mr. 400 said, holding the door open for Rogers. "Soldiers and police are afraid to question officers. I will be your aide,

Scharführer Müller. It's like a sergeant. I will do all the talking and carry your equipment." He tapped on the bulky brown leather bag hanging on a leather strap from his shoulder with a prominent red cross on its side.

"Where are we going?" Rogers said as he stepped out and straightened his tunic with both hands.

"Westerbork."

"Why not drive?"

Mr. 400 chuckled and handed Rogers an SS officer's gray wool cap with white piping around the crown, the Nazi eagle and skull on the front, and a silver bullion chin cord strapped across the shiny black Vulkanfiber visor. "We can't *borrow* it for much longer." He shut the door and saluted his colleagues away.

The two-hour train journey was uneventful. Rogers laid back in his seat with his cap over his eyes most of the time, pretending to be asleep as Mr. 400 had instructed. Dutch policemen in blue uniforms checking papers passed them by without any questions.

The train shuddered to a stop at the small Hooghalen train station, about five kilometers west of Camp Westerbork. Rogers and Mr. 400, carrying the First Aid bag, stepped outside the building and waited for the few passengers to disperse down the desolate road. Rogers tugged at his shirt collar in nervous irritation, wondering for what or whom they were waiting.

A German officer and two aides hurried out of the station and stopped beside Rogers, exchanging salutes and pleasantries. Silently, Rogers bowed his head in acknowledgment. When a black Opel Admiral Cabriolet pulled up, the officer motioned Rogers into the car as if offering him a ride, saying something in German. To answer, Mr. 400 jumped in, shaking his head.

Rogers pulled out a handkerchief and coughed into it repeatedly. Between coughing fits, he mouthed the word *danke* and rubbed his throat to indicate he'd lost his voice. With a shrug, the officer clicked his boots, bowed and, with his aide, sped off in the staff car.

Rogers fidgeted but knew better than to ask Mr. 400 anything in English. After an hour, a rusty, red Opel Blitz truck, its bed surrounded by wooden slats and full of tree limbs, bounced down the road and pulled up in front of the station. The word *Staatsbosbeheer* and a faint outline of a tree were etched on its door. Mr. 400 climbed in the passenger's side, followed by Rogers, who had to slam the door repeatedly before it would stay closed.

"This is our friend Ger from the *Van Dien* group," Mr. 400 said. "He works for the Dutch Forestry Commission around here. He will take us to a campsite in the woods where we can hide and observe Westerbork without being seen." He spoke to the driver in Dutch for several minutes.

"I speak some English," said Ger, who was blond and appeared to be in his twenties. He swerved off the main road onto a dirt track leading into a forest thick with spruce, birch, beech, and oak trees. "Maybe we see Werner tonight. He work on sewer and new crematorium."

"How do you communicate?" Rogers said.

"Special tree. He leaves messages and letters there. I leave identity papers and letters for him."

"Can you meet him in person? I need to talk to him."

"Sometimes at night. We wait," Ger said, veering off the path to cut between the trees. The truck crept along until it rolled to a stop at an embankment covered in thick foliage near what appeared to be an opening.

When Rogers jumped out of the truck and moved closer, he discovered it was the door, covered with leaves and branches, of a log cabin cut into the embankment.

"Stay here tonight," Ger said. "We wait for Werner."

"What about food?" Mr. 400 asked.

"Girl on bike will bring before sunset. Come, we look at Westerbork," he said and plunged into the woods, sweeping thick bushes aside, often checking over his shoulder that the two men were keeping up with him.

"How do you know so much about what goes on inside?" Rogers said, huffing and half-trotting to stay alongside Ger.

"My sister-in-law Trude is Jew. My brother Theo and I are not. They met during Spanish Civil War at Dutch hospital in Villanueva de la Jara. He was doctor. She was nurse. Both good communists, like their friend Werner. When Trude was arrested and sent to Westerbork, Werner stole her *Lagerkarte* from the *cartotheek,* uh—"

"Camp card from the Registry," Mr. 400 explained.

"Yes," Ger said. "So, she is safe. Her card cannot be selected for train.

She sends me information through Werner."

"Where is your brother now?" Rogers said.

"Dachau."

After about an hour, sweat covered Rogers despite the cool air. Ger raised his hand and dropped to his knees to crawl. Rogers and Mr. 400 followed suit until they reached the forest's edge.

"Dutch Jerusalem, some call it," Ger said, pointing ahead at Camp Westerbork, surrounded by a two-meter-high barbed wire fence and a moat on three sides, all overlooked by seven guard towers.

Mr. 400 rooted around the medical bag until he found a pair of binoculars, which he handed to Rogers; Ger had his own pair. They studied the flat, muddy heath in the middle of a desolate clearing a good distance from the forest. It resembled a bustling village with hundreds of men, women, and children in civilian clothes wandering about.

Some of the men wore coats and ties. The women wore dresses and caps, and some had on white turbans. Several of the adults had shaved heads. Children kicked soccer balls or played tag. Everyone wore yellow stars stitched on their shirts and coats. Jewish police, the OD in their green overalls with a yellow star, tall boots, and military-styled visored caps, patrolled inside the camp.

"Looks like a normal village except for the barbed wire," Rogers said.

"Yes. Designed to keep calm," Ger said. "Everyone has job farming or in construction, building furniture, binding books, making wooden horses and stuffed dolls for the children. Gives everyone false sense of hope."

Rogers counted about a hundred long wooden barracks and buildings lining a railroad track and a wide road, both cutting through the middle of the camp past a towering smokestack belonging to the camp's boiler. At the western entrance for the train, a Dutch policeman manned a glass-enclosed guard station, checking passes as people plodded in and out of the camp lugging bags of food or pushing wooden hand carts.

"They call road Boulevard des Misères," Ger said. "The train—the 'venomous snake' as it is known—comes with new prisoners every Monday and takes many people away on Tuesday to Poland. They say work camps, but we hear many Jews die at Auschwitz or Sobibor."

"Why don't they—"

Ger shoved Rogers' head down, "*Marechaussee*," he whispered, pointing at the guards who, before the war, had been Royal Dutch Military Police. In the brush, the three men lay as flat and as still as possible, controlling their breath. Two guards in long, dark-blue double-breasted coats with silver buttons, a thick leather belt, high black jackboots, and *Schirmmütze* (peaked visored caps), tramped in front of them, chatting and not paying much attention to their surroundings. Karabiner 98k rifles were slung over their shoulders.

When the squishing sound of the policemen's muddy boots faded, Rogers popped his head up and resumed his search with the binoculars. Marechaussee, at the southwest corner of the camp, also patrolled two entrances for train cars on narrow-gauge tracks.

A cacophony of pounding and buzzing saws and drills and grunting filled the air. The noise came from men in coveralls working outside the barbed wire on a slagheap of metal parts from wrecked vehicles and downed planes. They pounded the parts with sledgehammers and picked at the pieces to extract and separate valuable metals; other men inspected and tossed them into barrels marked *Kupfer* for copper, *Messing* for brass, and *Aluminum*.

Several men led horses out of the second entrance, pulling on a narrow-gauge track a row of small, open wagons filled with bricks that women wearing thick gloves tossed in a relay line from the wagons to construction sites for new buildings and sewers.

"There is new crematorium. Started working this month." Ger pointed to a T-shaped building with double doors and small rectangular windows about fifty paces south of the train entrances and out of sight of the guard station. Smoke drifted up from the chimney.

Farther south, two bored-looking Marechaussee guarded women in scarves and men laboring on a 100-acre farm, turning over fields with shovels, raking out the clods with hand-pulled metal drag harrows, and tilling the soil with a horse-drawn plow. Sheep, goats, pigs, and chickens grazed and pecked and rooted in their nearby pens while men on stools milked the cud-chewing cows.

Ger punched Rogers' arm and pointed at a young man leaving the main entrance, pushing a bulky cart. A single arm dangled from underneath a cover

over the side. The young man, with a big head of curly hair, a square jaw, and large ears, stopped at the crematorium's door and called out for two men to help him. After removing the cover, they lifted out four lifeless bodies and lugged them inside. The young man grabbed a tool chest from the cart and followed them, closing the door behind him.

"That is Werner," Ger said.

"The guards didn't even ask for his papers," Rogers said.

"Nobody wants to get near bodies. The smell," Ger said, pinching his nose. "And everybody knows Werner. He is one of the *alte Kampinsassen*, uh, senior camp inmates. One of the German Jews who has been here almost from beginning." He raised himself on his hands and knees and crawled backward, signaling with his head for Rogers and Mr. 400 to do likewise.

"What now?" Rogers said when he came alongside Ger and stood.

"We go. Hide. Eat. I will leave message at tree for Werner to meet us tomorrow night." He hiked back toward the hidden hut and stopped along the way at a towering oak, its branches largely leafless and spread wide like so many skeletal fingers. After scraping away some dirt, Ger lifted out a small metal box. From inside it, he removed letters and dropped in documents and a note in an envelope. "Another train comes tomorrow," he said, covering up the box in the hole.

"What if Werner doesn't come tonight?"

"It may be too late for your friend, I'm afraid."

CHAPTER 10

When they made it back to the hideaway, Ger handed Rogers and Mr. 400 blankets and a cup for dipping water from a bucket at the back of the hut. He told them to rest while he gathered wood for a small fire. Not long after Ger left, leaves crackled in the distance. Peeking outside, Rogers spotted a teenage girl heading their way on a bike with a basket strapped onto the back. He stepped into the daylight without thinking and, with a broad smile, greeted her with a friendly wave.

The girl slammed on the brakes and skidded, flipping over and scraping her bare knees. Rogers hurried over and reached down to help her up but she recoiled in horror at the arm of his Nazi uniform. With an involuntary scream, the girl abandoned the bike and basket, and fled on skinny legs into the forest with the frantic grace of a gazelle.

"Edda! Edda!" Ger shouted, dropping a bundle of kindling and running after her. He shouted something in Dutch that Rogers couldn't understand and flew with arms pumping into the thick foliage.

"She thinks we are Nazis," Mr. 400 said. "Ger is yelling that it is safe. That you are an American."

A stiff wind whisked through the spruce needles; a raven's rapid-fire caw-caw-caw warning echoed in the frigid air. Nothing else stirred. Perplexed and concerned, Rogers felt terrible about forgetting his uniform and scaring someone trying to help them. He stared at the spot where he had last seen Ger and cocked his head at the faint sound of footsteps. With his arm around her shoulder, Ger guided Edda out of the woods, her face ashen and lined with tears.

She was stunning with her beret, worn at a jaunty angle over her shoulder-length black hair. She also had on a school blazer with a plaid skirt. Her looks, her outfit, and her lithesome movements imbued her with an aura of elegance.

"Please tell her I am terribly sorry to have scared her," Rogers said.

"I thought I'd bought it," Edda replied in English spoken with a slight

British accent. She picked up the basket and handed it to Rogers. "I haven't been doing this for long, and I am here visiting relatives, so I don't know the territory well. When my cousin fell ill, I insisted on lending a hand. I hope you did not have to wait too dreadfully long."

"Not at all," Rogers said, handing the basket to Mr. 400.

"What unit are you two from?" she asked.

"Long story," Rogers said, unsure how much information he should reveal. "How did you learn English so well?"

"Boarding school in England."

"Edda here is quite a dancer," Ger said. "Does illegal performances at *zwarte avonden*— how you say, black evenings—in people's homes with blacked-out windows to raise money for people sheltering Jews and others. And she helps deliver food and documents to downed pilots."

Edda blushed. "I do what I can. Now I must be off. It wouldn't do for me to be on the road after dark."

Rogers picked up her bike and balanced it while she climbed on. "Thanks. For all you do," he said. She flashed an enchanting smile and rode off.

"Poor thing," Ger said as she disappeared. "Her uncle Otto was taken hostage by Nazis and executed as punishment for resistance attacks he had nothing to do with. Changed her name from Audrey Hepburn-Ruston to Edda van Heemstra because she was afraid it sounded too English." Before leaving, he demonstrated how to build a small fire inside the hut and warned them not to wander off during the night. "Light fire at dusk to hide smoke and flames. I will return tomorrow afternoon. Inside basket, you will find soap and razor. Please shave before I come. German soldiers always shave." With that, he drove off in the rusty Blitz.

The night was cold and full of strange sounds: creatures prowling on dried leaves in the gloom, owls' plaintive hoots, gusts of wind rustling the spruce and brush. Every one of those noises worried Rogers, who had trouble sleeping and at dawn woke up exhausted, his head full of vague images from strange, unremembered dreams. Ger returned at mid-afternoon and led them back toward the camp.

"When will we see Werner?" Rogers asked, again struggling to keep up with Ger's long strides.

"After train comes, when everyone pays attention to new arrivals. If he got message."

That weighed on Rogers' mind as they crawled to the forest's edge and scouted the scene with binoculars. The camp seemed almost empty compared to the day before. In their green overalls, a group of OD members lined up in formation near a train platform on Boulevard des Misères. A handful of Marechaussee and SS soldiers in gray uniforms wandered about with their 98k rifles slung over their shoulders.

"Where is everybody?" Mr. 400 asked.

"Train day. They are all locked in barracks," Ger said.

Standing on the platform, a tall officer surrounded by aides examined documents, a yapping Alsatian playing at his feet. He had three pips on his collar tab and an SD diamond patch on his left sleeve for *Sicherheitsdienst*, SD or security service, below the Nazi eagle.

"*SS-Obersturmführer* Albert Gemmeker," Ger whispered.

"The gentleman Kommandant?" Rogers said.

"He is no gentleman. It is true he does not beat prisoners himself or allow others to do so in his sight, and he does not yell at them. But he is monster all the same," Ger said and spat. "Trude works in hospital. She told me one time, a sick premature baby boy arrived on train, and Gemmeker had it rushed to the camp hospital. He claims to love children. He had special incubator brought in, and even a famous doctor. He visit the baby every day. Nothing was too good. Trude say she took care of baby day and night. When the boy recovered and puts on weight, the whole camp cheered. He was symbol of hope. But do you know what the gentleman commander did?"

"Adopted him?" Rogers said.

Ger shook his head. "Put him on next train to Auschwitz."

A train whistle triggered a flurry of activity inside the barbed wire. When the train came to a complete stop, OD members lining the platform scurried to unlock the cattle cars. Men in brown overalls and women—all wearing armbands with "FK" on them—helped the dazed passengers, holding their babies and luggage as they stepped out of the dark compartments, blinking their eyes to adjust to the light, and then loading the suitcases and bags into wooden carts. The *Fliegende Kolonne*, the Flying Column, were fellow inmates charged with helping new arrivals settle in and, later, depart—a sort of hospitality committee for the first level of hell.

Once the guards herded the hundreds of new arrivals into the building, a team of inmate-clerks manning typewriters would register them. Werner emerged from the main entrance hauling a hand cart full of bricks. He dumped them near the foundation for the new water treatment plant, picked up a shovel, and headed into the forest with the cart, not bothering to check behind for the guards' approval as if it were normal for an inmate to wander off on his own. Rogers figured it must not have been the first time because none of the guards paid him any attention.

Ger led Rogers and Mr. 400 deeper into the forest near the oak where he had hidden the message. When Werner appeared, he stopped dead, eyes wide and his body tense, preparing to flee. Ger gave him a hand signal that made him relax and join the three men.

"I got your message and a letter from Amsterdam," Werner said. "But I have bad news. Mr. Maduro says he will not flee with you because the Germans will kill too many others in revenge."

"Doesn't he realize this is his only chance?" Rogers said in exasperation.

"He said he has told others the same thing. And he will not change his mind."

"But haven't you gotten others out? Ger said you can remove their registration cards so no one will miss them."

"Yes. I removed their registration card and provided them with passes to leave the camp," Werner said. "But Solomon Maduro is a special case. All the guards know never to let him leave. The Germans fear he will bribe his way out with hidden money. They even have his picture at the guardhouse at the entrance."

"We can't wait," Mr. 400 said. "You have to return to your ship soon."

"There has to be a way," Rogers said, ignoring Mr. 400. He lowered his head in thought, rubbing his lower lip between his thumb and forefinger.

"You are beating *dood paard*," Mr. 400 said. When Rogers arched an eyebrow, Mr. 400 asked the others for help in Dutch.

"Dead horse," Ger said.

"Yes, you beat dead horse," Mr. 400 said. "It is not possible to rescue a man who does not want to be rescued. We must leave—now."

Rogers stared at Mr. 400, rubbing his chin; a ghost of a smile crept across his face. "Funny you should mention a horse. Before the Germans killed Mr. Maduro's brother on my ship, he told me a fable about teaching a horse to fly."

The three men stared at him, blank gazes on their faces.

"The point of the story, Rabbi Levy told me, was that nothing is hopeless," Rogers said. "That was true then, and it's true now. We'll just have to find a way to teach this dead horse to fly."

Rogers outlined his plan, a desperate scheme with a slim chance of succeeding. If it failed, all of them would either be killed or sent to a concentration camp. Rogers told them he couldn't live with himself if they didn't at least try. After expressing doubts, they all agreed to Rogers' ruse. With the plan set, Ger poured a bag of mushrooms into Werner's cart, which he rolled away.

The three remaining men followed Werner to the edge of the forest and watched him show off his harvest of mushrooms to the guards at the entrance. He offered them several handfuls and wheeled back into the camp.

Everything appeared normal for the rest of the day, with people hurrying between buildings, barracks, and work sites, hauling things, pounding things, dragging carts, and leading horses to the hoppers. Oberdienstleiter Schlesinger, creepy smile and all, strutted about in his riding breeches and black leather jacket, giving orders, stopping young women to flirt with, and letting everyone know who had the real power. At one point, Schlesinger shoved away a balding man bent over with age, who seemed to be pleading with him for something.

Then, the OD, SS soldiers, and Dutch policemen swarmed the compound, blowing whistles and herding and shoving people to the middle of the camp, beating anyone who slowed down or failed to comply with their orders without hesitation. Several thousand inmates lined up in silence and utter terror.

As soon as the desperate prisoners settled down, Schlesinger got up onto a wooden crate in front of them with Arthur Pisk, a former Austrian milliner who commanded the Jewish police, standing at his side. Rogers focused his binoculars as best he could on papers Pisk handed to Schlesinger, which appeared to be typed lists of something. With an eerie clarity, Schlesinger's voice carried over the wind-swept heath. One by one, he shouted names in alphabetical order, each greeted with shrieks and groans; people crumbled to their knees in tears, trembling as their loved ones hugged them.

When anyone dared to leave the formation or crawl through the mud to Schlesinger on their hands and knees, pleading and wailing, the guards pounced on them with fists and clubs or cracked heads with the butts of their rifles and laughed as they dragged screaming women and children back to the group. Kommandant Gemmeker was nowhere to be seen.

"What is happening?" Rogers asked Ger.

"It is the list of names for tomorrow's train to Poland. They have the night to prepare for departure," Ger said.

"But why tell—"

Ger tapped his forefinger on his lips for silence. With his hands cupped around his ears, he strained to make out the words. "Maduro's name is on the list. Your plan better work."

CHAPTER 11

After a hasty breakfast at dawn of powdered eggs and bread, washed down with tepid, green coffee, Rogers, Mr. 400, and Ger trudged in silence through the forest to their hiding place at the clearing, where they could see inside Westerbork. Anxious inmates were already lining up for a train, some lugging suitcases or large bags slung over their shoulders. Children clung to their mothers, who often knelt to whisper an encouraging word or scoop up a dropped toy.

Shouted orders punctuated the clamor of creaking wheels, shuffling feet, and grunts. Helpers in brown overalls with FC on their armbands were towing carts full of luggage. One rolled a strange makeshift wheelchair with oversized wire-spoked wheels like on old-fashioned bicycles, hauling an old woman apparently too feeble to walk to the train, even with assistance.

A tall man in horn-rimmed glasses and slicked-back hair scurried around filming the scene with a handheld 9.5mm Alef cine camera, doing his best to avoid capturing the chaos. Instead, he focused on anything that appeared calm or normal and encouraged people to wave and smile. Rogers raised an eyebrow at Ger.

"Gemmeker is making propaganda film to show world how humane he treats Jews and to show superiors how efficient he is," Ger said, curling his lips in disgust. "Werner says Nazi is quite proud of job he does."

The tall camp commandant paced along the platform, holding his hands behind his ramrod-straight back while chatting with other SS officers and reviewing documents; his Alsatian, its tail wagging wildly, trotted along.

Focusing his binoculars with difficulty, Rogers searched the crowd for Maduro. But it was almost impossible to make out faces as the inmates stepped forward when their names were called. They were gently assisted by the FC, or shoved and kicked by OD members up portable wooden stairs into the cattle cars.

An elderly nun in full habit, head down as if in prayer, appeared too weak to climb the stairs, so the helpers lifted her into a car. The grateful sister blessed them with the sign of the cross. Rogers lowered his binoculars to rub his eyes.

"Once a Jew, always a Jew, according to Nazis, even if convert," Ger said.

As each boxcar filled up, a fellow inmate rolled by with a cart full of small wooden barrels and handed two of them inside: one was full of water, the other was for use as a toilet during the three-day journey. Haunted faces stared out in despair as Dutch police, some in three-quarter-length blue capes, slid the creaky doors shut with a bang. After locking in the passengers with the flip of a metal bar, they scrawled the number of occupants on the side with chalk. The count was always somewhere between seventy and eighty.

In the middle of all the chaos, Rogers thought he spotted Maduro, whom he had only met once before, during his last visit to Amsterdam almost two years ago. The man, carrying a small suitcase, wore glasses, a long black overcoat, and a fedora. As he reached the boxcar door, where the crowd was thickest and most frenzied, he knelt out of sight as if to tie his shoes. When he rose, he wore a dirty pair of worker overalls and a flat cap, and the glasses were gone. On his left arm, he wore an FC armband. Seeming to be helpful, Maduro tossed his suitcase and overcoat and hat into the cattle car before blending into the surging crowd.

After several hours of loading, when the last door slammed shut on the twenty rolling tombs, Gemmeker hopped on a bike and pedaled on a slow tour from one end of the train to the other, inspecting each boxcar, his dog merrily yapping alongside him. Once satisfied everything was in order, he waved for the train to depart. The engineer waved back and sounded a piercing whistle blast as the train lurched forward in a hissing cloud of steam.

Turning his back to the train, Gemmeker handed his bike to an aide and laughed with the other officers as the last car for the camps in Poland rumbled out of the deathly still Westerbork.

Ger shook his head and lowered his binoculars. "Jews forcing Jews onto the venomous snake built by Jews."

Rogers twisted his head to look at Ger. "What do you mean?"

"It is a *Deutsche Reichsbahn's* Class 52 steam locomotive," Ger said.

"Jewish slave laborers built it for company in Germany. Henschel & Son in Kassel, I have heard."

Rogers rolled over on his back, fighting the urge to throw up.

☆ ☆ ☆

Several tense hours passed before Werner hauled a small, covered cart out of the camp entrance. The bored guards paid no attention to him. He paused at the crematorium, opened the double doors, and pulled the cart inside. After a few minutes, he came out again with the empty cart and returned to the camp, just as the skies opened, pounding the already muddy ground with torrential rain. There was nothing Rogers and the other two men could do but stay hidden and endure the cold and wet until long after the sun went down.

When, at last, nighttime came, it was difficult to see anything outside the well-lit camp and guard towers. Most of the Dutch police who were supposed to be patrolling the perimeter huddled in the dry and warm guard station at the main entrance. Lively music and singing from one of the long buildings, accompanied by tapping feet, filled the night air. Ger whispered to Rogers, "Gemmeker forces inmates to perform weekly musical revue on deportation night for him and his guests. I go now. You wait here." Ger slogged, crouched down, through the pouring rain toward the almost invisible crematorium.

A flashlight's glare blinded Rogers. He ducked, but it was too late. One of the few non-lazy Marechaussee shouted something at him and motioned with his rifle for Rogers to come out of the forest. He had no choice. Raising his hands above his head, Rogers stumbled toward the police officer, mumbling gibberish and swaying on his feet like a drunken fool.

The policeman inspected Rogers' SS uniform with his flashlight and lowered his rifle, appearing confused about how to proceed. Rogers laughed and danced around the incredulous policeman, who swiveled to keep an eye and his rifle on the crazy doctor.

Mr. 400 charged out of the woods and tackled the policeman, knocking his rifle out of his hands. As they wrestled in the mud, Rogers grabbed the rifle and smashed the butt into the policeman's head. Blood spurt out. The officer stopped moving.

In grim silence, Mr. 400 and Rogers dragged the policeman's limp body into the woods. Rogers handed the rifle to Mr. 400 and felt the policeman's neck. Finding no pulse, he closed the eyes on the now lifeless body. Mr. 400 shrugged and returned to the forest's edge, plopping down to wait with the rifle across his lap. Rogers knelt next to him and peered into the night, moving his head sideways to glance out of the corners of his eyes, which are better at seeing things in low light.

Not long after, the first shadowy figure emerged from the rain; a second one followed close behind, their feet making sucking sounds as they trudged through thick mud.

"We must hurry," Ger told Rogers as he made it to the forest with his soaked companion.

"We have a problem," Rogers said, pointing to the policeman's body.

"Capt. Rogers? Is that you?" the man with Ger said, putting on his glasses and stepping close to inspect Rogers' face.

"Yes, Mr. Maduro, it's me," he said, surprised when Maduro hugged him and wouldn't let go.

"Thank you, thank you."

"Plenty of time for that later. Let's get out of here before they come look-ing for the guard," Rogers said, concerned at how much Maduro had aged. When they first met in 1941, Maduro was a vibrant man in his late fifties. Now, with short black hair speckled with gray and an unshaven face that was gaunt and pale, he appeared far too old.

"We must take body with us," Ger said. "It cannot be found. That way, the Germans will wonder whether he deserted and not launch search right away."

Rogers blew out his breath and picked up the body's feet; Mr. 400 grabbed the hands, and together they hiked toward the hideout. Maduro strained to keep up but didn't complain.

"Where is Miriam?" Maduro said between huffs.

"Safe in Palestine. And so are all the kids."

"That is not possible."

"Really, I left them there with relatives safe and sound."

"But she was here two weeks ago."

Rogers dropped the body. "What do you mean?"

"She came to visit me and said she could help me escape. But I told her 'no' because of what would happen to the others," Maduro said.

"But how did she get back into Holland?"

"She did not say. But I almost did not recognize her. Her hair was blonde and she wore a cross."

Ger, shaking his head impatiently, picked up the body with Mr. 400, and together, they marched away. "Come. We must hurry."

Walking along with his mouth agape and his eyes struggling to focus, Rogers paid little attention to where he was going.

"I thought she came up with the idea to slip me out with the bodies," Maduro said. "Werner pulled my registration card, put me on the list for the train, and helped me with a disguise. Now, the Germans in Westerbork will believe I am on my way to Auschwitz. And the Germans there will not be looking for me because there is no card. No one will be punished. Brilliant. Was this your idea?"

"Where could Miriam be now?" Rogers said, ignoring the question. "We have to find her."

Maduro held onto Rogers as they plodded along, tripping and stumbling on roots and underbrush.

"I...I'm sorry about your brother," Rogers said. "The Rabbi was a good man. Died trying to protect the children from the German hostages on my ship."

"Yes, I know. Miriam told me all about it. I am proud of him. And I'm so grateful to you for everything you've done for my family."

"I'm not done yet."

By the time they arrived at the hiding place, the rain had let up, and rays of sun were piercing the thick clouds. They stripped the policeman's uniform and, using a shovel from Ger's truck, buried him in a shallow grave and disguised it with twigs and leaves. Ger instructed Maduro to recline in his truck bed and covered him with tree limbs.

"Where are we going?" Maduro said.

"The train station," Ger said.

Maduro shot up. "But I still have the yellow star and no papers. I cannot ride on a train."

"Don't worry," Ger said, nudging him back down and covering him again. "It is perfect disguise."

Rogers and Mr. 400 jumped into the cab, and Ger sped off to the train station. About half a mile before reaching it, Ger pulled off the road and, making sure no vehicles were approaching, helped Maduro down to the pavement and handed him some documents.

"Here is your ticket, your identification papers, and your pass from Gemmeker himself to pick up medicine in Amsterdam. Jews from the camp are a common sight on train. Now, you must walk to Hooghalen train station. Your friends will be on same train. Follow them from some distance once you arrive in Amsterdam."

"How can I ever thank you?" Maduro asked.

"Build home for Jews in Palestine." They shook hands, and Ger drove the other two men to the train station.

As he found his seat in one of the first-class cars, Rogers spotted Maduro shuffling through the station. But when Maduro was about to board, he was roughly stopped by a *Bahnhofswache*, a regular Wehrmacht soldier assigned to train station security. The soldier, wearing a 6.5-inch-wide aluminum identification gorget that hung on a metal chain around his neck, checked Maduro's papers, taking his time to humiliate the Jew even though he had permission to be out and about.

When finished, the soldier tossed the papers back and shoved Maduro toward the train door. After that, the two-hour journey to Amsterdam passed without incident. Rogers pretended to be asleep again; Maduro rode in a separate car where no one would meet his eye or notice his presence.

☆☆☆

When they arrived, Amsterdam Centraal buzzed with activity, so no one took note of the two unshaven SS medical personnel in muddy uniforms or the Jew trailing behind them in overalls with a yellow star. After a three-minute walk to Zeedijk Street, Rogers and Mr. 400 ducked into a narrow, ivy-covered brick building with *v. Vollenhoven's Bieren* in foot-high letters above the entrance and *Café Gooiland* painted on its front picture window.

Maduro, following several paces behind, paused to scan the cobblestoned street. Jews were not allowed in cafés and restaurants. Satisfied that no one was watching him, Maduro slipped inside.

A waiter in a white apron latched the door and flipped a sign on it saying *Gesloten,* meaning closed. Without a word, he led Maduro to the sparse storage room in the back of the café, where he found Rogers and Mr. 400 already stripping off their uniforms and putting on their dungarees and work shirts.

They tossed Maduro a pair of baggy Volendam worker pants, a shirt, boots, and a flat newsboy cap. After he had changed clothes, Maduro handed the waiter his forged documents and backed up against a blank wall to have his picture taken. "It will take a few minutes to transfer the picture to your new identity paper," the waiter said. "In the meantime, eat."

The three ravenous men gathered around a small table in the backroom for a plateful of a beef version of *braadworst*, a traditional Dutch sausage, typically served on top of steaming *hutspot*—mashed potatoes with kale, onions, and carrots. Vegetables were hard to come by, and meat was even more scarce, so the dish was mostly carrots.

"No, that will not do," Mr. 400 said, snatching the fork out of Rogers' right hand. "Here, do this." He cut the tiny sausage with the fork in his left hand and the knife in his right and shoved the bite into his mouth with his left hand. "Do not eat like an American. Do not switch hands. Understand?"

Rogers said he did but knew he would have trouble remembering the different technique.

As they ate, the waiter returned with Maduro's new photo and set to work on another table where he had gathered pens, tweezers, rubber stamps, sharp knives, and scalpels. With a scalpel, he scraped off the "J" for Jew and Maduro's name from his ID and dabbed it with a cloth soaked in bleach.

When it dried, he wrote in a new name with the same first letter and the same number of letters as the original: Servass Mathus. Then he used fumes from a bottle of acetone to remove the official, transparent seal that was half on Maduro's black-and-white photo and half on the document.

After peeling off the picture with tweezers and a scalpel, he pressed Maduro's index finger on an ink pad and on the back of the new picture. He used special glue to affix the new picture over a transparent seal. The final step involved a wooden contraption called "the hinge," resembling two square ping pong paddles connected on the fat ends by a hinge, which aligned the picture so the stamp could be replaced in the same position as before.

By the time the three men had scarfed down the last bit of food, the waiter had handed Maduro his new ID card and other papers. Rogers grilled him for a few minutes to help him memorize his new identity, and then Mr. 400 led everyone to the docks. He promised to return as soon as he learned anything about Miriam's whereabouts.

☆☆☆

"You can relax a bit now," Rogers said as he led Maduro onto the ship. "This is the last place in Europe the Germans will inspect." Rogers led him to the wheelhouse to meet Griffin.

"Welcome aboard, Mr. Maduro," Griffin said, extending his hand between puffs on his pipe.

"Mathus now," Maduro said, holding up his new ID card.

"I see," Griffin said. "Anyway, Capt. Swift sends his regards."

"Ah! Now, this makes sense to me," Maduro said, pumping Griffin's hand and smiling like a man released from a death sentence, which, indeed, he had been. "But the last I heard of him, Bob had joined the Irish parliament and no longer smuggled for the IRA."

Rogers and Griffin exchanged hard glances, which Maduro appeared to notice.

"I am only assuming that is the case now. Aren't many of the IRA pro-German?" Maduro said and waited for a reply. After a brief, strained silence, he cleared his throat. "But it is none of my business. I am just thankful you came."

Griffin looked at Maduro with a big grin. "'Tis no matter, a cara," he said, putting his arm around Maduro's shoulder. "Come and have a taste of poteen. Ye'll be wanting to celebrate your freedom, no doubt." The two men left Rogers in the wheelhouse and headed to the captain's quarters.

Rogers gathered Obasi, Nidal, and Cookie on the poop deck, out of earshot of the rest of the crew, and filled them in on what had happened. "I'm hoping to find out more about Miriam from the resistance. But it doesn't look good."

"We must find her soon," Nidal said. "Capt. Griffin said the repairs should be finished in a couple of days."

"We can't leave without Miriam!" Cookie shouted. "That lovely lass saved all of our skins more than once."

"I like her very much, Captain," Obasi said, surprising everyone that he had something to say. Miriam had patched up wounds in Obasi's chest and legs after being machine-gunned by a German captive who had joined some of the *Peggy C's* crew in a mutiny.

How Miriam ended up back in Nazi-occupied Holland was a mystery to Rogers, one he was determined to solve once he found out where she was. Later that afternoon, he got his answer.

"We found Miriam," Mr. 400 told Rogers after sneaking onto the ship with a worried look. "She's in the *Oranjehotel*."

"Thank God," Rogers said. "Where is it? How can we smuggle her onto the ship?"

"We cannot."

"What?" Rogers said. "You sneak people around all the time."

"Yes. But this is not something we have ability for."

"How hard could it be to check someone out of a hotel?"

"Oh, I am sorry. I was not clear," Mr. 400 said. "The Oranjehotel is what you call, a... nickname?"

"For what?" Rogers said in exasperation.

"A prison."

CHAPTER 12

Feeling lightheaded and unable to focus his racing thoughts, Rogers silently led Mr. 400 to the crew's mess and mumbled for him to wait there while he rounded up Maduro and his crew. When they returned, Mr. 400 sat sipping coffee and smoking a Christo Cassimis, a colorful pack of hard-to-find Egyptian cigarettes set on the table in front of him. The others declined his offered cigarette and joined him at the table.

Shaking his head to clear his mind, Rogers asked, "Where is this Orange Hotel prison?"

"In Scheveningen," Mr. 400 said.

"It is a district of The Hague about an hour south of here," Maduro added for the others' benefit. "Do they still allow visitors?"

"Sometimes. Mostly Red Cross and the prison chaplain."

"Good. Then we must go there," Maduro said to Rogers.

"Whoa, matey, you can't go anywhere," Cookie said. "This is the only place where you're safe. Besides, how would we even get there? We ain't got no proper papers."

"And even if we could go to the prison, what would we do to help Miriam?" Nidal said.

"Can't Group 2000 do something?" Rogers said.

"We help *onderduikers,* and *Engelandvaarders* and downed pilots escape," Mr. 400 said, referring to people in hiding and those fleeing to England. "We do not have the military capacity to attack the prison. Many of our members are in hiding now because of the attack on the Amsterdam Civil Registry Office."

"What attack?" Maduro said.

"A few days ago, Mr. 2200 and a dozen or so men disguised as police entered the registry pretending to do an inspection. They overpowered the four guards and dumped all the registration cards on the floor and set them on fire," Mr. 400 said, stubbing out his cigarette with his boot. "The Germans are offering a 10,000-guilder reward, and many of the men have been arrested. The others are in hiding. We dare not do anything now."

"Can you at least take us to Scheveningen with documents that give us a cover story?" Rogers asked.

"And do what? Captain?" Nidal said. "We do not look Dutch."

"I don't know yet. But if we can get there and connect with some resistance group, maybe we can figure out a way."

"But the train is under too much scrutiny now, and what you ask takes money. That is something we do not have now," Mr. 400 said.

"Money I can find," Maduro said, standing to pace around the room, hands clasped behind his back "Yes, yes, I can find it. And maybe other help. But I need to get to an office near the Municipal University Library."

"We cannot do anything for you now," Mr. 400 said. "It is dangerous for me even to be out on the street."

"Then I will walk. It is no more than thirty minutes away," Maduro said.

"You can't go alone," Rogers said. "But what are you going to say if we are stopped?"

Maduro shrugged. "We can say we are looking for an open bar. They believe us, or they don't. I must do this. I will not leave without Miriam." He rushed out of the mess.

Rogers yanked on his newsboy cap and hurried after him. Hands in pockets and head down, Rogers followed Maduro southwest through Amsterdam side streets, avoiding Dam Square and other more crowded areas and frequently stopping to peek around corners before moving on. All the weaving and waiting meant the journey lasted more than an hour, but they weren't stopped.

Maduro crossed a bridge over the seventeenth-century Herengracht Canal, the oldest of the city center's three main canals, veered left, and wove past stately narrow canal houses with gables and cornices, some equipped with a crane on the roof. He turned onto Leidsegracht, a narrow cobblestoned street on a tree-lined side canal, and stopped at Number 5, a five-story brick building with the city's traditional tall and narrow windows.

As soon as Rogers caught up with him, Maduro stepped down a shallow stairwell and knocked on the front door. A tall, thin man in a rumpled suit and tie inspected them through the door's six small windowpanes before opening it and letting them in, checking the street to be sure no one was watching.

"Solomon, thank the Lord," said the man, who appeared to be in his late thirties, wrapping his arms around Maduro in a bear hug. "When did the Germans release you from Westerbork?"

"Wally, my boy. You are a sight for sore eyes," Maduro said, pulling away. "This is my friend Capt. Rogers. He helped me escape Westerbork. And now I need your help."

"Oh, I see," Wally said. He led them to an office where they sat around an antique coffee table stacked with papers and magazines. "Of course, I will do anything I can for you. Do you need money or identity papers? I can put you in touch with the Comet Line or another group that handles escapes."

"We will probably need all those things. But the main reason I am here is because of Miriam," Maduro said.

"Miriam? I heard she was in Palestine," Wally said with a slight New York accent while scrutinizing Rogers. "Wait a minute. Are you Capt. Jake Rogers of the *Peggy C*?"

"Yes," Rogers said.

"Oh, my goodness," Wally said. "We all read about what you did for Solomon's family in *Vrij Nederland* and all the other underground newspapers. Did you really—"

"Miriam is not in Palestine," Maduro broke in. "She is in Holland. In the Oranjehotel. I want your help to get her out."

Wally slumped back in his chair, his jaw dropping in stunned silence. "I am so sorry. I didn't know."

"Do you know if George stayed around The Hague after being released from the Oranjehotel?" Maduro asked.

"Yes, I believe he is still in the city."

"Good. I need a way to find him, plus money and documents. I, of course, will repay it all after the war. You can use the bonds you are holding for me as collateral."

"Please," Wally said, holding his hand up. "Don't worry about that." He went to his tidy desk across the room and retrieved a pen and a piece of paper from a drawer. "I should be able to send a radio message to the OD in The Hague. I believe they can help you find George and with the escape."

"The OD? Isn't that the Jewish police at Westerbork? Why would you contact them?" Rogers said.

"Yes, same name, Ordedienst, Order of Service in English, but not the same group. George was involved with the *Van Hattem Group*, which is now part of the OD," Wally said. He explained that it was one of four main Dutch resistance groups was founded in The Hague by someone code-named "Uncle Alexander." "The OD is mostly made up of former cadets and midshipmen, so it has the expertise and equipment you might need."

"So, how will my crew and I travel to The Hague?" Rogers said. "We can't take the train. The Germans will be double-checking everybody because of the registry bombing."

Maduro gazed at Wally for an answer. He didn't have one.

"You know," Rogers said, "when we sailed into the North Canal, I saw hundreds of men under guard working on the bunkers and fortifications. They obviously weren't all Dutch. Could we pretend to be foreign laborers going to work at another fortification?"

"The Germans did recently start tearing down houses and digging ditches all around the Oranjehotel for what they call Fortress Scheveningen," Wally said, his hand running over his neatly parted hair. "It's part of the *Atlantikwall*. Like what you saw at Ijmuiden. They are building it with *Arbeitseinsatz*, forced labor. And you are right; many of them are foreigners caught up in the war."

"Yes, yes. Wally, how soon can you get us employment record books saying we work for Organization Todt and are returning from here to The Hague?" Maduro asked. He was referring to the German engineering firm in charge of the wall's construction along 3,100 miles of Atlantic coastline in conquered Europe, a series of minefields, and concrete barriers, bunkers, and barbed wire stretching from the Spanish-French border to the northern edge of Norway.

"Less than a day for an Arbeitsbuch für Ausländer once we take photos of the men who will accompany you. And you will need a Sonderausweis," he said, referring to employment record books for foreigners and an official travel order signed by the SD and local Grüne Polizei. "We can steal a truck with no problem and provide a driver to take you there and back."

"We can't wait long," Rogers said. "Our ship is sailing soon."

"Then you will have everything by tomorrow," Wally said. "I owe my friend Solomon quite a lot, Captain. Like you, I was a merchant marine, and because of him, I became a third mate on one of his ships."

"You did all of that on your own. You'd have your own ship by now if your eyes weren't so bad," Maduro said. "And you have done more than enough. Do you know, Captain, that Wally helped set up the secret *Zeemanspot*, a fund worth millions of guilders to aid the families of more than 18,000 Dutch seamen stranded abroad because of the war, including many of my employees."

"And Solomon was one of the first to donate to the cause," Wally said.

Rogers stared at Solomon. "Do you donate to every good cause?"

"What is the point of money, Captain?" Maduro asked. "I haven't worked as hard as I have to sit on my riches. God has blessed me with success and wealth, and I honor him by using it to help others. As it says in Proverbs, 'A generous person will prosper; whoever refreshes others will be refreshed.'"

"I am so happy you are free," Wally said. "What is the name of your ship, Captain?"

"*Erin Go Bragh*," Rogers said.

"I'll have someone come by before dark to take everyone's picture. And in the morning, we'll see if we can't requisition a truck from the street and pick you up," Wally said, leading them to the door. "Good luck."

Once outside, Rogers whispered to Maduro: "Who was that?"

"Some know him as *Bankier van het verzet*—the Banker of the Resistance," Maduro said. "But you know him by another name."

"What?"

"Oom Piet."

☆☆☆

Not long after dawn the following day, a field-gray three-ton Ford G917T cargo truck, with a canvas tarp covering its wooden bed and the letters OT atop a large triangle painted on its doors, parked at the end of the quay. Rogers spotted it in the pale light and led Maduro, Nidal, Obasi, and Cookie to the truck. Maduro now wore ill-fitting dungarees, a dirty pea jacket, and a wool watch cap to fit in with the others. They all wore orange-brown cotton armbands saying *"Arbeitet für OT."*

"What does this mean?" Rogers asked Maduro, tapping on his armband.

"Works for Organization Todt. They handle all of the Nazis' construction projects."

A man in a brown uniform with "OT" on his collar tabs and a red armband with a swastika in a white circle with the words "Org. Todt" emerged from the truck's cab and directed the men to the covered bed, handing each one his papers as they climbed in. "We are unlikely to be stopped," the driver said, adjusting his brown wool M43 field cap. "But if we are, hand them your documents and keep quiet. Let me do all the talking." He pulled down the flap and returned to the cab, where another man in an SS uniform rode in the passenger's seat.

The drive to The Hague was slow going because the German and Dutch police had set up frequent roadblocks to inspect the few civilian vehicles and pedestrians on the roads leading southwest out of Amsterdam. At each roadblock, guttural shouts rang out as officers checked papers and searched vehicles. They were angry voices. Maduro explained that the Germans were asking about the registry attack, and not in a nice way.

Their truck was always waved through, until they were on the city's outskirts. Maduro tapped a finger on his lips for everyone inside the truck to remain silent while he strained to hear what the police at the roadblock were saying. The voices grew louder and more emphatic. "Trouble," Maduro whispered. "Something about a stolen truck—"

Before he could finish, the Dutch police ripped open the flap and shined flashlights into the gloomy back of the truck, examining each person and shouting: "Persoonsbewijs!" Rogers and the others looked at one another as if confused before pulling out their documents and handing them over. Two Dutch policemen examined the cards and trained a flashlight on each man to verify his identity.

A German SS officer accompanied by a soldier holding a submachine gun snatched the IDs from the policemen and studied them, peering often into the back of the truck. He called over the OT driver and the fake SS guard and berated them in a harsh voice before shoving them away and sticking his head inside the flap. He pointed at the man sitting in the back.

His hand signal was unmistakable in any language: "You, come outside." There was also no mistaking whom he was pointing at: Maduro.

CHAPTER 13

Miriam had no idea how she'd ended up in prison. For several weeks, she had been traveling in Holland with papers falsely identifying her as Hedda ten Boom. According to her identification, she was a representative of the Amsterdam Red Cross who had permission to move about without restrictions, delivering care packages to prisons and concentration camps. Her long, black hair had been cut short in a pageboy style and dyed blonde, as were the thick eyebrows above her soft chestnut eyes.

Even with little or no makeup, her fragile smile and sculpted cheeks turned heads and made her appear much younger than her twenty-five years. A small crucifix on a necklace hung around her neck; on her left arm, she wore a dirty white armband with a red cross and the words *Roode Kruis Afdeeling Amsterdam* in small letters.

In Amsterdam, she had contacted Geertruida Wijsmuller-Meijer, known as Truus to her family and Auntie Truus to the hundreds of Jewish children she helped flee Europe before and after the war began. French soldiers she helped escape knew her as Madame Odi. She also was the secret head of Red Cross Services for Group 2000 and organized the shipment of food packages to Westerbork. With her help, Miriam traveled to Westerbork and distributed food and medicine to the inmates, including her shocked father.

Under the pretense of helping her distribute packages, Maduro was able to talk to her for some time without drawing attention from the OD or other guards because they whispered in *Ladino*, a hybrid of Spanish, Hebrew, and other local languages used by Sephardic Jews. The OD members were Ashkenazi Jews who spoke Yiddish when not speaking their native German. After her father refused her help to escape because he feared German retaliation against the other prisoners, Miriam fled in tears.

Once back at a safe house in Amsterdam, she tried to devise another escape plan. Only the German police raided the house and captured her, giving her no time to take the poison "L-pill" sewn into her shirt collar, even if she had wanted to. She hesitated because her will to live was too strong, and there was always hope she could get out of this mess. The tiny L-pill—for Lethal pill—composed of deadly potassium cyanide would kill her within two minutes of crushing it between her teeth.

She would never do that, no matter how bad things became. But it comforted her to know she could if the pain became unbearable. She tried not to dwell on it as the police hauled her off to the notorious police prison in The Hague's Scheveningen district known as The Orange Hotel, a nickname honoring all the resistance members who had been imprisoned there. Orange was the Dutch royal family's color and the symbol of a free Netherlands.

Miriam didn't know what to expect when the police van she rode in stopped at the red brick prison's castle-style entrance. Its double wooden doors under a stone arch were flanked by four-story-high watchtowers shaped like chess rooks. It didn't take long for her to learn how bad things would be. The guards dragged her to brick barracks with wooden ceilings, built behind the main building in 1919 as a temporary solution for overcrowding. They shoved her into one of the 500 sparse, six-by-twelve-foot cells and locked the door.

At the far end of the cell, stretched from wall to wall, was a built-in narrow bunk with a straw pillow and mattress covered by two flimsy brown blankets. The bunk sagged between tall wooden planks like a bed buried inside a rectangular coffin. Relentless flies swarmed in one corner around a lid-covered metal bucket that served as a malodorous toilet. A single exposed lightbulb hung over a retractable desktop on the sidewall. On one wall, there were three metal hooks for hanging clothes.

The only outside light came through a row of small-paned windows above the door, too high up to see through. Previous prisoners had scribbled messages and prayers on the walls; some had created makeshift calendars to mark the duration of their dreadful stay.

In the dead of night, the terror began. Stone-faced guards dragged Miriam from her cell to a windowless interrogation room, where an SS officer seated at a metal table directed her to take the chair across from him. Two SS soldiers stood guard as the officer examined Miriam's papers and compared her appearance to her ID.

"What is your name?" the officer said in German. Miriam stared at him as if she didn't understand, although she spoke perfect German. The officer glanced at one of the guards. He slapped Miriam so hard that she flew from the chair onto the cold cement floor. "What is your name?" the officer repeated, his voice stern. When Miriam didn't answer and continued to groan, one of the soldiers kicked her in the stomach, jerked her up, and threw her back onto the chair.

"Hedda ten Boom," Miriam whispered between gasps of air, her head on the table.

The officer studied her papers. "These are excellent forgeries. Too good for the locals, which tells me you are working for someone else. Who?"

"I...work for the Red...Cross."

"Do not waste my time," the officer said, leaning forward and placing both hands flat on the table. "What is your real name, and who are you working for?"

"My name is Hedda—" Without warning, the officer jerked her head up with both hands and cracked it several times on the metal table, bloodying her nose. She screamed in pain and yelled gibberish at the officer, having been trained that anger could lessen pain. But she didn't utter a word. The interrogation went on and on and on—she couldn't remember how long—until a short soldier with pointed ears stepped in, jingling a heavy ring of keys in his left hand. He wore an SS uniform with two pips and one line on his collar tab.

"*Hauptscharführer* Schweiger," the officer said to the master sergeant. "Take this lying scum back to her cell and make her comfortable."

"With pleasure, Herr *Untersturmführer* Krüger," Schweiger said to the second lieutenant. He yanked Miriam by her hair and shoved her, stumbling through the door, jangling his heavy keychain as they tramped along. The clicking of his hobnail boots on the stone-tile floor echoed down the long, gloomy hallway, which reeked of sweat and feces. It was one of seven housing more than 1,500 prisoners accused of being resistance members, communists, Engelandvaarders fleeing the country, or *Deutschfeindlichkeit*—anti-Germans whose crimes ranged from listening to BBC broadcasts of Radio Orange to attacking Germans.

And then there were the Jews, often imprisoned for no other reason than being a Jew caught in hiding. For them, there was special treatment. Occasional screams and shrieks and the sound of fists and clubs on flesh terrified Miriam, but she refused to show fear. At the open door to her cell, Schweiger whacked Miriam on the back of her head with his key ring and kicked her sprawling onto the floor inside. He clicked the door shut and locked it with a laugh as if sealing her last ray of hope in a brick-lined crypt.

Soft hands lifted Miriam onto the wooden bed and helped her stretch out. "Would you like some water?" a young woman in her twenties asked in a whispering voice.

"Thank you. Yes, please," Miriam said with a whimper, hugging her sore ribs and straining to breathe. The woman lifted Miriam's head as she sipped from the lone wooden cup in the cell. "Who are you?"

"My name is Ilse Sloos. I'm from Haarlem. What did you do to be thrown in here?"

"I don't know. I haven't done anything," Miriam said, sitting up with her feet hanging over the side of the bed and tenderly touching the back of her bloody head.

"Oh, dear," Ilse said. "Let me help you." She dampened a towel with water from a jug and used it to wipe the blood off Miriam's head. "*Das Flurschwein* can be so cruel."

"The Hall Pig?"

"That is what we call Hauptscharführer Schweiger. He is second in command, but he's the one who runs things. You must be careful around him," she said. "Behind his back, the other guards make fun of his shortness, and he knows it. He takes it out on everyone any chance he gets."

"Why are *you* here?" Miriam said, taking the towel from Ilse and pressing it on her head.

"There is not enough room for all the inmates, so they make us share cells, sometimes with as many as five people. It doesn't matter, though. I won't be here much longer."

"Are you being deported?"

"Oh, no. I'm being released soon. Someone on the outside denounced me, so I was brought in for questioning. But they have found no evidence of me participating in the resistance," Ilse said with a wink. She leaned over to whisper in Miriam's ear. "I am like you, fighting these damn Huns."

Miriam gazed at Ilse. "I have done nothing."

"Of course not, dear," Ilse said with a knowing smile. "I know certain authorities here and, after I'm released, I could smuggle in some medicine for your cuts."

Miriam shook her head.

"Or I could take letters to your friends on the outside."

"No, thank you." Miriam lay down with a moan.

"Are you sure? No one you want to..." she mouthed the word "warn?"

Miriam rolled over to face the wall, racked by pain and trembling in the cold.

For a few days, Miriam and Ilse were left alone in their vermin-infested cell, rising at 6:30 a.m., when the Germans forced prisoners out of their beds. At 8 p.m. each night, on German instructions, they turned out their solitary light, taking turns on who got to sleep in the bed and who had to use sacks of straw on the floor; that is when the guards hadn't confiscated the sacks because of a violation of one of the prison's arbitrary and often mysterious rules.

Meals consisted of fetid soup and moldy bread. Some days, they were denied hot food for unexplained reasons. On other days, they were given reduced rations because Schweiger stole some of their food to fatten the geese he raised. Friends or relatives were allowed to come once a week to pick up the laundry of non-Jewish inmates. No one ever came for Miriam's.

With nothing to read or do, and forbidden to rest on the bed, they spent most of their days pacing—only four steps back and forth between the bunk and the door—or chatting in low voices about mundane things like the ordinary lives that seemed so far away now. But somehow, Ilse always managed to bring their conversations around to Miriam's background; where she was from or where she attended school, who were her parents, whether she was married or had a boyfriend, and where she worked.

At first, the questions were innocent enough. Miriam would offer a vague answer about being an orphan from Breda in the south of Holland who had to drop out of nursing school at the beginning of the war and was lucky to find work with the Red Cross in Amsterdam.

"Breda?" Ilse said. "I've been there once. Lovely town. I particularly enjoyed that church, the famous one whose name escapes me."

"Grote Kerk."

"No, not that one. The Gothic one with the tall tower."

"That is it. Perhaps you know it as Onze Lieve Vrouwe Kerk."

"Yes, that is it."

If Ilse had asked, Miriam could have told her the minister's name, the times for services, and even the hymnal's color although she had never been to Breda. She had what was known as a "true-false" identity, meaning that if the Germans checked the registry in Breda, they would find a card for Hedda ten Boom with details matching her description, a card surreptitiously added by another agent.

During the day, guards often led Ilse away for questioning. She would return grim-faced but without any visible signs of abuse. And she would always want to talk about it. "I don't know why they keep asking me the same questions over and over. Did they do that with you?"

"I don't remember much," Miriam said as she swept the cell for the umpteenth time using a short-handled whisk broom and dustpan.

"Did they ask you about the SOE?"

"I do not know what that is?"

They both jumped when the door swung open, surprised that, instead of a soldier, a civilian in a threadbare suit stepped in and offered them a Red Cross package. "Good morning, ladies. I'm Reverend Henri van Nooten, the prison chaplain. I have a package for you." Ilse grabbed the package and tore it open, spilling the contents onto the floor: toiletries, chocolate, and fruit—all unbelievable luxuries in the Oranjehotel.

As Ilse scooped up the bounty and shoved it in her mouth, Miriam noticed something she had missed: a roll of peppermints. She slipped it into her pocket while keeping eye contact with the smiling minister, who nodded ever so slightly. *They know I am here. There is hope still.* The clergyman settled on the small wooden stool in front of the foldable desk and asked how they were doing and if they would like to pray.

"Oh, yes," Miriam said, clutching the crucifix around her neck and bowing her head. Ilse kept wolfing down the treats.

Schweiger stormed in unannounced with one of his henchmen, Josef Kotalla, who carried a long leather whip with a braided handle. Ilse dropped her food and cowered by the bed. "No food allowed for this scum, Reverend," Schweiger said, pointing at Miriam, who stood her ground. "Now, leave."

"But—" the reverend said.

Kotalla, who was as short as Schweiger, shoved the minister out of the cell and whipped Miriam until she fell to the ground and covered her head. He gathered all the food and toiletries and strutted out of the cell with a smirk. As Schweiger followed him out, he snatched the straw sack bed on the floor and pointed at Miriam. "No bed for you. Tomorrow, we are taking you to the doctor."

After the Germans locked the door, Ilse comforted Miriam, who tried swallowing her tears. "You should tell them what they want to know. The doctor is the worst at using *Verschärfte Vernehmung*," Ilse said. Miriam, knowing "enhanced interrogation" meant torture, curled up into a ball on the floor and sobbed.

That night was the most disturbing of all her nights in prison so far—a series of screams and moans echoed throughout the hallways, sounds that penetrated the cell's thin walls with terrifying clarity. In addition to the usual chaos, feet pounded up and down the hallway as the drunken guards laughed and shouted insults. Agonized voices howled for mercy, followed by thumps of clubs on flesh and bones.

"*Judensport*," Ilse said to Miriam. "They make the Jews run and do gymnastics until unconscious. And then they beat them some more."

With her thin blanket, Miriam curled up on the icy stone floor, covered her ears with her hands, and drifted off to a fitful night's sleep.

Morning came all too soon. The guards dragged Miriam from the cell and hurled her into Cell 607, the interrogation room. Inside sat an SS officer with thinning blond hair and a wispy blond mustache that gave him a perpetual frown. Forty-three-year-old Untersturmführer Ernst Knorr was known as "the Doctor," a title Germans used for anyone who had earned his Juris Doctor law degree, which Knorr did before joining the Gestapo. The guards thrust Miriam into the chair across a metal table from Knorr, who had no fingers on his left hand. His right hand clutched a rubber baton on the table.

"Where is your wireless operator?" Knorr said.

"I do not know what you mean," Miriam said, bracing for the inevitable blow to fall.

"We found the two parachutes buried near Garderen where you parachuted in, but not him or her. So, please, do not lie again," he said, clasping and unclasping his hand on the baton. When Miriam failed to answer, two burly guards jerked her up from the chair, tied her hands in front of her, and hung her from a hook in the ceiling. The tips of her toes brushed the ground. Knorr sneered, and his droopy eyes lit up as he wailed away with his baton, hitting her in the stomach and back, concentrating with particular viciousness around the kidneys.

Every time she passed out, the guards revived her with buckets of ice-cold water poured over her head. "What's this?" Knorr said, inspecting Miriam's drenched hair, where the dark roots showed. "Now, why would you dye your hair blonde?" He grabbed her head with both hands and examined it with a practiced eye. "You're not only a spy. You're a Jew, aren't you?" He didn't wait for an answer.

The next thing Miriam remembered was being dragged by two guards through a hallway and stopping in front of a different cell door. On it was a sign written in Dutch: "Strict solitary confinement / is a Jew / is not allowed to write / is not allowed out for an airing / nobody is allowed to speak with her / is not allowed to read." They threw her inside and clanged the door shut, leaving her alone in total darkness and shaking uncontrollably.

After several hours, or maybe days, a somber Reverend van Nooten and a man in a suit she didn't recognize came to visit her.

"Would you like to pray?" van Nooten said.

"Who is that?" Miriam said, pointing at the stranger and squinting to adjust her eyes to the painful light.

"This is Herr *Staatsaanwalt* Giskes, the prosecutor in your case."

"I am to go on trial?"

"No, dear," van Nooten said, shaking his head. "You have already been convicted. That is why you are in the *D-gang*," he said, referring to the middle corridor of the barracks. Miriam stared at the two men with red-rimmed eyes, confused.

"Death row," Giskes said, pulling a document from inside his coat and waving it at her. "You've been convicted of espionage and Deutschfeindlichkeit. You will be executed by firing squad—soon."

CHAPTER 14

To comply with the German officer's command, Rogers jumped up as if he thought he was the one being summoned. After the officer screamed another command, Maduro nudged Rogers aside and crawled out from the back of the truck. The officer examined Maduro's identity papers and studied his face before handing them back.

Then he called out Obasi, whom he and his fellow soldier delighted in humiliating. They patted him down, rubbed his head like a pet monkey, asked him questions at the top of their voices, and slapped him with his papers for not answering because he didn't speak German. When they tired of their taunting, they checked out Nidal, who jabbered away in French until the frustrated officer tossed his papers back to him. The officer repeated the same routine until everyone had stepped out of the truck and passed inspection.

As they milled around, trying not to act nervous, a blaring horn startled everyone, making the officer spin around, ready to give someone hell. The driver of a Mercedes-Benz 170 V two-door officer's sedan laid on the horn and waved for the truck to move out of his way. Flustered, the officer returned the documents to Rogers and his crew and ordered everyone back into the truck. The OT driver revved up the engine, jammed the clutch into gear, and screeched away, heading south to The Hague.

In less than an hour, the truck bounded down the narrow Wassenaarseweg in The Hague's upscale Benoordenhout district and past a long row of identical three-story brick homes with bay windows and small balconies. When the truck stopped, Maduro made sure the street was deserted before climbing out and knocking on the door at Number 98.

A slender young man, perhaps in his twenties, of medium height, dressed in a dapper, three-piece gray suit, opened the door and hugged Maduro, who patted him on the back. They spoke briefly, and then the young man grabbed an overcoat and fedora and hustled into the back of the truck with Maduro.

"This is George," Maduro said, introducing him to the others. "He was in the Oranjehotel."

"Twice," said George, whose swarthy, tropical complexion, dark hair, and warm brown eyes made him appear somewhat exotic compared to his fair-skinned Dutch compatriots.

"It'll be a third time if you don't flee home to Curaçao," Maduro said of the Dutch Caribbean colony.

"I am making plans. But first, we must help Miriam," George said, playing absentmindedly with a gold ring inlaid with a square of topaz and what appeared to be a family crest. "Here is what I know. The last we heard, she had been moved to solitary confinement for unknown reasons. But we fear it is because they suspect she is Jewish. I am trying to find out more from the prison chaplain and other sources. In the meantime, we need to get all of you and the truck out of sight."

"What can we do for her now?" Rogers said.

"Nothing until we know more," George said, peeking out from the flap before turning back. "We know that the Germans sometimes take prisoners from the Oranjehotel to their headquarters in the Binnenhof for questioning," he said, referring to the complex of government buildings in the center of The Hague. "They travel in a single staff car without many guards. That may present an opportunity. I will join you tonight, and we can discuss it more." He hopped from the truck and, lighting a cigarette, wandered down the block.

The fake OT official drove the truck on a winding path through the city, pulled into an alley, and swerved through a warehouse's open double doors. As soon as the truck entered, two armed men slammed the doors shut. "Follow me," one of the men said in Dutch, which Maduro translated. The man chatted with Maduro as he led them into a crowded storage room with cots, a bucket of water, and bread.

"He said we must wait here until George returns."

They ate in silence.

A couple of hours later, George slipped in through a side door with some apples in his hands. "We have some time before our meeting. Eat," he said, handing out the fruit.

As they munched, savoring every bite, Maduro said, "How is the *Aktie*

Portugesia going, George?"

"What's that?" Rogers said.

"Do you want to explain, or should I?" Maduro said. When George shrugged and grabbed a seat, Maduro continued. "It means 'Portuguese Action,' which I'm afraid stems from the belief among some of my Sephardic brothers that we are not only superior to the Ashkenazi Jews from Eastern Europe but not even of the same race. And, therefore, we are not actually Jews, according to the Nazis' racial theories."

"Jews look down on other Jews?" Cookie said in amazement. "Don't you have enough problems?"

"It is not that simple," George said. "I have spent days and days at the National Archives researching my family and other so-called Marannos. Some of them had converted to Christianity and intermarried with Catholics in Spain and Portugal before their expulsion during the Inquisition."

"The theory, as I understand it," Maduro jumped in, "is that because we never intermarried with Ashkenazim, we are not a Semitic race at all but rather a Western Mediterranean one. That theory was supported by reams of research by anthropologists, lawyers, and academics that went so far as to include measurements of Sephardims' skulls—if you can imagine."

"I did not take part in that," George said. "The research was supposed to convince the Germans that we are Aryan and should not be discriminated against or deported. And it worked for a while." George showed him his ID card stamped with the words *"Inhaber diese Ausweise ist auf Arbeitseinsatz freigestellt."* "It means that the ID card holder is exempt from employment—meaning forced labor—until further notice."

George explained that deciding whether, when, and to whom to issue that life-saving stamp was in the hands of a sympathetic German lawyer named Hans Calmeyer, whose job was determining who was a "true Jew" with four Jewish grandparents. By accepting flimsy arguments and dubious evidence, he inscribed several thousand people on the so-called "Calmeyer List," which protected them from being seized during raids. "The stamp is useless for us now," George said. "The Nazis have decided that the 'Portuguese of Mosaic faith' are no less Jews than the Ashkenazim."

"It was worth a try, George, even if it only saved a single Jew, I suppose, no matter how flawed the premise," Maduro said, leaning back as everyone fell into a long silence.

At 6 p.m., George instructed Maduro and Rogers to follow him outside and into the back of an adjacent building, where they climbed four flights of stairs to an attic overlooking Prinsegracht Street. Along the way, they passed signs and posters with an inverted red triangle stamped with the Dutch initials "CJMV" for Christian Young Men Association. George explained that the Germans wouldn't suspect an athletic club of housing resistance activities.

At the top of the stairs, George tapped out a signal on the wall, and a hidden door opened. Inside, they found two men near a primitive radio set that had a Morse straight key with a flat knob. To dampen any sound, it was anchored on a block of wood nestled on top of a cloth. One of the men was taking off his headphones as the other, older man, closed the door.

"Ton, Pieter," George said. "These are the men Oom Piet messaged us about. Any news from the chaplain?"

Ton stared at his telegraph key.

"Yes," Pieter said. "And it is not good. She has been condemned. A firing squad will execute her at the Waalsdorpervlakte in the morning. I am sorry."

Rogers caught Maduro as he collapsed, then helped him into a chair. "Are you sure?" Rogers said.

Pieter nodded.

"What is that place? Where is it? What do we know about the routine? Can't you—"

"Please," Ton said, rising from the telegraph and holding his hand up for silence. "There is nothing we can do."

"I refuse to accept that!" Rogers shouted. He inhaled sharply and closed his eyes to calm himself.

Pieter placed his hand on Rogers' shoulder. "I became head of the OD after the Nazis rounded up our group's entire leadership. They were valiant resistance members. But they were rash and sloppy. I will not risk a military action without knowing precisely what we are getting into."

"George," Rogers said, "you were a prisoner there. How will this execution work?"

"Shortly after daybreak, the Grüne Polizei will put her on a truck and drive two-and-a-half kilometers to a flat area in the Meijendel dunes known as the Waalsdorpervlakte. A firing squad will execute her and throw her body into a pit in the sand and cover it with quicklime."

"How do you know this, George?" Maduro said in a shaky voice.

"I have not seen it, but I have been told about it by a man named Kuijt. It is his job to plant beach grass that reinforces the dunes. He said he hides and waits for the Germans to leave. Then he plants marram grass in a special shape so the graves can be found after the war."

"But why do they do the executions there?" Rogers said.

"German efficiency. No one can see or hear what they do. Easier to hide the bodies, too."

"Can't be seen, huh?" Rogers rubbed his lower lip between his thumb and forefinger. "Can this Kuijt lead us to the spot and describe the executions?"

"Most likely," George said.

"Good," Rogers said. "Now, Pieter, as Sun Tzu said, 'Opportunities multiply as they are seized.' What do you say?"

Pieter steepled his fingers and lowered his head, contemplating, and then searched the anxious faces in the room. "I believe he also said, 'Never venture, never win.'"

☆☆☆

As word of Miriam's sentence spread throughout the D-row barracks, inmates tapped Morse code messages of encouragement and exhortations to be brave. Others sang hymns and prayed. Miriam lay on her bunk in the blacked-out Cell 601 and tried to stop trembling by reciting the first stanza of *The Song of the Eighteen Dead* that Jan Campert had written about the execution of eighteen resistance fighters at the Waalsdorpervlakte two years before:

> *A cell is only two meters long*
> *and narrowly two meters wide,*
> *but smaller still is the piece of ground*
> *that I do not yet know,*
> *but where I will rest nameless,*
> *my comrades besides,*

RESCUE RUN

we were eighteen in number,
none will see the evening.

She tried not to dwell on regrets but on sweet pre-war memories of life in Amsterdam, of her family and her poor father, of her life in Palestine, and especially of Jake and the brief, lovely time they had together.

Remembering her time on the *Peggy C* made her smile. There was Cookie struggling to patch a wound, or whipping up an amazing feast out of nothing, or teaching the boys to fish and calming everyone's fears with his daffy sayings. Nidal, trying to act tough, finally cracking a smile as they were rescued. And Obasi, the gentle giant who was willing to sacrifice his life to save everyone. Other faces and snippets of conversations flashed through her mind, and she deeply inhaled the rancid air that, to her, now smelled as comforting as the aromas of Shabbat dinners at home. The sweet smell of being alive.

The door creaked, and a shaft of light fell on her. She knew her fate was sealed, so she struggled to her feet, head held high, and hobbled from her cell, not letting them see her cry or show fear. A Grüne Polizei officer clasped her wrists with bulky, double-locking, swing-through handcuffs and clutched her arm. He led her toward the prison's narrow, arched side portal through the brick wall, where Reverend van Nooten waited, Bible in hand.

As she emerged outside, the sunlight hurt her eyes. Ahead, one person laughed behind the phalanx of armed police and soldiers: Ilse, her cellmate, the *Vertrauens-Frau* or V-Frau, an informant for the Nazis, who sometimes called them "confidential advisers." Each step to the idling Mercedes-Benz L-3000 truck, with the German military's white, straight-armed cross on its doors, stung like walking on cut glass; *the Doctor must have whipped the soles of my feet.*

Ignoring the pain, she fought to control the shivering from her head to her toes as two policemen hoisted her into the truck bed and shoved her down on a side bench. Behind the truck, the reverend and Prosecutor Giskes followed in a police car.

What to think about? I have only minutes to live, and I'm frightened and lonely and terribly sad. But that can't be it. No, don't think about him. That is too sad. No, focus on something else. Jake had always told me about struggling to do the right thing. I have done that, my love. I am doing that, and I will not let them win by showing weakness. I will not make it easy for them by taking the L-pill. We will be victorious in the end because we are doing the right thing. We will be Isaiah's Oaks of Righteousness.

When the truck jerked to a stop, the guards dragged her out. Her vision was spinning, and her heartbeat was so loud in her ears that she wasn't sure what was happening. Then, her feet squished and skidded in the sand. Waves crashed in the distance. Briny ocean breezes filled her lungs. Carefree seagulls squealed as they swirled above her. *Another lovely day at the beach.*

Two policemen propped her up as she stumbled on wobbly legs over a dune covered with spiky, green-gray tufts of marram grass. They stopped in front of the reverend and the prosecutor. Van Nooten read the Lord's Prayer and some New Testament passages unfamiliar to her. When he finished, the prosecutor read out the charges and the sentence and then, as if swatting a fly, made a perfunctory gesture for the police to proceed.

"Wait," Miriam said, grasping the crucifix on her necklace. "Reverend, could you please remove this?"

With a doleful look, he reached around her neck and unclasped it.

"Give it to someone of your faith who truly understands the words of your Jesus," she said, glaring at the prosecutor, who avoided her eyes as he and the reverend climbed into their car and sped off.

Not wanting to be dragged, Miriam tromped ahead of her two guards, pointing their Karabiner 98k rifles at her and a Grüne Polizei officer armed with a J.P. Sauer & Sohns 38H police pistol. She was the lone condemned prisoner that day, so the firing squad was small. Together, they slid down a steep dune and up another two-story-high one before emerging into the flat Waalsdorpervlakte.

"Quien quiere ser servidor, es mal sufrid." She thought of that Ladino saying, meaning, "The person who desires to serve suffers the most." Despite her best efforts, the tears began to trickle from the corner of her eyes, making it difficult to find her way. Ahead, an armed German soldier and an SS officer guarded a crew of laborers finishing up a pit that must be her final resting place.

"You're early," said the SS officer supervising the gravediggers.

"You are late," the Grüne Polizei officer said. "You should have been finished hours ago. Now, leave, or we'll shoot you, too."

Why are the Germans arguing over who was late and who was early? The laborers crawled out of the hole and hustled behind the firing squad along with their angry officer. Miriam's executioners removed the handcuffs, positioned her on the grave's edge, and stepped back.

Behind her, the firing squad commander unsnapped his black leather holster, and bolts clicked, chambering bullets into the soldiers' rifles. Silently, Miriam recited David's prayer in Psalms 17: *Hide me in the shadow of your wings from the wicked who are assailing me.* She closed her eyes tight. *They will have to shoot me in the back. My dear Jake. I love you.*

"Ready!" the officer shouted. "Aim!"

"*Sh'ma Yisra'eil Adonai Eloheinu Adonai echad,*" Miriam whispered, reciting the beginning of the Sh'ma prayer, meaning, "Hear, O Israel, the Lord is our God. The Lord is one." From behind them, the sound of whacks and thuds bewildered Miriam. She felt no pain. *Would it take another round of shots to end this agony?*

She swayed; her knees buckled; she teetered toward the hole, but as she swooned, someone grabbed her from behind and twisted her around. Fighting to focus her eyes through the tears, Miriam spotted the laborers with their shovels and an armed Waffen-SS officer standing over her three would-be executioners, two of them lying face down in the sand. Next to them, their commander trembled on his knees, shaky hands in the air.

"Miriam. You're safe," the man holding her said.

"What? Joopie? Oh, my God!" she hugged George, calling him by his childhood nickname. "I got the peppermints. They gave me so much hope." As Miriam peered over George's shoulder, an older laborer in ragged clothes hurried over to her and joined in the hugging. "Father! How? What?!"

"Come, my dear. We must hurry. We will explain later," Maduro said, tears of joy streaming down his cheeks.

"They'll be expecting gunshots soon," someone said.

Miriam wheeled around to see who was speaking and couldn't believe her eyes. "Jake!" She charged over and almost knocked him down with her leaping embrace and kisses on his face. "I love you, I love you, I love you. I never thought I'd see you again."

"I love you, too," Rogers said, hugging her before easing her back onto her feet and instructing the other men to tie up the Germans. He picked up the rifles and tossed one to Nidal and the other to Obasi, causing Miriam to gasp in recognition. The two men waved and smiled at her and aimed the rifles in the air. But Miriam moved quicker. She snatched the 38H police pistol from the sand where the Grüne Polizei officer had dropped it and pointed it at his head.

With terror in his eyes, the officer struggled in the loose sand to rise from his knees while lifting his hands higher over his head and pleading for his life. "Please, don't shoot me. I'm only following orders. Please, I have a family."

The bullet slammed into him right between the eyes, blowing out the back of his head and knocking him to the ground. "And Jews don't?" Miriam said as she pivoted and, with cool, military precision, fired two more shots into the heads of the squirming, prostrate policemen. No one moved.

Overcoming his shock, Rogers whispered to Obasi and Nidal, "Shoot, now. It has to sound like a firing squad." They pulled the trigger several times. "Throw the bodies into the pit and cover them up, fast. But remove the clothes first."

The men stripped the bodies, dragged them into the hole, and shoveled and kicked sand over them. Rogers snatched the gun from Miriam's hand and wrapped his arms around her. This wasn't the first time Miriam had killed a Nazi. But this time was different. On the *Peggy C*, a German ensign, a captive freed by mutineers, had a gun to Rogers' head and would have handed them all over to the approaching U-boat. Miriam did not hesitate to pull the trigger. Although she felt ill afterward, there was no remorse. This time, there was no remorse and no queasiness, just cold, all-consuming anger and a serenity she hadn't experienced for months. *This is war, and I am prepared to fight to the death.*

"That's good enough," said Pieter, disguised in the Waffen-SS officer uniform. "Everyone to the truck."

They fled over several dunes, with Pieter walking backward at the rear, brushing away their tracks with an uprooted bush. After reaching the waiting OT truck, they scrambled into the covered back.

"We have a little time before the Germans' truck driver realizes that the soldiers are not coming back and tries to sound the alarm. His tires have been slashed, so he'll have to walk," Pieter said with a snort as he closed the flap.

The fake, Nazi-attired OT soldier drove away with Pieter in the passenger's seat, holding the dead soldiers' rifles and pistol. After a few blocks, he climbed out with the weapons and trotted into a building. Not long after, the truck stopped again, and George bid his farewells, giving Miriam a long embrace and a kiss on the lips.

"Please come with us, George," Maduro pleaded, holding his hand. "Flee while you can."

"There are others I have to help escape. I'll see you soon in England," George said, sliding out of the truck.

Rogers frowned at Miriam as the truck rumbled away. "Old boyfriend?"

Her lips cracked into a faint smile, and she shook her head. "Are you jealous?" she said.

Rogers shrugged.

"Don't be. He's a distant cousin. His family is in the shipping business in Curaçao. Dutch boys come over to Holland for schooling." She collapsed into Rogers' arms. "Where are we going?"

"Amsterdam, where we have an Irish ship waiting to take us all away," Rogers whispered as he kissed the top of her head. "The Germans are focused on people fleeing Amsterdam, so we shouldn't be stopped going into the city. But if we are, you'll have to hide in there." He pointed to the back of the truck bed, where a truck-wide tool chest with a false bottom flipped on its side. "We'll cover you with shovels and tools."

Miriam slipped out of his arms and hugged and kissed the cheeks of the men from the *Peggy C*, thanking them for saving her life and for taking good care of Rogers. Her father could barely speak as she snuggled up beside him and held his hands for a few minutes before returning to Rogers. They whispered and kissed and hugged for almost the entire hour-long trip to the docks in Amsterdam.

They made good time because there hadn't been much traffic on account of fuel shortages and, as predicted, they were routinely waved through roadblocks. When the truck parked at the Eastern Docklands, Rogers handed

Miriam a man's shirt and denim pants with a wool watch cap and boots. "Put these on after we get out and tuck your hair under the hat. Wait for my signal to follow us aboard the *Erin Go Bragh.*"

Once comfortable that the coast was clear, Rogers and the other men jumped out of the truck, closing the flap behind them. Inside, Miriam stripped and tugged on the men's clothes and waited. When the flap flew up, she leaped to her feet, but her father flung her back and climbed back in, followed by the other men in a frenzy.

Outside, Rogers said something to the fake OT driver and scrambled in, snapping the flap down. The truck rumbled away.

Miriam gave him a quizzical look.

"It's gone," he said. "Sailed this morning. Now we're stuck."

CHAPTER 15

Dries Janssen kicked the sand at Waalsdorpervlakte, furious at the idiot Dutch police and SS soldiers stomping about the crime scene. They were leaving so many footprints and smells that even the cadaver dogs wouldn't be able to pick up a scent. As a result, they would never find where the firing squad members were buried in the sand, if they were dead, or in which direction they had been led at gunpoint by the resistance members fleeing the scene.

Technically, the forty-year-old Janssen had no business wandering around the dunes. Dressed in a double-breasted suit and a gray silk homburg in his right hand, he fanned his sweaty face, his armless left sleeve tucked into his jacket pocket. At six-foot-seven—tall even for the Dutch—he was a physically imposing man. With close-cropped blond hair and crystal blue eyes, he could have been a poster boy for Hitler's Aryan *Übermensch*, except for the nasty red birthmark spattered over most of his right cheek. That flaw, his lumbering gait, and ever-present scowl made him seem less a superman than an ill-disguised ogre in blue pinstripes. Bitter, canny, and dangerous.

He wasn't a military investigator or police detective, although he had been one before the war. But when an informant had phoned him earlier from the Oranjehotel and told him an inmate had escaped and the firing squad was missing, he sped over from Amsterdam. He didn't care that Hedda ten Boom was considered a spy; other services dealt with those. What piqued his interest was how the informant had described her: a Jew on the run. That was fair game for someone like him, a bounty hunter for Jews working for head money.

As a Colonne Henneicke member, Janssen received a regular salary of 230 guilders a month and substantial overtime pay, plus the money he made off the books by accepting bribes and stealing confiscated Jewish possessions. That was an enormous increase from the 60 guilders a month he had received on welfare and more than enough to make him well off. But the real money was in the head money bonuses for captured Jews, and he was sure this Jew would bring in far more than the regular 7.50 guilders. In March alone, he and the other Colonne members had rounded up close to 3,200 Jews.

"What are you doing here?" said Untersturmführer Knorr, the prison interrogator known as the Doctor, his arms akimbo in belligerent imitation of Hitler. "This is a matter for my men in the Gestapo."

"Yes, Herr Untersturmführer. I am only here to help. I understand she is a Jew and, as you know, I have a certain expertise at capturing them."

"They may call you 'The Bloodhound,' but do not interfere with my investigation," Knorr said with an embarrassed sneer.

"I'll be off then." Janssen donned his homburg and started to leave before turning back to Knorr. "You might want to have your men dig up where you are standing."

"What the hell for?"

"The marram grass," Janssen said with a polite smile. "It's falling over. Looks like someone didn't have time to bury the roots deep enough." Knorr glared at him and shouted for his men to bring their shovels.

✩✩✩

"What now?" Rogers said to Miriam.

"I know a place where we can hide, at least for a while," she said and directed the fake OT official to drive them to her former medical school classmate's home at 282 Nieuwezijds Voorburgwal, a three-minute journey south from the Royal Palace on Dam Square.

"Are you sure?" Rogers said.

"Yes, Tineke hid our friend Tirzah there after the Nazis kicked her and me and all the other Jews out of medical school. Since then, she and her mother have hidden many others in their boarding house."

"Why didn't you go into hiding?"

Miriam eyed her father. "It is my fault," Maduro said. "I thought we were safe because my brother was a member of the Jewish Council. All his family members were exempted from being deported, called a *Sperr*. Like thousands of others, I should have paid closer attention to the stamp that said *bis auf weiteres*, which means 'for the time being.' That notice came for me and will come for all the others soon. It was another trick that we should not have fallen for."

After a short drive, the truck swung into an alley off the wide, cobble-stoned Nieuwezijds Voorburgwal. Miriam tugged her watch cap down over her ears to cover her hair, scurried across the street, and knocked on a door with an ornate wooden frame at the front of a three-story brick rowhouse. A young woman with dark, shoulder-length, curly hair opened the door, pulled Miriam inside, and searched the street before closing the door.

A few minutes later, the woman emerged with a coat wrapped around her shoulders and strolled across the street into the alley. When Rogers lifted the flap on the truck, she raised her hand for him to stay put.

"You must come one at a time every few minutes to avoid attracting attention from our neighbors," she said. "Do not knock. Enter like you are staying at our boarding house." Without looking at Rogers, she continued on her way out of the alley.

For the next hour, one man after the other made the trip; Rogers was the last one. He thanked the driver and waited for the truck to exit the alley before striding to the front door and letting himself inside. An older woman whispered a greeting, "I am Marie, Tineke's mother. Follow me." She led him up the stairs of the six-bedroom rowhouse, which resembled a former school.

On the third floor, they found the others waiting. "You must pay close attention," Marie said. "You will stay on this floor. If you hear a bell, go to the hiding places." She took them up to the attic and opened a hidden door into one of the gables lined with rifles and pistols. "We store them for the resistance. Two, maybe three of you will hide here. Make no noise no matter what horrible things you may hear on the outside. The others will go out the window and across the roof to the school next door and hide there."

"How long should we stay hidden?" Rogers said.

"You all must hide until I or someone else comes to get you," Marie said. She made them practice the procedures several times, sneaking up the stairs, opening the hidden door, and slipping out the window to be sure that they could move quickly and quietly into hiding. "My mother will bring you food and water. Do you require anything else?"

"I have no identity papers or ration cards," Miriam said.

"I will take care of those. And I will connect you to an escape line," Marie said. "But you must stay on this floor and away from the windows." She stepped toward the door but stopped. "Oh, and one more thing. Our house-keeper, Lize, is not to be trusted. Stay away from her as much as you can. For all she knows, you are boarders."

Later that day, Tineke returned, hopped up the stairs two at a time, and barged into the room to find Miriam and Rogers sitting on a couch talking. "This is bad," she said, trying to catch her breath and holding out a flyer. Miriam gasped and showed it to Rogers. The wanted poster had her real name and a current picture. A10,000-guilders reward was being offered for her capture.

"How could they know your name?" Rogers said.

"That reward is worth more than most Dutch earn in years," Miriam said. "Someone who knew me must have seen my picture and told them in hopes of getting some of the reward."

"The flyers are everywhere," Tineke said. "And they warn that anyone who helps you will be executed."

"We must leave," Maduro said, standing in the doorway. "We cannot endanger you and your family."

Marie brushed past him and snatched the flyer. "I won't hear of it. You're safe here. We've been raided many times, but they have always found noth-ing. We'll have Lize take a few days off. For that amount of money, we cannot trust anyone, and neither can you."

"What about a disguise?" Miriam said.

"We can dye your hair and perhaps make you look pregnant," Marie said.

"That would be good," Rogers said. "But we still can't risk riding a train or walking outside, even after a few days."

"I will talk to some resistance groups to see who can smuggle you out," Tineke said.

The sudden, urgent ring of a telephone startled everyone. Tineke ran down the stairs to answer it. Her muffled voice carried up to the third floor, but her words weren't clear. She hung up the phone and bounded back into the room, out of breath and frantic. "Hide! Now! The Gestapo are coming."

"This is strange," Marie said as she hustled them into the attic. "Usually, we get that call the day before."

"From whom?" Miriam said as she led her father into the secret compartment.

"We don't know," Tineke said. "We guess it must be someone at Gestapo headquarters. We don't know why he calls us. But he is never wrong."

"Does that mean they know I am here?" Miriam said.

"I doubt it," Tineke said. "They seem to be raiding every suspected safe house, and we are at the top of their list. As I said, they haven't found anyone here before. And they won't find you." Tineke and her mother hurried downstairs.

Following their training, Nidal and Obasi climbed out the window. When Rogers tried to follow, Cookie grabbed his arm. "I'll go, Cap'n. You stay with Miriam."

"Are you kidding? With your bad hip?" Tires squealed and car doors slammed outside, followed by a banging on the front door. "Get in and close the door." Cookie followed orders and sealed off the hiding place. Rogers climbed out the window, slid it shut, and tiptoed across the roof to the adjacent school to hide with the other two.

☆ ☆ ☆

In a tiny space inside the pitch-black gable, Cookie, Miriam, and her father huddled together and tried to control their breathing. When Cookie trembled, Miriam grasped his hand. Hobnail boots pounded on the wooden stairs and clicked up and down the hallway. Angry voices in German and Dutch echoed throughout the house as the soldiers opened and dumped drawers, punched holes in walls with their rifle butts, overturned dressers probing for secret doors behind them, and flicked on flashlights to scour the attic's murky corners.

Someone opened the window. Soldiers grunted as they climbed out to the roof. After they crawled back in, they tapped on the walls, searching for hollow places. One of them rapped a pistol butt around the door to the hiding place. Miriam squeezed Cookie's hand, stifling her breath and hoping the pounding of her heart wasn't audible to others. The German searched around the room, tap-tap-tapping on all the walls, and then moved downstairs.

Directly below the hiding place, Tineke used her sweetest voice to chat up the Germans, who responded with shouts and curses. When Tineke laughed, a German yelled at her and pounded something on the wall. Marie screamed. "Stop! You are killing her! She told you. We aren't hiding anyone. Please." A sharp slap ended the conversation.

Maduro grabbed his daughter's hand. For two terrifying hours, the Germans had ransacked the house, finding nothing. For two more excruciating hours, everyone huddled out of sight to be sure the Gestapo didn't surprise them with a return visit.

☆☆☆

Once the sun had set, Tineke snuck out the window and fetched the men, who tiptoed back inside. As Rogers closed the window, Marie, using a flashlight, tapped a code on the hidden door in the attic to let Miriam and the others know it was safe to come out. Once they all had filed down to the third floor, Rogers recoiled at what he saw. Marie's face was still bright red from the slap, and Tineke had a bandage around her head.

"They tried to use my head to knock a hole in the wall," Tineke said with a short laugh, trying to lighten the grim mood. "We brought you food. Try to eat and rest. We'll make plans tomorrow."

Still shaken, they merely toyed with the food laid out for them on a table. But they did drink acorn coffee, slurped small spoonfuls of soup, and nibbled at the bread. The silence continued until Tineke returned and showed them to their rooms. Miriam and Maduro got their own rooms while Rogers bunked with Obasi. Nidal and Cookie shared a room.

Rogers waited until he could hear the men's soft snoring before sneaking down the hallway to Miriam's room. When he opened the door, Miriam was peeking around a blackout curtain. Startled, she spun around at the squeaking hinges, bolted to the door, and pulled him down onto the bed. Tears ran down her cheeks as she clutched him to her as if to hold him for eternity. As Rogers returned the hug, Miriam groaned. He released her and leaned back. "I'm sorry. Did I hurt you?" Rogers said.

Miriam stripped off her shirt, revealing the festering cuts and bruises all over her black and blue torso. "I am a little tender."

Raising his hands in horror, Rogers rolled off the bed and stood beside her. "Oh, my God. What have they done to you? You poor thing. I'm so sorry." He scoured the room, found a hand towel, dipped it into a water basin, and kneeled to clean her wounds. At each touch, no matter how soft, she winced and groaned. Then, he removed her pants, shoes, and socks and washed the blood off her body. She covered her mouth to muffle the screams when Rogers dabbed the shredded soles of her feet. When he'd done all he could, he wrapped her in a blanket and sank onto the bed's edge. He was on the verge of tears.

"Can you just hold me?" she said in a weak voice.

"Of course, dear." He laid down beside her and wrapped his arms around her shoulders, surprised by her trembling. "Are you cold?"

"No. Afraid. All the time. But I can never let it show. I have to play the part, except with you."

"Do you feel like talking?"

She nodded yes.

"How did you get here?"

"Gaylord."

"Basil Gaylord? Flight Lieutenant Basil Gaylord?" he said, rubbing the backs of his forefingers above his lips as if smoothing down a pencil mustache, something their old friend always did. They had rescued Gaylord from the North Atlantic Ocean after his plane had been shot down, and Miriam used her medical skills to save his life. He returned the favor by helping them quell a mutiny by some crew members and captured sailors from a U-boat boarding party.

"Yes, that Gaylord," Miriam said. "Not long after you left Haifa, he approached me about helping defeat the Nazis. He could no longer be a pilot because of his wounded arm, so he began to work for something called MI9. He told me it was a British intelligence agency that helps downed pilots escape occupied Europe. He said a unit called Jewish Parachutists of Mandate

Palestine worked with MI9 and another agency called the Special Operations Executive."

"SOE? The agency that helps resistance groups?" Rogers said. "You work for them?"

"Yes. Gaylord said I was a good fit because I speak so many languages and because of my medical training."

"That explains a lot," Rogers said, sitting up.

"Explains what?"

"We were able to sneak into Holland because someone at SOE helped us travel on a neutral Irish ship. Until now, I didn't understand why. They wanted me to find out what happened to you through your father or the resistance groups. I guess they didn't tell me that because they feared I'd spill the beans if I were captured."

"Why would you have beans?"

Rogers chuckled. "Not beans, literally. It's an expression meaning to reveal secrets."

"You Americans speak such funny English," Miriam said, pulling Rogers closer and wrapping her legs around him. "We trained not to spill beans at RAF Ramat David airstrip outside of Haifa. Our instructors said the mission Churchill had given the SOE was to set Europe ablaze. So, we learned shooting and hand fighting, sabotage, Morse code, how to operate a radio, and how to parachute."

"So, you jumped out of a plane to get here?"

"Yes. But something went wrong. Right after my wireless operator and I buried our parachutes after our landing, a man who said he was from a resistance group came to guide us to a hiding place. But he asked too many questions. We knocked him out and fled in different directions. As I hid in the woods, I saw German soldiers sneak up. It had all been a trap. I made it to Amsterdam but never saw Fennel again."

"Fennel?"

"That was his wireless operator's code name. I didn't know his real one," Miriam said. "We all had vegetable code names."

"And you were?" Rogers asked.

"Rhubarb."

"Well, Miss Rhubarb, was rescuing your father part of your mission?"

"It was not. But it crossed my mind that if I volunteered, I might be able to get him out."

"But what about Truus, Wim, Julius, and Arie? Who's taking care of them?" Rogers said, concern in his voice. He had grown quite fond of Miriam's sister and her three young cousins on the *Peggy C.*

"It was hard to leave them all, especially after..." Miriam's voice drifted off, tears welling in her eyes.

"Especially after what?" Rogers asked, using a handkerchief to dab away her tears.

"There are more important things than family," she said, ignoring his question. "Jews must fight, and this was my chance. Besides, we have lots of family in Palestine to care for all the children until I return."

"I'll get you back to Palestine soon."

"Not soon. I do not trust any of the SOE contacts here. With help from friends I trusted, I had to operate on my own. Now that Father is free, I must return to England to warn them the whole operation has been compromised. Many lives may depend on my doing so." She grabbed Rogers' face with both hands and covered it with kisses. "I never thought I'd see you again, you know. What happened in America?"

"Not what I'd expected," he said. After he had been released from the hospital at Haifa and recuperated for a month at the home of Miriam's relatives, Rogers hitched a ride on a Red Duster, a British merchant ship, in a convoy to New York, working as an able seaman. Even though he was over-qualified, he was happy to do the work and, for once, not be in command.

After the ship docked, he bought a train ticket to Annapolis to find out what had happened to the fellow Navy midshipman he thought he had killed in a fight at the US Naval Academy more than two decades before. Rogers had been jailed after the fight, and much to his surprise, the grandfather he never knew had bailed him out and arranged a job for him as an apprentice on a cargo ship heading to Europe.

His grandfather, a well-known admiral, warned him never to return because the boy who had attacked him was not expected to live and was from a prominent family that would make sure Rogers was sent to prison. It didn't matter that the trouble started when the boy and several other midshipmen attacked Rogers after he defended a friend they were bullying.

"Turns out I didn't kill him," Rogers said. "He recovered and went on to become an admiral. When I visited him to apologize, he actually apologized to me and said it was all his fault and how sorry he was to have ruined my career. So, he got me into the US Merchant Marine and a commission as captain of one of the new Liberty ships."

"Where is your ship now?" she asked.

"In Davy Jones' Locker," he said, grinning at Miriam to see if she understood the slang.

"I give up," she said and slapped his arm, forgetting for a moment what a horrible situation they were in.

"It means at the bottom of the sea. Split apart. We ended up in Ireland, where I heard about your father. And that's how I got here."

"I am so happy you did," Miriam said. They clung to each other in the cool night. Dim moonlight peeped around the curtains' edges. They felt safe for the moment, warmed by the soft human touch they had missed for too long. Both felt alive with expectations and hope, yet nagged at by unrelenting fear. Blustery winds swished the young leaves outside on the elms lining the misty streets.

"Why were you staring out the window when I came in?" Rogers asked.

"Always have a way out."

CHAPTER 16

A soft tapping woke Rogers. Obasi was peeking around the door, waving for him to come along. As Rogers snuck away, the sun's first rays lit the horizon. Later, when the others started moving about, he headed to the second floor, where Marie, on a dining room table, had laid out some bread and butter and coffee with condensed milk. Everyone was busy eating when a shrill horn blast and tire squeals startled them. *"Pulsen,"* Marie said in disgust after she reached the window.

"Pulsen!" Maduro threw down his napkin and hurried over with the others to check it out, careful to stand far enough back to be out of sight of the people below. Across the street, a black semi-trailer idled in front of one of the luxury rowhouses. Large white lettering on the trailer's side read: "A. PULS. AMSTERDAM."

"Bloodsucking removal company," Maduro said.

"Moving houses in the middle of a war?" Cookie said. "Don't seem right."

"They are not moving. That house, like thousands of others, was owned by Jews who have been deported. For the Nazis, Abraham Puls and his company remove all the furniture and valuables that the neighbors haven't stolen. *Roven* is the Dutch word for 'to rob.' Now, *pulsen* is the slang word we Dutch use to describe those official robbers."

Tineke, who had risen much earlier than everyone else, shuffled through the front door with a pained expression. "I stopped by a funeral and stole these from someone's pocket. She looks something like you," she said, handing the identity card to Miriam.

"Thank you," Miriam said, examining the black-and-white photo. "I'll have to darken my hair. Maybe a light red."

"I'm afraid no one will help us now. I talked to several people in resistance groups, all of whom had heard from others that Miriam might come to Amsterdam looking for the help of friends," Tineke said. "They all said it was too dangerous and to stay away if I heard from you. There were raids all over the country last night, and they will likely do them again tonight. The Germans were already cracking down because of the registry attack, but whatever you did has upset them even more."

"Don't you know what she did?" Rogers said.

"The flyers and posters do not say, nor do the underground newspapers. No one seems to know exactly."

"Have they taken any hostages?" Maduro said.

"Not that I've heard."

"They must be too embarrassed to make the exact details public," Maduro said.

"Mother," Tineke said to Marie, standing near the window. "I have more bad news. They caught Johan." She explained to the others. "Johan Brouwer is a friend of mine from the university. He formed his own resistance group, and we helped him hide weapons and explosives and forge documents."

"Those were his guns in the hiding place?" Miriam said.

"Yes," Tineke said. "He was one of the men who attacked the registry, and almost all of them were arrested in less than a week. Someone must have betrayed them for the 10,000-guilder reward."

"That means we are not safe. We should move," Nidal said, returning to the table and buttering a slice of bread. "If the police come back, it is only a matter of time before they punch or shoot a hole in the right wall or catch us in the school."

"He's got a point, Cap'n," Cookie said. "Maybe we could hide in that truck. Nobody'd be looking for us there. Now would they?"

Everyone gawked at him, making him raise his hands as if to say, "Sorry for the bad joke."

"I doubt we'd survive for long in the back of the truck," Rogers said with a chuckle and peered out the window, rubbing his lower lip between his thumb and forefinger. "Where does it go?"

"The truck?" Maduro said. "It will go to the Puls' Argentina warehouse at the Eastern Docklands, where it could wait for days to be unloaded. Even with dozens of barges coming every day to haul the furniture to the Rhine River and then Germany, the warehouse is almost always out of storage space."

"Dutch barges?" Rogers said.

"Yes, mostly," Maduro said.

Rogers stared out the window, observing the movers hauling furniture from the house, showing it to a man who wrote in a ledger, and then lifting the pieces into the truck. The driver, sitting on a running board smoking a pipe and paying no attention to the haulers, didn't lift a finger to help. No guards or police hovered about, only neighbors and occasional passersby stopping to watch.

"They are right. We must leave before tonight," Miriam said, hugging Rogers' arm.

"Unfortunately," he said. "But we need one person we can completely trust, who would not be tempted by the reward. Know anyone?"

☆☆☆

"What are you doing back so soon?" Wim Henneicke, the thirty-three-year-old leader of Colonne Henneicke, demanded of Janssen as he entered their office in room twenty-five in a converted secondary school on Adama van Scheltemaplein in South Amsterdam. "She's probably halfway to England by now."

"I have reason to believe she's here in Amsterdam," Janssen said, settling into a chair behind a desk. On it was a framed picture of his young son Stefan surrounded by photos, documents, and tip letters from his regular sources and others hungry for rewards. He tossed his homburg at a hat rack in the corner, but it missed the hook and flopped to the floor.

"That's stupid," Henneicke said with a slight German accent. The former taxi driver and auto mechanic with underworld connections had been born in Holland to German immigrants but had never been naturalized as a Dutch citizen. "Why would she come here? This is the most dangerous place for Jews in all of Holland."

"Yeah, you'd think so. But one of my informants said she saw a solitary Organization Todt truck near Waalsdorpervlakte this morning, and it was heading north," Janssen said. He did not mention that he beat the tip out of several area residents and might have left one for dead. Even had to scrub for almost half an hour to clean the blood off his new suit coat.

"That is pretty weak," said Henneicke, shaking his head. His towering shock of curly reddish-blond hair resembled an upside-down shaving brush.

"I checked with the local commander, and he said none of his trucks was in that area this morning, and none traveled alone. However, one *was* reported stolen from Amsterdam yesterday and found abandoned here today."

"Even if that is somehow connected to her, it could still be a trick to throw us off the scent. Or it could mean nothing at all," Henneicke said, putting on a midnight blue double-breasted overcoat of wool twill and heading out the door. "I have other duties now. Go find her. I will not be happy if we miss out on that 10,000-guilder reward."

Stuffing a note from his desk into his pocket, Janssen snatched his hat from the floor and followed behind his boss, who oversaw one more link in the Nazis' elaborate robbery chain. The Colonne Henneicke was one of four divisions of the Hausraterfassungsstell, the Office for the Registration of Household Effects, which had been set up to keep an inventory of property belonging to deported Jews.

Henneicke's fifty-four-man unit was originally the investigative arm that tracked down stolen or misappropriated Jewish goods. That job evolved into hunting Jews in hiding and those without an exemption from deportation. The caseload exploded in March 1943 when a bounty was put on Jews' heads.

Janssen loved his job because he loved money, and he hated Jews. He tolerated the gruff Henneicke because he rarely questioned Janssen's brutal methods or inflated expense accounts. All the boss cared about was results and splitting the reward from those results. Janssen believed he had found his life's calling.

Unlike his father and his father before him, he never wanted to be a tulip farmer. Instead, he had joined the Dutch fascist party, the National Socialist Movement or NSB, and became a member of its military wing of black-shirted young men called the WA, short for "*Weerafdeeling*." It could have a double meaning of Defense Department or Weather Department, an allusion to Germany's stormtroopers.

He used his NSB connections to obtain a job with the Amsterdam police, where he rose to detective despite his reputation for brutality and cutting corners. Not long after the Germans invaded, he joined the Dutch Volunteer Legion, and was sent to the Russian front, where he lost his left arm in a battle near Lake Ilmen in the Soviet Union's Toropets-Kholm offensive in January 1942. He was awarded the Eastern Front Medal, with a "wound badge," and was discharged after his recovery.

Appalled by his wound, his wife deserted him and took their 10-year-old son Stefan with her, refusing to let the boy ever see his disfigured father again. Naturally, that infuriated and saddened Janssen no end. Since the police had no job for a cripple, he was on welfare until Henneicke hired him.

Janssen's first stop after leaving his office was the Hollandsche Schouwburg where captured Jews were detained for days while being processed for shipment to Westerbork transport center or concentration camps. Janssen had delivered dozens of Jews to the "Jewish Theater," as the Germans called it, being careful to fill out the arrest reports because the bonus was doubled for anyone caught in hiding. "Penal cases" they were called, and almost all his terrified arrestees had been in hiding.

Janssen flashed his ID card at the Dutch police guard at the entrance. "Inspector Janssen. I have business inside," he said and brushed past the officer. Colonne Henneicke members often called themselves detectives, but they had no such official capacity. They weren't supposed to arrest anyone, but they did, saying they were "picking someone up." They didn't have a gun permit, either, but they carried weapons.

They often claimed they were from the SD, the Nazi security service. They weren't. The card Janssen carried was a simple ID with a seal. Despite all that, their authority to pretty much do as they pleased was rarely questioned; in the case of the hulking Janssen, never.

In the theater, Janssen found the stench overwhelming as he shoved through crowds of overwrought men and tearful women huddled on the floor or standing in line to register their names and turn over their valuables. From the looks of it, some of them had been there for days, if not weeks, crying, arguing, and dodging blows and kicks from the police and SS guards.

Janssen caught the eye of a young woman seated at a table at the front of the crowd, interviewing people and filling out forms. He signaled for her to come with him. She spoke to a colleague, grabbed her coat, and followed

Janssen outside and down the street.

"Why haven't you called me?" Janssen said, backing the woman against a wall with an ominous sneer.

"I don't know anything new."

"Now, now, you always know something, Lieke. You're my best V-Frau," he said, pressing closer to her quivering body.

Passersby stared straight ahead or crossed the street to avoid getting involved.

"What do you hear about this Miriam Maduro?" he said.

"Nothing. Nobody's heard anything… Honestly." Janssen wrapped his enormous right hand around her throat and lifted her until only the tips of her toes touched the ground. "There was something," she said in a squeaky voice, her face reddening.

Janssen lowered her but didn't release his grip.

"I heard that somebody was asking around for a place for her to hide," she said.

"Who?"

"I don't know. They didn't tell me."

"I would hate for something to happen to your mother's exemption, Jew girl. If I don't get answers soon, even the Jewish Council won't be able to protect her or you." He threw her against the wall, cracking her head on a low windowsill, and spun around to leave.

"Wait, please! We were at the university together. She had many gentile friends. Ask them."

Janssen stopped and glared at her. "Names."

"I…I didn't know them." When Janssen lurched at her with his raised fist, Lieke screamed. "Talk to her professors. They'd know." The fist stopped within a millimeter of her nose.

"They'd better, or we'll be having a longer talk," he said, shoving her away.

The Municipal University of Amsterdam, where Miriam had studied medicine, was in turmoil. German officials had ordered students to take a loyalty oath, but most refused, and fights and screaming matches disrupted classes. Janssen didn't have much luck with the professors. All the Jewish ones had been fired, and the remaining ones claimed not to know anything about Miriam, who hadn't attended classes for three years.

Frustrated but refusing to throw in the towel, Janssen rested on a bench in the middle of the campus and pondered what to do. He could try to intimidate administrators into helping, but they probably didn't know much either.

Unlike most Colonne Henneicke members, Janssen had graduated from high school and even attended a year of college. He tried to draw on memories of that year. *Where did one go to find out things? Of course. The library.* So, he drove to the sixteenth-century Handboogdoelen building at 421 Singel, which had served as a longbowmen's shooting range for the city's civic guard and later as a hotel before the city donated it to what became the university.

He scoured student publications and directories inside the library until a photo caught his eye. The picture showed a group of medical students in 1940. He compared the faces to the one on the flyer for Miriam, and spotted her standing near another woman whose name rang a bell: Tineke Bucher.

CHAPTER 17

Near sundown, the last of the furniture had been loaded into the A. Puls truck across from Tineke's house. The driver inspected the contents and, seemingly satisfied with how everything had been stacked, released the loaders, who hopped on a flatbed truck for the ride back to the warehouse. Most of the gawkers had wandered off, except for a small cluster of men, some with dark skin.

As the driver crushed out a cigarette under the toe of his boot, one of the men approached with a smile. "We'll pay a handsome price for that Dutch marquetry side chair you loaded," said Maduro, wearing a tie and an ill-fitting brown suit. "Eighteenth-century, I believe. How about 100 guilders?"

"Not a chance," the driver said, grabbing the truck's door handle and placing his foot on the sideboard, ready to leave.

"What about 200?" Maduro said, pulling out his wallet.

The driver hesitated momentarily, looked over his shoulder, then shook his head and climbed into the truck's cab. He gasped as Miriam, who had squeezed into the passenger's footwell, pointed a gun at him, a 9mm FN military-style pistol favored by the resistance because it was flatter and easier to hide than most weapons. "Do as you are told, and we will let you live," she said.

"I don't got no money. Take all the furniture you want. I won't tell anyone."

"Keep your hands on the steering wheel until I tell you to start the engine," she said, never breaking eye contact with the petrified driver.

The truck's rear double-doors squeaked and, after a moment, banged shut, followed by three knocks.

"Now, take your usual route to the warehouse," Miriam said. "If you do not, or if you say anything to anyone, I will not hesitate to kill you. I have nothing to lose. Drive."

☆☆☆

As the truck rumbled down Nieuwezijds Voorburgwal, it passed Janssen, who was strolling in the opposite direction on his five-minute journey from the library. He stopped in front of Tineke's rowhouse and paced, waiting for the police to arrive. He had called R. Dahmen von Buchholz, the head of the municipal police's Bureau of Jewish Affairs, and tipped him off that Miriam might be hiding there with her medical school chum, whom they both knew quite well.

Janssen had taken part in a couple of previous raids on the house, and though nothing was ever found—even after Tineke and her mother had been arrested and subjected to intense interrogations—he remained suspicious. He didn't care who arrested Miriam because he would still collect the reward. Plus, smashing a few walls, or heads, would be fun.

☆☆☆

At Miriam's direction, the truck driver, now soaked in sweat, stopped on a side road out of sight of the quay at the Eastern Docklands and let the truck idle. Peeking out the window, she opened the door and made room for a young man to climb in while she slid back to the floor and told the driver to cruise along the quay until the young man instructed him to stop.

"Pull up next to that one, the *Noordster*," the man said to the driver, pointing at one of the long canal barges and leaning over to whisper to Miriam. "It is scheduled to leave at daybreak."

He leapt from the cab; his footsteps crunched on the gravel going to the back, and the rear metal doors creaked open. Miriam climbed back into the seat, never taking her gun off the driver, and raised herself high enough to see the barge out the side window. Her father approached it alongside Rogers and Obasi. Each of them carried an antique Dutch marquetry side chair made of elm and walnut; they had exquisite inlaid designs of cherub and upholstered seats resting on cabriole legs.

Wearing an armband with the inscription "Im Dienst der Einsatzstabes

RR," meaning in the Service of the Task Force RR, Maduro waved a paper at the barge captain and pointed to the chairs. "Got a last-minute request that must leave soon. Straight from *Reichsleiter* Rosenberg himself," he said, referring to Alfred Rosenberg, the Nazi Party's chief ideologue who created the *Einsatzstab Reichsleiter Rosenberg* to oversee all of Hitler's cultural looting.

When the befuddled captain came over to examine the paper, Rogers flashed a Mauser P.38, the German army's standard pistol. It resembled a Luger but had a shorter barrel. He pressed it against the captain's side and led him into the barge named after the North Star. The truck driver's door flung open, Nidal and Cookie dragged the driver out, and the young man crawled in.

"They will tie him up and gag him in the back of the truck," Miriam told the young man. "Don't take too many chances, Willem. Abandon the truck as soon as you find a place where it won't be noticed for a couple of days." He saluted as Miriam dashed to the barge. Nidal pounded on the truck's rear, signaling Willem to speed off into the night.

Rogers forced the captain at gunpoint into the cramped wooden wheelhouse at the stern of the boat, a steel-hulled 1929 Luxe motor Dutch Barge. Cargo holds covered by duckboards—wooden planks—and topped by a tarpaulin and a tall wooden foremast folded in half lined the deck of the twenty-four-meter-long *Noodster*. Miriam joined Rogers and the captain while the others led the two crew members at gunpoint to the small cabin below and behind the wheelhouse.

"Tell the Captain that we leave at first light," Rogers said.

"I speak some English," said the captain, whose wrinkles and arthritic hands made him appear to be in his late sixties. "And my name is Henk Cuyper."

"Do you know who I am, Capt. Cuyper?" Miriam said. When he hesitated, she pointed her Mauser at his chest. "Do not make me ask twice."

"Yes, of course," Cuyper said. "I have seen the flyers. You are Solomon's daughter."

"Do you know him?" Miriam asked.

"We've never met, but I know of him," Cuyper said, folding his arms over his chest as if to show he wasn't afraid. "I have carried many loads for his companies, and my brother was the first mate on one of his ships until he got stranded in Spain."

"Then you know he helped fund the Zema-something." Rogers looked at Miriam for help.

"Zeemanspot," she said.

"Right, the fund to help the families of stranded sailors like your brother," Rogers said.

"No, I did not know that," Cuyper said. "But I am not surprised. Solomon Maduro has always been more than kind to us." He stared at the gun in Miriam's hand. "You do not need that. I will not betray you. *Hallo!*"

"*Hang alle landverraders op!*" Miriam replied, lowering the gun. For Rogers' benefit, she added, "It means 'hang all traitors.' It is what Dutch people mean now when we greet each other with hallo."

"What about your crew?" Rogers said. "Can we trust them?"

Cuyper chuckled. "They are my twin sons."

"Good, good," Rogers said. "Can you show me a map of your route?"

The captain spread out a folded map and drew his finger south from Amsterdam down the Merwede Canal, past Utrecht to the Waal River, and then east to the Rhine River and Germany's Ruhr region. It was about 35 kilometers to Utrecht and twice that to the Waal River.

"How fast can she move?" Rogers asked.

"Maybe six knots,. It has a one-cylinder hot-bulb engine with water injection. Gives me trouble sometimes, so I cannot always guarantee that speed."

Rogers did the math: 70 kilometers was around 38 nautical miles. At 6 knots—which means nautical miles an hour—it would take at least six hours to reach the city of Gorinchem at its intersection with the Waal River. "What if we went west on the Waal toward Rotterdam instead of east?"

"Why?"

Rogers drew a line with his finger from Gorinchem to Kanaal van St. Andries that connected to the Maas River, also known as the Meuse River, and through several canals south to France. "Could we make it that far?"

"No."

"Okay. What about here, to Maastricht?" Rogers pointed to the south-eastern tip of Holland near the border with Belgium. The city was about 100 nautical miles from Amsterdam as the crow flies, but much, much longer and slower on winding waterways. "Miriam, could we catch a train here or find someone to help us sneak into Belgium and France?"

"It is risky to go to small towns," she said. "But maybe."

"It would be impossible, my friend," Cuyper said and tapped on the Kanaal van St. Andries. "There is a German fort here right before the lock between the Waal and Maas. We would be stopped before we began. No, Utrecht is your best choice."

"But that is, what, three-four hours away? And we'd arrive in broad daylight," Rogers said, rubbing the back of his neck. "Not much of an escape."

"I know people there who will help you," Cuyper said. "And no one knows how fast we sail. If I do 1 or 2 knots, we will arrive around sunset."

"And a couple of hours before the curfew," Miriam said. "I will tell Father and the others."

"Father? Is Solomon that man with the armband?" Cuyper said.

"Why don't you go with her, Captain?" Rogers said, shaking Cuyper's hand. "You can meet him in the flesh. Plus, you'll need to get some rest. I'll sleep up here. Getting kind of crowded in the cabin."

☆☆☆

Janssen stood outside Tineke's house, watching the police meander about, when his furious boss arrived.

"Are you out of your damn mind?!" Henneicke screamed. "Why the hell did you tip off the Bureau of Jewish Affairs? They're always trying to steal our rewards."

"It is my tip. So, we get the reward if they find her," Janssen said. "Anyway, I needed police who would come in a hurry and be, uh, thorough. That is their training."

"Well, you should have called me first," said Henneicke, who enjoyed going nose-to-nose to intimidate people but couldn't with Janssen, who was a head taller than him. That infuriated the five-foot-nine Henneicke even more.

Janssen stifled a laugh at the spittle running down his boss' cleft chin. "Doesn't matter now."

"Why the hell not?"

"She's not here. But she was."

"What?" Henneicke shook in anger. "How do you know that?"

Like a magician about to pull off a trick, Janssen paused for dramatic effect, stuffed his right hand into his coat pocket, pulled out a bundled handkerchief, and used his teeth to unwrap it. Inside was a green tin about the size of a teacup with the words "L'Oreal-Henna" in black letters and the slogan *"La Plante Merveilleuse"*—"The Marvelous Plant." On the top was a woman's face with long, flowing blue hair. That brand of red hair coloring had been invented earlier in the century by French chemist Eugène Schueller, who named his company the *Société Française de Teintures Inoffensives pour Cheveux*—The Safe Hair Dye Company of France. He was also a strong supporter of French fascists and the Vichy government and, as a result, enjoyed a booming business during the war.

"What am I looking at?" said a disgusted Henneicke, who didn't speak French well and didn't recognize the brand despite having been married three times.

"It is a powder for red hair dye. I found it buried in the trash."

"So what?"

"No one in the house has red hair. And when I asked them about this, they said it must have belonged to one of their boarders," Janssen said, using his teeth to wrap up the tin. "But, of course, they couldn't remember any names."

"Beat it out of them, idiot."

"I tried, but they had nothing to say, and the police said they had nothing to arrest them for."

"You're wasting my time," Henneicke said with a snort and spun around to leave.

"Wait. I can prove it."

Henneicke turned back to face him.

"take the tin to Scheveningen Prison and have them check it against her fingerprints," Janssen said. "I can almost guarantee there will be a match. If not, you can fire me."

"I'll bet my share of the reward that you are wrong, Bloodhound. This time, I'm sure you are *barking* up the wrong tree," Henneicke said with a cackle as he pocketed the wrapped tin, apparently amused at his own cleverness.

Janssen shrugged and wandered back to his car at the library with a nagging feeling he had missed something.

In the middle of the night, he jolted out of a dead sleep and clicked on a lamp. He grabbed a pocket-sized moleskin notebook, wrote down the hunch that had occurred to him, and drifted back to sleep.

☆ ☆ ☆

Not long after Rogers had settled down on the wheelhouse deck, unable to stretch out his long legs or make himself comfortable, Miriam returned with a plate of beans, bread, and a cup of tea. He set the plate down and pulled Miriam into his arms, holding her for a long time before saying a word. "I'm sorry," he said. "My plan wasn't very well thought out, was it?"

Miriam kissed him over and over. "It doesn't matter. My father and I are free for one more day. That is your gift to us."

At dawn, Cuyper nudged Rogers awake. "Time to heat the engine."

Rogers wasn't sure what that meant, so he followed him into the engine room to find out. From a long-spouted can, Cuyper squirted oil onto various parts of the 35-hp engine, turned a small crank a dozen times, and squirted more oil.

He lit a slow-burning wick on the end of a metal stick and pumped oil into the glow-head at the top of the engine, nicknamed the "Vicar's Hat" because that's what it resembled. Flames shot out, preheating the engine until a thin stream of white smoke poured out of a small pipe on the side. Lodging a long metal bar into a hole in the flywheel—a metal wheel about the size of a car tire—Cuyper rotated it until it was positioned correctly and switched on the engine, which roared to life, shaking the entire boat.

"That's quite a process," Rogers said. "Nothing like that on Liberty ships."

"You have to warm up the engine and align the gears properly, or you never will get going in the right direction," Cuyper said. "Once underway, I can switch on the water injection and give it 10 percent more power. But we won't be needing it."

For ten hours, the four-meter-wide *Noodster* put-put-putted and rattled along the canal. Poplar trees and lush farmland coming to life in the spring lined the way. The boat was moving so sluggishly that Cuyper was forced to signal faster barges to pass him, and other times, he had to pull over near shore, pretending to do maintenance. After a few hours, one of Cuyper's sons went ashore with a bike and rode south to make arrangements with resistance members in Utrecht.

By late afternoon, as shadows covered the canal, Cuyper and his other son tied up the barge north of the city, where the canal was separated from the Vecht River by a small strip of land. "Over there, you will find my son," Cuyper told Rogers, pointing at the Vecht. "He will take all of you by a smaller barge into the city, where there is a safe place to hide for a day or so."

Rogers thanked him and prepared the others to make the crossing. Maduro hung back to talk to Cuyper. "This was the best canal ride of my life, even if I did almost lose all my teeth from the shaking," he said with a wide grin. "After the war, we'll buy you a modern engine."

Cuyper shook his hand and laughed. "I don't think I could get used to the quiet, so thanks anyway. And good luck."

No one was around to watch Rogers and the others scurry across the fifty-meter-wide strip and climb aboard a barge less than half the *Noodster*'s length. With the wooden wheelhouse in the bow, this type of boat was used for transporting goods and supplies around the smaller canals in the city center. Cuyper's son led them into a small cabin where they huddled on the floor for the hour-long trek along the winding river. After passing the sixteenth-century brick Zuylen Castle, they chugged into the Oudegracht Canal, a scenic waterway flowing between brick houses, and under arched brick bridges through the heart of Utrecht's old town.

The canal, unlike the ones in Amsterdam, was cut several meters below street level and was lined with windows, arched double doors, and an occasional staircase. The doors led to the city's wharf cellars, carved out under homes so the owners above could take in supplies and store them without having to haul them up to street level. Most of the 700 in existence had been abandoned after rail and road traffic began to dominate transportation.

The boat docked at a narrow quay under a double-arched bridge, making it almost invisible to anyone at street level. Cuyper's son told everyone to stay hidden as he vaulted off the boat and into a door under the bridge. After a few moments, he waved a dim lantern from the doorway and motioned them inside the cool, pitch-black cellar.

Once inside, he turned up the lamp, revealing another young man at the rear of the cavern, standing in the shadows and smoking a cigarette. "This is where I leave you. He will take care of you now," Cuyper's son said, indicating the smoker standing by a stairway. He hurried out the door before anyone could thank him, then leaped back onto the barge, which chugged away.

The young man stubbed out his cigarette on a wall and stepped into the lantern's light. He appeared not even twenty, with an oval face, thick lips, and round glasses. "My name is Rut," he said. "We usually deal with Jewish children. But we know who you are and, if we can, we will help you escape."

"How long will we have to stay here?" Miriam said, wrinkling her nose at the stench of the moldy, water-stained stone walls.

"A few days, maybe more. It depends on how long it takes to forge new documents and devise a plan to get you all to Brussels," Rut said.

"Brussels?" Rogers said. "Why not Paris?"

"You will eventually travel there. But the direct route is through Brussels," Rut said. "It is too risky to go through small towns and change trains. And you will need new papers for each leg of your trip. Each region has local paperwork allowing you to pass through. The forgers in Brussels can make it possible for you to enter France. We cannot."

"You realize there is a substantial reward being offered for Miriam?" Maduro said. "How can we protect her as we move?

"We are reaching out to *Knokploegen*. They have more experience with adults and military operations. I'm sorry that we did not have much time to prepare for you. So, bread and water were all I could bring. There are blankets on the shelves. I'll be back in the morning with more food."

After he departed, Miriam sprinted up the stairs, shouldered open a cantankerous door at the top, and slipped inside for a moment. Afterward, she joined the others at their meager meal. "The house is empty, and there are three exits," she said, drawing blank stares from everyone except Rogers, who knew she was scouting an escape route.

Once everyone had eaten, Rogers and Miriam huddled in a blanket, shivering. The others settled in for the long night. "Who are the Knock-whatever?" Rogers whispered to Miriam. "How do we know we can trust them?"

"I have not heard of them before, but their name gives me hope."

"What's the name mean?"

"Goon squad."

CHAPTER 18

Earlier that day, Janssen dragged himself out of bed and struggled to decipher his notes: "If there...how...where...timing." At least, that is what he thought it said. He was born left-handed and, since the amputation, had struggled to learn to write with his right hand. He had figured out how to dress himself and cook and even how to drive one-handed by never shifting out of second gear, or by using his legs to hold the wheel while shifting.

Although he hated being dependent on anyone, he did have to pay the baker's son below his apartment to tie his shoes and silk tie, something he always wore with a hand-tailored suit. Appearances were important to him; expensive clothes drew attention away from his missing arm and instilled fear in anyone the well-dressed giant approached. Someone this important must mean big trouble.

What the hell did the notes mean? He pondered that over a cup of coffee made with roasted barley and sweetened with saccharine. *There?* There was no doubt Miriam had been there, and it wasn't just because of the hair coloring tin; the beds at Tineke's house had been rumpled as if made in haste; the housekeeper had been given extra days off. He had intimidated neighbors, who told him several people, whom they assumed to be boarders, had come in the day before, one by one, without luggage. Tineke and Maria had both said there had been no boarders for several days. *Why lie unless they were hiding someone?*

How? Janssen had asked neighbors, not always politely, about any traffic in the area, something they would have noticed because fuel shortages meant few vehicles on the road. One elderly man approached him on the street wearing an NSB membership pin on his lapel. The triangular pendant—half-black and half-red with a gold lion over the Dutch colors of orange, white, and blue—had "NSB" in gold letters.

As a good party member, he was eager to help and described every vehicle and person he had seen the day before, as well as all the aches in his body, and the time he saw Hitler. Janssen was about to leave when the old man finally said something interesting.

"My eyesight isn't that good anymore, but I keep on the lookout for Jews and spies as best I can. And the Germans appreciate it. They even waved at me yesterday."

"Who waved at you?"

"The Organization Todt truck driver who stopped in the alley. My dog wanted to pee on the tires, but I pulled him away."

"Does that happen often—an OT truck stopping in the alley?"

"Not in the alley," the old man said between coughs. "They're always passing, though."

Janssen thanked the man, hurried to his car, and squeezed into the front seat. He knew how they had come.

Now, sitting in his car the next day, he had to figure out *where*. He waited for the engine to heat up in his car, a Volkswagen KdF Wagen, a small "producer gas" vehicle with a bulbous front end known as a *"Holzbrenner,"* a wood burner. The engine could take up to thirty minutes to heat up, driving Janssen crazy. He had no idea where Miriam could have gone.

But what about timing? Miriam hadn't been at Tineke's house long enough to concoct an escape plan with all the necessary documents and transportation. So, how could she get out of the neighborhood so fast without being noticed? Janssen remembered that, at Tineke's boarding house the day before, he saw an A. Puls moving van drive past him. It would be a perfect way to smuggle someone out of a neighborhood.

He screeched away for the short drive to Puls' office at 303-305 Kerkstraat, an eighteenth-century, five-story brick warehouse with two wide garage doors. The street had once been part of a thriving neighborhood where Jews and Gentiles lived and worked together. They ran a bicycle shop, a blanket factory, and a printing shop. Now, the Jews were gone, and the most notorious business was A. Puls, with fourteen moving vans and sixty employees.

Janssen flew up two flights of stairs and found Puls himself perched behind a messy desk, flipping through invoices. With his puffy face, thin, sneering mouth, and broad nose, the forty-year-old businessman appeared to be every bit the bully he was reputed to be. "What do you want?" he said, dropping the papers and opening the top desk drawer to pull out a gun, which he placed on top of his papers and tapped with his right hand.

"I'm Inspector Janssen," he said, flashing his ID card. "You had a truck doing a removal yesterday on Nieuwezijds Voorburgwal. I need to talk to the driver."

"You can't," Puls said, leaning back in his chair and grabbing the lapels of his suitcoat to emphasize his five-year NSB membership pin.

Janssen rested his right fist on the desk and leaned in, towering over Puls. "Why? Got something to hide?"

"No," Puls said, scoffing at the threatening posture. "You can't because he never showed up at the warehouse. I called his wife, and she said he didn't come home last night. I told the police that this morning. If you were a real cop, you'd know that. Now get the hell out of my office," he said, adding with a sarcastic sneer, "Inspector."

For a big man, Janssen could move surprisingly fast. He grabbed Puls by the throat before he could even consider reaching for his gun, dragged him over the desk, and pinned him down on the floor with one of his enormous, imported John Lobb black-and-white spectator shoes. He pointed a gun at Puls' head, a Walther PPK—*Polizeipistole Kriminalmodell,* or police pistol detective model—favored by the Waffen-SS and the Gestapo.

"If I had a truck full of expensive furniture and one of my employees ran off with it, I'd be a bit more upset than you," Janssen said in smooth, calm tones that belied his furious scowl. "Any chance he unloaded it at one of your other properties? And you just forgot?"

"No. Of course not," Puls said, pleading with trembling outstretched hands and talking as fast as he could. "He's not a drinker, and he's been one of my best drivers for years. He didn't steal it. I mean, what would he do with it? Who's got the money to buy stuff like that in Amsterdam?"

After holstering his gun inside his coat, Janssen let up the pressure on Puls' chest but kept his size 14 shoe on him. "True. Why would a guy run off with loot he couldn't sell? Is it possible he unloaded it on the wrong canal boat?"

"I'm telling you, he was kidnapped right off the Eastern Docklands."

"What makes you suppose that?"

"We checked with the canal boat captains this morning, and none of them loaded a shipment last night. One of them said he saw one of my trucks leaving there after sundown, and it wasn't heading in the direction of my warehouse," Puls said, gently moving Janssen's foot so he could sit up.

"How many barges are leaving today?"

"Let's see," Puls said, standing to read from a list on his desk. "The *Noodster* sailed first thing. Then the *Groningen* and the *Prinses Albertina* a couple of hours later. Two more will head out in the afternoon."

"Were any of them searched today?"

"No. Why would they be?"

"I suggest you check for stowaways on the ones still here and contact the barges that sailed if you don't want my friends in the Gestapo paying you a visit."

"They aren't my barges." Puls flinched at Janssen's threatening glare. "But I'll make some calls," he said, sinking into the chair behind his desk and dialing the phone. After a few calls, he leaned back in his chair. "This is strange. The *Groningen* and the *Prinses Albertina* have already passed Utrecht, but no one has seen the *Noodster*. It should have been there hours before the other two."

Janssen made a move to leave but thought better of it and stopped to glare at Puls. "What about cargo ships? Any arrive from overseas?"

"We don't get many of those anymore. Wait ... There was an Irish tramp. But it sailed three days ago, I believe."

"That's why!" Janssen said and hurried off without explanation, leaving the perplexed Puls tilting his head to one side. *That's why she came to Amsterdam, to sneak aboard that Irish ship. And that means she must have help from foreign sailors. Something must have gone wrong. And now she, and probably her helpers, are on a slow-moving barge.* He glanced at his black-faced watch—an expensive, stainless steel Longines Calatrava. If he hurried, he could catch the next train to Utrecht; his car would never make it before curfew.

Without a moment to spare, he made the train for the quick ride to Utrecht.

There he found one of his contacts in the local police and convinced him to help for a share of any reward. Together, they parked along the Keulsekade overlooking the Montsluis, a lock on the Merwede Canal west of the city center, and checked with neighbors, who said they had not seen the *Noodster* pass by. So, the two men returned to the police car, shared Janssen's flask of scotch, and waited as the sun dropped low on the horizon.

An hour later, their prey glided into the lock. The police officer flagged down Capt. Cuyper with a flashlight and he and Janssen boarded, guns drawn. Despite Janssen's best efforts at intimidation, nothing was found after an hour of tearing apart the barge's holds and cabin. When they returned to the lock, and the barge puttered away, a young man on a bicycle skidded to a stop on the bank. Janssen shined a flashlight on the rider, who fled.

"He shouldn't be out. It's almost curfew," Janssen said, looking at his watch, which had luminous radium-painted hands. He stopped to briefly ponder what he had just observed. "I've seen that face before." His shoulders slumped as it hit him. "Damn it. He looks exactly like the crew member on the barge."

"I wondered why there was only one of them," the policeman said. "Must be brothers. Perhaps he was picking up supplies."

"Or dropping off passengers," Janssen said.

Everyone in the wharf cellar had been awake for hours, unable to sleep in a frigid, drafty room that reeked of long-ago rotting supplies and mold. Footsteps clumped outside. Rogers and Miriam pressed their backs against the wall on either side of the door, pistols drawn; the others crouched in a corner. The doorknob rattled. As the wooden door's hinges creaked, Miriam knelt behind it with her gun pointed up, and Rogers slid farther back into the shadows, holding his breath.

Daylight flooded in as two men stepped inside. Like a shot, Miriam kicked the door closed and pressed her Mauser against the man carrying a suitcase. Rogers grabbed the other man and shoved him against the brick wall, knocking the wind out of him. Maduro lit the lantern and moved in close to examine the intruders. One was a priest. The other was Rut.

"You must leave," Rut said, swatting Miriam's gun away from his head. "They've increased the reward to 15,000 guilders and announced that Miriam is believed to be somewhere in Utrecht."

"How could they know that?" Miriam said.

"A V-Frau or V-Mann or the barge crew. Who knows?" Rut said. "It doesn't matter. We have to move you sooner than we had planned."

"In broad daylight?" Rogers said.

"That is why the monsignor is here," Rut said. "Archbishop de Jong sent him to help because we haven't much time."

"Why would he agree to help?" Miriam said, knowing the Vatican had signed a Concordat ten years earlier with Hitler, a lapsed Roman Catholic whose attitude toward all Christianity fluctuated between ambivalence and hostility and who once called Jesus an "Aryan fighter" against the corrupt Pharisees and Jewish materialism.

"Archbishop de Jong is different," Maduro said to Miriam. "Since you've been gone, he has ordered his priests to refuse what Christians call their sacraments to Dutch Nazi sympathizers, and he and the other bishops have made public statements condemning the deportation of Dutch workers and Jews."

"Unfortunately, the Nazis retaliated by deporting more than 200 Catholics of Jewish descent," the Monsignor said, shaking his head. "That may be one reason, I'm afraid, why His Excellency and the Vatican have not been more vocal since. But it doesn't mean we can't help in other, less public ways."

"The archbishop has given our Children's Committee more than 10,000 guilders," Rut said as he set up his forging tools on a table. "That helps pay parents 50 guilders a month to care for the Jewish children they are hiding."

As Rut got to work, the monsignor, a middle-aged man with a slick bald pate, paced around Miriam, looking her up and down as if inspecting a thoroughbred at auction. "Brother Paulis should do nicely." He glanced at Rut. "Who else?"

After Rut pointed at Rogers, Cookie, and Maduro, the monsignor nodded. "And the other two?"

"They are foreigners and have proper IDs," Rut said, rummaging through his suitcase. "I'll only have to forge travel papers for them."

"Then I will leave you and take care of the rest," the monsignor said. He opened the door to leave, but had to step back to make way for an older man with long, flowing gray hair, a blue capelet draped over his shoulders, and a burlap bag.

"Where's my diva?" the man asked in a theatrical voice.

Rut pointed to Miriam.

"Ah, come, my dear Cordelia, you shall be king after I work my magic." The man grabbed Miriam's hand and led her to a chair where a tiny ray of light pierced through a hole in the curtains onto her bruised face. With a flourish, he flung off his cape, rummaged around in the bag, and pulled out an assortment of makeup bottles, brushes, and compacts. As the man dabbed gray powder on Miriam's thick, black eyebrows and drew light brown lines under her eyes and around her cheeks, Rogers raised an eyebrow at Rut.

"Stadsschouwburg Utrecht. Our new theater," Rut said and added with a chuckle, "It drives the Nazis crazy that someone like Pim is such a popular actor. They have no idea how important he and other artists like him are to the resistance. Look at this." He handed Rogers a piece of paper with what appeared to be poetry stanzas in Dutch, topped by illustrations of a dead person, tulips, barbed wire, destroyed buildings, and tombstones. "We are raising lots of money for the Utrecht Children's Committee by selling copies of this poem about the Nazis' execution of eighteen patriots."

Rogers handed back the paper, all the while staring at Miriam in concern and thinking how close she had come to being one of them.

☆☆☆

The monsignor's destination—the archbishop's palace on the stately Maliebaan outside the city's canals—was lined with double rows of linden trees. As such, it was a holy island in a sea of fascists. On one side of a railroad magnate's former home was the German SD intelligence service headquarters. Down the street, the NSB national headquarters flew "the Movement's" flag with horizontal red and black halves with a triangle and a golden Dutch lion in the middle wielding a sword. Still other buildings on Maliebaan were occupied by the German army, the SS, the *Sicherheitspolizei* (Security Police or SiPo), and the Grüne Polizei.

Ironically, the street was also a hotbed of activity for the resistance. The Grund Garage, where the Germans fueled their vehicles, was the print shop for underground newspapers and a hiding place for Jews. Dr. Max, the code name for Dutch feminist Marie Anne Tellegen, lived in an apartment adjacent to the SS building. Here she organized the hiding of Jews and the distribution of the underground magazine *Vrij Nederland*, put out by the same organization Miss 2000, a.k.a. Jacoba van Tongeren, was involved with.

The archbishop's palace itself was where the Utrecht Children's Committee, founded by Jan Meulenbelt and Rut Matthijsen, stashed coded records about the hundreds of Jewish children they had rescued and hidden.

Once the monsignor had assembled all the necessary supplies, he dispatched several priests with instructions to travel different routes to the same destination, where they would find a young woman with something red on her head and a school satchel over her right shoulder. They were to give her the supplies and return by different routes. They also knew not to ask any questions.

A gentle tapping on the cellar's wooden door made everyone inside stop talking and hold still. Rogers reached for his gun, but Rut swept his hand away and darted to the door. He tapped three times, and when it was repeated by whoever was on the outside, he opened it. A woman carrying a large suitcase and crutches stepped in and kicked the door shut with her heel. The freckled twenty-something woman wore a gray two-piece wool suit, low-heeled black Oxford pumps, and a red crocheted snood covering her abundant strawberry-blonde hair.

"I am Leida. Bertus sent me with these presents from the archbishop," she said, setting the suitcase down and clicking it open. "He said our lookouts in the area are concerned. Seems like the whole city is on high alert—the train station in particular. Everyone must hurry." She examined the cellar. "Where is she?"

Rut pointed at a blanket strung up on a wire in a corner with some kind of light behind it. Leida scooped up a black garment in the suitcase and the crutches and carried them behind the blanket.

"Who is Bertus?" Rogers said.

"A leader of Knokploegen," Rut said. "He and some others will keep a watch over you until you board the train." He called Maduro and Cookie to join Rogers and, from the suitcase, handed them black Benedictine habits with pointed hoods. "Put these on and practice walking in them with your shirt sleeves and pants legs rolled up so they don't show. I will help you tie the belts in a moment."

"What about our boots? Not very priestly," Rogers said.

"These days, people wear all kinds of footwear. No one will notice," Rut said. He handed them their new identity papers, travel documents, and forged funeral programs. "You are returning to Mont-César Abbey near Brussels from a visit to the Cathedral of St. Catherine, where you attended a funeral for the brother of your colleague, who was too ill to travel alone. I will fill Mr. Maduro in on the details because the two of you should never speak out loud," he said, pointing at Rogers and Cookie.

"What about us?" Nidal said, patting Obasi's shoulder.

"You are traveling to Marseille to work on the construction of the new U-boat bunker for the Todt Organization," Rut said, handing them their papers. "Thousands of workers are heading that way."

"Good idea," Rogers said. "You can put on your OT armbands, too."

"I do not like this plan," Nidal said as he removed the armband from its hiding place inside his socks. "We should not go to the train station now. It is too risky."

"Yes, stay in hiding," Obasi added, shaking his head and eyeing Rogers for support.

"You cannot stay," Leida said from across the room near the hanging blanket. "Someone from the Colonne Henneicke is in town throwing around money and beating people for information." The men's puzzled faces gave her pause. "He is a headhunter—or do you say bounty hunter—who wants that 15,000-guilder reward. The longer you stay here, the less we can guarantee your safety."

"She's right," Rogers said. "Hiding is what they'd expect Miriam to do.

And, yes, Mr. Nidal, going to the train station is risky. But the odds are better than staying put."

"And Miriam? What's her opinion?" said Maduro.

"Who?" a crackly voice said from across the room.

Pim, slipping out from behind the hanging blanket, beamed and swung his arm out like an impresario. He was about to introduce an ancient Benedictine monk in a black habit and leather belt, balancing with difficulty on one leg with the aid of crutches. "May I present Dom Veremund," he said, swirling a flashlight over the stooped monk like a Klieg light at a movie premiere.

Assisted by Leida, the monk wobbled over to the others and, with cracked dry lips, repeated, "Who?" Droopy chestnut eyes behind wire-rimmed spectacles stared out from the craggy face. Strands of longish gray hair hung over both ears from a balding pate.

Still struggling with the leather belt around his habit, Cookie inched closer to examine the monk from head to toe. "Well, I'll be gobsmacked!"

"Miriam?" Rogers said in astonishment. "Is that you?" The monk smiled, revealing a mouthful of blackened teeth. As Rogers moved closer, he snapped his head back and grabbed his nose. "My God, what is that smell?"

"Dramatic, isn't it?" Pim said with a delighted grin. "We don't want anyone getting too close to the mourning brother. I can only work so much magic in these primitive conditions."

"The Germans are looking for a blonde woman," Leida said, holding up a wanted flyer with Miriam's picture on it. "They are not going to waste much time checking men, especially a wizened old monk with one leg who smells like death itself."

"You all have your documents, and you know what to do. So off we go to the train station," Rut said as he cracked open the door. "Leida will travel in the same train car with you and then take you to your next contact in Brussels. Walk behind her in separate groups. The station is ten minutes away. Do not act nervous. It could get us all killed."

CHAPTER 19

Like a snorting bull ready to charge, Janssen paced in front of the new Station Utrecht Centraal, destroyed by a fire in 1939 and rebuilt in the "functionalism" style using an undulating glass facade with scalloped concrete canopies under tall palladium windows. Janssen had positioned himself far enough in front of the building that he could observe the faces of people rushing into it. Its two-story-high ground-floor windows served as a perfect mirror.

An unlit cigarette dangled from Janssen's lips; his gold-plated S.T. Dupont gas lighter had gone missing—stolen no doubt by one of his office mates. Lighting a match with one arm was too much trouble, and no one was kind enough to offer one to the disfigured giant. *Just as well. It's a stupid habit, and I need to quit.*

Scrutinizing the faces of the people rushing by, Janssen made mental notes about which ones he was sure were Jews with fake IDs. Typically, he would have stopped anyone with dark hair whose nose was too large, or who had thick lips, or who didn't seem Aryan enough. But it wasn't worth the time and effort now for a few guilders. He needed a big score. It was getting harder and harder to find any Jews, and he knew his income would dry up soon, ending his lavish lifestyle.

Going back on welfare was out of the question, and another job this lucrative—or any job during the war, for that matter—was unlikely. And more importantly, he needed that 15,000-guilder reward, almost five times his annual salary, if he was ever going to win his son Stefan back. He'd hire the best lawyer money could buy or bribe a judge, or both. And, if that didn't work, he'd snatch him away from his bitch mother, and together they would flee to South America.

The police—Dutch and German—and the SS, Gestapo, and German soldiers had been chasing rumors all day, rushing to follow up one tip after another. They were stopping every woman regardless of age or hair color, and even breaking down doors without warning. What they weren't doing was focusing on the train station anymore.

After a few hours, officials re-positioned most of them because they were convinced Miriam would never show up at such an obvious place. No, they all agreed; the Jew-spy-murderer would hide out for many days and then try to escape. It was only logical. And that is why Janssen stayed; he had learned long ago that the obvious was almost always wrong.

A striking young woman in a gray suit with her hair in a red knit snood caught his attention as she hurried to the entrance. Janssen compared the picture of Miriam on the wanted flyer to this young woman's reflection in the station windows. *Could be? Was her hair red or blonde?* Stuffing the flyer in his pocket and flicking the unlit cigarette to the ground, Janssen trotted after the woman, but a group of four slow-moving monks in black habits and hoods blocked his path.

"Move, damn you!" Janssen said and swept them out of his way with his one arm, knocking over the small monk on crutches. For a moment, Janssen caught a glimpse of Rogers' face as he and Maduro assisted the fallen monk, whose head remained hidden by the pointed black hood.

Cookie, craning his neck to stare at Janssen, shook his head in disgust. His jowls and chubby body reminded Janssen of someone he had seen in the Errol Flynn movie *The Adventures of Robin Hood* before the war. "Out of my way, *Broeder Tuk*," Janssen said with a mean laugh. Cookie, who didn't speak Dutch, clutched a prayer book close to his chest and neither moved nor smiled at the joke. Janssen balled his beefy fist and glared.

In the crowd, Rogers spotted the two men in long coats who had been following the group from the wharf cellar. Rogers could only hope they were from the Goon Squad, coming to help, and not the Gestapo.

"Brother, let this gentleman pass," Maduro said in Dutch, pulling Cookie back. "Please excuse us, my son. *Vade retro satana*, and may you have a blessed day." He was careful to keep his head down while making the sign of the cross with his right hand, a rosary clutched in the other. Janssen brushed his hand away, held his nose at the stench, and jogged off to catch up with that woman in the red snood.

The two men who had been following the monks withdrew their hands from their pockets and veered away, disappearing into the crowd. The four monks continued their slow procession, watching Janssen elbow his way through the busy entrance ahead.

"You are lucky he doesn't speak Latin, Father," Miriam said under her breath to Maduro, who gripped her arm to keep her steady on the crutches.

"Why?" Rogers said.

"It means, 'Begone Satan,'" Maduro said with a chuckle. "And it worked."

"Did you notice that red birthmark on his cheek?" Rogers said.

"Hard to miss. Why?" Maduro said.

"Could be a coincidence, but Bob Briscoe said that if I were captured, I should say my contact was a big man with a large birthmark on his right cheek," Rogers said, searching the crowd until he spotted Nidal and Obasi being questioned by Marechaussee, the Dutch military policemen in blue uniforms. After a cursory inspection of their papers, the officers sent them on their way. With a silent sigh of relief, Rogers led the monks through the station until Leida hopped into one of the globe cars, their carriages painted gray with rounded ends. They followed her, as did Nidal and Obasi shortly afterward.

Rogers helped Miriam navigate the narrow side corridor, passing already full second-class compartments. In one, Leida was reading a copy of *Das Reich*, a Nazi newspaper; next door, Obasi and Nidal were jammed in with four other passengers. In the middle of the passenger car, they passed the first-class compartment, where Janssen sprawled across one of two facing benches designed to hold two people each.

They found seats in the last of the nine compartments, a second-class one with facing upholstered seats, and settled in for the three-to-five-hour journey to Brussels. How long depended on customs stops, mechanical problems, and destroyed track. Although there were two empty seats, Rogers was sure no one would join them because of Miriam's stench.

Not long after the train rumbled out of the station, railroad police officers in field-gray uniforms called *Bahnschutzpolizei* entered the monks' compartment and asked to see their papers. After barely inspecting the documents, they beat a hasty retreat when the foul odor assaulted their noses.

☆☆☆

Pacing up and down the corridor, Janssen paused often to check out Leida, whose nose was always buried in the newspaper, something the Bloodhound found suspicious. After about an hour, he approached two Bahnschutzpolizei and flashed his ID card. "Inspector Janssen from Amsterdam," he said in an arrogant tone as if he were somebody important. "I believe a fugitive is on this train, and I require your assistance."

The older officer with scars all over his forehead studied Janssen and snatched the ID out of his hand "You are not a police officer. This says your job is to search for stolen furniture," the officer said, throwing back the ID. "What is your business here?"

"I'm in pursuit of this woman," Janssen said, showing him and the younger officer the wanted flyer. "I believe she is in the first compartment."

The policemen scowled.

"She killed three police officers," Janssen said. When the officers remained unmoved, Janssen waved the flyer at them. "There is a huge reward for her capture, one that we can share if I'm right." Of course, Janssen had no intention of sharing the money with anyone.

The older officer plucked the flyer out of Janssen's hand. "We will check her papers again, but you must stay here." The two officers stepped into the compartment and shut the door behind them; all Janssen could do was watch through the door window. The young woman lowered her newspaper and listened to the elderly police officer, after which she smiled and giggled, handed over her documents and flirted with the younger officer, whose cheeks reddened. While holding the flyer up to her face, the two officers checked back and forth from it to Leida, who chatted away. The officers stormed out of the compartment. "It is not her," the elderly officer said.

"But—" Janssen started to say.

"Do not harass any more of our passengers, or we will arrest you. Do you understand, *kaaskop*?" the older officer said, using the Germans' derisive nickname for the Dutch, meaning cheesehead. He wadded up the flyer and tossed it on the floor.

Janssen, stifling the urge to punch the officer, bent over to retrieve the flyer, humiliated by the appearance of bowing to the officers, an insult he was sure they had intended. He stewed in his seat until the train reached the Dutch-Belgian border, where everyone had to exit the train and show all their documents again to customs border guards in green uniforms and peaked green visor caps. Janssen flashed his ID card at the border guards, saying he was a police officer. This time, he got away with his ruse and stepped to the side to watch them examine passengers.

While the border guards checked Leida, Janssen studied her face and kept comparing it to the wanted flyer. He wasn't sure. There was a resemblance to Miriam, and the blonde hair did have a red tint, but he couldn't approach her because the two Bahnschutzpolizei glared at him from a train window. Janssen had to be careful; he had already exceeded his authority and was traveling without authorization to Belgium, where he had no authority.

No one would care what he did if he was right about the woman being Miriam, but there would be hell to pay if he was wrong. To confront the woman in the red snood, he would have to wait until arriving in Brussels, and he would need the help of Belgian police. They would be more receptive to a Dutchman offering a substantial reward than the damn *Moffen*, the Dutch derisive name for Germans.

☆☆☆

When the train stopped at the Gare du Nord, Rogers waited until all the passengers had gotten off and crowded the platform before lifting Miriam onto her crutches. Cookie helped her down the steps to the platform, with Rogers and Maduro holding her from behind. Ahead, amid the swirling dust motes, light poured down from glass insets in the towering gabled roof. Leida's red snood wove through the crowd, with Nidal and Obasi following at a distance on the lengthy platform. Behind them, a familiar gray silk homburg glided above the crowd like the dorsal fin of a ravenous shark.

Rogers was surprised to see yet another checkpoint, where railroad officials were inspecting documents of people leaving the platform. When it was his turn, he handed over his ID. The official subtly shook his head "No," slipped back the papers without a word, and motioned for Rogers to move on.

As Rogers glanced back, Cookie handed the official his ticket. That explained the funny look from the official. Nobody had warned Rogers that they do things backward in Europe and take tickets from passengers at the *end* of the trip, not the beginning, as in America. Luckily for him, the official let him get away with it.

As the four monks shuffled out of the station through the main entrance of the nearly 100-year-old neoclassical building, Janssen argued nearby with two gendarmes, Belgian police officers wearing dark tunics, riding breeches, and distinctive dark-blue shakos with red and gold trimming on their heads. Janssen held up the wanted flyer and pointed toward Leida, strolling across the large Place Charles Rogier/Karel Rogierplein, jammed with people rushing to and from electric trams.

One of the policemen removed his tall, cylindrical cap, flicked it at Janssen to move along, and turned his back to him. Unlike in other occupied countries, most Belgian police—also known as *Rijkswacht* in the French- and Dutch-speaking country—had refused to cooperate in the Nazis' deportation of Jews. As a result, the Germans relegated them to administrative and traffic duties.

But the second gendarme talking to Janssen had no such qualms. He drew his Belgian-made Browning Model 1922 pistol and raced after Leida, shouting in French and Dutch, "Halt, Jew, halt!" People in the crowd screamed. Some, including Nidal and Obasi, raised their hands; others fell to their knees in shock or crawled away.

"Wait!" Janssen shouted, drawing his Mauser P.38 and running after the gendarme. "Don't shoot! I need her alive."

Glancing over her shoulder at the commotion, Leida picked up her pace. Nearby, Gestapo and SS officers heard the shouting, saw Janssen and the gendarme weaving through the crowd, and joined the chase with guns drawn. With no way to escape, Leida stopped and casually turned around.

She was the lone person still standing in the square. In an apparent effort to charm her way out of trouble, she smiled and waved at the gendarme, reaching with her other hand into her jacket pocket. Shots rang out from every direction, riddling Leida with bullet holes and blasting her body apart like a piñata.

Taking advantage of the confusion, Rogers led his three companions toward the side of the station and away from the swarming police and soldiers, who shoved aside the monks and anyone else in their way.

"Where are Nidal and Obasi?" Cookie whispered in Rogers' ear.

Rogers scoured the crowd in the square until he spotted his two friends and got Nidal's attention. He raised his chin, signaling for the pair to follow him. "They'll have to catch up. We can't wait," he mouthed to Cookie and shook his head.

Cookie's eyes widened in surprise, but he continued moving along with Rogers and Maduro, who helped Miriam maneuver as fast as she could on her crutches. When they rounded the corner onto Rue d'Aerschot, Rogers whispered to Miriam, "What do we do now?"

Without revealing too much of her dazed face to passersby, Miriam twisted her lowered head to peek out from her hood. "I do not know. I have no contacts here."

Glancing over her head at Maduro, Rogers raised his eyebrows and mouthed the words, "Where to?" Maduro steepled his hands as if in prayer.

Rogers mouthed the words, "Good idea."

CHAPTER 20

Janssen, his face twisted in fury, holstered his pistol as he reached Leida's body in the middle of the square. "Why the hell did you shoot? Didn't you hear me?"

The gendarme didn't answer, staring wide-eyed at the oozing pool of blood spreading around the body, his warm gun trembling in his right hand.

Janssen shoved him back, dropped to one knee, and pulled Leida's hand out of her pocket, appalled by what she was holding: an official SD identification card with the vertical crossed-green strip and her picture on it. It said she was a contract employee assigned to the SD branch in Pau, France, near the Spanish border, whose job was to interrogate Dutch and Flemish prisoners. Her official travel documents were signed by several German authorities on the route, and she had a *Bescheinigung,* an official certificate, issued by the police. Janssen's stomach flipped, but he didn't hesitate to pocket the documents, hoping no one would notice in all the confusion.

As he rose, a shadow fell over him. He whirled around. A man who barely came up to his chest tapped out a cigarette from a flat red-and-white Reemtsma Sorte R6 pack. As he cupped his hand against the wind to light it, the man never took his cold eyes off Janssen. "Why are you stealing those documents?" he said in German.

"None of your damn business. I'm Inspector Janssen, and this woman is a Jew who I've been pursuing. Now, move out of my way," Janssen said, knocking aside the much smaller man, who was wearing an ill-fitting brown suit and rumpled tie.

With lightning speed, the man sidestepped Janssen's outstretched hand, clutched his wrist, twisted his arm behind his back, and kicked him hard behind the right kneecap, driving the giant to the ground. With Janssen yelping in pain, he jammed a gun against the back of Janssen's head. "I am a real inspector, and you will hand over those documents and your ID, or I will add your brains to hers," the man said.

Janssen handed him Leida's documents, dug his ID out of his pocket, and passed it behind him, careful not to make any sudden movements. "I'm one of you!" he yelled, hoping to be heard over the din of screams, shouted orders from police, and running feet swirling around them.

"Stand up," the man said. After Janssen rose and brushed off his trousers, the man handed back his ID but didn't lower his Luger P08. "I am *Inspektor* Gunter Brosan of the *Geheime Feldpolizei*," he said, referring to the Secret Field Police, or GFP, the German military's version of the Gestapo, which specialized in counter-espionage and fighting the resistance movement. In Belgium and France, the GFP often worked in plain clothes alongside local police, who couldn't always be trusted to carry out Nazi policies. Instead of a badge, he wore a silver dollar-sized *Erkennungsmarken,* an ID disk that resembled a bronze dog-tag hanging on a chain from his lapel with "Geheime Feldpolizei" and his ID number on it. "Why are you in Belgium chasing an employee of the SD?" he asked, flashing his green GFP identity card.

"Those IDs must be fake. She's a Jew and a spy whose escape involved the murder of three Grüne Polizei," Janssen said, moving his hand toward his coat pocket. "May I?" Once Brosan nodded, Janssen retrieved the wanted flyer and showed him. "I followed her here on the train from Utrecht. I wasn't sure she was this Miriam Maduro until she started to run away."

Brosan glanced at the flyer. "I'm afraid there's not enough of her face left for me to tell," he said. "You will come with me until we sort this out." He waved over two Belgian gendarmes and instructed them to disarm Janssen and guard him as they trekked to the GFP's office on the nearby Rue Traversière. "If he doesn't cooperate fully, shoot him."

☆☆☆

"Can't you move any faster?" Rogers asked Miriam, who kept stumbling on the crutches.

"Stop," Miriam whispered and slipped into the entryway of an abandoned storefront. "Block the view."

The three monks gathered around her and lowered their hooded heads as if praying. Miriam lifted her habit and tugged off the rope holding her calf to her thigh, the trick Pim used to make it appear she had only one leg. After shaking the leg, rubbing it, and stomping on the ground to get the blood flowing, Miriam tossed the crutches aside. "That's better." When she stepped back onto the sidewalk, followed by the others, she whispered to Rogers, "Where are we going?"

Rogers pressed his hands in prayer and pointed to his right, at the back entrance of the small Church of Saints John and Nicholas with its white facade and red brick sides. He turned the handle on the narrow double doors at one end of the neoclassical building and waved everyone inside. "This is the first Catholic church I've seen," he said, closing the door. "Where else would four monks seek help?"

As Rogers' eyes adjusted to the dimly lit hallway, a door swung open at the other end. An ancient priest, wearing a green chasuble and stole over a long white linen robe, stopped in his tracks and gawked at the four monks. "Welcome, brothers," the priest said in French after overcoming his surprise. "I'm sorry, but you just missed Mass."

"We are not here to pray, Father," Miriam said in French, not disguising her voice. She flipped back her hood. "We need help."

The ancient priest's wide eyes made clear he realized the old monk addressing him was a woman. He glanced over his shoulder into the church and kicked the door closed. Pushing past them, the priest locked the back entrance and led them toward an office off the hallway. Banging on the entrance made the priest hurry the monks along and shut the office door, putting a finger to his lips for silence.

He took his time unlocking the door and cracked it open. Two dark-skinned foreigners stared back. "I'm sorry, my children, but we have no food today. Try Église Royale Sainte-Marie on Place de la Reine," he said in French, trying to close the door.

But a hand shoved back, and the two foreigners lunged inside. "We are here for the monks," Nidal said in French.

The priest bit his lip. "I don't know what you mean."

"It's all right, Father," Miriam said, stepping into the hallway. "They are with us."

"Ah," the priest said in relief, locking the entrance again. "Then come this way." He led them back into the office, removed his vestments and his black, three-cornered biretta, and eased into a seat behind his desk. "Now, why do you need help?" he asked in French, looking directly at Rogers.

"Non, uh, parlay Frenchie," Rogers said. "Do you speak English?"

The priest laughed. "I speak English. My question was, why do you need help?"

"We were escaping to Spain, but our contact was killed, and now we have nowhere to turn," Miriam said before Rogers could respond.

The priest set his elbows on his desk, clasped his hands together, and leaned his chin on top of them, moving his watery eyes from one person to another, seemingly mulling over how he should respond.

Rogers and Maduro pulled back their hoods so he could get a better look at them.

"I cannot help you," the priest said.

"If you are worried about trusting us, you should know that I am a Jew with a large price on my head," Miriam said.

"It's not that," the priest said, his jowls quivering. "It's simply too dangerous."

Maduro sprang up and leaned over the desk. "What would your Cardinal van Roey do?"

"The Germans would not harm His Excellency," the priest said, taking a furtive glance out a side window at the deserted street.

"But he was not afraid to help Rabbi Salomon Ullman and five other Jewish leaders get released from a concentration camp last year," Maduro said.

"Yes, but he was joined by Queen Elizabeth," the priest said.

"But he has not been afraid to criticize the fascists and ordered that they should be denied communion if in uniforms," Maduro said, speaking faster. "I even read his speech saying Belgians have a duty of conscience to combat fascism and resist. If he is not afraid, why are you?"

"I am a lowly parish priest. If I were caught, the Germans would not hesitate to arrest me along with many members of my flock. I must protect them."

"We are not asking you to do anything other than put us in contact with an escape line," Miriam said. "Surely you know someone in the resistance."

The priest glanced around, uneasy. "I might know someone, but—"

"We'll leave as soon as they can safely get us out of here," Rogers cut in.

"I was going to say, I don't know this person personally. I've heard rumors, but I'm unsure how to contact him."

"Can't you ask around?" Rogers said.

"Yes, I suppose I could do that," the priest said as he rose. "I will ask some of the other priests. But you must stay out of sight in this room. I will have food sent in."

"Thank you, Father," Nidal said in French.

"It is only for tonight," the priest said as he opened the door. "Tomorrow, you must leave."

After the priest closed the door behind him, Nidal asked Miriam, "Did you notice his accent? Was that Dutch?"

"No," she said. "German."

"Then we should go, now," Cookie said, standing with difficulty on his bad hip.

"To where?" Rogers asked.

"I don't know," Cookie said, "Maybe another church?"

"He's right, Captain," Nidal said. "I do not trust this priest."

☆☆☆

Janssen sat across from Inspektor Brosan's desk as he hung up the phone. "It will take us several days to drive the fingerprints to The Hague and get the results back," Brosan said. "You will stay in custody until that happens."

"What if I could get you the results today?" Janssen said.

"That is not possible."

"Yes it is. I can have Miriam's fingerprints from Amsterdam sent here so you can have your experts compare them to the dead woman's."

"That is more than 200 kilometers away. Because of all the roadblocks, it would take all day to travel there and back. Besides, The Hague is closer."

"I didn't say drive. I can have them here within the hour if you let me use your phone to call my office."

The inspector hesitated, then slid a phone across his desk.

Henneicke answered the phone and, as usual, was furious at Janssen. "Where the hell have you been!? I need you here now. The fingerprints on the tin were hers."

"She's not in Amsterdam."

"How the hell do you know?"

"I followed her to Utrecht and then to Brussels, where I am now. I assume she's dead, but I need you to send me a copy of her fingerprints to verify that."

"Dead?"

"I believe so. But I need to prove it to the GFP. Take the prints you got from the Oranjehotel to *Deutsche Zeitung's* office and have them transmitted to the *Brüsseler Zeitung.* Tell them it is urgent."

Henneicke yelled some more before agreeing to do as Janssen had asked and slammed down the phone.

"How will newspapers help?" Brosan said.

"They have AP Wirephoto machines," Janssen said. The inspector didn't seem to understand. "One newspaper transmits the photo by telephone line to the other in a matter of minutes. It will work the same for fingerprints. We've done this many times in Holland."

Brosan sent an aide to the newspaper office. While they waited for the picture, he handed Janssen a cigarette from his R6 pack and lit it with his lighter. They only had to wait a little over an hour to receive the finished product; analysts only required a few minutes to review it and deliver their findings to Brosan by telephone.

"It's not her," Brosan said through clenched teeth as he hung up the phone.

"But maybe—" Janssen said before the inspector raised his hand for him to stop talking.

"She wasn't an SD employee either. So, you're in luck. We have no idea who she was or why she came to Brussels."

"I do," Janssen said, pounding his fist on the desk. "I was right about Miriam being in Amsterdam. I was right about her being in Utrecht. And I was right to have followed that dead woman with forged papers to Brussels. The instincts of de Bloedhond are always on target."

"Your instincts are worthless."

"Don't you see? If she wasn't Miriam, then she was her guide from the resistance. Miriam is here in Brussels!"

CHAPTER 21

Footsteps echoing down the church hallway startled Rogers and the others, but there was nowhere for them to run or hide. When the door creaked open, an old woman dressed all in black shuffled in, carrying in her shaky hands a tray with bowls of a watered-down version of *Taatjespap,* a traditional Flemish porridge normally made of potatoes mashed with buttermilk, browned butter, salt, and pepper with a dash of nutmeg. Usually, it was poured over soft-boiled eggs, but none were available.

A young priest followed behind the old woman with a loaf of bread, a bottle of wine, glasses, and a jug of water. They set the food and drink on the ornate desk and departed without speaking.

"I still don't like this," Nidal said, picking up a spoon and a bowl. "We should leave as soon as we've eaten."

"When can we take off these stupid robes?" Cookie said as he swallowed a mouthful of warm porridge and smacked his lips.

"They are not robes," Maduro said. "They are called habits."

"How come you know so much about monks, Mr. Maduro?" Cookie said.

"Solomon, please. Our ancestors were what the Spanish derisively called Marranos."

Cookie dipped his spoon in for one last bite. "What's a—?"

The young priest, out of breath, threw open the door. "You must come with me. Now!"

Everyone sprang up and hurried after him, down the hall to the back entrance.

"Put your hoods up, please," the young priest said. Behind them in the main church, hobnailed boots clicked on the floor, heading in their direction. With shaking hands, the young priest opened the door and glanced outside before closing it again. "I called someone who another priest told me helps downed pilots. But I have a feeling that Father Köhler does not approve."

"Did he call someone?" Rogers said as the bootsteps grew louder.

"Yes, but I could not understand all he said. My German is not so good." The priest took another anxious glimpse outside. "They are here. Hurry. Get in the cars, and they will take you to another hiding place."

A slender man motioned the four monks into a bulky, black, four-door 1939 Graham Paige with Swiss diplomatic plates. The American manufacturer called the four-door car "Spirit of Motion," but most people called it "Shark Nose" because of its pointed front end." Nidal and Obasi scooted into a trailing red car, a dented, two-door 1938 HP Chevrolet driven by a dark-haired woman.

When Rogers jumped into the front seat, the driver extended his hand, which was missing most of the right little finger, and said, "I'm Capt. Bill Jackson."

"Drive! The Nazis are inside looking for us!" Rogers said.

Jackson ground the car into gear and sped off.

Rogers gazed out the window and then back at Jackson. In his fifties, he had greased-back dark brown hair with a broad white streak starting from his forehead. "Where are we going?" Rogers said.

"Don't worry about it," Jackson said, pronouncing *about* as *a-boot*. "I've done this dozens of times. I'm taking you to a safe house."

"Are you Swiss?"

"Me? Oh, no. The plates are stolen. I'm Belgian, but I spent years in the Canadian and Belgian armies." Jackson tapped a lapel pin of the Belgian veterans' group Confédération des Fraternelles d'Après-Guerre, or COFAG. "Stayed here after Dunkirk and have been running an escape line for British Intelligence ever since. By the way, the priest didn't know what unit you're with."

"We're not military. We're foreign sailors, and we need to escape to Spain. We're ... what's the word?"

"Engelandvaarders," Maduro said from the back seat.

"Oh, I see. I don't usually handle those," Jackson said, his blue-gray eyes focused on Miriam's face in his rearview window. "And what about the girl? She a sailor too?"

"She's our guide from Holland," Rogers said. "She's been betrayed and needs to escape with us. Is that a problem?"

"Complicates things, but no, no, that will not be a problem. As luck would have it, we're putting together a convoy that leaves for Paris tomorrow."

The twenty-minute drive took them past the Royal Palace of Brussels, after which the two cars pulled into a basement garage at 369 A. J. Slegers Avenue, a modern apartment block in the Woluwe-Saint-Lambert suburb. With a slight limp, Jackson led everyone up a green marble staircase to the first floor, where they were greeted by a man in a leg cast who said he was a downed Royal Air Force pilot and too severely wounded to leave the safe house any time soon.

On the next floor, they came to an L-shaped lounge. Two men, playing cards and smoking, asked Rogers what unit he was from and didn't seem to mind when he gave an evasive answer. Jackson and the woman driver led Rogers and crew to a large bedroom and told them to change out of their habits and clean up as best they could in the washbasin.

"How can we leave tomorrow? We don't have any IDs," Rogers said, pulling the habit over his head and rolling down his pants legs and shirt sleeves.

"Not to worry. My associate and secretary, Miss Anny, will take you to have your pictures taken," Jackson said, putting his arm around the woman's shoulder. Much younger than him, she had dazzling black eyes, a pointed nose, and a tawny complexion. "Belgian IDs are much easier to forge than Dutch ones."

"The two of us probably don't need new ones," Nidal said, indicating Obasi as he showed Jackson their travel papers.

Retrieving his horn-rimmed reading glasses from his green sports jacket, Jackson examined the documents. "These will get you all the way to Spain. We can create similar ones for the rest of you. Well, except for the young lady. We'll have to come up with a different cover story, won't we, Miss Anny?"

"She could be a nurse," Miss Anny said with a slight Spanish accent. "How good is your German?"

"*Sehr gut*," Miriam said.

"I'm pretty sure we have a *Betreuungshelferinnen* uniform that would fit her," Miss Anny said, referring to the women's army auxiliary for the German Red Cross, the Deutsches Rotes Kreuz, which was no longer an independent organization but under the Wehrmacht's control. "Go bathe and scrub off that horrid smell in the bathroom down the hall, and I'll bring it to you."

"Wait," Miriam said. "How do we know we can trust you?"

With a smile that revealed a gold filling in his front tooth, Jackson said, "Good question, young lady. Take a look at these." He pulled several papers from a desk drawer and handed them to Miriam. They included documents with British government seals and letters with British stamps from RAF members who had escaped safely to England. "Satisfied?"

"No. These could be forgeries."

"You'd make an excellent SOE agent," he said without missing a beat. "I can prove I work for British Intelligence. Give me a sentence in French that you'd like to hear on the BBC tonight."

"*Il a précipité dans la mer le cheval et son cavalier,*" she said.

"'He threw horse and rider into the sea,'" Jackson repeated in English. "Lovely. Is that biblical?"

"It's from the *Song of the Sea*, which the prophet Miriam sang to celebrate the Jews' escape from the pharaoh across the Red Sea," Rogers said, giving the current-day Miriam a wink. It was what Miriam had said of Rogers to her Uncle Levy, Maduro's rabbi brother, on the *Peggy C* after Rogers had saved them from a U-boat the first time.

"I will arrange it," Jackson said. "Now, I'm off."

Miriam went to the bathroom to clean up while the men did the same in the bedroom. An hour later, as the men waited in the lounge area, the bathroom door opened and out stepped Miriam, a small bun at the nape of her neck, her dyed red hair under a gray wool side cap. She was almost unrecognizable in her military uniform—gray wool pleated skirt and matching double-breasted jacket with wide lapels over a white shirt. Her black tie had a round DRK pin clasped to it, indicating she was a *Helferin*, a helper.

The national emblem adorned the jacket's right breast pocket, left shoulder, and front of her cap. Above her left cuff was a white armband with a swastika over a red cross. Miss Anny had even managed to find a pair of dark hose and black, laced, low-heel shoes and a leather handbag with a long shoulder strap. Miriam looked stunning—and utterly miserable.

"Chin up, *liefje,*" Maduro said, using the Dutch word for "sweetheart."

"You are using their own weapon against them. It makes me proud."

A dour Miriam traveled with Miss Anny in her red Chevrolet. A fat man with ginger hair and a mustache, who called himself Philippe, picked up Rogers, Maduro, and Cookie in a black, four-door Ford V-8 with red leather seats. He drove them past the downtown Parc de Bruxelles to Boulevard du Jardin Botanique, where they stopped at a seven-story department store with "Au Bon Marché" in giant letters on the roof.

"Mind you, not a word in English," Philippe said, peering over his pince-nez glasses as he stepped out of the car. "Follow me in separately and pick out work clothes made in Belgium that fit you. We can't have you wearing anything from another country. It is a dead giveaway." He handed them some money and led them inside. As each one finished his purchase, Philippe waved him over to a photo booth and watched from a distance as he posed for black-and-white headshots.

When it was Rogers' turn, a German officer with a young woman on his arm thrust him aside and escorted the woman into the booth, where they laughed and mugged for the camera. Ducking his head, Rogers pretended to shop and waited impatiently for them to leave. Once they were gone, he hurried inside the booth, snapped his pictures, and headed for the exit, passing Miriam and Miss Anny on their way in but acting as if he didn't know them.

Philippe collected the men's photos and drove them back to the safe house. "I'll bring you the documents and train tickets in the morning."

That night, after a hearty dinner of *Waterzooi*—a creamy chicken stew with vegetables—everyone crowded around an illegal Audiola Radio, a small Danish-built receiver made of brown Bakelite, an early form of plastic.

A second radio set, a small German receiver, blared by the front door. The nine-inch-square Bakelite box, with a circular speaker and Nazi eagle stamped above the dials, played patriotic music to cover the sound of the BBC. Nicknamed "Goebbels' *Schnauze*" for the nose of Propaganda Minister Joseph Goebbels, the radio had been mass-produced so cheaply that every German could afford one and listen to Nazi propaganda on its limited channels. Unsurprisingly, they didn't include shortwave for foreign broadcasts.

Miriam, who had stripped off her German uniform as soon as she could and donned her men's work clothes, got comfortable on the floor close to the

Danish radio and translated the French version of the BBC broadcast known as *Radio Londres* for her friends and the two pilots. They tuned in for its flagship program, *Les Français parlent aux Français,* meaning "The French Speak to the French," featuring a team led by journalist Pierre Bourdan.

The broadcast kicked off with its familiar call sign—the first four notes of Beethoven's Fifth Symphony, imitating the three dots and one dash of the letter "V" in Morse code and representing "Victory." "Before we begin, please listen to some personal messages," said the announcer, who read a series of phrases that were coded messages to résistants, members of the resistance, and SOE agents like Georges Bégué, a French officer who came up with the idea and was the first SOE agent to parachute into France in May 1941.

Miriam's face grew darker and darker as she listened. Then she gasped. "They said it. They said the phrase."

"So, Jackson is what he says he is," Rogers said. He pulled Miriam aside so the others couldn't hear their discussion. "You could use him to send your messages to the SOE—your suspicions about the agents being betrayed."

"They would not believe such a message. I must do that in person so they can interrogate me and make sure I am not a double-agent," she said, with a sideways glance at Jackson across the room. "Besides, I still do not trust Jackson completely."

"Why?"

"Little things. There was too much chicken in the Waterzooi. Meat is strictly rationed and hard to find in any quantity."

"Maybe he knows a farmer."

"Everyone knows a farmer, and they all want food. Plus, we were trained to expect a BBC message to take more than a day. He did it in less than twelve hours. And how does he find gasoline for his big American cars?"

"What do you want to do? Should we leave?"

"Not now. There is one staircase, and the windows are too small or too high for an escape. And, even if he is a V-Mann, he will not turn us in here. That would reveal him to the Belgian resistance." She turned her back to the others. "But, if I am correct, once we are in France, we may be in danger."

Not wanting to alarm the others, Rogers and Miriam joined them to listen to the latest developments in the war. The broadcaster said there were reports of a growing armed insurgency by Jews in the Warsaw Ghetto. And, he noted, Field Marshall Erwin Rommel had not returned to North Africa from Germany since his once invincible Afrika Corps had been repulsed at the Battle of Medenine the month before by the British Eighth Army.

That came on the heels of the Germans' stunning defeat at Stalingrad, a battle that began almost by accident, much like Gettysburg in the American Civil War, and then escalated into an existential threat for both sides because of two men's egos: Hitler, the self-described military genius who wanted the propaganda coup of capturing a city named after the Soviet leader, and Stalin, who believed it would be a crippling psychological defeat to lose his name-sake community between the Don and Volga rivers.

After everyone retired for the evening, Rogers couldn't sleep, tossing and turning on the bedroom's hard floor amid the other men's loud snores and coughs. Grabbing his thin blanket, he headed out the door to try the couch in the living room. But he paused at the sound of voices and half-closed the door.

Miriam and her father were having an animated discussion in Dutch, at once happy and serious, then turning grim. Maduro wagged his finger at Miriam and raised his voice, only stopping when Miriam covered his mouth with her hand and shushed him. For a moment, they stared at each other in silence. With tears rolling down his cheeks, Maduro wrapped his arms around Miriam and kissed her cheeks, holding her tight.

Rogers closed the door without a sound. *What that was all about?*

☆☆☆

Inspektor Brosan returned to his office long after lunch the next day. "Come with me," Brosan said to Janssen, who had been waiting there. "The Gestapo may have something for us." They drove south to Avenue Louise and stopped at a twelve-story Art Nuevo apartment building that was riddled with bullet holes.

"What is this? I haven't heard of any attacks on Brussels," Janssen said, amazed none of the other buildings near Number 453 displayed any sign of damage. "Was it a resistance group?"

"This is Gestapo headquarters," Brosan said. "Some crazy British pilot shot it up and dropped a bunch of miniature Belgian and British flags. Killed several high-ranking police and Gestapo officers."

Inside the building, Janssen and Brosan met with *Kriminalinspektor* Oberg, who led them to a basement interrogation room holding the old woman from the Church of Saints John and Nicholas. Screams from other rooms filled the hallway as they questioned the woman, who was cowering in a seat behind a long table. "Tell them what you told me," Oberg said.

"Why are you treating me like this?" she said between sobs. "I called you. I am loyal."

"Yes, and we will release you soon," Oberg said, softening his tone to calm the hysterical woman. "But you must help us first. Now, what did you see?"

"Father had us prepare food for four Benedictine monks. But when I served them, there was an African and another foreigner in the room. And the smallest monk wouldn't look at me. That made me suspicious," she said, taking a sip of water from a glass Oberg handed her. "So, I listened to them talk from the other side of the door. And what I heard made me call the authorities. I am very loyal, you see. But the police arrived too late. They were already gone."

"I questioned the parish priests," Oberg said. "They said they didn't know the monks, where they came from, or why they left so suddenly,"

"So, what made you suspicious?" Inspektor Brosan said. "What did you hear?"

"A woman's voice," she said.

Janssen's eyes widened. "Where did they go?"

"I don't know," the woman said.

Janssen tugged the inspector out of the room by the arm. "It's Miriam. We must find her and her accomplices before they disappear again."

"And how do we do that? They would have gotten rid of their habits by now and found another disguise for her," Brosan said, clenching his jaw. "We have no idea who we are looking for."

"Yes, we do," Janssen said. "There were four monks and an African on the train from Utrecht. And the dead woman was in the same car. I've seen their faces. And de Bloedhond never forgets a face."

The inspector vaulted up the stairs.

"Where are you going?" Janssen said.

"I might have an idea how to find them," Bronson said as Janssen hustled after him.

CHAPTER 22

Jackson assembled everyone in the lounge and handed out their new documents, travel papers, and tickets for the night train to Paris. Two young women, a blonde and a brunette, distributed small suitcases to everyone containing a change of clothes and toiletries, the bare minimum for a laborer heading to a project.

"You two will go with Skylar," Jackson said to the two pilots, indicating the brunette. "The rest of the men will go with Chantal."

"And me?" said Miriam, again in her German nurse's uniform.

"Miss Anny will drive you," he said. "Chantal will be everyone's *passeur* on the train. Once you arrive in Paris, she will hand you off to another guide. He will be wearing a green tie and standing at the entrance to Metro Line Five with Charles Péguy's book about Joan of Arc under his right arm. Remember, if it is under his left arm, do not approach him. Never speak to one another, and never, ever speak English."

Miss Anny and Miriam headed out first, followed ten minutes later by the pilots with Skylar. After a few more minutes, Rogers and the other men departed with Chantal, who had the assured air of a dimpled coquette with china-blue eyes behind fashionable glasses, shoulder-length hair, stylishly voluminous and curled under, and a winsome smile. Leather pumps with 2.5-inch spool heels and rouged cheeks on her milky skin added to her allure. She would be easy to follow through a crowd in her red plaid skirt, white blouse with long pointed collars, and long-sleeve dark brown cardigan.

They took a short ride on the electric tram to the Gare du Midi. A nineteenth-century neoclassical building, it featured a towering entrance resembling a triumphal arc topped by a statue of Nike, the Greek goddess of victory, riding a chariot. The station was much busier than the ones in Holland, and Rogers was surprised when a man approached him, offering to sell him silk stockings, which were exceedingly hard to find, even in the United States.

After arriving, they had to sit around for several hours, pretending to read newspapers or nap.

At one point, Obasi, sitting across from Rogers, appeared panicky at the sight of German and Belgian police checking everyone's documents. The African held his ticket in one hand and his ID and travel papers in the other. He raised his eyebrows at Rogers and lowered his eyes at one hand, then the other, as if asking what he was supposed to show the officials. Rogers didn't know and was afraid to ask because he, like Obasi, didn't speak German or French. And he didn't dare seek help from Miriam and the others, who were sitting too far away.

Knowing the wrong choice could be fatal, Rogers rose from his seat for a long stretch and yawned, all while trying as nonchalantly as he could to spot what the police were inspecting. He couldn't tell. As the police moved closer, he felt a tightness in his chest and forced himself to breathe normally.

Someone nudged his leg. He lowered his eyes at an elderly woman sitting next to him, a brown knit kerchief on her lowered head. She held a ticket in her left hand. Without looking up, the woman opened her right hand, showing it was empty. With a quiet sigh of relief, Rogers flashed his ticket at Obasi and flopped back into his chair. He supposed the police wanted proof that they had a good reason for being out after curfew and didn't care who they were—for now.

☆☆☆

Janssen was growing more agitated by the minute. Brosan had driven him all over Brussels, stopping at Café du Globe, then La Taverne Alidor, then Café Sirius, and then seedy bars in Hotel Scheers and Hotel du Canterbury. At each stop, Brosan would sit at the bar or a corner table, sipping water and smoking an R6, observing the gloomy, smoke-filled rooms. When pressed by an impatient Janssen, all Brosan would say was that he was searching for one of his confidential advisers, a V-Mann, who might be able to help them.

While hanging around Café des Arcades on the corner of Rue Hancart and Chaussée de Haecht, Janssen said he was ready to call it a night. But Brosan said he had one more stop: 94 Rue Vandeweyer, a nondescript street of three-story rowhouses with small cast-iron balconies.

"What the hell are we doing here?" Janssen said in exasperation as they climbed the stairs and stopped at an apartment door. Brosan ignored him and knocked. When no one came to the door, Janssen pressed his ear against it. Voices whispered inside. In a flash, he kicked in the door. "I'm tired of waiting," he said to a speechless Brosan.

Capt. Jackson and Miss Anny froze in the hallway, mouths open in terror. "Who's he?!" Jackson screamed at Brosan.

"He's with the Dutch police," Brosan said, stepping carefully over pieces of the shattered door frame.

"You shouldn't be here," Jackson said, closing the remains of the door. "Someone might see you. Why didn't you contact me in the usual way?"

"We're in a hurry," Brosan said. "Did any of the priests you deal with contact you today about helping some fake monks traveling with an African?"

"And a woman," Janssen said. He loomed over Jackson and Miss Anny, who cowered behind the captain.

"I don't work for you," Jackson said, stepping back and looking at Brosan. "Can he be trusted?"

"Answer the question," Brosan said. "He's not going to tell anyone, Prosper."

"Well, yes. A priest did call me about some fugitives dressed as Benedictines."

"And?" Brosan said.

"We picked them up and got them ready to move on to Paris. I made all the usual arrangements with the *Abwehrstelle*," he said, referring to the local branch of the *Abwehr*, the German military intelligence service.

"We told *Sonderführer* Kohl all about it," Miss Anny said in their defense, referring to the leader of the Brussels' Abwehrstelle Group III in charge of catching downed pilots. "Didn't he let you know?"

"Where are they now?" Janssen said, ignoring Miss Anny.

"At the Gare du Midi, waiting for the Berlin-Paris express," Jackson said.

Janssen was halfway down the stairs before realizing Brosan was not following, forcing him to trudge back up the stairs to the apartment. "What are you waiting for?" he said to Brosan, pointing at his watch. "We don't have much time."

"You can't pick them up now," Jackson said.

"Who the hell are you to tell me what I can and cannot do, or when?" Janssen said, waving his massive, clenched fist in front of Jackson's nose.

Brosan lowered Janssen's arm. "He's right. If we arrest them here, it will expose Prosper. We must wait until they arrive in Paris."

"Then let me ride on the train so they can't escape," Janssen said.

"No," Brosan said. "They will be captured out of sight in Paris so everyone in Belgium will be convinced they have escaped. That way, they will continue to use the services of our friend here."

"But I have to be there to identify Miriam," Janssen said. "Remember, she's a trained agent. We can't chance her slipping through our fingers again. It'll be the end of both our careers. I must be on that train." He didn't mention that he had to be in on the capture to guarantee getting the 15,000-guilders reward.

"You said you had seen their faces close up, which means they likely have seen you close up. And you are a hard man to miss," Brosan said, glancing at Janssen's red birthmark. "However, there is another way that will not compromise one of our most successful operations. He has helped us capture hundreds of British soldiers in hiding by befriending priests and leaders of religious organizations."

☆☆☆

By the time Rogers and the others entered the 11:30 p.m. express to Paris, it was nearly full, and there weren't enough seats for everyone. So, Rogers, Cookie, Obasi, and Nidal settled on the floor apart from each other in a narrow corridor packed with men sitting on suitcases, backpacks, and duffle bags. Maduro and the two pilots jammed uncomfortably into a six-seat compartment already occupied by five other people, a situation that put them in greater danger of being exposed.

A German officer offered Miriam a seat; she accepted with a bright smile and *"danke."* Chantal was in another second-class compartment. Much to Rogers' relief, the Bahnschutzpolizei, the uniformed railroad police, barely glanced at anyone's papers. They had enough trouble maneuvering around and over the mass of bodies and luggage blocking the corridor, all of which reeked of sweat and cigarette smoke.

For the next few hours, Rogers tried not to dwell on food or the cold or being caught as he labored to sleep through the carriage's incessant shuddering and the rhythmic clack-clack of the iron wheels on poorly maintained track. Unlike the two downed airmen in his convoy, Rogers and his crew had no dog-tags to prove their military status and, therefore, were subject to execution as foreign spies.

The grinding screech of the train's brakes jolted Rogers awake. His heart raced as the police herded him and the other passengers outside in a small, chilly French border town. All the passengers, except Miriam and others in uniform, had to file through long sheds so their luggage could be inspected by Belgian agents for contraband—*Douaniers*, as French customs officials were called—and by German officials to check their papers.

As Rogers returned to the train, Chantal waited outside a car that appeared to be reserved for German soldiers. She motioned for Rogers to join her, which he thought was dangerous but did as she asked anyway. She waved over a few other men who had been sitting in the train car corridor as well as her wards: Maduro, the two pilots, and the rest of Rogers' crew. Much to Rogers' consternation, she climbed the steps into the car half-filled with soldiers and beckoned him and the other men to follow her aboard. *This is insane.* It was hard enough to avoid glancing at the police or engaging in conversation with other passengers, but now Chantal was leading them into the lion's den.

In the doorway, Rogers hesitated at the sight of the German soldiers, some stretched out over two seats. Ahead of him, Chantal wagged her finger at the soldiers, scolding them with her cute, dimpled smile to make room for other passengers in the overcrowded train.

Maduro whispered in Rogers' ear without moving his lips. "Smart. Soldiers are not allowed to speak to civilians." Chantal moved the chagrined soldiers around and interspersed Rogers and the other men among them, smiling and saying "*danke schön*" or "*vielen dank.*" The charmed soldiers smiled back; some even offered her their seats. She waved them off with a warm grin and found a seat by herself at the rear. For the final six hours of the trip, there was blessed silence.

At 7:30 a.m., the train rumbled into Paris' Gare du Nord train station, a Beaux Arts wonder of towering iron pillars supporting a glass-and-cast-iron roof. Its iron beam ran the length of two football fields. Early morning light flooded the cavernous train shed. This time, Rogers flashed his ticket at the harried officials as he filtered through the platform into the main building.

Chantal waited inside with Miriam at her side, both looking up as if studying the train schedules. Rogers made eye contact with Obasi. Maduro, Cookie, and Nidal were headed in the right direction toward the women.

Farther ahead, the two downed airmen hustled toward the Metro entrance, where a man wearing a bright green tie waited, carrying a copy of Charles Péguy's *Le Mystère de la charité de Jeanne d'Arc* under his right arm.

As Rogers and Obasi wandered toward the Metro entrance, Miriam caught their attention and shook her head, indicating with her eye movements and tilted head that they should follow her and Chantal. *What's wrong?* Rogers scrutinized the bustling crowd. The airmen lingered around the man in the green tie, pretending they didn't notice him. Nidal, Cookie, and Maduro walked separately through the bustling crowd toward the airmen.

Gendarmes and German police milled about, spot-checking people's documents and chatting among themselves. Over the shoulder of the man in the green tie, Rogers spotted a stocky man in an ill-fitting suit with an unlit pipe peeking over a newspaper. Even from a distance, Rogers could detect the telltale sign. He was watching them. *We are walking into a trap.*

CHAPTER 23

Vomit shot out of Janssen's mouth as the Fieseler Fi 156 Storch military aircraft plunged and regained altitude, an aerial ping pong ball in the stormy weather. Lightning flashed all around, and rain pelted the three-seat, single-engine liaison plane, one of the hand-me-down aircraft the *Polizeifliegerabteilung,* the Police Aviation Department, used to move officers, equipment, and documents around occupied Europe. Brosan and the pilot glanced at each other, shaking their heads in amusement.

The flight from the Fliegerhorst Melsbroek military airbase north of Brussels to Orly Air Base south of Paris should have taken less than two-and-a-half hours at the plane's cruising speed of 130 kmh. They had taken off shortly before 7 a.m. at the first glimmer of sunlight and were already more than an hour behind schedule.

Janssen hated to fly, even in good weather. This trip was torture. As the plane rattled and swayed on its approach to the runway, Janssen had nothing left in his stomach yet couldn't stop retching.

Once on the ground, it took another hour for the drive through the heart of Paris past the Eiffel Tower, draped with swastikas like so many other buildings and monuments all over town. Nearby, they drove around the Vélodrome d'Hiver, the indoor sports arena where the Germans detained 13,000 Jews they had arrested the previous July in the notorious Vel' d'Hiv Roundup. The Jews were held for days with little to eat or drink and no bathrooms before being shipped off to concentration camps. There was no mention of that history as Brosan and Janssen drove by on their way to the GFP headquarters.

The GFP was one of a dizzying array of military, civilian, and paramilitary law enforcement organizations under Nazi Germany. But it was unique in that its officers had the authority to pass through military roadblocks, commandeer military vehicles and communication equipment, and enter any military building. They also worked with local police and paramilitary forces in occupied territories. The GFP was as feared as the better-known Gestapo, especially because of its notorious shooting range in Paris, where prisoners were tortured and executed.

Around noon, when they arrived at GFP headquarters in the confiscated Hôtel Bradford on Rue Saint Philippe du Roule, Brosan led the still queasy Janssen to a washroom to clean off the vomit from his leather overcoat and then to an office on the second floor. An aide handed him a note that made Brosan smile. "They've got them," he said.

"Who? Where?" Janssen said.

"The *Brigades Spéciales* followed them to a safe house and arrested them. They are being held for us at the Prefecture of Police," Brosan said and scurried back down the stairs, with Janssen hurrying to keep up with him. Janssen was unaware of the Brigades Spéciales, a French police force in charge of hunting down resistance members, Jews, communists, and other enemies of the state. It reported to Brosan's GFP and had an even worse reputation for cruelty to prisoners.

Brigades Spéciales' agents specialized in disguises, including at times a yellow Star of David, and used a "spinning mill" technique that involved pairs of agents following suspects for days or weeks, collecting information on all their contacts. Once satisfied the whole network had been identified, BS agents would swoop in for mass arrests. Just the month before, they had rounded up fifty-nine foreign Jews, many of them part of a Communist youth resistance group.

After another long drive past French and Gothic-lettered German signposts, they arrived at the Prefecture of Police, a sprawling nineteenth-century building once used as a barracks near Notre Dame Cathedral. On the second floor in room 47, Brosan introduced Janssen to Commissioner Fernand David, head of a BS division. With his sparse strands of greased-back hair, owlish eyes, and petite handlebar mustache, he more resembled a cartoon character than the feared "David les main rouges"—"David the Red Hands." With him was Chief Inspector Sodoski, known as "the Jew eater" for his aggressive roundup of Jews in public places, especially train stations.

"Where are they?" Brosan said.

"Come with us," David said in his high-pitched voice, smoothing down his mustache with a satisfied smile as he led them into a nearby interrogation room.

"What the hell?" Janssen said, his voice rising in anger at the sight of two men handcuffed to a table. "These aren't them. And where's the woman?"

"I can assure you, these are the ones who approached me in the train station," Chief Inspector Sodoski said. "I led them to the safe house and arrested them there, out of sight as instructed. No one told me how many to expect."

"Who are these two?" Brosan said.

"*Luftterroristen*," Sodoski said, meaning "air terrorists," the Germans' name for downed Allied pilots. "They were wearing RAF dog tags."

Seeing his reward slipping through his hands, Janssen slapped one of the airmen. "Where is the woman? And the others?" he said in English. "Capt. Jackson told us she was part of his convoy along with several other men, including an African and an Arab. So, don't tell me you don't know what I'm talking about."

"I don't know what you are talking about," the airman said, bracing for another slap.

"Arab?" Chief Inspector Sodoski said. "Now that you mention it, I thought an Arab and two other men were heading toward me, but they stopped to talk to a Red Cross nurse. She pointed them toward the exit for the Number Two line down the street, and they wandered away. Didn't think anything of it at the time."

"Damn it!" Janssen said, raising his voice. "She was disguised as a Betreuungshelferinnen. That was her, and you let her escape, you fool."

"Now look here," David said. "I will not have you misuse my men or interrogate my prisoners without my permission. Get out!"

Brosan grabbed Janssen's elbow and tugged him out of the room. "Let's find out what happened before we burn all our bridges." Once back at GFP headquarters, Brosan tracked down Prosper on the phone in Brussels and asked if he knew what had gone wrong.

"Got a call from my passeur a little while ago," Prosper, a.k.a. Captain Jackson, said. "She said the others got cold feet for some reason and abandoned her at the station. She tried to follow them, but they got on the Metro, and she lost them."

"Now what?" Janssen said after Brosan slammed down the phone and relayed what Jackson had said.

"Well, after your performance, we can't expect any more help from the Special Brigades. And I have been ordered to fly back to Brussels immediately. I, of course, will issue a bulletin for my men to keep an eye out for the fugitives. But you are on your own."

"What about the *Carlingue*?"

"What?" Brosan fell back in his chair and studied Janssen for a long moment before replying. "Be careful what you ask for."

"I don't have much choice. I don't know my way around France."

"But they are no more than a band of ruthless thugs with a blank check from the Gestapo to do whatever they want to whomever they want."

"I am aware of their reputation. Can you introduce me to them?"

"If I must," Brosan said with a sigh. "I will have my men provide you with a police pass so you can travel freely and enlist the help of gendarmes. But you must understand I cannot guarantee your safety."

☆☆☆

Miriam and Rogers paraded arm-in-arm like a loving couple out for a stroll around the circular Place de la Nation, above the last stop of the Number Two Metro line they had used to flee from the Gare du Nord. At a distance behind them, Maduro followed along with Chantal; Cookie, Nidal, and Obasi rested on benches, appearing to admire the giant bronze statue in the middle of the park known as the Triumph of the Republic. It depicted Marianne, symbolizing the Republic, standing on a globe in a chariot pulled by lions. With their heads close together, Miriam and Rogers whispered to one another.

"Can we talk now?" Rogers said.

"Keep your voice very soft and your head down so no one can see your lips," she said.

"What happened at the train station?"

"Chantal said she did not recognize the passeur with the green tie but was not able to warn the airmen away," Miriam whispered, glancing around to be sure no one was paying attention to them. "She said she had only done this a couple of times and was becoming suspicious of Capt. Jackson."

"Why?"

"He would never tell her where the airmen were taken after she dropped them off. She even gave one of them a postcard to mail to her once he made it safely to Spain. It never arrived, even though Capt. Jackson assured her the airman was safe in London."

"So, the strange face spooked her?"

"Spooked?"

"Scared her away."

"Yes, it spooked her," Miriam said, resting her head against Rogers' arm. "That and she thought she spotted some strange men following her. And their shoes had rubber soles."

"So?"

"Those are hard to come by. Most soles are made of cardboard or wood these days. Undercover police use rubber soles so they can follow people without being detected." She slowed down to allow her father and Chantal to catch up.

The two women greeted each other as friends in French, kissing cheeks and introducing the men, who shook hands and appeared to exchange pleasantries. With sweeping motions, Chantal spoke in French, gesturing at the statue in the circle as if pointing out highlights to tourists.

Rogers faked a smile and rapt attention but comprehended nothing in the conversation. "What's she talking about?" he whispered in Miriam's ear.

"She is saying there used to be a large pond here with statues of sea monsters protecting Marianne from enemies of democracy, or so the socialists liked to think." Miriam turned her head to follow Chantal's pointing hand as if she was enthralled with the tour. "The Nazis did not like that, so they filled in the pond and melted down the statues. They've done the same thing to hundreds of other statues and works of art that offend them all around Paris."

Chantal kept chattering and pointed to the southern part of the square.

"She says that's where a guillotine was set up during the revolution," Miriam said.

"Perfect place to bring us," Rogers said.

While keeping up the fake tour, Chantal switched to English when she was sure no one could hear her. "We must hide. Capt. Jackson has surely given them our description by now."

"Where?" Miriam said.

"The one person I know in Paris is a distant relative. But I'm not sure he would want to risk helping us," Chantal whispered. "Stay here, and I'll find a phone to contact him."

"Make it quick," Rogers said, handing her a wad of French francs that Capt. Jackson had given him to buy food and tickets for everyone. "And see if you can find a long raincoat to cover up Miriam's uniform."

A half an hour later, Chantal returned with a gabardine raincoat and a floppy, wide-brimmed, black fedora that covered most of Miriam's hair. "He said he cannot help us. But he has a doctor friend named Petiot who might. I have his address. It is near the Arc de Triomphe, so we must take the tram."

"No," Miriam said as she slipped into the coat and stuffed her field cap into her pocket.

"If you are afraid of the tram, we could pair off and take a *vélo-taxi*," she said, pointing to a nearby line of bicycle-powered rickshaws that could hold one or two passengers.

"I said no," Miriam said, steel in her voice.

"But we must go there. I do not know anyone else," Chantal said in a whiny voice, pulling on Rogers' arm and using her doe-eyed charm in an apparent plea for support.

"That is too far away, and it takes us right back into the heart of Paris," Miriam said. "We must get as far away as possible."

"It wouldn't have been if we had gone west on the Metro as I had wanted," Chantal said.

Watching his daughter with growing concern, Maduro asked, "How do you propose we get away?"

"We walk. South. As far as we can. Out of Paris," Miriam said.

"Don't be foolish," Chantal said. "I'm afraid. Let us go to the doctor's house and be safe for one more night."

Miriam frowned and stomped off past Nidal, Obasi, and Cookie, gesturing with a flick of her head for them to tag along. Rogers and Maduro shrugged and followed Miriam. A distraught Chantal hesitated, grimacing at her uncomfortable shoes. She finally gave in and scurried after the group.

☆☆☆

As they reached the outskirts of the city, Cookie clutched Chantal's arm to help her along. "Us cripples have to stick together," he said, hobbling on his bad hip. Gaunt women carrying empty baskets hurried past them; others lugged baskets half-full of vegetables back toward Paris. Cookie gave Chantal a quizzical look.

"*Système de Débrouillage,*" she said. "Everyone is starving because of rationing and because the Nazis take most of the food for Germany. So, they visit farmers to buy what little food they can spare."

"Like a black market?"

"Yes and no," Chantal said. "Only the Germans and the wealthy can afford the black market. Prices for things like butter and eggs are triple the official price. And wages have been frozen since the war started. So, my French friends tell me they survive with *Système D*, using farmers and anyone they know to beg, barter, or bargain for food. It is very sad."

"Such a bugger of a thing," Cookie said. "Makes me hungry."

☆☆☆

Two unsmiling bruisers frisked Janssen as soon as he stepped into the hallway at 93 Rue Lauriston, a four-story, gray and beige stone building in the sixteenth arrondissement, a fashionable neighborhood near the Eiffel Tower. The area was headquarters for the Gestapo, SD, Abwehr, and other Nazi agencies. The two big guys removed Janssen's Walther PPK and led him through high-ceiling salons up the stairs past the cold stares of other bulky men in tailored suits and Borsalino hats, the kind favored in American gangster films. Janssen recognized one of the men but couldn't place his face at first. It wasn't until the man flashed a dazzling smile while gliding down the stairs that Janssen recognized the famous actor Maurice Chevalier.

Once inside a palatial second-story office, Janssen was surprised to see the walls lined with steel. *For soundproofing?* Dozens of rare orchids and dahlias covered every surface, including the claw-footed coffee table, where a beefy man lapped up foie gras and slurped oysters from an ice-covered silver tray. With his lacquer-dark hair and slight double chin, the man appeared to be a banker or accountant in his forties. But when he raised his penetrating eyes, the first tingle of fear struck Janssen.

"Please sit down, Mr. Janssen. May I offer you some champagne?" the man asked in a high-pitched voice unexpected from such a big man. Lifting a bottle of Dom Pérignon from a silver bucket, he said, "Or perhaps you'd prefer some of this delicious Meursault 1928."

"No, thank you, Monsieur Lafont," Janssen said as he settled on the edge of an exotic sphinx-legged chair and removed his homburg. "I believe Inspektor Brosan told you why I'm here."

"Vaguely," Lafont said, pouring himself another tall glass of champagne. "This woman must be very important for a member of Colonne Henneicke to have traveled so far out of your territory."

"She is a British spy who killed some policemen. And she is a Jew."

"What's she worth?" Lafont stopped mid-slurp and locked eyes with Janssen.

"There is a 15,000-guilder reward, which we, of course, would be willing to share if you can help us," Janssen said. He didn't hesitate to tell the truth because he assumed Lafont already knew everything and was just testing him.

Lafont waved his hand in dismissal. "Not necessary. I like doing favors for the Colonne and the GFP. Comes in handy from time to time. Besides, that reward wouldn't cover a week of my bills at the One-Two-Two," he said with a laugh, referring to one of the most expensive bordellos in Paris, famous for fine dining and topless waitresses at its restaurant, Le Bœuf à la Ficelle. The bordello itself featured twenty-two "fantasy rooms," including an Orient Express mock-up cabin that rocked like a moving train. *Reichsmarschall* Hermann Göring, Hitler's second in command, almost always visited there when he came to Paris for one of his frequent shopping sprees.

"Thank you," Janssen said. "I tracked her and several men who helped her to Paris but lost them at Gare du Nord. I am hoping your sources can help me find her again." Muffled screams and thumps from a room above them made Janssen flinch; Lafont didn't seem to notice.

"I thought bloodhounds never lost the scent of their prey," Lafont said, obviously letting Janssen know that he knew everything about him and that he needed to be careful with the most dangerous gangster in France.

Lafont, whose real name was Henri Chamberland, had been a petty criminal before the war. He spent years in prison learning his profession and building up invaluable contacts in the underworld. He parlayed those connections into doing dirty work for various Nazi security forces, being careful to share the proceeds from his robberies, shakedowns, protection rackets, black market activities, confiscation of deported Jews' valuables, and murders.

He entertained lavishly at Maxim's and other luxury restaurants and, with impunity, drove around Paris after curfew in his new white Bentley, a rare luxury in a metropolitan area of 6.7 million people. Paris had 350,000 parking spaces but no more than 7,000 permits for private vehicles. Many of those cars and trucks were powered by *gazogène* engines that burned wood, charcoal, or coal.

Lafont's army of underworld crime thugs called themselves La Carlingue, literally an aircraft cabin, implying a strong structure. The public called them the French Gestapo. The Nazis, for all their feared efficiencies, became increasingly dependent on groups like Lafont's because they were not only short-handed but hobbled by intense turf wars and personal rivalries among military, police, paramilitary groups, and intelligence agencies.

That was especially true when it came to capturing resistance members and Jews. Lafont was so good at his job that he was made a German citizen and a captain in the Gestapo. The once small-time crook who was barely literate was now a gang boss, and he was untouchable.

"Boss, we've administered a correction, but he won't talk," said a man who stuck his head inside the room, blood covering his knuckles holding the door.

"Well, take him to the basement and see how he likes the *baignoire*," Lafont said, almost gleeful. "Care to watch?"

"No," said Janssen, who didn't mind roughing up people for information but didn't care for holding victims' heads under ice-cold water until they almost drowned. "I need to move on." He showed Lafont the wanted flyer. "She doesn't look like that anymore. I believe she has red hair and may be disguised as a Red Cross nurse. She was traveling with several men, including an African and an Arab."

Lafont glanced at the flyer and burped. "They will need to find an escape line to flee Paris. A group like that would not go unnoticed. So, we will put out some feelers offering them assistance. It just so happens that one of my associates is quite adept at drawing flies to his web and dealing with them in, shall we say, creative ways. He's a doctor. Everyone trusts a doctor," he said and cackled.

Janssen thanked him and set out with one of Lafont's goons, who introduced himself as Pierre Bonny. Janssen knew the name. He had been the most famous detective in Paris, and later dubbed "*Le Premier Flic*," France's top cop, by newspapers; that is, until he was caught making up evidence and convicted of corruption. Once out of prison, he joined Lafont in what became known as the Bonny-Lafont gang.

Tall and lean, Bonny wore shaded glasses and bore a lampshade mustache; he dressed gangster-style in a tailored suit, black shirt, and black tie. Driving his expensive Jaguar, he sped north past Place Victor-Hugo to Rue le Sueur 21, a two-and-a-half-story townhouse with a black and gray stone facade. The first-floor shutters were closed, as were all the curtains on the other floors, and there was a vague scent of coal smoke in the air. Bonny rang the bell.

When a man opened a wooden double-door that had once served as a carriage entrance, Bonny explained who Janssen was and why he was there. "This is Doctor Eugène, Inspector Janssen," Bonny said, using Janssen's fake title, apparently to add some gravitas. "Henri says he'll help you. I'll wait out here."

"Please, come in," Doctor Eugène said with a broad, charismatic smile. Almost as tall as Janssen, he had a bushy, chin-strap beard and mustache, wavy hair pomaded back and parted in the middle. Black circles underlined his shifty eyes. Elegantly dressed in a double-breasted suit and silk tie, the doctor led Janssen by the arm through a grand salon, a library stuffed with medical journals and crime novels, a formal dining room with a crystal chandelier, and a billiards room, ending at a petite salon.

Despite all the oriental rugs, Louis XV furniture, oil paintings, and marble statues, Janssen scrunched his nose at the filth. Cobwebs, dust-covered stacks of suitcases, and upturned chairs were everywhere. Wallpaper hung loosely from the walls. And the air was nauseating. Trying not to gag, Janssen showed the doctor Miriam's wanted flyer and explained what he needed.

"Now, this is most unusual," Doctor Eugène said. "I had a call from a colleague this morning asking if I could help arrange an escape for a group of foreigners such as you describe. In fact, I've been expecting them."

"Here?" Janssen said, unable to believe his luck.

"Yes, but that was several hours ago, and I cannot wait any longer. I have many others who will be leaving soon for Argentina, and I must prepare for them. Monsieur Lafont insists that they be taken care of," the doctor said in a haughty, self-important tone.

"How did your colleague meet the fugitives?"

"Didn't say."

"Did he say where they were?"

The doctor hurried Janssen toward the door. "I believe Place de la Nation," he said as he tripped over a bag. A half-burned skull and a dismembered hand tumbled out as he opened the entrance. With an annoyed sigh, the doctor kicked them aside as if they were nothing more than children's toys cluttering the floor, shoved Janssen out, and slammed the door so hard it rattled the frame.

CHAPTER 24

"I can't do no more," Cookie said, agony in his voice after hobbling along with the others for several hours. Obasi and Nidal had tried to help him, but his pain was overwhelming. They had traveled through the outskirts of Paris and were passing by farms and groves toward a distant village in the dying light.

"We have to stop soon," Rogers said to Miriam. "What about there?" He pointed to the top of a hill, to a large farmhouse, light shining through its windows.

"No. We must keep going."

"But Cookie can't make it any farther."

"Neither can I," said Chantal. "My feet are killing me."

"Why not take our chances at the farmhouse?" Maduro asked as he caught up with them.

"It's too big," Miriam said. Rogers and Maduro stared at her, confusion on their faces. "The Nazis always take over the largest houses. We cannot take that chance."

"What about that barn on the other side of the road?" Rogers said. "At least let Cookie rest a bit before we press on."

She nodded in reluctant agreement. Nidal and Obasi, followed by the others, half-carried Cookie across a damp field into a ramshackle barn, where they laid Cookie down in some straw and made themselves as comfortable as they could in the darkness. They were cold, hungry, and desperate.

Hay swished as if brushed by something or someone. Miriam rose without a sound, motioning for the others to stay still. As she crept toward the sound, Rogers clutched a pitchfork in both hands. More swishing. Miriam and Rogers paused, holding their breath, hearts racing. Rogers sprang in front of Miriam and drew back the pitchfork, ready to hurl it at the sound. Dim moonlight, shining through cracks in the barn, fell on the tearful eyes of several children huddled together, trembling and muffling moans of fear.

Rushing over, Miriam spoke to them in soft, reassuring tones. Four boys and two girls, none older than twelve, hugged her and sobbed. Chantal joined them and tried to calm down the terrified children.

"Who are they?" Rogers said. "Why are they here?"

"Jews," Miriam said. "Their parents hid them here and have not returned."

"They haven't eaten in two days," Chantal said.

"We must bring them some food and water," Miriam said.

"From where?" Rogers said, throwing up his hands. "We can't make it to the village and back before curfew, even if we got lucky enough to find someone to help us."

"As you always say, we must take our chances," Miriam said to Rogers.

"But that is not wise," Chantal said. "If the wrong person sees you ..."

"I will not let them starve," Miriam said, taking Rogers' hand. "Come with me. The rest of you stay in hiding."

"But—"

Miriam didn't wait for Chantal to finish as she guided Rogers into the night through the soft, dewy fields adjacent to the road, stopping often to listen and watch for approaching vehicles. Clouds covered the moon, making the trip safer yet more difficult as they stumbled over roots and loose rocks.

"Why are you so tough on Chantal?" Rogers whispered. "She's only trying to help."

Miriam didn't slow down. "You like her?"

"What? No. I mean, sure. She seems nice enough."

"She tries too hard," Miriam said, glancing at Rogers through the corner of her eyes. Startled by a noise, she dragged him down into the long grass. Behind them, the gentle clop-clop-clop of a horse pulling a wagon approached. Its single occupant, dressed in blue overalls and a flat beret, held a lantern to light the way. Miriam peeked over the grass, but Rogers grabbed her shoulder, shaking his head. She jerked away, ran into the road, and waved at the driver of the wooden cart, which was loaded with hay.

Once the horse stopped with a whiney, Miriam jogged over. The driver doffed his beret and leaned over the side as Miriam gestured and appeared to plead for help. In the lantern's flickering light, Rogers could see the man's stern visage but couldn't tell how he was reacting to Miriam's story.

Much to Rogers' dismay, the man flipped on his beret, tightened his grip on the reins, and urged the horse forward. Miriam backed up to the side of the road and glanced over to where she had left Rogers, who couldn't make out her expression. The horse plodded along toward the village, then swung off the right side of the road toward Miriam, who waved for Rogers to follow.

Together, they huddled in the back of the cart for the bumpy ride to the barn. "He will help us," Miriam said, leaning on Rogers.

"Thank goodness."

Once they arrived back at the barn, Miriam herded the children onto the cart and covered them with hay, telling them they were going to play a game of hide and seek and that they had to remain absolutely still for the ride. Obasi and Nidal lifted Cookie into the back and arranged hay on top of him, too.

"He will take them to his home," Miriam said. "We will follow in the fields, away from the road." In a gathering fog, they traipsed behind the lamp's eerie glow to a tidy farmhouse at the edge of the village. The cart rolled behind the building at the same time as Miriam and the men made it across the field. Chantal, shoes in hand, brought up the rear. Quietly, they helped the children and Cookie down from the cart and through the rear kitchen door.

A sad-faced woman wearing an apron directed them to sit at a knotty wooden table, where she served them rye bread and watery rabbit stew with rutabaga. Though despised and primarily served to livestock, rutabaga substituted for hard-to-find potatoes, just as nettles substituted for spinach. There was barely enough to go around, so the adults shared smaller portions.

In the fire's flickering light at the far side of the kitchen/living room, Rogers could see for the first time the children were wearing the yellow Star of David, and their dirty faces were tear-stained and gaunt from starvation, exhaustion, and worry. "What happened to their parents?" Rogers asked Miriam.

"They do not know," Miriam said. She asked the farmer's wife something in French. "Madame Garnier says the Brigades Spéciales caught them foraging for food. They will not be coming back."

"Can the children hide here?" Chantal said, using her bread to sop up the last of her soup.

"Not for long," Miriam said. "We must take them with us."

"That is impossible," Chantal said in her most woeful voice. "Our group is too large as it is."

Miriam glared at her. "If you are so afraid, why don't you go back to Brussels?"

"You know I can't," Chantal said, sticking out her lower lip. "By now, they know I'm helping you. They would kill me."

Miriam ducked her head in disgust and, under her breath, so Rogers alone could hear her, said: "I'm not so sure." Rogers looked askance at Miriam and Chantal, again wondering the reason for the antagonism. The youngest child, perhaps six years old, moved over to sit beside Miriam and played with a doll. Miriam stroked her head. "They go with us."

"Where are we?" Rogers said.

Miriam spoke with Madame Garnier. "She said we are near Villeneuve-Saint-Georges, about fifteen kilometers south of Paris."

"Not bad for a couple of gimps," Cookie said, elbowing Chantal with a chuckle.

The young girl in Miriam's lap tapped on her shoulder and whispered something in her ear. Lifting her head in surprise, Miriam got her father's attention. "She said it is Friday and wonders when we will celebrate Shabbat."

"Oh, my. I'd lost track of the days," Maduro said. "But we've already eaten."

"Maybe we could sing *Zemirot*," Miriam said, referring to traditional hymns sung during or after the Jewish sabbath on Friday evenings. She spoke to the children in French, and they all nodded their heads up and down in eager agreement. "But I don't remember as many hymns in Hebrew as I do in Ladino."

"*Shalom aleichem malachei hash-sharet malachei Elyon.*" Nidal stunned everyone into silence by singing the first line of the traditional hymn "*Shalom Aleichem*," meaning "peace be upon you," in tune and in perfect Hebrew.

"Where did you learn Hebrew, my friend?" Maduro said. "I assumed you were a Muslim."

"I am," Nidal said. "When I was young, my father went to sea and never returned. So, my mother took me to Cairo to find relatives. But she died, leaving me alone on the streets. An old Jewish couple kindly took me in for a while and helped me learn English. They insisted that I follow my father's faith, but I learned their ways, too. I very much enjoyed Shabbat after Friday prayers at the mosque."

"Were they Ashkenazi Jews?" Miriam said. "I didn't realize they were in Egypt."

"There were a few in Cairo who fled pogroms in Ukraine, Poland, and Romania last century, mainly in the Darb al-Barabira quarter. But I did not know there was a difference back then," Nidal said and looked at Maduro "Does it matter?"

"Of course not. Sephardim, Ashkenazim, Mizrahim—we are all Jews," Maduro said. "Please, continue."

Before doing so, Nidal broke into a rare, fleeting smile at Rogers, whose mouth was still agape. "You looked surprised that I know some Hebrew, Captain."

"No, that's not it," Roger said, shaking his head. "It's that I can't believe you know how to sing. I've never heard you even hum before. Have you, Cookie?"

"Nay, Cap'n. It's hard enough to get words out of his mouth, much less the dulcet tones of an Al Bowlly," Cookie said, laughing at his reference to a singer and jazz guitarist popular in Britain.

As usual, Nidal displayed no emotion at the ribbing and instead gathered the children around him, instructing them to hold hands while they sang hymns in Hebrew. Miriam and Maduro joined in for the ones they knew. Rogers' eyes widened in amazement at his friend Nidal's hidden talent.

They ended Shabbat with a rousing version of *Hava Nagila*, meaning "Let us Rejoice," even though it was not a hymn but a Jewish folksong, and put the children to bed in a sea of blankets in front of the crackling fire.

Once the children were asleep, the adults discussed their options with the Garniers, who hated the Germans because they had drafted their son and hundreds of thousands of other men between the ages of eighteen and fifty into forced labor. The *Service du travail obligatoir*, Compulsory Work Service or STO, drove thousands of men into hiding as draft dodgers.

As they lingered around the table talking, it became clear there was no easy answer about how to continue their escape. Walking was out of the question; taking a train with Jewish children was too risky. But they couldn't stay much longer with the Garniers, who didn't have enough farm produce or *carte d'alimentation*—ration cards with color-coded postage stamp-like coupons called "tickets"—to feed them all. Madame Garnier and her husband talked over something with Miriam.

The only thing Rogers could make out was the phrase, "*on dit que,*" which the Garniers repeated over and over. Looking at Maduro, Rogers whispered the phrase and asked what it meant. "It means, 'it is being said.' It is what French people say when discussing rumors," Maduro whispered. "No one has much real information these days. So, we all live on rumors."

"So, what are the rumors?"

"They hear that many raids have been conducted in the area recently and that some sort of new police force has been activated to reinforce the Brigades Spéciales. So, it is too dangerous to stay much longer."

"Any ideas on how we get out of here?"

Miriam overheard and replied, "They said that a friend of their son is in hiding with the resistance. They will try to contact him tomorrow for help."

"Why not use the monk disguises again?" Cookie said.

"We don't have the habits or proper IDs," Maduro said. "Plus, the French have a mixed history with the Catholic Church and religious orders. That might not be the best disguise."

"There you go again, mate, talking like you are Catholic," Cookie said. "Is that what you Maranios do?"

"Marranos," Miriam said, patting her friend on his arm. "But we do not use that word about ourselves. We are descended from Crypto-Jews."

Cookie frowned.

"Secret Jews," she said.

Rubbing his forehead in frustration, Cookie said, "Well, if it was a secret, why are the Nazis after you?"

"Many centuries ago, our ancestors in Spain and Portugal were forced to convert to Christianity. Those who refused faced death," Miriam said. "Some did convert. But many pretended to be Christians while practicing Judaism in secret. They were called Marranos, which some believe means "swine." Our family eventually fled to Amsterdam and resumed our Sephardic traditions for all to see."

"But our ancestors preserved their Spanish and Portuguese heritage, including some Christian artwork and even a beautifully illustrated Christian Bible," Maduro said. "Our past always intrigued me. So, when my brother Levy and I attended what you British would call secondary school at Saint Ignatius Gymnasium, I made it a point to learn as much about Christian traditions as I could. Now I wonder how followers of Jesus could support Hitler or Mussolini or Franco?"

"Didn't Jesus say something about rendering unto Caesar?" Chantal said. "Most of the people I know don't support the fascists. They do what they must to survive."

"Is there any distinction between support and allowing evil to continue by your selfish indifference?" Miriam said.

"I am not indifferent," Chantal said, the blood rushing to her cheeks and slapping her hand on the table. "I am doing my part to resist. I resent—"

Rogers wrapped his arm around Chantal's shoulders, pleading with Miriam with his eyes. "Yes, you are," Rogers said. "And we all thank you. Don't we, Miriam?"

Sitting erect in her chair, Miriam glared at Rogers. Grim-faced, she jumped up, snatched a blanket, and stormed out the back door. Rogers scurried after her into a stable, where he found her curled up in the blanket in an empty stall. He laid down with her, hugging her close to him. "I can never forgive," Miriam whispered.

"I know," Rogers said. "I don't blame you. I just wish I could make the pain disappear. But you can't let your hatred turn you into one of those killers."

Turning over to stare at him, Miriam said in a flat, matter-of-fact tone, "I am a soldier. I do not kill people. I kill my enemy."

The cold fury in her chestnut eyes worried Rogers. No amount of affection could soften the pain and determination in them, or the soul-deep suffering that cried out for vengeance. "You seem to be arguing with your father a lot," Rogers said. "What's going on?"

"I'm sorry. It's a subject I do not wish to discuss with you."

When Rogers opened his mouth to insist, Miriam pulled him under her blanket, kissed him hard on the lips, and unbuckled his belt, causing him to pull his head back and whisper, "The others."

"I don't care," she said and kissed him again. "I want to feel alive."

☆☆☆

"I want her alive," Janssen said earlier in the day as he pulled shut the door of Bonny's Jaguar, still shaken by what he had seen inside Dr. Eugène's house. "The others I don't care about. Dead or alive for them is fine. Can you take me to Place de la Nation? The doctor said they were seen there not long ago."

"Sure," Bonny said, ramming the car into first gear and screeching off.

"Who was that guy? He made my skin crawl."

Bonny laughed. "Someone we find useful."

"But there were body parts all over the place. And that smell."

"He does have some unusual methods. I'll grant you that. We don't care, and neither does the Gestapo, as long as he makes our problems disappear."

Once they crossed town to the square, it didn't take Bonny long to extract the information he wanted. Janssen couldn't help but notice the fear on the faces of the local shop owners questioned by the former detective. They avoided eye contact but didn't hesitate to answer Bonny, pointing to the south with trembling fingers.

"They couldn't have gotten very far," Janssen said. "Can you drive me around for a look?"

"No. Can you drive?"

Janssen shook his head. "Only for short distances."

"I have other work to do," Bonny said, parking in front of a café. "I'll phone one of our men to pick you up."

Janssen waited on a park bench for more than two hours before a black Faux Cabriolet 7C—a rare two-door coupe model of the Citroën Traction Avant—arrived, and the young driver waved him into the car the French called "*Reine de la Route*," meaning "Queen of the Road." The driver introduced himself as Pierre Loutrel and offered Janssen an unfiltered Gauloises Bleu cigarette, lit it with his metal Leica lighter, and lit one for himself. Having a real cigarette was a rare treat for most people in France, where tobacco was so scarce the *tabac national* was mixed with grass and herbs.

"Where to, mate?" Loutrel said, blowing smoke out his nose. Like all La Carlingue members, he had neatly trimmed, slicked-back hair and wore a tailored suit. Even in Holland, Janssen had heard about *La Valise*. The expelled merchant marine and veteran of *Bat d'Af*, an army penal battalion in Algeria, had a reputation for brutality, a quick trigger finger, and utter contempt for authority—civil, military, or criminal. The nickname came from Loutrel's habit of keeping a doctor's bag with him loaded with guns and burglary tools. "The Mad" would be a better nickname, Janssen thought as he glanced from Loutrel's crazed eyes to the P.38 on his lap, to the doctor's valise and submachine gun on the back seat.

"Drive south," Janssen said. "We'll have to stop often to ask if anyone's seen the fugitives walking by."

"There are a lot of roads out of Paris they could have taken," Loutrel said through a cloud of blue smoke.

"Don't worry, I'll sniff them out," Janssen said as he tossed his cigarette out the window. "Avoid the main roads and zigzag."

"I suppose, if they are heading south, they would have to cross the Pont de Charenton over the Marne," Loutrel said. "We'll start there." Like Bonny before, Loutrel had no trouble getting pedestrians and café owners to talk to him. Displaying the same fear on their faces, they treated the pair with deference. Even a nervous gendarme went out of his way to be helpful, probably aware Loutrel was known to shoot anyone who displeased him. None of them had seen a red-haired nurse pass by, but several remembered seeing an African or two and maybe even an Arab.

On the south side of the Marne, Loutrel pointed to a large man coming out of a bar with an envelope in his hand. "*Nez de Braise*," he said to Janssen as he pulled to the curb and rolled down his window. "Jean-Michel, come here." The man stuffed the envelope inside his tailored jacket, steadied himself with both hands on the car door, and leaned in.

"Bonjour, Pierre," Jean-Michel said. Janssen could smell his alcohol breath from the passenger's seat and assumed that was the source of his nickname, which, in English, was "Glowing Nose." Despite his inebriated state,

Jean-Michel was a keen observer, as only someone expecting a knife in the back at any moment can be. Scanning his surroundings and checking reflections in shop windows for an angry husband, a gendarme with bad intentions, or someone he'd left for dead at Lafont's orders was a matter of survival for a man with many enemies. And, yes, he said, he had observed an African and Arab walking together behind a pair of women, one with a raincoat and floppy hat that didn't quite cover all her red hair. "Nice legs, she had." Jean-Michel saluted with two fingers and staggered down the street into another bar.

"They're walking, so they won't make it far before curfew," Janssen said. "Let's keep heading south and make a wide loop. We should stop every kilometer or so and ask if anyone has seen them."

"I don't have all day, mate," Loutrel said. "I have my own business to attend to."

"How far to the next train station?"

"Ten, maybe fifteen kilometers," Loutrel said, lighting another cigarette on the butt of one he had almost finished.

"If you're trying to be inconspicuous and taking back streets," Janssen said, "you can't get too far, even in a full day's walk. You can drop me off there if we don't find them. They can't walk all the way to Spain. So, I'll bet they'll eventually show up at that station or the next one. What's the name?"

"Villeneuve-Saint-Georges."

CHAPTER 25

Shortly after Monsieur Garnier returned from town early the following day with word that he had contacted the resistance for help, a middle-aged man with an aquiline nose and full beard arrived on a bicycle with wooden wheels. "You cannot travel together. We will have to divide you into three groups," the man, who identified himself as Gilou, told Rogers and the other fugitives.

"We can't split up," Rogers said. "That's too dangerous. Can't we at least be on the same train but in different cars?"

Gilou slipped off his flat cap and mulled the question as he sipped a cup of steaming tea in the Garniers' cozy combined kitchen and living room. "As I understand from Monsieur Garnier, you were betrayed at the Gare du Nord, where the Nazis captured two airmen who know your faces. No?"

"That is correct," Rogers said.

"Therefore, *mon ami*, they will be looking for your faces. More particularly, they will be looking for the color of your faces together," Gilou said, eyeing Obasi and Nidal. "And the color of the women's hair," he added, pointing at Miriam's red hair and Chantal's blonde hair.

"We can always dye our hair," said Miriam, who still wore the Red Cross uniform.

"Even so, you all cannot travel together with the ..." He stopped to count the six children. "Just you," Gilou said, pointing at Miriam. "We do not have much time and must work with what we have. Do you have papers that match the uniform?"

Miriam handed them to Gilou, who mouthed what he was reading as if memorizing them. After he handed the papers back, he led Miriam into a corner away from the children and whispered to her, "And the men?"

"They have travel permits from the Todt Organization to go to Marseille, where I have papers assigning me to the Hôtel-Dieu de Marseille. And we all have a *Grensbescheinigung*," she said, referring to the travel pass for the Belgian-French border. Until abolished the previous March, it was the demarcation line in France between occupied and Vichy zones. "I don't know about her," she said, flicking her hand dismissively in Chantal's direction.

"Do you mean me?" Chantal said, setting down one of the young boys. "I won't have any problems. I'm a V-Frau."

Audible gasps and angry shouts of "Damned informant!" and "How could you!" erupted in a furious cacophony. The terrified children scattered, hiding behind the couch and chairs. Miriam snatched a butcher's knife from a cutting board on the table and charged across the room. "I knew there was something wrong with you," Miriam said.

"That is what my travel papers say," Chantal said, holding the documents in front of her. "They say I work for the DSK," she said, referring to the *Devisenschutzkommando*, the Foreign Exchange Protection Commando, a unit of SS soldiers officially assigned to oversee currency transactions. But in reality, it was a band of thieves authorized to confiscate anything of value, particularly from Jews.

Rogers wrested the papers away from Chantal while Obasi and Nidal pinned her arms behind her back. Miriam pressed the knife against her neck. "Why should I not kill you now?"

"I didn't say the papers were accurate," Chantal said, wide-eyed and shivering.

"No, no," Maduro said, gently moving his daughter's hand holding the knife away from Chantal's throat. "What do you mean?"

"Capt. Jackson provided these as my cover," she said in a trembling voice. "They are excellent forgeries. So, I can travel almost anywhere."

"If that is true, why did you flee with us from the station?" Miriam said, pointing the knife at Chantal. "You had nothing to fear."

"Because once I warned you, I was no longer safe. And I wanted nothing more to do with that traitor." Holding back tears, she glanced from face to face as if pleading for understanding. "Now, I can never return home."

"Let her go," Rogers said. Obasi and Nidal released her arms and stepped back. "Miriam, please." After a long pause, she lowered the knife and, returning to the kitchen table, thrust it into the cutting board, never taking her fiery eyes off Chantal. Gilou sat at the table, unmoved.

"What do you think?" Miriam said.

"I think we have a plan," Gilou said. "I will return this afternoon. But I'm not sure I can obtain hair dye so quickly."

"Do not worry yourself. I have an idea,"

After Gilou rode off on his bike, Miriam had a long discussion in French with Madame Garnier, who picked up a large kettle and spoon, grabbed Miriam's hand, and led her outside to a cellar door.

"Captain, this is not good," Nidal said under his breath to Rogers. "You must make peace between the women, or their bickering will give us away."

Rogers agreed and approached Chantal to begin the mediation process, but she didn't let him speak.

"Thank you for believing me," Chantal said, putting her hand on Rogers' arm. "What did they say?" Chantal asked. In explanation, she said she hadn't heard any of the conversation because she had been entertaining the children with silly games on the floor while Cookie had them giggling and rolling with laughter.

Rogers raised the palms of his hands and shrugged as if to say, "I don't know," and tried to change the conversation. "Look, Chantal, you and Miriam—"

Chantal clutched his hand with both of hers and squeezed it tight, making Rogers squirm. "Did they come up with a way for us to leave the children here and escape to Spain?"

"Uh, I don't speak French," he said, blushing at Chantal's attention, especially when she pressed her breasts against his body and tilted her head up to whisper in his ear.

"I could teach you French," she said with a devious grin that accentuated her dimples. "And I bet a man like you could teach me a few things, too. I've always wanted to go to America."

When Miriam breezed back inside with blackened hands and a pail full of unshelled black walnuts, Rogers wrenched his hand from Chantal's grasp as if he were a schoolboy caught doing something to feel guilty about. His reaction visibly irritated Miriam and made her glare at Chantal, who snickered and rejoined the children. Madame Garnier followed Miriam in with a handful of onions that she placed on a cutting board near the butcher knife. Taking the pot of walnuts from Miriam, she filled it with water and set it down on the stove to boil.

After pulling down a meat mallet from a hook on the wall, Miriam dumped onto the cutting board all the peppermints George had sent her in the Oranjehotel and covered them with a dishtowel. She banged away, shattering all the mints into tiny pieces, and scraped them into a petite, green-tinted, metal-hinged glass-canning jar. She added some cooking oil, secured the lid, and dropped the jar into another pot of water over a lit burner.

As she did that, Madame Garnier retrieved what appeared to be a ragged bedsheet from a cabinet and cut it into pieces. Monsieur Garnier joined them from outside, carrying a headless chicken in a pail. After dipping her hands in the pail, Madame Garnier flicked her fingers at each rag, covering them with specks of blood. While the men watched in curiosity, Miriam spooned ashes from the fireplace into a bowl.

Cookie couldn't take it any longer. "What are you two about, lass?"

"Using my training," Miriam said, flashing the type of joyous smile that hadn't been on her face since Palestine. It vanished as soon as she caught Rogers staring at her. For two hours, the two women puttered around the kitchen, chatting away in French, stirring the pots, and then setting them aside to cool. Miriam used tongs to pull the canning jar out of the smaller pot and set it aside.

Once satisfied that the canning jar was cool enough, Miriam rubbed some of the oily mixture under her eyes. After a few minutes, she motioned to Chantal and said, "Come here."

"Oh, goodness. Are you crying?" Chantal said, studying Miriam's eyes.

Rogers and Cookie hurried over. "Your eyes are all red and swollen," Cookie said, concern in his voice.

"Good," Miriam said.

"Good?" Rogers said. "What's good about you crying?"

"I'm not. It's an old actor's trick the SOE taught us," she said. "Peppermint oil under your eyes makes them water up like you're crying."

Chantal scrunched up her face. "Why would you want red, puffy eyes? It is so very unattractive."

"You will see. Lean over the large pot." Although reluctant at first, Chantal followed orders. Then Miriam lowered her head and dipped the end of a long strand of her blonde hair into the black walnut concoction. She shook the strand, patted it with a cloth, and then repeated the procedure with her own red hair. "That might do," Miriam said, examining the two strands in a handheld mirror.

"What is this stuff?" Chantal said, waving the odor away from under her nose.

Ignoring her question, Miriam wrapped a towel around Chantal's shoulders and bent her over the sink. "Hold still," she said as she ladled more thick black liquid over Chantal's hair. By now, the children and the men were intrigued and crowded around to watch the show. When Chantal's hair was entirely black, Miriam wrapped her wet head with the towel, draped another one around her own shoulders, and leaned over the sink. "You do my hair."

During the process, Miriam explained that enough dried black walnut hulls had been discarded on the cellar floor or were still attached to the uncleaned shells to extract the natural hair dye. When Chantal finished and wrapped up Miriam's hair, they both stepped outside into the cool, sunny day. "We have to dry our hair in the sun," Miriam said, taking off the towel, leaning over, and shaking her hair, careful not to stain her clothes.

As Gilou rode up on his bike, a stiff late afternoon breeze was rustled the grassy fields behind the Garniers' farmhouse. Red-faced and out of breath, he removed his flat cap and scraped off his feet before entering the kitchen, where everyone waited in anxious silence to hear his plan. Miriam and Chantal, their hair now black and dry and tied up in tight buns, stood as far apart as possible.

"These are for you," Gilou said, handing Miriam transport papers for each child and an official-looking document. "It says you are transporting the children to one of the tuberculosis sanatoriums in Saint-Hilaire-du-Touvet near

Grenoble, which means you would have to switch trains in Lyon. There you will be met by someone. We leave soon." Pointing to Rogers, Chantal, and Obasi, he said, "I will return and take you three to the bus station. Together, we will take a bus tonight to Sens, a local train to Dijon, and then to Lyon."

"What about us?" Maduro said about himself, Nidal, and Cookie.

"A passeur will take you to the train station tomorrow morning for another train to Lyon," Gilou said, wiping his brow with a ragged handkerchief. "This way, there will be a French speaker with each party. And we can regroup in Lyon and plan the next stage for Spain."

"But they will be looking for a Red Cross nurse," Maduro said.

"Not with six children who are ill with tuberculosis, Father," Miriam said, holding up a sign Gilou had brought with him for her to position in the railcar's window. It explained to other passengers that ill children were aboard and should be avoided.

"But the bairns look in rude health to me," Cookie said, tossing the youngest boy in the air, much to the child's delight. "See? The babies look ruddy... not a bit sick."

"They will," Miriam said.

"I don't like you traveling alone," Rogers said.

"I know what I'm doing," she said, brushing past him to the children. "I will tell them we are playing a game." She had them sit in front of her to watch as she dabbed the ashes in the bowl on her cheeks and forehead, giving her skin a gray pallor.

After opening the canning jar with the gooey peppermint concoction, she passed it around for them to smell and then rubbed a little under her own eyes with a piece from the cut-up sheet. Pretending to be sick, Miriam sneezed and coughed into the rag, making the children snicker. One by one, the children squirmed as Miriam applied the goo under their eyes and patted ashes on their faces.

But the eldest, a freckle-faced boy around twelve, refused the make-over, turning his back and shaking his head. "*No, ça pue,*" he said, holding his nose. Miriam spoke to him in soft, gentle tones and finally convinced him to turn around so she could apply the peppermint mixture under his nose. He immediately teared up.

"*Très bien*, Rémy," Miriam said. Now that the crisis had passed, she handed each child a blood-speckled rag and had them practice coughing into it when she winked at him or her. "The Germans are terrified of tuberculosis, with its bloody coughs," she explained to the adults, watching dumbfounded. The children enjoyed the game immensely, mugging for each other and laughing. That stopped when Miriam shushed them with a dramatic frown, which the children comically imitated.

"I do believe they are ready," she said to Gilou. She returned to the cutting board and chopped the onion into large chunks, wrapped them in a rag, and stuffed it into her jacket pocket.

"What's the onion for, lass? Teatime?" Cookie said.

"Back-up for the menthol. If need be, I can open the rag, put it under their noses, and make them tear up," Miriam said.

"I doubt they'll need it," Rogers said. "They look terrible." He ushered Miriam outside by the arm. "Look, there is nothing between me and Chantal. I didn't travel halfway around the world and risk everything just to throw it all away for the first floozie who made a pass at me," he said, holding her shoulders with both hands and staring into her red, puffy eyes. "The day we rescued you was the happiest of my life. I don't want to lose you again. I love you, Miriam. Don't you see?"

Real tears rolled down Miriam's ashen cheeks and quivering chin as she wrapped her arms around Rogers. "I love you, too. I am sorry. The things I have been through...you cannot imagine how they have changed me. They have made me suspicious of everyone and everything. And I have become... *hardvochtig*...how do you say? With a hard heart. Will you forgive me?"

"You never have to ask that," Rogers whispered, tearing up. "I understand, and I will always be on your side. But I can't bear to let you out of my sight. I should travel with you."

"No, Gilou is right. I must go alone with the children. But we will be together again. I promise."

"We must leave now. The ambulance is here," Gilou said, standing in the doorway.

Miriam kissed Rogers one last time and loaded the children into the ambulance for the short ride to the train station. Gilou followed on his bicycle.

☆☆☆

After a restless night in a third-rate boarding house near the Villeneuve-Saint-Georges train station, an exhausted Janssen refused to abandon the hunt. He had stayed at the station until the last overnight train from Paris to Lyon had come and gone, checking out women's faces a little too closely for the local gendarmes, who demanded his papers and warned him about harassing passengers. Now, he puffed on a cigarette and, in the brisk morning air, paced on the cobblestoned street outside the three-story station.

A familiar black Citroën Traction Avant screeched to a halt in front. Loutrel hopped out and strutted toward the station, stopping to talk to two French gendarmes before heading inside. Janssen stubbed out his cigarette with his shoe and followed him in. "I thought you had had enough," Janssen said when he caught up with the dapper gangster, who was wearing his Borsalino hat at a cocky angle on his head.

"I reconsidered," said Loutrel, whose bloodshot eyes and alcoholic breath made clear he, too, had had a long night. "Are you sure you can recognize her?"

"Yes."

"Good. Then we will wait together. I can be of some help," he said, opening his suit coat to reveal his holstered Walther P.38 pistol. "And I've made sure the gendarmes are prepared to help." They found seats on a bench facing the entrance and waited.

Loutrel fidgeted, tapped his foot, and jumped up to pace up and down the hall, checking out faces. A predator in constant motion, he stopped cold at a window. Outside, a Red Cross nurse was unloading children from an ambulance and herded them inside, holding hands and walking toward the train platform. All were using rag masks to cover their mouths and noses.

"*Schnell, schnell!*" Miriam said in a harsh tone to speed the children along.

Loutrel caught Janssen's eye and tilted his head toward her. Janssen leaped up and said, "That's her. Let's go."

Much to Janssen's surprise, Loutrel grabbed his arm and spun him around.

"How can you be sure? She has black hair, not red. And the sick children ..." Janssen hesitated.

"Plus," Loutrel said, "I don't see an African or Arab with her."

"From what I could tell from this distance, I'm pretty sure," Janssen said, yanking his arm free from the smaller man. "Let's stop her so I can get a better look."

Instead of agreeing or joining him, Loutrell motioned to the two gendarmes he had spoken to earlier. Their high leather boots clicked on the floor as they approached and unsnapped their holsters.

"Papers, please," said one of the gendarmes, who had a thick mustache and a single stripe on his sleeve, indicating he was a sub-lieutenant.

"I'm a consultant for the Dutch police, and I'm convinced that I spotted a fugitive Jew who's a cop killer," Janssen said, flashing his ID and the GFP pass from Brosan while swatting the officers aside to chase Miriam.

"Halt!" the gendarmes shouted in unison. When Janssen froze and slowly turned around, he found himself staring down the barrels of two drawn MAB Type C pistols. The junior gendarme frisked Janssen, finding his Walther PPK and holding it up for his superior to see.

"Do you have a Waffenschein for this?" the sub-lieutenant asked, referring to a gun permit.

With fire in his eyes, Janssen shook his head.

"Come with us," the officer said, pulling out handcuffs, which he sheepishly reattached to his belt when it became obvious that he couldn't handcuff a one-armed man.

"But I told you. I'm with the police!" Janssen yelled. "Look at the GFP pass, damn—"

The junior gendarme smashed his pistol into Janssen's jaw, staggering the giant. After regaining his balance, Janssen rubbed the blood off his chin and looked to Loutrel for help. It didn't come. "What? Are you double-crossing me? Your boss said he didn't want the reward."

"My boss may not need the money, but I have gambling debts and several expensive girlfriends, and, well, you see my point, mate," Loutrel said, stepping back and out of Janssen's reach.

"Then we can split the 15,000 guilders, you and me, if we capture her now."

"Oh, no. That won't do," Loutrel said, wagging his finger at Janssen. "Imagine how much more the Germans will pay to roll up an entire escape line, something I can do for them by simply following her for a few days."

"She's getting away!" Janssen yelled at the gendarmes. "And that will be on your heads, I promise."

"Now, who do you suppose they fear more: you or me and the Carlingue?" Loutrel said with a smirk. He shook the gendarmes' hands, which Janssen could see was Loutrel's way of passing them several hundred francs. "Gentlemen, this foreigner has fake papers and an illegal weapon. He's all yours."

They thanked him and dragged the furious Janssen away.

Humming a show tune, Loutrel lit a Gauloises Bleu cigarette and ambled toward the platform for the Lyon-bound train, where Miriam waited with the children.

CHAPTER 26

With iron wheels screeching, the train to Lyon juddered to a stop, smoke pouring out of its chimney, clouds of steam hissing from underneath. A *contrôleur*, or conductor, in a dark blue uniform jacket and flat-brimmed cap, led Miriam, in her nurse's uniform and field cap, and the masked children to the rear of a dark green SNCF third-class passenger car, where he seated them on facing wooden benches. Miriam stuffed the two-sided warning sign in the bottom of the window frame and took a seat facing the engine.

She had warned the children that she must pretend to be a real, imperious German as part of the game to fool the Nazis. She winked at Rémy to cough. He ignored her. Trying not to show her exasperation, Miriam winked at another one of the boys, who erupted in a symphony of coughing and wheezing, drawing giggles from some of the others and a disapproving stare from Miriam.

Once the children calmed down, a stern-faced SS-*Untersturmführer,* accompanied by an armed soldier, entered the crowded car and worked his way down the aisle, checking papers. Miriam snapped to attention and clicked her heels with a stiff-arm Nazi salute. "Heil Hitler!" she shouted, waving her other hand for the children to do the same. All of them followed suit.

All except Rémy. He refused to stand, crossing his arms across his chest and sticking out his lower lip in defiance. Without hesitation, Miriam slapped him hard, knocking his mask askew, and screamed at him in German and French to stand and show respect.

The stunned child, rubbing his cheek with real tears streaming down it, staggered to his feet and half-heartedly saluted the soldiers. "Heil Hitler," he mumbled, collapsing into his seat and staring daggers at Miriam. She felt terrible but couldn't allow herself to show it.

After enthusiastically returning the salute, the two soldiers ignored the other passengers and marched straight to Miriam. The second lieutenant, breaking into a polite smile, held out a green pack of German-brand Jan Maat cigarettes. "Cigarette, *Fräulein?*"

"Danke, Untersturmführer," Miriam said, taking a cigarette and leaning in for the officer to light it. She inhaled deeply, blew the smoke out slowly, and picked tobacco pieces off her tongue as if she had been smoking all her life— at the SOE Finishing School at Lord Montagu's Beaulieu Estate in England, she had been trained to smoke.

Over the officer's shoulder, Miriam caught a matronly Frenchwoman staring at her cigarette with longing; French women did not receive any cigarette rations and rarely smoked in public.

"Here are the transportation orders for the Jews," Miriam said to the officer. "I am taking them to a tuberculosis sanatorium. Please do not come too close."

Stepping back with furrowed brow, the officer looked over the children with their red eyes and ashen, mask-covered faces before glancing at Miriam's orders and holding them out to her. He leaned in and extended his arm, looking closer at her bloodshot eyes and pallid complexion.

Miriam blew out a stream of smoke and slid into the aisle to exchange the transportation order for her voluntary nurse's ID, a blue-gray booklet with a red cross, a Nazi eagle, and the word *Bermendungsbuch*, indicating it was a record of her activities.

The officer flipped through the pages without taking time to inspect them and returned the booklet. "Heil Hitler," he said, clicking his heels with a curt head bow before moving quickly to inspect the other passengers' documents.

Miriam and the children saluted and plopped down. Feeling a weight lifted off her shoulders, Miriam wrinkled her nose at the onion fumes wafting from her jacket pocket. She felt miserable that she couldn't somehow comfort the children. But she had to remain in character. *It truly is for their benefit.* Ironically, their escape was on a railway line once owned by PLM and financed by the Rothschilds and the Pereires, two distinguished Jewish families, one Ashkenazi and the other Sephardic.

Black smoke and sparkling embers from the engine streamed by the window as the train rumbled out of the station. Lost in thought, Miriam caught a glimpse of a disturbing reflection amid the fire show outside: a man in a dark, tailored suit and hat at the far end of the rail car was staring at her. When she faced forward for a better look, he tipped his Borsalino hat with a greasy smile. His jet-black vampire eyes were so intense a shiver shot up Miriam's spine.

Despite the seriousness of their situation, Rogers had to laugh when they arrived at the bus station for the trip to Sens, some 100 kilometers to the southeast.

"What do you find funny?" Chantal asked, wrapping her arm around his as if they were a couple about to embark on a vacation together.

"There," he said, freeing his arm to point at the bus. "It looks like it has a rubber mattress on top. What is that?"

"Shhh," Gilou whispered to Rogers. "You must not speak English."

With Obasi in tow, they all boarded the bus, which didn't have a mattress on the length of its roof but a four-foot-tall silk bag that had been soaked in rubber and filled with what Gilou told Rogers was "town gas," a fuel derived from processing coal for coke. Rubber straps and metal hooks secured it to a rack on the roof. It took almost four hours to make the trip because, to preserve fuel and prevent the wind from ripping off the gas bag, the bus wheezed along no faster than 50 kmh. It also made frequent stops to refuel, avoided steep hills, and traveled a circuitous route to dodge low bridges.

Once in Sens, they wended separately behind Gilou through the first-century BC town known to Julius Caesar as Agedincum. It's also where Pope Alexander III and Thomas Becket, Archbishop of Canterbury, took refuge together. To get to the Gare de Sens, they passed by the Cathédrale Saint-Étienne de Sens, with its single tower topped by a campanile, the first Gothic cathedral in France, as well as the marriage site for Louis IX.

The Gare de Sens, still in some disrepair from the German invasion, was bustling with activity by the railway workers. Road maintenance crews, uniformly dressed in brown cotton moleskin pants and dirty shirts, hustled about, some lubricating the iron wheels with long spout oil cans; a security chief tapped the axels with a hammer and rubbed his hands over them to be sure they weren't loose or overheating. Still others unloaded canvas sacks from the mail car or wheeled away luggage and packages on carts and dollies. The engineer and a coal stoker called a driver leaned out of the engine's cab, goggles propped on top of their stiff-brimmed caps, waiting for the station master to blow his whistle, clearing the train for departure.

Few gendarmes or Germans were around, so getting on the train for Dijon was uneventful. When they found their second-class compartment, Chantal slipped down beside Rogers and leaned her head on his shoulder, making Rogers squirm. Gilou and Obasi, sitting opposite them, frowned.

A middle-aged couple joined them, sat facing each other, and never stopped talking. The man sitting next to Rogers elbowed him and howled with laughter, waiting for a reaction to what must have been a funny story. Raising his voice, the man gestured wildly at Rogers in apparent disbelief that he didn't find the joke funny.

Not knowing what to do and afraid of being discovered as an American fugitive if he spoke, Rogers stared at his feet. An uneasy silence filled the compartment. With a smile, Chantal said something to the man, grasped Rogers' head with both hands, and kissed him, refusing to let up. Relieved at his rescue yet embarrassed at his predicament, Rogers let Chantal behave like they were lovers, too engrossed with each other for conversation the entire trip. Gilou kept the middle-aged couple occupied by listening to their endless tales and asking questions. Obasi fell sound asleep.

By the time Miriam's train arrived at Lyon's Gare de Perrache, the children were cold, hungry, and exhausted from the painfully slow trip on the swaying and rattling train. Once all the other passengers had exited, Miriam dabbed more peppermint goo under the children's eyes, made them inhale onion fumes, and told them to remove their masks and cough every so often into the blood-spattered rags. When soldiers or gendarmes saw those hacking children with bloodshot, dark-rimmed eyes and the warning sign under Miriam's arm, they backed away and let them all pass without inspecting their documents.

As they crossed the platform, Miriam scanned the crowd, her body growing more tense by the minute when no one approached her to guide them on the next part of their journey. Not knowing what else to do, she marched the children in a row out of the station.

A matronly woman in a Red Cross nurse's uniform greeted Miriam like an old friend with a hug and kisses on both cheeks. "Gilou *dit bonjour*," the nurse whispered in Miriam's ear. She explained in French that she hadn't waited on the platform because she would have had to pay a fee and would have been too conspicuous standing there.

Since their next train didn't leave until the following morning, the nurse said she would lead them to a place to spend the night farther north in the Presqu'île neighborhood, the peninsula where the station was located between the Saône and Rhône rivers.

Miriam carried the youngest girl, who wrapped her arms around Miriam's neck. Holding hands with the children as a group, the nurse led them away from the station. They passed the grandiose Hôtel Terminus to their left, built by the Jewish-financed PLM and recently commandeered for Gestapo headquarters. "If anyone asks, tell them we are taking the children to see doctors at the Hôtel-Dieu de Lyon," the nurse said under her breath, referring to Lyon's historic hospital.

All along the way, Miriam stopped and twisted around without warning or slowed down to check reflections in store windows to ensure they weren't being followed by the man from the train in the Borsalino hat, or by anyone else. After twenty minutes, they arrived at Place Bellecour, the center of historic Lyon and one of the largest pedestrian squares in Europe. "Wait here," the nurse said. "They look exhausted. I will find some food while they rest. They must be starving."

Miriam led the children to a row of trees on the edge of the square and had them sit together on benches facing a bronze statue of Louis XIV in the middle of the square. The six-story-tall monument depicted the Sun King as a Roman emperor on a horse without saddle or stirrups. Nearby rose the grandiose wings and dome of the Hôtel-Dieu de Lyon. Trying not to look nervous, Miriam smiled and nodded politely at a group of passing pro-Vichy students wearing the *francisque*, the symbol of the regime with a tricolor ax and fasces.

When the nurse returned, she handed Miriam and each child a piece of bread and some cheese. "It is not much, but it is the best I can do here."

It didn't take long for the food to be devoured by the famished children, who whined for more.

"There will be food when we reach our destination," the nurse said. "Come."

They continued heading north, passing the hospital, and walking for half an hour until they stopped outside a textile shop at 13 Rue du Griffon, where a dark-haired man with a jutting jaw, wide mouth, and thick-rimmed glasses paced. "This is Monsieur Segers," the nurse said. "He will lead you to a safe house." She turned on her heels and hurried away.

Without a word, Segers picked up one of the young boys, who seemed too tired to continue, and led everyone around the corner into a rowhouse. Miriam scouted down the hallways for a possible escape route on the way up to the third floor, where a haggard middle-aged woman let them into a small apartment.

"How long?" she asked Segers.

"Marcel will come and stay here tonight and take the children on the train to Annecy first thing in the morning. I will send my secretary to help prepare the children."

"I cannot go with them," Miriam said in French. "I must return to England."

Segers shocked her when he replied in Dutch, "You couldn't go with them even if you wanted to. The Swiss rarely allow entry for what they call 'racial refugees.' You will stay here until the rest of your convoy arrives."

"You are Dutch?"

"Yes. But I was born in Brussels and grew up in Switzerland," he said with a toothy grin, pulling her aside and continuing to speak Dutch. "That is why my Dutch is not as good as my French, I am sorry to say. And that is why I do not fear that you will reveal our secrets if you are caught...Miriam." Her eyes widened at the mention of her name, the one attached to a huge reward she feared few could resist. "Your secret is safe with me."

"Thank you"

"Don't thank me yet. I have a dangerous favor to ask of you."

"Anything."

He handed her a small tube of toothpaste. "Deliver it to the SOE as soon as you arrive in England. You have a right to know that it contains microfilm with critical military intelligence. If you arc caught, you will be shot."

"If the Germans get their hands on me, I will be shot, microfilm, or not. *Your* secret is safe with me," she said, stuffing the tube into her purse. "How will we escape?"

"Once all the members of your convoy arrive, we will try to get you to Toulouse and then over the Pyrenees into Spain."

That route through the heart of Vichy France, Miriam knew from her SOE training, had become even more dangerous by two recent events: the German occupation of Lyon and all of Vichy's so-called Free Zone in southwestern France; and the creation of a new paramilitary force to hunt Jews and résistants known as *la Milice*, a feared band of thugs who used torture and summary executions in a reign of terror.

Shaking his head, Segers said France's total descent into fascism seemed unthinkable at the beginning of the war. Now, France's famous motto extolling individual rights, "*Liberté, Égalité, Fraternité*," was debased to the more authoritarian one of "*Travail, famille, patrie*," meaning "Work, family, fatherland," often mocked as "*Trahison, Famine, Prison,*" or "Treason, Famine, Prison."

For many demoralized French men and women, if not most, Segers said, it was a time to keep their heads down, to not get involved, to do what was necessary to survive; a time they themselves called "*le temps des autruches,*"— "the time of the ostriches."

CHAPTER 27

A lanky teenage boy arrived that night carrying a battered suitcase and, as Miriam and the children gawked, set up a workspace on the kitchen table, which he covered with blank documents and the typical forger's tools: stamps, pens, acetone bottles, and razor blades. With a goofy grin, he curled his long, slender index finger to urge the children to come closer. "Who is the oldest?" he said.

Rémy raised his hand.

"Please sit and give me your identification card."

Rémy glared at him suspiciously and didn't move.

"Do not worry. My name is Marcel, and I am going to be your friend." With that, he made a funny face, crossing his twinkling brown eyes at his prominent nose.

The children tittered, but Rémy remained standoffish.

"Very well. I see I'll have to use force," Marcel said with an exaggerated frown. He hopped up, raked his fingers through his curly hair, and rummaged around inside his suitcase, moving his head from side to side as if hunting for something of great importance.

"No," Rémy said, stepping back and sticking his chest out like a tough guy in the movies.

"Ah, here it is," Marcel said, pulling hand-over-hand to reel an imaginary rope out of his bag, all the while making more funny, wide-eyed faces, tilting his head in confusion, and sticking out his tongue. When he whirled the imaginary rope over his head and flung it to lasso Rémy, Miriam and all the children erupted in boisterous laughter.

Unable to resist the game, Rémy chuckled and pretended to be caught, stepping closer every time Marcel tugged the imaginary rope. Eventually, he collapsed into a seat facing Marcel.

Working almost non-stop for several hours, Marcel created fake papers for each child. None included the usual word "*Juif*" in red letters. Meanwhile, he continued to clown around and got the youngsters to relax and forget about their troubles for a while.

"You are quite talented. And funny," Miriam said to Marcel after he had finished with the last child.

"It seems to calm them down," he said, stuffing his tools in his suitcase.

"How did you learn that?" she said, taking a seat across from him.

"The forgery or the comedy?"

"Both."

"When I was young, my parents took me to the cinema to see Charlie Chaplin movies. I was enchanted and knew at that moment that I wanted to be a mime. I painted on a mustache and wore my father's pants, trying to imitate him." He paused to take a deep breath before continuing. "After the Germans invaded, my family fled from Strasburg to Limoges. I studied ceramics and art for a while, but my brother and I wanted to do something for the resistance. So, our cousin in Paris got us involved with *Oeuvre de Secours aux Enfants* to help lead Jewish children to safety."

"You are Jewish?" Miriam said, jerking her head back in amazement. "How have you survived?"

"I am a very good forger. My documents say I am Protestant and seventeen years old, too young for the military or compulsory service in Germany."

"Why are you in Lyon?"

"To help a friend who needed help in a hurry."

The children clamored for Marcel to entertain them in front of the fire.

"*Excusez moi, mademoiselle*, but my audience demands an encore." He made a dramatic bow to Miriam and waddled like Charlie Chaplin, twirling an imaginary cane as the children giggled.

Miriam watched transfixed as Marcel performed silent skits; one as a hapless hunter trying in vain to net elusive butterflies, his eyes jittering around wildly as if overwhelmed. In another skit, he was a prisoner using his enormous hands to press against the walls of a relentlessly shrinking box closing in on him and squashing him to the ground. The glorious performance ended all too soon.

The following morning, as the children ate a meager breakfast of bowls of barley with bits of carrots and small chunks of stale bread, the messenger from Monsieur Segers arrived. The young woman wore a sweater over a round-collared shirt, a jacket with padded shoulders, and a short, pleated skirt that made her appear to be a schoolgirl. She carried a bulky canvas duffle bag. "I am Raymonde," she said. "Where is Marcel?"

As if on cue, he stepped out of a bedroom. Miriam's jaw dropped at the sight of Marcel in a Boy Scout troop leader's uniform: a flat blue beret, a light blue shirt, a red and blue neckerchief, shorts, knee socks, and boots.

"*Voilà*. We are going on a hiking trip," Marcel said with a flourish, giving a two-finger salute.

The children clapped and jumped for joy as Raymonde pulled out similar uniforms from her bag for the boys and girls, holding them up to see which would fit each one.

As Raymonde helped the children try on the uniforms, Marcel called Miriam into the kitchen. "We must make sandwiches for the trip. You can cut the baguettes while I prepare the ID cards."

Miriam did as he asked but stopped mid-saw when Marcel wrapped an ID card in waxed paper and slathered it with mayonnaise.

"What are you doing?"

"They will need their real papers once they arrive in Switzerland," he said. Miriam didn't seem to understand, so he cut two slices of a baguette, stuffed a mayonnaise-wrapped ID inside, added cheese slices, and rolled the sandwich up in more waxed paper. "The German soldiers will never look inside. They are afraid of getting mayonnaise on their uniforms because those oily stains are almost impossible to remove."

He laughed so hard that Miriam couldn't help but join in. The very thought of the big, bad Nazis being undone by a gooey sandwich was hysterical.

Once everything was ready, Miriam hugged and kissed the children. Rémy refused to come close, apparently still angry about the slap. Miriam knelt in front of him. "I am a Jew like you. I hope you can forgive me someday. I did what I did to save your life." She stretched out her arms, tears slipping from the corner of her eye. "Please."

Refusing to look at her, Rémy let Miriam take his lowered head in her hands and kiss him on the forehead before breaking away to join the other children.

Marcel shook his head but said nothing and led the children away. Before Miriam could close the door, Rémy scampered back and hugged her tight, tears rolling down his cheeks. "Thank you," he said, trembling. "I am so afraid."

"Can I tell you a secret?" Miriam whispered in his ear.

Rémy nodded.

"I am always afraid, too."

"Really?" he said, eyes wide in disbelief.

"I only pretend to be brave. But you need not worry. Your troop leader is truly brave and will keep you safe."

And then they were all gone. No more laughter, silly faces, or excited chatter; only the gloom, dread, and anxiety that had been Miriam's constant companion. "What will he do with them?" she asked Raymonde, dabbing her eyes with a handkerchief.

"Monsieur Segers has a shop selling silk goods in Annecy where Marcel can hide them until it is safe to travel by bus toward Collonges-sous-Salève near Geneva. There is a Seventh-day Adventist seminary in the hills near there where Segers' father taught. Its members will sneak the children across the border, where they will be placed with several families."

Miriam wandered over to the window to watch the children marching in a line behind Marcel, all high-stepping and arms swinging. She could almost hear the laughter. Then her heart skipped a beat. The man from the train wearing the Borsalino leaned on a building, smoking a cigarette. "We are being followed," she said, pointing across the street at Loutrel. "He was in our train car. Now, we cannot go to the station for the others."

Raymonde gasped. "We must leave immediately. There is a back way out."

Continuing to stare out the window, Miriam mulled something over in her mind. She yanked her head back when Loutrel gazed up at the building's upper floors. "Why is he watching instead of doing something?"

"Please," Raymonde said. "We must leave. Now. It is not safe. The Germans could be here any minute." With a tinge of fear in her voice, she tugged Miriam's arm.

"Why did they not come last night? Or this morning?" Miriam said.

"What difference does it make?"

"It means he is not looking for me alone. He must want me to lead him to more résistants for a bigger reward."

"Oh, I see," Raymonde said. "In that case, I have an idea."

The two women sauntered out the building's entrance, arm-in-arm, gaily talking as if they hadn't a care in the world. Raymonde's wooden sandals clicked on the sidewalk as they headed west instead of south toward the station. Loutrel's ominous reflection in store windows floated close behind.

After a few minutes, they came to the Passerelle Saint Vincent footbridge over the Saône near the Église Saint-Paul, a Romanesque- and Gothic-style cathedral with an iconic tower lantern. "We are in luck. No guards today," Raymonde said. "The man following us will have to hang back until we have crossed the river. Otherwise, he would be too obvious on such a narrow bridge."

"Good idea," Miriam said, looking at Raymonde with a newfound respect for her cleverness. On the other side of the river, they turned left down a wide, tree-lined sidewalk along the Saône and continued for about ten minutes until they reached the imposing stone Court of Appeals building. There, they veered right suddenly onto the narrow Rue du Palais de Justice and picked up their pace.

At the end of the block, they dashed left where the street dead-ended at Rue Saint-Jean. With a furtive glance over her shoulder, Raymonde pulled Miriam faster, almost running, and stopped at Number 54, which had a green wooden door and an ornate iron transom. She twisted the doorknob, made sure they weren't being followed, and dragged Miriam into the narrow, arch-roofed corridor, closing the door behind them without a sound.

"Where are we?" Miriam said, blinking her eyes to adjust to the dim passageway.

"La Longue Traboule," Raymonde whispered, explaining that the word traboule derives from the Latin *"trans-ambulare,"* meaning to pass through or to cross. She said La Longue Traboule was one of hundreds of hidden passageways built in Lyon around the fourth century. They were designed to provide residents with easier access to freshwater than the winding streets. In the nineteenth century, Raymonde said, thousands of silk workers known as *canuts* used this particular traboule, the city's longest, and others as hiding places during their bloody revolts over pay and working conditions. Now, they came in handy for resistance members desperate to evade capture.

After stripping off her clunky sandals, Raymond hurried Miriam down unlit, musty corridors, under four buildings, and across five courtyards surrounded by four stories of balconies, then past a spiral stone staircase before emerging into the sunlight on Rue du Boeuf. "Even if he finds the door, he won't know how to follow us," Raymonde said, slipping her sandals back on.

"But we have to go to Gare de Perrache to meet the others," Miriam said.

"Me. Not you. I have another place for you to hide near here, and I will go to the station."

"But how will you recognize them?"

"Don't worry. I know Gilou."

☆ ☆ ☆

Janssen's swollen black and blue jaw still throbbed when he emerged from the train in Gare de Perrache. It had taken the gendarmes at Villeneuve-Saint-Georges several hours to get in touch with Inspektor Brosan at GFP headquarters in Brussels. Once he verified Janssen's identity and his authority to pursue Jewish criminals, the gendarmes freed him—with no apology. It was too late to catch another train, and the boarding house he had stayed in the night before had no vacancies. So, he spent a miserable night on a bench in the frigid, smelly train station.

Now, he was ready to kill Loutrel. Only, he couldn't. Nor could he beat up the gangster to within an inch of his life. That would be easy. No, if he did anything so obvious, the Carlingue would hunt him down. Still, he was determined to find Loutrel and make him suffer in one way or another. *But how?*

He couldn't be sure that Miriam got off at Lyon or that Loutrel hadn't already captured her. All he could do was go with his instincts, and they told him Lyon was Miriam's most likely stop. After all, Janssen had heard, it was not only a hotbed of resistance, but also the railroad crossroads for the various escape lines smuggling fugitives east to Switzerland or southwest to Spain via

Toulouse.

So, here he was in Lyon, one of the biggest cities in France, on what was turning out to be a fool's errand, with him being the fool. He had no choice but to wait outside at a nearby café, where he could observe the station's entrance, smoking and sipping lousy-tasting Café Pétain—coffee from roasted acorn or barley—while browsing *Je Suis Partout,* Vichy's largest circulation newspaper called "I am Everywhere" in English. Janssen laughed to himself, knowing that French partisans often mocked it as "*Je Chie Partout,*" meaning "I shit everywhere." It was edited by Pierre-Antoine Cousteau, a virulent anti-Semite and fascist whose younger brother Jacques-Yves had recently released the first French underwater documentary to much acclaim.

Scanning every man and woman was as tedious as watching individual grains of sand slip through the narrow neck of an hourglass, but necessary because it was the one place anyone coming to or leaving the city would have to pass through.

Shouting voices distracted him. Scowling, he looked around to find the source: two teenagers were picking on a young boy who appeared to be about the same age as Janssen's son Stefan. They goaded and shoved the boy, who was half their size. But rather than back down, he held his ground and, raising his fists, taunted the teenagers with obscenities. Baring his teeth in righteous anger, the bigger teenager punched the boy's chin, knocking him to the ground.

As the smaller boy rose, his hands curled into fists, the bigger teenager laughed, then cocked his right fist to throw another punch at the scrappy pipsqueak. A massive hand grabbed his arm in mid-swing and twisted it behind his back. He screamed in pain at the crack of his arm breaking. Janssen tossed the howling teenager to the ground and glared at his companion, who, in wide-eyed terror, was petrified.

"Take your friend and never come back," Janssen said. "And, never, I mean never, pick on someone smaller than you again. If you do, know that I will find you and rip out both of your arms."

A puddle spread around the teenager's feet as he lost bladder control while helping his friend to his feet. Together, they fled. Janssen pulled out a ten franc note and handed it to the boy, who held back, skittish as a fox sensing a trap.

"Buy some food, kid. I hate bullies," Janssen said, oblivious to the irony of a bully saying that. "And next time, keep both of your fists up high."

The boy snatched the money and ran off without a merci.

As soon as Janssen returned to his seat at the café table, he got lucky. A man leaving the station with a woman on his arm seemed out of place. He was too tall, his face too full, his pace too broad to be a Frenchman. *He must be an American.* And there was an African farther back, following him. The man and woman passed right by him.

The woman wasn't Miriam, but he had seen the man before, and de Bloedhond never forgot a face. *He is one of the monks at the Utrecht train station.* Janssen flipped up the folded paper to cover his face because he knew they had seen him at the Brussels station during the shooting. Looking around to be sure Loutrel wasn't doing the same thing as he was, Janssen followed the American at a distance.

As he progressed north, the American appeared to be following another woman. Janssen's hunch was confirmed when the woman turned onto the Pont Saint-Georges, a footbridge suspended over the Saône on cables hung from metal poles in the shape of silk weavers' shuttles. Her flock—the American with the other woman and the African—trailed behind.

When they were halfway across, Janssen tagged along, ducking his head, hunched over, his hand behind his back as if in deep thought, but actually trying to hide his massive frame by bending down behind other pedestrians.

The flock continued north and appeared to be going toward the neo-Byzantine Notre-Dame de Fourvière basilica high above the city on "the hill that prays," a nickname derived from all the churches and religious communities there. Its four rook-like corner towers made it resemble an upside-down elephant with long, needle-like spires sticking out of its feet.

Coming to an abrupt stop, the woman spun around and flicked her head to the side, signaling for the flock to scatter into side streets. Janssen, unsure what was happening, ducked into a doorway and peeked out, spotting what had spooked the flock: Loutrel, searching faces, questioning passersby, and tipping his Borsalino in thanks.

Now what? Janssen was torn about whom to follow but decided the flock was worth more to him. Besides, Loutrel wasn't likely to end his pursuit in the neighborhood anytime soon. So, when the gangster slipped around a corner, Janssen chased after the others.

He caught up with them on the narrow, cobblestoned Montée du Chemin Neuf in time to see the woman, the flock, and another man slip into a three-story ocher-colored building at Number 33 adjacent to a gated courtyard. He had them trapped now.

Unlike Loutrel, he didn't care who was helping them. The reward for Miriam would be plenty, but the first order of business was to make sure that he alone received the reward. Getting even would kill two birds with one stone.

Janssen retraced his steps to where he had last seen Loutrel and paced up and down the hilly streets, glancing around corners before proceeding in a grid pattern. It seemed impossible given the irregular-shaped city blocks, but it didn't take long. Loutrel hadn't gone far; in fact, he had stopped for a drink at an outside café. Janssen backed into an alley where he could watch Loutrel in the reflection of a shop window across the street.

After gulping down several glasses of wine, Loutrel paid his bill and resumed his hunt. He strode down a side street barely wide enough for a single car and stumbled downhill toward the river. Janssen jogged past the café, deftly stealing a thick walking stick from an elderly man dozing with his chin on his chest.

Hustling around the corner, Janssen snuck up on Loutrel and slammed the cane down on the gangster's head so hard it broke in half with a resounding crack. Like an expert thief, he patted down Loutrel, splayed in an oozing pool of blood on the street, and stripped him of his identification papers, expensive cigarette lighter and gun.

Having also snatched money from Loutrel's wallet, he threw the wallet down near the gangster's bleeding head, and placed the pistol beside Loutrel's hand as if he had dropped it. After making sure no one had seen him, Janssen sprinted into a nearby bakery and spoke in a panicked voice. "Some man has been beaten and robbed outside. You'd better call the gendarmes."

The baker hurried to the window and gasped. "Yes, yes, I will."

"You do that, and I'll see if I can help him," Janssen said, doing his best to sound concerned.

"Here, take this," the baker said, handing Janssen a dirty towel. "I can see blood."

Janssen thanked the baker and scurried away as fast as possible, tossing the towel over his shoulder. When the gendarmes arrived, they would find an unconscious man with an illegal gun and no identification papers, no travel permit, and no money. They might take him to the hospital, or, more likely, straight to jail, or turn him over to the Germans. It would take Loutrel a day or two to prove who he was—if he recovered consciousness. By that time, Janssen expected to be a wealthy man on his way to destinations unknown with Stefan.

All he needed was a little help raiding the building where the flock was roosting. And, as luck would have it, Janssen had become acquainted with the Gestapo's newly appointed head in Lyon when he was a young, up-and-coming SS-Obersturmführer in Amsterdam. The man loved to personally lead raids for Jews and résistants, so much so that he earned what Janssen felt was the perfect nickname since his promotion: "the Butcher of Lyon."

CHAPTER 28

When Rogers and the others entered the apartment, Miriam stopped staring out the window, watching for them and the man in the Borsalino, who thankfully hadn't returned, and raced to the door. She hugged Rogers and Obasi, thanked Gilou, and ignored Chantal. Raymonde conferred with Gilou. "We cannot use the train station again," Gilou said to the others.

"But my father and the others," Miriam said.

"The train from Villeneuve-Saint-Georges arrives soon," Gilou said. "I will meet it and bring them here. Then we can come up with another escape plan."

"Why can't we all go to the train station?" Rogers said.

"We were followed to our last safe house, and whoever it was may have alerted the Germans about her," Raymonde said, indicating Miriam.

"What? By whom?" Rogers said.

"A man who traveled on the same train as I and the children did," Miriam said. "I kept catching him staring at me with eyes that made me nervous. Then we saw him again this morning outside the safe house. He must have followed us. So, we had to sneak away to here."

"He may know what you look like," Rogers said to Miriam, "but he doesn't know me. So, I'm going to the station with Gilou."

"That is not necessary," Gilou said.

"I've already lost Solomon and Mr. Nidal once before. I'm not losing them or Cookie again," Rogers said.

☆☆☆

Repeatedly checking his expensive watch, tapping his feet, and sighing loudly, Janssen cooled his heels in the wood-paneled lobby of the Hôtel

Terminus. All around him, hobnail boots clicked on the marble floor as SS officers hustled about, passing plainclothes Gestapo agents in their long black leather coats huddled in whispered conversations; harried clerks, loaded down with papers and boxes, scurried after their officious-looking bosses in baggy suits.

Armed guards dragged in handcuffed prisoners, staggering and barely able to walk. The stench of their wounds and their fear intermingled with the sweet fragrance of the abundant bouquets in ceramic vases all around the lobby. It was a surprisingly busy place for a Sunday.

For the third time, Janssen sprang up and asked a young officer at the front desk about meeting the Gestapo commander. "Tell him who I am and why I'm here. He will want to see me immediately," Janssen said.

"Yes, you said that the last time," the officer said. "And, as I told you before, he is a very busy man."

"Show him this," Janssen said, pulling out the wanted flyer for Miriam. "Let him know she is in Lyon. And I know where."

The officer raised an eyebrow at the flyer and waved over a soldier. "Take this to the *Hauptsturmführer*, he said referring to the captain, then glared at Janssen until he returned to his seat.

Janssen didn't even have time to pull out a cigarette before the young officer returned with two soldiers, who frisked Janssen and confiscated his pistol. The officer said he would get it back later and escorted him into a palatial second-floor office. "Wait here," the officer said and hurried out of the room.

Studying the office, Janssen admired the tools of the trade: Leather-bound, weighted coshes resembling long blackjacks lined an antique desk along with whips, a spiked ball on a chain, pliers, needles, and screw-levered handcuffs. A moan startled him, making him spin around and instinctively reach for the gun in his empty holster. Across the room groaned a tied-up man in bloody clothes and a bandaged head sprawled on a chaise lounge.

"Where is she, Dries?" a young man with a pointed chin demanded as he flew in, waving the flyer in one hand and, in the other, holding a white-and-brown Persian cat close to his rumpled gray suit. After taking a seat behind the desk, he stroked the flat-faced cat, who "responded" with its perpetual frown.

"I can show you, Herr Hauptsturmführer, is it?" Janssen said.

"Congratulations on the promotion, Klaus."

The 29-year-old Klaus Barbie was a man on the move who not only knew Janssen but, in a way, had already crossed paths with Miriam and Rogers. Infamous for his cruelty yet famous for his efficiency, he had been at the heart of almost every German atrocity while stationed in Amsterdam. Barbie had personally captured Hermannus van Tongeren, Grand Master of the Freemasons in The Netherlands, who, unbeknownst to the Germans, had assisted his daughter Jacoba in creating the Group 2000 resistance group that later helped Rogers free Maduro.

After being transferred to Lyon in late 1942, Barbie further burnished his reputation for sadism. He hated the French, as did his alcoholic father, who was wounded at Verdun during World War One and forbade his son to study theology or pursue an academic career. Instead, he became a Nazi's Nazi.

The man on the chaise lounge moaned again through swollen lips, irritating Barbie, who gently released the cat from his lap, barreled over to the couch, and punched the man hard in his bleeding head. "I admire you, I really do," he said over the man's screams. "How many days has it been?" He retrieved a red document from his desk and held it an inch away from the semi-conscious man's eyes. "Fourteen days. See, right here is your signature on the *Schutzhaftbefehl*," he said, referring to the form the Gestapo cruelly required prisoners to sign requesting protective custody.

Blood trickled from the man's nose and he raised a single bloody hand as if to ward off more blows. All of his fingernails had been ripped out.

"Quite admirable to last this long. But, in the end, everybody talks." Barbie slapped the man's head, wiped off his hand with a handkerchief, and returned to his desk. "Now, tell me where we can find this terrorist," he said, holding up the flyer about Miriam.

"I believe she is in an apartment on Montée du Chemin Neuf," Janssen said.

"Believe?"

"I saw several people who were traveling with her enter the building. She must be there," he said, not mentioning Loutrel or the Carlingue's involvement. *No need to complicate things.*

With menacing pale green eyes, Barbie glared at Janssen. "I do not have enough men or time to act on a hunch, even one from de Bloedhond. We have more leads from *mouches* than we can handle right now," he said, using the French slang for informers. He picked up a stack of letters from his desk and waved them at Janssen. "And we get hundreds of these from *corbeaux* every day," he said, referring to the writers of anonymous denunciations.

"She is a Jew and a spy who killed three Grüne Polizei," Janssen said. "Isn't that worth at least checking out?"

Barbie leaned back, his head supported by clasped hands, and stared at the ceiling momentarily before picking up the phone on his desk. "Send in Francis André," he said.

Within seconds, the door opened, and a man rushed in as if he had been a puppy waiting outside the door for his master's call.

"Take Monsieur Janssen and two other men to search a building where he suspects a terrorist is hiding," Barbie said in perfect French. He pointed to the moaning prisoner. "And I don't want to see this idiot again. *Nacht und Nebel,*" he said, using the Wagnerian-sounding euphemism "night and fog" for the Nazi policy of making some prisoners disappear without a trace in clear violation of the Geneva Convention.

"Vernebelt," André replied, meaning the prisoner would be transformed into mist. Janssen snatched the flyer from Barbie's desk and followed André into a four-door, black Citroën Traction Avant. Two uniformed soldiers armed with MP-40 submachine guns sat staring straight ahead, emotionless, in the back seat.

As they drove away, Janssen tried not to gawk at André's grossly distorted face—a bulging left eye and a mouth slanting down at the left corner like a gaping wound under a thin mustache. There was no conversation until they parked on Montée du Chemin Neuf.

"Are you sure?" André said as they climbed out of the car and slammed the doors.

"Yes, Number 33, there," Janssen said.

The soldiers clasped their submachine guns at their waists, supported by leather straps around their shoulders. Janssen and André chambered a round into their pistols and snuck up on the entrance, keeping an eye on the building's windows for any sign of danger.

☆☆☆

"Oh, no!" said Raymonde, who had peeked out the window at the sound of closing car doors. "Germans!"

Miriam checked out the street. "I know the one-armed man. He was following us at the Brussels train station. What is he doing here? And who is with him?"

"*Gueule Tordue*. He is the worst of Barbie's collaborators," Raymonde said, pulling Miriam away from the window. "We have to leave." She darted to the door and called for Obasi and Chantal to hurry.

As the four of them skipped down the stairs, Miriam wondered why Raymonde called the man "twisted face," but she was not going to stay around long enough to find out. At the bottom of the stairs, Raymonde guided them into the next-door courtyard and through another traboule, where they passed sculpted corbels beneath dripstones, used three staircases, and traversed three courtyards before emerging into the sunlight on Montée du Gourguillon. They hurried south and then east toward the Saône.

"It will take them hours to search all the apartments and find the traboule," Raymonde said, picking up her pace.

"What about the captain?" Obasi whispered in English. "I will not leave him."

"He's right," Miriam said in French. "They will walk right into the trap if we don't warn them."

Raymonde paused, locked arms with Miriam, and strolled with a carefree air down the street. "I'm not sure what we can do," she whispered. "I don't know their route."

"Will they not have to take the same footbridge over the Saône as we did?"

"If it is not guarded. But there is another bridge they could use, Pont Kitchener-Marchand, near the station."

"When does the train arrive?"

"Soon," Raymonde said, glancing at her slim wristwatch.

"Then we will have to split up and watch both bridges."

"And how are we supposed to find each other again?" said Chantal, who had been eavesdropping.

Rolling her eyes, Miriam peered over her shoulder at Chantal and then at Raymonde. "Is there somewhere we could rendezvous this afternoon?"

Raymonde mulled over the question for a moment. "Yes, there is a safe house south of the station on Quai des Étroits. It runs along this side of the Saône. Number 7. It is easy to find. It is white and has seven stories. Let's meet there in the courtyard at, say, 3 p.m."

"With or without the others?" Chantal said.

"Yes," Raymonde said in a tone that brooked no dissent. She wrapped her arm through Chantal's arm. "You will come with me. You two go back to the Pont Saint-Georges. And try to be inconspicuous."

☆☆☆

Under his breath, Rogers asked Gilou, "Where are they?" They scoured the thinning crowd pouring out of Gare de Perrache. Gilou raised his hands, palms up, and rolled his shoulders. Most people had boarded electric trams or horse-drawn carriages. Others had trudged away, heads down, lugging bulky suitcases or dragging unruly children by the hand.

"It is dangerous to stay. Too many Germans. Something is wrong," Gilou said, watching soldiers and gendarmes stop almost everyone to check identifications. As Rogers stepped toward the station, Gilou clutched his arm. "They must have missed the train. We will come back tonight for the next one."

"No," Rogers said, tugging his arm free. "I will not leave them."

"*Est-ce votre bagage, monsieur?*" a man behind them said.

Not sure what he wanted, Rogers pretended he didn't hear and kept his eyes focused on the station. Gilou glanced over his shoulder and nudged Rogers. He flicked his eyes, directing Rogers to look behind them, where a blue-suited conductor pointed at a bag on a cart being wheeled along by two railway workers in their brown jackets and pants. Without raising his eyes, Rogers shook his head.

"I believe it is," the conductor said in English.

Rogers' heart raced. *What have I done to tip off the conductor? Should I run for it?* There were too many soldiers around to make a clean escape. He glanced out of the corner of his eye at Gilou, who had a strange expression, something between a grimace and a smile.

"It is safe, Captain," another voice behind him said in English with a distinct French accent, one he had heard many times before.

When Rogers turned, Nidal winked at him. Gilou shuffled away, and Nidal and Cookie resumed pushing the cart, trailed by Contrôleur Maduro, who dropped a suitcase at Rogers' feet. He picked it up, waited a few moments, then followed the others at a distance, with Gilou in the lead.

☆☆☆

Reading a copy of *Je Suis Partout,* Miriam lounged on a separate bench from Obasi at the Place de la Commanderie side of Église Saint-Georges, a neo-Gothic nineteenth-century church. From there, they had a clear view of the suspension footbridge across the Saône. Tied-up barges and smaller boats dotted the quays. Obasi was the first to spot Rogers and the others crossing the bridge. Standing to stretch and yawn, he motioned for Miriam to go ahead.

As she rose, a truck full of German soldiers screeched to a halt in front of the bridge. They piled out and split up, submachine guns and rifles at the ready. As one group rushed around the far side of the church, six soldiers jogged in formation toward Obasi and Miriam, both of them frozen in silent terror. Without so much as a glance, the soldiers hustled past her and rounded the corner to the front of the church.

Miriam sank back onto the bench and buried her head in the newspaper. Shouts and pounding boots filled the air. Miriam peeked over the paper. The truck blocked her view of the footbridge. Moments later, German soldiers dragged a priest and another man past Miriam and Obasi and threw them into the truck, which sped away, opening the view again for Miriam to the footbridge. Empty!

Trying not to appear panicked, Miriam signaled with her hand for Obasi to stay seated while she meandered toward the footbridge, pausing when she could peer around the rear of the church up and down Quai Fulchiron alongside the Saône. The ordinarily bustling thoroughfare was practically deserted.

Her stomach lurched. *Where had they gone? Had they turned around when they saw the Germans?* If not, the safe house was northwest of the footbridge, so Gilou most likely went north and then west. *But on what street?*

She waved for Obasi to follow and, scooting along as fast as she could without being obvious, made it to the other side of the church. Looking down Place François Bertras, she spotted someone who resembled Rogers turning the corner.

Miriam picked up her pace and veered right on Rue Sainte Georges, a winding one-lane street heading north uphill. Rogers roamed some distance up the hill, but she feared that calling out to him would draw too much attention to herself. Nidal was even farther ahead, following someone who walked like her father.

She wasn't sure how far they had to go to the safe house, but she suspected it wasn't much farther. Fighting the urge to run, she speed-walked up the hill and around several curves, closing in on Rogers but still too far away to catch his attention.

Obasi blew past her in a dead run. Ahead at Place de la Trinité was a street sign for Montée du Gourguillon, the street where their escape traboule had led them, the one where the Germans could be passing through at any minute. Rogers glanced backward at the sound of Obasi's pounding feet and smiled, then frowned in concern when his friend raced ahead without a word, passing Nidal and Maduro, arms pumping, and made a desperate vault to tackle Gilou as he was about to turn the corner.

Stunned, Gilou rolled over and opened his mouth to yell at the mugger, who covered his mouth with his black hand. Rogers, Miriam, and the others caught up with them and helped Gilou to his feet. Miriam peeped around the corner and jerked her head back. "Go, go, go," she whispered, her complexion turning white. "The one-armed man might have seen us. We have to get to the safe house near the train station. Now!"

☆☆☆

Janssen caught what he thought was a glimpse of someone's head jerking back out of sight from around the corner at the end of the street. "Who was that?" he asked André.

"Another one of your ghosts," André said, lighting a cigarette without offering one to Janssen. "We've wasted enough time. Are you coming?"

Unable to stomach the sight of André's hideous face any longer, Janssen kept his back to him and dismissed him with a flick of his enormous hand. "I'll walk."

"What shall I tell Hauptsturmführer Barbie?"

"You can tell him that the men I saw enter the building were no longer there. I don't know why. But I know they are with Miriam. And I will find her." He stormed off with an outward show of confidence he did not feel. He spied around the corner, but no one was on the street. Now, he had no idea how he would find her in a strange city. He only had one option: start all over at the train station.

☆☆☆

At the Pont Kitchener-Marchand, Gilou bid farewell and headed across the bridge to the station to catch a train home. Just south of the bridge, there were tears and hugs when Rogers and the others rendezvoused in the safe house's courtyard. Even Chantal seemed happy to see everyone. Miriam hugged her father and laughed. "When did you become a contrôleur?"

"Every boy's dream," Maduro said, taking off his hat and blue uniform jacket. "We couldn't go into the station because the Germans were out in force checking papers. One of the cheminots saw us and guessed we didn't have proper papers. He didn't ask why. But he snuck us into an office and outfitted us with the uniforms. He said no one ever checks railway workers. So, we followed him into the station, and he stashed us in the mail car."

Raymonde led them into an apartment, where she gave new clothes to Nidal and Cookie and a different jacket for Maduro so they wouldn't seem out of place in their railway uniforms. The men kept their Organization Todt armbands in their pockets in case they were stopped and had to produce their travel papers for the company. "You will have to stay here for now until we can arrange another way out of town," Raymonde said.

"We can't wait," Rogers said. "We need to leave now."

"But that is not wise," Raymonde said. "You can't go near the train station, and buses will be under extra scrutiny. You must wait a few days."

"He's right," Miriam said. "We've been spotted twice in Lyon already. Someone or something is giving us away. It is too dangerous to stay."

"It is too dangerous to leave," Raymonde said. "Please, allow Monsieur Segers enough time to work out a new plan."

"Eliminate the impossible," Miriam quipped to Rogers.

"What?" Raymonde asked.

Rogers smiled. "Good memory. It is impossible to stay and impossible to leave by train or bus. So, what remains?"

"I still do not understand," Raymonde said.

"The captain reads too many books," Nidal said, shaking his head. "But maybe Sherlock Holmes is right this time."

"'Once you eliminate the impossible, whatever remains, no matter how improbable, must be the truth.' Ain't that right, Cap'n?" Cookie said, beaming like a schoolboy.

Raymonde stared at them. "What is the truth, then?"

CHAPTER 29

Across the street from their latest safe house, Rogers wandered down the stone quay on the Saône inspecting more than a dozen docked barges and smaller boats and listening for any sounds of crew members inside. Nothing moved, and no one was around. Not unusual for a late and lazy Sunday afternoon.

One of the steel-hulled barges caught his eye, a twenty-four-meter-long Luxe motor Dutch Barge with duckboard-covered holds and a folded mast, similar to the *Noodster* they had ridden to safety in Utrecht. He flashed a thumbs-up at Raymonde, standing on the street at the top of the ramp.

Within minutes, all the others had joined Rogers on the quay while Raymonde served as a lookout on the sidewalk above. "I watched Captain Cuyper start the engine on one of those," he said, pointing to the barge. "Once it's warmed up, I'll signal for each of you to follow the plan. Understood?"

They all nodded and split up, so each one waited near one of the other barges.

It didn't take Rogers long to find the oil can and to begin squirting lubricant on the engine parts. While pumping in oil, he turned the small crank several times, lit a slow-burning wick on the end of a metal stick, and used it to light the glow-head at the top of the engine. Once white smoke flowed from a small pipe, the engine was warmed up.

The next crucial step, lining up the gears, was a struggle. Over and over, Rogers tried to rotate the flywheel with a long metal bar but couldn't get everything aligned. *There clearly is more of an art than a science to this.* Sweat poured down his brow, stinging his eyes. At last, everything clanked into place, and he switched on the engine. It rumbled to life. Satisfied that everything was in order, Rogers climbed up onto the deck and signaled to the others.

They scrambled from boat to boat, tossing off hawsers and ropes from metal bollards and shoving the boats and barges into the swirling current with long boathooks or their feet, then scrambled to untie Rogers' barge before hurrying aboard, giving Nidal time to kick its bow clear of the quay and spring onto its stern. He landed on cat's feet and signaled all clear to Rogers, who ground the boat into gear and steered downriver at a low speed to reduce the engine's normal put-put-put racket. Raymonde waved goodbye from the shore.

"How long can we afford to do this?" Maduro said.

"A few hours, I hope," Rogers said. "When someone finally notices all the loose barges, it will take quite some time to round them up and figure out which one is missing. We can probably run until sunset." He switched on the water injection to give the engine more power and settled into the captain's chair, his hands on the wheel, as they sailed south past the end of the Presqu'île peninsula into the Rhône River. *This is where I belong.*

☆☆☆

With a loud slurp, Janssen downed the last of his *potage paysanne*, a traditionally rich peasant's soup loaded with vegetables that now, because of rationing, was largely carrots and water. *When this damn war is over, I will never eat another damn carrot.* Lighting a cigarette with Loutrel's lighter, he settled back in his chair at the café across from the station and continued scrutinizing faces. Night was beginning to fall when a commotion broke out among people crossing the nearby Pont Kitchener-Marchand. They stopped and pointed at the Saône, shook their heads, some laughing, others hurrying away.

Janssen couldn't resist. He lumbered to the bridge and gazed over the water, where everyone was pointing. Loose barges were clustered in the middle of the channel; others floated farther downstream. On the quay below, angry captains paced, waving their arms in frustration, apparently waiting for someone in authority to retrieve their boats and explain what had happened.

"A prank?" a young boy standing near Janssen asked of a one-legged man on crutches leaning over the rails.

"Sabotage, more likely," the man said with a chuckle. "*J'irai le dire à la*

Kommandantur," he added, using a phrase that literally meant "I'll go and tell the Germans about it," but which had gained a double meaning during the war, mocking people who denounced others to the Nazis.

Janssen scanned the water for a while and then got bored. As he headed back to the café, he stopped abruptly when a thought occurred to him. *The men who helped Miriam were sailors. What a perfect distraction to cover your escape on the river in a stolen barge.* He jogged back to the bridge for another look. "Can you tell if any boats are missing?" he asked the one-legged man, still leaning on the rail.

Flashing Janssen a dismissive glare, he spat andwatched it splat on the water, and remained silent. Undeterred, Janssen hustled down to the quay and quizzed the captains and other bystanders and gendarmes. What he was told made him head straight to the nearby Hôtel Terminus. *Barbie would surely want to know.*

Once again, Janssen had to bide his time for more than an hour before being escorted into Barbie's office.

"What is it now, Dries?" said Barbie, scribbling on documents on his desk without looking up.

"I have a hunch where she is."

Barbie set his pen down and shook his head. "Again with this terrorist?"

"A few hours ago, several barges were cut loose from their moorings on the Saône."

"I know that, you kaaskop."

Janssen ignored the "cheesehead" insult. "One of the captains told me his barge is missing."

Barbie stretched out his arms and hands up as if to say, "So what?"

"Miriam was traveling with sailors from Amsterdam," Janssen said. "I believe they sailed away on the missing barge after pushing the other boats away from the quay to create a diversion."

"Or it might be stuck on a bank around the next bend," Barbie said, his voice rising as he pulled at his collar. "You are trying my patience."

Janssen rubbed his forehead and mulled over what he was going to say next. It wouldn't do to have the Gestapo upset with him. "I am staying at least until tomorrow. If the barge is found more than a short distance away, will you believe me?"

"I will reconsider, yes. How can I reach you?"

"I haven't found a hotel yet."

"Then stay here. We have plenty of unoccupied rooms. And the other guests won't mind," Barbie said with a sneer.

☆☆☆

Controlling the barge proved surprisingly tricky for such an experienced sailor as Rogers. The Rhône was no North Atlantic with its monstrous waves and howling gales. Still, the spring thaw had sent oceans of water hurtling down from the Alps toward the Mediterranean, and the cold, northerly wind was whipping up troublesome waves and crosscurrents, all of which made for a wild ride. Several times, Rogers had to fight the wheel to keep from ramming the banks.

The one good thing about the situation? The current propelled the barge downriver by an additional three to four knots. By sunset, the barge had covered nearly thirty nautical miles in less than four hours. "Mr. Nidal, prepare to dock on the right bank before that village," Rogers said, pointing toward the tiny town of Saint-Pierre-de-Boeuf, surrounded by heavily forested hills rising to the Mont Pilat mountain range to the west.

"Aye, aye, Captain," Nidal said.

Once everyone was ashore, Rogers and Nidal used boathooks to shove the barge away from the bank and into the current, where it drifted downstream in the dying evening light.

"Eventually, they will find the barge and know we are here," Maduro said to Rogers.

"They'll know we're somewhere south of Lyon but not exactly where. With this current, the barge could travel another thirty nautical miles before they find it."

"What do we do now?" Miriam said.

"Find another friendly farmer who can house us until we can find a train or bus out of here?" Nidal said.

"And then where?" Cookie said. "How long can we keep running from place to place? My hip won't take much more of this."

"What else can we do, mate?" Nidal said, his voice rising in obvious irritation.

Rogers stepped in between them, "Calm down, everyone. I know this is tough. But we can't fight the Germans if we're fighting among ourselves. Nidal's right. We need to find someone to help us. Where we go after that, I don't know."

"Marseille," Chantal said.

"Why not Toulouse?" Miriam said.

"To go there by train, we'd have to pass through Marseille. I have heard of another escape line there called Pat O'Leary," Chantal said. "If we can contact someone with that group, they can get us over the Pyrenees into Spain."

"How would you know about them?" Miriam said.

"Capt. Jackson. He talked often about the group and how he would like to connect with its members so they could help him."

"Since Capt. Jackson is a V-Mann, that group, if it even exists, is probably compromised by now," Miriam said with a scoff. "Your information is worthless."

Maduro interrupted the spat. "I have visited several shipping merchants there, both Jews and Gentiles, who might be willing to hide us in the Old Port area. Don't you know some of them, Captain?"

"Unfortunately, most of the ones I dealt with were *Le Milieu*," Rogers said, referring to the French mafia. "I would imagine that Paul Carbone and the others are collaborating with the Nazis. More profita—"

Suddenly, gunshots exploded nearby. Everyone on the bank dropped to the ground and tried to stay as still as possible. At some distance ahead, on what appeared to be the town's main street, a crowd gathered outside a cinema, holding their hands in the air. They were surrounded by half a dozen armed men in brown shirts and neckties, with blue tunics and pants, thick leather belts with holsters, and leather boots. Some wore dark blue berets tilted on their heads, while others wore steel Adrian helmets with white front emblems in the shape of the Greek letter gamma, the zodiac sign of Aries the ram.

They dressed like soldiers, but Rogers had never seen the uniforms before. The soldiers—if that's what they were—forced each boy and man in the crowd to step forward and show his papers. Some were released, but several older men were handcuffed, lined up, and ordered to march away at gunpoint.

Bullets ricocheted off the cinema's walls, striking a young soldier, who threw up his hands, flinging his Smith & Wesson Model 10 revolver high in the air, and collapsed. The remaining five soldiers crouched behind the civilians or ducked for cover behind the few cars parked on the street, searching all around, trying to figure out where the shots were coming from. Muffled footsteps made Rogers and the others duck, but it was too late.

Two men with their faces covered with scarves and wearing muddy dungarees and work shirts pointed their ancient World War I-era Lebel Model 1886 rifles down the bank at them. They were joined by a masked, skinny black man in a tattered, olive-khaki French army uniform and a dark, tall kufi. With a machete in his hand, he signaled for quiet. Then, with the other two men, he crept toward the soldiers by the cinema, who were firing in the opposite direction, not realizing they had been surrounded.

As the trio snuck down the shadowy street in a crouch, another soldier slipped around a building behind them and raised his rifle. Obasi charged over the embankment. At the sound of Obasi's pounding feet, the soldier looked over his shoulder, but not fast enough to stop Obasi from making a flying tackle, knocking him to the ground with a loud crash and punching him senseless.

Stifling a scream, Chantal rose to run away but slipped on the muddy embankment and landed on her hands and knees with a squish. The black man glanced over his shoulder and yelled a command. His men opened fire, killing three soldiers outright and badly wounding a fourth. The one still standing dropped his weapon and raised his hands. Three other armed civilians in masks emerged from the shadows and surrounded the soldier.

Rogers sprinted over to drag Obasi off the fallen soldier, who was semiconscious. Blood squirted from his nose. They froze when the black man, who seemed to be in command, picked up a fallen soldier's revolver and waved it at them, yelling something in French neither man understood. They raised their hands high over their heads, assuming that was what he meant.

Miriam shouted at the man in French, bolted over to stand in front of

Obasi and Rogers, and stretched out her arms to protect them. The other armed men stripped the soldiers—both the dead ones and the ones still alive—of their uniforms and weapons and checked the pulse of the wounded soldier, who by now had died. They tied up and blindfolded the standing survivor and marched him over to wait behind the commander.

"Merci," the commander said, pulling off his mask and lowering his weapon to give Obasi a hand up. He knelt and snapped open the holster of the soldier Obasi had beaten. It was full of paper. Tossing the paper wad away in disgust, the man rose. The armed civilians lifted the downed soldier and bound and blindfolded him.

"*Suis-moi,*" the black man said.

"He said to follow him," Miriam said, waving for Cookie, Nidal, her father, and Chantal to join them.

"Wait!" Cookie shouted. "Chantal's been wounded." He got down on one knee and pressed a handkerchief on her wounded left arm to stanch the bleeding.

Miriam hustled over and examined Chantal. "It's a flesh wound," she said, tying the handkerchief around the arm. "Can you walk?"

Chantal, who appeared to be in shock, stared ahead with glazed eyes and, with help from Cookie, rose to her feet on wobbly legs.

Rogers and Nidal took turns with Cookie helping Chantal along as the group marched out of the village into a forest so dense Rogers not only had trouble seeing where he was going, but also keeping his footing. Along the way, the armed men freed the two prisoners several minutes apart, still with their hands tied behind their backs and blindfolded. Rogers was relieved they weren't going to be executed. It was smart to let them return to the village with tales of the savage fighters who had them grossly outnumbered. Word of mouth was a powerful weapon.

After an hour of hiking up hills and bumping into trees and each other, they came to a stop. The commander whistled. It was returned, and a boy with a shotgun stepped out from behind a tree. The man patted the boy on the shoulder and led everyone through a small opening, where other armed civilians mingled around a low fire between crude sheds used by hunters all year, and by shepherds during the summer.

The man pointed to the fire, indicating they should sit down. After making room for Rogers and the others, the civilians offered them pieces of roasted roe deer and water and wine. A weakened Chantal rested her head on Cookie's shoulder and rubbed her muddy feet as one of the civilians cleaned her wound, wrapped it with a bandage, and clad her in a boy's jacket so the wounded arm wouldn't be visible.

The commander reclined across the fire from Rogers and Miriam. She spoke to him in French and then to the others in English. "I explained that I am not really a German nurse and that we are foreigners who need help getting to Spain."

"Which one is the American?" the commander said in English. Rogers raised his hand. "Are you a pilot?"

"Sailor. Who are you?" Rogers said between chomping on the tough venison.

"My name is Yora. And we are the *Maquis Guépard.*"

Rogers raised his eyebrows at Miriam for a translation. "Guépard means cheetah," she said. "But I do not understand Maquis. Is that not some kind of Corsican bush?"

"It does not translate well," Yora said with a short laugh. "Resistance fighters is what it has come to mean. There are more Maquis bands every day."

"Who were you fighting back there?" Maduro said, gratefully accepting a blanket from one of Yora's men. "They looked like some sort of army."

"La Milice," Yora said and spat on the ground. "It is the new militia created by that snake Pétain to hunt réfractaires and résistants like us and Jews. But even the Germans don't entirely trust the *miliciens* and won't provide enough weapons for them. Some of them have to stuff their holsters with paper to appear armed. They have no honor. They work for *shanghaillage.*"

"*Shanghaillage*? I am sorry, but I do not know that word either," Miriam said.

"It is a bounty they are paid for each captured réfractaire who is eligible for the forced labor. That is why they were at the cinema, for the *rafle,*" Yora said, using the French word for a roundup. "We had come to steal ration cards from the *mairie.*"

"Townhall," Miriam said to Rogers before he could ask.

"But we stumbled into the Milice. We could not let them continue," Yora said. Focusing on Obasi, he continued. "And we would not have succeeded, mon ami, without you. Merci *beaucoup*. You would make a fine warrior."

"Why are you here?" Obasi said.

"Why do you ask? Because I am an African?"

Obasi nodded.

"I am a *Tirailleurs Sénégalais*," Yora said, proudly waving his *coupe-coupe*, the customary machete of West African colonial troops, like the Senegalese Riflemen, in the French army. "And I vowed on the bodies of my fallen brothers to remain in France until the last Nazi is dead."

"So, you're part of de Gaulle's Free French?" Cookie said, wiping his mouth with his sleeve.

Yora scoffed and sat up bolt straight. "Who is this general no one had heard of before the war to tell us *attendre*? To play the waiting game while hiding in England will not defeat the Nazis. De Gaulle does not control us. And neither do *Combat*, or *Libération*, or the communists of *Le Franc-Tireur et Partisans*, nor any of the other resistance groups that cannot stop fighting among themselves. Nor can we trust the British, who seem only prepared to fight to the last Frenchman. We *maquisards* alone fight the Nazis. And the Maquis Guépard fights now." He waved his coupe-coupe in the air to the cheers of his men around the fire.

"But why would a Sénégalais stay to fight the Germans for the French? Why be *une poire*?" Nidal asked, using the slang for a sucker. "I am *Tunisien*, and I owe the colonists nothing."

"Neither do I," Yora said. "But I owe the Nazis." He disappeared into a shed, returning with something he handed to Obasi. "I owe them, also." Obasi stared for some time at the crinkled, blood-stained photograph of dozens of Tirailleurs Sénégalais standing at attention in formation, then passing it around for the others to see.

"Who are they?" Obasi said.

"My brothers of the 25th Regiment," Yora said, taking a seat close to the crackling fire. "We were fierce. And the Germans hated us for it. They called us savages and '*Affen*.'"

"Affen? They called me that in Dam Square. Remember, Captain?" Obasi said. Rogers said he did, angered and saddened at the memory of the SS officer deliberately bumping into Obasi and his own inability to do anything about it. "What does it mean?"

"Apes," Yora said. "They even called us 'the black horror of the Rhine' and rapists from the time we were part of the Allied occupation of the Rhineland after the Great War."

"That is horrible," Miriam said, scooting closer to Rogers, who wrapped his arm around her shoulders.

"That is the way they treat us Jews, like subhumans," Maduro said.

"Where are your brothers now?" Obasi said.

"Dead," Yora said, his eyes glistening. "But we made the Germans pay. We stopped them cold for a day north of Lyon the June after they invaded. When the Panzers broke through, some of us occupied a small castle in the village of Chasselay. All day and night, we fought. We fought to the last bullet. We fought until we had no choice but to surrender. And then ..." His voice drifted off as he wiped a tear from his eye.

"You do not have to continue," Miriam said with a gentle voice.

"Yes, I must, so you can let the world know," he said. "And then they separated all fifty black prisoners from our white officers. They told the officers to lie face down on the ground. We thought they were going to make us watch them be executed. But then they ordered us into a field like this." He raised his hands over his head. "When we turned around, there were Panzers lined up. Several of the German officers laughed and shouted at us in German. And then they screamed in French: *"Fuyez! Fuyez! Fuyez!"*

"Run away," Miriam translated.

"Many of my brothers hesitated, thinking maybe it was a bad joke. I did not wait. I ran. I heard the Panzers fire their machine guns, and I ran harder." He paused to take a sip from a water bottle. "Many men collapsed around me. I do not know how, but I found a clump of trees and hid. I watched the Germans slaughter them. Some fell to their knees and raised their hands, screaming for mercy. But the Germans cut them down with their own coupe-coupes," he said, waving his machete in the air. "To be sure they were all dead, the Panzers drove over the bodies. Over and over and over. You could hear their bones crunch and their screams. And then it was silent. The Germans left the bodies where they were and drove off. I waited until dark and crawled among the bodies, whispering for any survivors. But all I heard were the flies and crows picking at the bodies. Rats scurried everywhere."

Rogers patted Miriam's hair as she started to sniffle. Maduro lowered his head in prayer.

"The stench of death, the sweat, the shit, the decaying flesh—it was overwhelming," Yora said. "There was nothing I could do for those brave, unarmed *black* heroes. Nothing. So, I fled. And all I have left of them is this picture in my pocket. That is why I fight."

Obasi, tears welling in his eyes, tried to comfort Yora, sitting down close to him and putting his massive arm around Yora's heaving shoulders.

CHAPTER 30

A chilly mist rolled over the verdant forest at dawn as Yora and his maquisards led Rogers and the others to a ledge overlooking Saint-Pierre-de-Boeuf, which was just coming to life. "You will follow that road to cross the river," Yora said, pointing with his coupe-coupe. "On the other side, it is a short walk to the Gare de Péage de Roussillon. There, in a few hours, you can catch the train to Marseille." He handed each of them one of the ration cards his band had stolen the night before. "Get food for the ride. Do you need money?"

"No," Rogers said. "We have enough. Thanks for everything. And good luck." He shook Yora's hand and waved his thanks at the other maquisards. As he headed downhill, Chantal collapsed behind him with a moan. Nidal and Cookie hoisted her up and supported her with her arms over their shoulders.

"I'm sorry," Chantal said, turning pale and struggling to focus her eyes. "I'm fine. A little woozy is all."

"She has lost a lot of blood," Miriam told Rogers. "She would be better off staying here until she recovers."

Rogers glared at Miriam. "She saved our lives, Miriam. She goes with us." He looked back at the group. "Let's go."

"I cannot, Captain," Obasi said.

"What? Why?" Rogers said.

"I must stay."

Like a boxer stunned by a haymaker to his jaw out of nowhere, Rogers stood immobile on wobbly legs, his vision blurred, unable to speak, and unsure how to counterpunch. They had been friends and fellow sailors for years, sailing from Cape Hope to the North Sea and across the Mediterranean. They had survived the loss of two ships and saved each other's lives on more than one occasion. Together, they had risked everything to rescue Miriam and her family—twice.

Raging seas, aerial attacks, and fights on land and sea had bound them to one another like brothers. They never talked about that bond, even when Rogers spent hours teaching Obasi to read or when Obasi tried and failed to teach Rogers how to throw a knife. Now, Rogers had been caught cold, pinned against the ropes, paralyzed by an overwhelming sadness.

Miriam broke the silence. "Are you sure, Obasi? You don't even speak French."

"We talked about that last night after all of you went to sleep," Yora said. "We have Poles and other foreigners in our group. He will learn fast enough. And he knows we need good fighters like him."

"But we can fight the Nazis on another ship," Rogers said, finally finding his voice.

"I want to fight them face to face," Obasi said. "On a ship, they cannot see the color of my skin. They cannot see my eyes. They cannot feel the sting of my knife. I am sorry, Captain. But I must stay. You will always be my friend."

Rogers fought back tears as he bear-hugged Obasi and patted his back. "You will always be my friend, too."

Miriam barged in and wrapped her arms around Obasi's neck. They, too, had saved each other's lives and would never forget how Miriam had patched up Obasi's life-threatening wounds after the U-boat sailors tried to take over the *Peggy C*. "I am so glad to have known you. You will be in my prayers."

Even Nidal, always the stoic, appeared moved when he shook Obasi's hand. "Good luck, old friend. And stay alive."

"*Ígwè nile ga-eje n'ụzụ*," Obasi said. "It is Igbo saying that 'every iron will go to the blacksmith's furnace.' We all die. I hope my death means something."

"*Inshallah*," Nidal said in Arabic, meaning "God willing."

Cookie couldn't hold back the tears. "Now, who's going to keep the captain safe, mate? And who's gonna keep the captain from getting us all killed?" Obasi threw his head back and howled with laughter, his mouth wide open.

After Cookie finished his blubbering farewell, Maduro shook Obasi's hand. "Thank you for what you've done for my family," Maduro said. "As the Prophet Samuel said, 'Be of good courage, and let us prove strong for our people.'"

Now sullen, Rogers marched down the hill, tears flowing down his low-ered head. The others followed in silence.

"Captain!" Obasi shouted, holding both fists in the air.

Rogers whirled around to look up the hill.

"Yo-ho-ho!"

Despite the tears, Rogers laughed at the quote from *Treasure Island*, the book he used to teach Obasi to read. The phrase "yo-ho-ho" had stumped Obasi. When he had asked what it meant, Rogers told him, "Nothing really. It's a cheer for when you're happy."

☆☆☆

"Hauptsturmführer Barbie needs to see you in his office right away," the young Untersturmführer said to Janssen, half-awake in his hotel bed.

"I'll be there shortly," Janssen mumbled, his mouth so dry he could barely talk. He had a splitting headache and a vague recollection of what he had done the night before. Waving for the second lieutenant to leave, Janssen pulled himself out of bed, shaved, and dressed with the help of a bellboy who tied his tie and shoes. Then, it was off to Barbie's nearby office.

"I hate to admit it, but you were right," Barbie said. "The barge turned up more than fifty kilometers from here, stuck on a bank. It couldn't have drifted that far."

"What's the nearest town?"

Barbie glanced over at the aide.

"Saint-Pierre-de-Boeuf, Herr Hauptsturmführer," the aide said, spreading a map over Barbie's desk and, with a pencil, pointing right at the city.

"Does it have a train station or one nearby?" Janssen said, leaning over the map.

The aide pulled out a book of train schedules and compared it to the map before pointing to Gare de Péage de Roussillon.

"How many soldiers can you provide me?" Janssen said to Barbie. "And trucks?"

"None. I said you were right about the barge. I didn't say that is where they are. They could be anywhere between Lyon and there. Or even farther if they caught a train."

The aide consulted his train schedules. "No trains stopped there last night. But ..."

"But what?" Barbie said in a sharp voice.

"I'm sorry, Herr Hauptsturmführer. I placed a report on your desk earlier about a terrorist attack there last night against the Milice during a rafle."

Barbie barked at the aide. "And what of it?"

"Two of the Milice survived. They said there were two dozen terrorists, including two women, two Africans, an Arab, and—"

"What were the women wearing?" Janssen said.

"That is the strange part," the aide said. "One of them had on the uniform of a Red Cross auxiliary nurse."

"That's her, don't you see?" Janssen said. "If you won't send troops, will you at least provide me a ride so I can investigate further?"

Barbie sighed. His eyes flicked from Janssen to the aide and back again. "Untersturmführer Hölzer will drop you off at the Gare de Péage de Roussillon," Barbie said, indicating his aide. "If you find her, you will call me immediately. Otherwise, you are on your own."

Although there wasn't much traffic, it took Hölzer close to two hours to work his way through roadblocks and security checks to reach the train station. As soon as Janssen stepped out of the gray Mercedes-Benz 170v staff car, Hölzer sped away. Inside the station, Janssen found the station manager and confirmed what he had suspected. Several foreign workers and a Red Cross auxiliary nurse that morning had taken the morning southbound train.

"Seemed odd for foreign workers to be catching a train in such an out-of-the-way place," the station manager said. "But their papers were in order. And they were wearing Todt Organization armbands."

"Can I use your phone?" Janssen said.

"Yes, but not for long," the station manager said, leaving Janssen alone in his office.

Janssen called Henneicke at the Amsterdam office. "I've got her," he said.

"Where the hell are you now, Dries?!" Henneicke shouted.

"On my way to Marseille," he said, pulling the receiver away from his ear in anticipation of the inevitable outburst.

"You mean you don't actually, physically have her!" Henneicke shrieked. "I'm tired of your damn excuses. We are up to our necks here in Jews, and you are running around wasting our limited resources on just one. Let me be clear; if you don't capture her soon, don't bother coming back to Amsterdam." The line went dead.

So much for getting assistance from him. Plus, the station manager's information would not be enough to convince Barbie to help him. There was, however, one other person with as many contacts in Marseille as Barbie, someone who might be of assistance. So, he made a quick call and bought a ticket on the afternoon train to Marseille. He smelled blood.

☆☆☆

Around the same time, another train pulled into Gare de Marseille-Saint-Charles, Marseille's central train station on a hilltop, a fifteen-minute walk from the *Vieux-Port*, the Old Port in the second arrondissement. Maduro led the way out of the station into the bright sunshine and down the 104 steps and seven landings of the monumental Grand Staircase. Art Nouveau lampposts decorated with bronze dolphins ran down the middle flanked by palm trees and ornate statues representing Marseille's naval history.

Layers of dust covered everything. Maduro marched south onto Boulevard d'Athènes and then veered west. The Germans had occupied the city for only a few months, yet all the buildings were festooned with swastikas, and SS officers lounged at sidewalk cafés.

When he reached the seaside Quai du Port, Maduro stopped in his tracks, slapped his forehead with his palm, and shook his head. Rogers caught up with him and gawked at the devastation in front of them: building after building lay in ruin to the north of the small harbor. Partial remains of dusty brick walls teetered over the rubble-filled streets like exhausted skeletons. Rays of light flickered through the stripped-clean bones of ancient apartment buildings in the once vibrant neighborhood.

Only three buildings remained standing in a thirty-two-acre area—the size of six city blocks in Manhattan. The destruction stretched from the seventeenth-century Fort Saint-Jean at the small Old Port's entrance to the

new commercial port in the La Joliette neighborhood. The skyline was domi-
nated by the 230-foot-high main cupola of the nineteenth-century Cathedral
of Sainte-Marie-Majeure, whose green marble and white stones reflected its
Byzantine and Roman Revival style architecture. Dozens of workers used
shovels, picks, and brooms to remove the debris as women scavenged clothes
and any furniture that could be hauled away.

Rogers hadn't heard of any Allied bombings of Marseille, and it seemed
odd that the destruction was confined to such a compact area of the city that
he had visited often on the *Peggy C* before the war. There was no obvious
damage to the Old Port. Dozens of brightly colored Pointu fishing boats tied
to wharf poles bobbed in the sapphire-tinted water. Similar boats with pointed
bows tacked to-and-fro beyond the harbor, their triangular Lateen sails flap-
ping in the wind.

To the north, an undamaged 820-foot-long concrete U-boat bunker was
swarming with hundreds of construction workers. And in the Gulf of Lion,
two German gun batteries on the Îles du Frioul archipelago, bristling with
155mm guns in concrete pillboxes, also appeared unharmed.

Rogers couldn't ask Maduro what had happened, so he stepped back into
the shadows to wait with the others. Miriam strolled up to her father and
appeared to be speaking to him.

A stooped-over elderly man, shuffling along with a cane, paused in front
of the Maduros and shook his cane toward the vanished neighborhood, tears
rolling down his wizened cheeks. When the old man hobbled off down the
Quai des Belges, Maduro gestured for the others to come along.

Miriam wrapped her arm around Rogers' waist, and they paced several
yards behind her father, who trailed the old man. Chantal locked arms with
Cookie as they followed, with Nidal close behind.

"The old man says the French police did it for the Germans," Miriam whispered in English, keeping her lips as still as possible. "He said they expelled
more than 30,000 residents with only a two-hour warning and rounded up
some 2,000 Jews, who they shipped off to concentration camps."

"What happened to the buildings?" Rogers said, being sure no one could
see him speaking English.

"The Germans blew up more than 1,400 of them because they suspected the resistance and Jews of using the alleys and twisting streets as hiding places."

"That explains all the dust everywhere. Where are we going?"

"There," she said, pointing ahead at an intact four-story, Gothic-Renaissance-style building on the edge of the destroyed area. "Past the Hôtel de Cabre, the oldest existing house in Marseille. The Germans let it remain along with the Hôtel de Ville, which is the town hall, and the ancient Maison Diamantée behind it."

They passed the intersection with La Canebière, the wide boulevard considered the Champs-Élysées of Marseille, where waiters in white coats and bow ties served German officers under the striped awning of Le Mont-Ventoux on the corner and other cafés lining the block.

Rogers slowed his pace so he could watch the Pointu fishing boats tacking through the harbor and farther out to sea, admiring the skill of their captains as they prepared their boats for sailing. A stiff, cold wind ripped down La Canebière, making Miriam shiver. "The Mistral," Rogers whispered.

"What is that?"

Rogers tilted his head, signaling Miriam to look beyond the harbor's entrance at the waves being whipped up, smashing against the concrete barriers and sending foamy spray high in the air. Threatening clouds and fog, seemingly out of nowhere, rolled toward the shore, obscuring the view of the smallest island in the archipelago and the Château d'If, the sixteenth-century fortress where the fictional hero of *The Count of Monte Cristo* was imprisoned. "Trouble for ships," Rogers said.

When Maduro came alongside the Hôtel de Cabre, he ducked his head and kept walking. The others followed past the building with its blown-out windows and pockmarked masonry, where German soldiers and gendarmes had kicked people out and shoved them away.

The old man led them farther north onto narrow streets through the parts of the Le Panier district, where the buildings were still standing but abandoned. At the top of a stone staircase on a side street, the old man paused, lifted his cane toward a *Tabac* shop with a shattered display window and a door that was ajar. Maduro slipped inside; the others quickly followed. They made their way past newspapers, empty cigarette boxes, and broken glass on the floor to the back, where they found stairs to a second-floor apartment. "We'll be safe here," Maduro said, inspecting the small, two-bedroom apartment with a sparse kitchen off the sitting room. Half-opened drawers and overturned furniture were clear signs of the residents' hasty departure.

When Cookie, moaning in pain from taking the stairs, brought Chantal into the sitting room, he eased her down onto a red tufted settee. She immediately kicked off her pumps and rubbed her blistered feet. Miriam and Rogers rifled through drawers and opened doors while Nidal scoured the kitchen.

"There is some food," Nidal said, holding up a bunch of carrots and half a baguette.

"And candles," Rogers said. He pulled the pewter candle holders down from the fireplace mantle and set them on a coffee table in front of the settee.

"I must somehow try to contact members of the Pat O'Leary line," Chantal said, standing barefoot on unsteady legs. "Marseille is like Lyon. Full of résistants. So it shouldn't be too difficult to find someone trustworthy to connect us."

"You're not strong enough to go anywhere," Rogers said. "Let one of us try."

"No. I must do it. It is not safe for any of you. I'm strong enough, even if I have to crawl all the way back to Le Mont-Ventoux," Chantal said, slipping on her shoes with a wince.

"You might try the café beside it—the Wolf something," Rogers said.

"La Brûleur de Loups?"

"Yeah, that one. When I was there, it was always full of writers and artists. I even saw Max Ernst there once. I bet you'll find plenty of anti-Nazis there."

"Good idea," Chantal said, flashing her V-Frau card. "And, if anyone stops me, I can show them this, and they will leave me alone."

Once Chantal had limped away, Miriam disappeared into one of the bedrooms and returned holding sheets. "Help me make knots in these. We can tie them on the radiator under the window in the back bedroom."

"What are you doing?" Rogers said.

"Always have a way out."

CHAPTER 31

As soon as he stepped off the train at Gare de Marseille-Saint-Charles, Janssen knew precisely where he had to go. Holding onto his homburg and leaning into the swirling wind, he raced down the grand staircase and hailed a taxi for the four-kilometer ride south to 425 Rue Pardis—Gestapo headquarters. Once again, he had to cool his heels in the front room of the villa before he convinced a young aide to take him to his boss.

Janssen thought he had been taken to the wrong place or was being put on when the aide led him into an office and introduced him to a master sergeant, not a high-level officer. *Oberscharführer* Ernst Dunker, in his early thirties and with receding hair, glanced up from his cluttered desk as he waved Janssen to sit.

"My friend, Monsieur Lafont, was quite mysterious about your purpose in Marseille," Dunker said in perfect French. "If it has to do with Carlingue business, I am surprised he didn't send you to Paul Carbone or François Spirito. They rule Marseille."

"No, it's not about that," Janssen said, sliding across the desk the wanted flyer for Miriam. "I believe she is in Marseille trying to escape to Spain. But this is a big town, and I need the Gestapo's help."

Danker seemed skeptical as he read the flyer.

"She's an extremely dangerous spy," Janssen said. "Escaped from prison and killed three Grüne Polizei."

"And is worth a substantial reward, I see," Dunker said, sliding the flyer back to Janssen and staring at him in disgust.

"And she nearly killed one of Lafont's men in Lyon. Crushed in his skull."

"Pierre Loutrel?" Dunker said. "I heard La Valise was in the hospital. When I was assigned to the Gestapo in Paris, we used to go to L'Étoile de Kléber together quite often to hear the marvelous Edith Piaf sing. No wonder

Monsieur Lafont wants to find her. How can I help?"

Despite his low rank, Dunker was exactly the person who could assist Janssen. A petty thief in and out of prison most of his life, Dunker floated from job to job as a waiter and bartender in Rome and London and even managed a restaurant in Hoboken, NJ, for a while before joining the German army in 1939. After being wounded and receiving an Iron Cross Second Class, he was transferred to the Abwehr, the army's intelligence service, to work as a translator because he was fluent in French, English, and Italian.

In 1942, he was transferred to the Gestapo in Paris, where he hung out with gangsters, including Carlingue members. He was arrested again and imprisoned for a month before being reinstated and promoted, a criminal record being no impediment to working for the Gestapo. Dunker had been in Marseille for a few months but already had gained a reputation for efficiency and brutality, a reputation burnished by his feared gang of torturers operating in the villa's basement known as the "Cellar's Brigade."

☆☆☆

"I am so, so sorry," Chantal sobbed as she stumbled into the apartment and collapsed on the settee, kicking off her pumps. "I couldn't find anyone to help. Now we're trapped."

Cookie plopped down beside her and held her in his arms. "There, there, lass, you tried your best. We'll figure out something else, won't we, Cap'n?"

Rogers and Miriam glanced at one another. "Do you feel like telling us what happened?" Miriam said, her voice softer than her usual brusque tone with Chantal.

"I did what Capt. Jackson had taught me to do: make contact with résistants if I needed help," she said, blowing her nose in a handkerchief. "I sat at the bar and flirted and made subtle insults about the Germans. You know, calling them "the dirty Germans" or "Huns" and such under my breath. I even asked some of the bartenders—discreetly, mind you—if they knew anyone with the Pat O'Leary line. But nobody would help. I feel like such a fool. Now we are all going to die." She dropped her head on Cookie's shoulders and sobbed.

He patted her head and looked around the room, distraught, seeking answers from the others.

"I could try to find some of my business associates," Maduro said. "But I don't know how to find them anymore. Everything's gone."

"We'll figure something out," Rogers said. "Cookie, why don't you help Chantal into the bedroom to rest? She looks exhausted."

With Nidal's assistance, Cookie lifted Chantal, walked her between them into one of the bedrooms, laid her down on the bed, quietly closing the door behind them, and returned to the sitting room.

Everyone flinched at a flash of lightning and booming thunder. Rain pounded the roof and windows. "We'll have to wait out the storm and try to find help tomorrow," Rogers said. "Cookie, see what you can fix for us to eat. And let's close the blackout curtains tight so we can light the candles." Rogers entered the back bedroom, where Miriam had tied up the sheets and strained to close the thick blackout curtains.

"Men," Miriam laughed, shaking her head. "Helpless. Here, let me do it." She reached up and slid the curtains closed with no trouble. Sitting on the bed, she patted the mattress for Rogers to join her. "Are you not going to say it?"

"Say what?"

"That you were right about Chantal," Miriam said, "and I was wrong."

"Never crossed my mind," he said with a smile. "She's just a scared little girl. But she's right. We're dead if we don't figure out how to get out of here."

"I can find some clothes here to change into and go out in the morning to look for someone to help us. Marseille has a reputation for being rebellious." She clasped Rogers' head in both of her hands and kissed him. "Like me."

Later, dinner was a sparse affair—bits of boiled cabbage and carrots with one stale half a baguette cut into tiny pieces. But there was plenty of wine. Chantal had stopped sobbing and apparently fallen asleep, so they didn't wake her for the meal. Miriam had changed from her nurse's uniform into a flowery skirt she had pinned up and an oversized blue jacket with buttoned pockets. She had replaced her hose with white Bobby socks and let her hair down.

Everyone ate in glum silence around the candle-lit coffee table in the sitting room, seemingly lost in their thoughts, exhausted by their long journey, and hiding their anxiety about what to do.

They didn't hear the door swing open.

☆ ☆ ☆

"Stand with your hands in the air, or I will shoot," Janssen said as he stepped into the room, a Walther PPK in his hand and rain dripping off him onto the floor with a splat.

Expressionless, they all rose and faced the giant one-armed man whom they'd only seen at a distance and in their nightmares.

Janssen glanced at his watch. "Turn around and raise your hands above your heads. All except you, Miriam. I want to see your face."

They did as they were told.

"You sound Dutch, traitor," Miriam said in Dutch.

Janssen shook his head. "You are the terrorist. I'm doing my duty for my country."

"I am serving my country. You are nothing more than a bounty hunter for the Nazis."

"Yes, and one who will soon be quite wealthy, thanks to you," he said, sneaking another glance at his watch.

"Expecting someone?" Miriam said.

Rogers peered over his shoulder.

"Gestapo," Janssen said. "Once I heard the tip they had received, I couldn't wait to meet you. They'll be here straight away, I assure you. So don't move."

Rogers spun around and motioned the others away, gesturing with his head for them to face Janssen and separate. "We are five. You might be able to shoot one or two. But not all of us."

As they spread farther apart, Janssen swung the pistol from one to the other.

"I only have to kill one of you," Janssen said, pointing his pistol at Miriam's chest. Now it didn't matter whether she was dead or alive; the reward would be the same. "Stop moving."

They all stood still.

"Now it is only—" *What was I going to say? Ow. My ears hurt. Tulips in bloom everywhere. But not tall enough. I can't hide. He'll find me and beat me again. Mother, help me. Something hurts. Why am I thinking about her now? Look at their faces, full of fear. I told them to stop moving. I'll have to shoot one of them. Send a message. Where's my hand? Mother, help me. Why is my gun on the floor? Any minute, they'll be here, and I'll be rich for you, my sweet Stefan. We'll...we'll run away and be safe somewhere she can't find us...If only that pain would go away. Did they blow out the candles? Stop moving, damn it. Have to steady myself. Be strong. Stand up for myself. Show them how tough I am. Mother stands there and does nothing. Nothing...nothing...can't breathe. Help me, Mother...Nothing...Bitch.*

☆☆☆

With eyes bulging and his mouth wide open in a silent scream, Janssen stared in disbelief at the blood spurting between the fingers of his only hand. He pressed it against his chest and tumbled like a marble statue to the ground.

Standing barefoot behind him, Chantal gripped a small nickel-plated Dreyse m1907 pistol in her stone-cold, steady hand.

"Thank God for you, Chantal," Rogers said. "Let's get the hell out of here."

He stepped toward the other bedroom along with the others.

BANG!

Everyone froze. "Put your hands up. Now!" Chantal screamed. "You are not going anywhere."

"I knew it," Miriam said. "I should have listened to my instincts. You called in the tip, didn't you?"

"As a matter of fact, yes. But I have no idea who this buffoon is. Too bad for him, but I always carry this little beauty for protection," Chantal said, holding up the pistol. "And I am not splitting the rewards with anyone."

"Rewards?" Rogers asked.

"For Miriam, for all of you spies, and for all the members of all the escape lines that the Germans will be able to roll up because of Miriam," Chantal said. "It was all Capt. Jackson's idea. Why settle for one reward when we can get multiple rewards that'll be enough to live on forever in South America?"

"But why did you save us?" Cookie asked, inching closer to Chantal, who trained her gun on him.

"Don't try that five-on-one trick with me. I'm an excellent shot," she said. "The plan was for all the men to die in Paris at the hands of Doctor Eugène, whose real name is Marcel Petiot, by the way. Capt. Jackson had a deal with him, just like the Carlingue, to eliminate troublesome people. He seems to enjoy it."

"But why kill us? Aren't we worth something?" Cookie said, inching closer.

"Cookie, don't," Rogers said.

"Listen to your captain and step back," Chantal said. "With all of you gone, Miriam would have had no choice but to travel with me, which would have made it easier to arrest her once we reached Toulouse. But it seemed like we were never going to make it there. So, our plans changed."

In the distance, car doors slammed; hobnail boots echoed and splashed down the deserted, cobblestoned streets. Chantal glanced at the kitchen window and smirked. Cookie leaped at Chantal and fought her for the gun. The others rushed her.

BANG!

Cookie slumped over Chantal, holding tight to the pistol as Rogers and Nidal wrestled her to the ground and pinned her. Maduro scooped up Janssen's Walther PPK and aimed it at Chantal. Clutching a gushing wound in his stomach, Cookie rolled over and tossed Chantal's pistol to Miriam.

"Oh, no!" Miriam cried out, rushing into the bedroom, where she grabbed her nurse's skirt and sped back to press it against Cookie's wound. "Hold this here," she told Cookie. "I can patch you up. You will be all right, *liefste*," she said with false bravado, using the Dutch word for "dearest."

"Now, lass, I may not have a medical degree, but I'm a good enough doctor to know there ain't no surviving a gutshot like this," Cookie said between coughs.

Nidal cut down a curtain drawstring and tied up Chantal. Rogers shoved a rag in her mouth. "We must go, Captain. The Germans will soon figure out where we are," Nidal said. "Let's lower Cookie out first."

"No!" Cookie shouted, clutching his stomach and wincing in pain. "Leave me with the guns, and I'll give you time to get away."

"But, Cookie, we can't—" Miriam burst into tears, unable to finish.

Cookie squeezed her hand. "You must, lass. I'm old, and I've had a good life. And I could not bear the thought of anything happening to you—or me mates," he said, smiling at Rogers and Nidal. "My dear, sweet girl, you are needed to defeat these Nazi bastards."

"You don't have to do this, my friend," Nidal said with watery eyes. "I cannot live without your burned pumpkin."

Cookie chortled and coughed up blood. "Get on with ya. And keep the good captain safe."

"What do we do with Chantal, Captain?" Nidal said.

"Put a bullet in her head," Miriam said, checking the pistol's chamber for a bullet and pointing it at Chantal, who shook her head frantically with a muffled scream.

"No," Rogers said, taking the gun away. "She wants rewards. So, let's give them to her." Miriam gaped at Rogers as he bent over Cookie and whispered something in his ear, making him grin and nod.

"Help me with him," Rogers said to Nidal and Maduro, who hoisted up Cookie and gently lowered him into an armchair facing the apartment door. After fetching a wooden chair from the kitchen, Rogers positioned it in front of Cookie to also face the door. With Nidal's help, Rogers lifted the squirming Chantal, terror in her eyes, and tied her to the wooden chair. "And here is where you can get your *just* rewards."

"I'll fire two shots to draw them here," Cookie said, taking the pistols from Rogers and Maduro. "Your brother Rabbi Levy was a fine man."

"I will pray for you," Maduro said.

"Is this a *mitzvah*?" Cookie said, remembering what Maduro had said in a letter to Rogers about saving Miriam and his other family members on the *Peggy C.*

"No greater kind, my friend," Maduro said, touching Cookie's shoulder as if giving a blessing.

"Now run. And don't worry about her, Captain. I'll make sure she won't be tellin' no tales," Cookie said, steadying the Walther PPK on Chantal's shoulder. He gripped Chantal's gun in his other hand, pressed it on the cloth covering his wound, and pointed it at her back.

Rogers led the others into the bedroom and held the knotted bedsheet for them. Nidal scaled down first so he could help catch anyone who slipped in the pouring rain.

Maduro was next, making it almost all the way down before falling into Nidal's arms, knocking them both to the ground.

Miriam trotted back into the sitting room, kissed Cookie's cheek, and fled out the window, followed by Rogers, his tearful eyes lingering on Cookie for a long moment before he climbed out the window and slid down the sheet.

They sloshed along the slippery cobblestone alley and rounded a corner toward the sea when two gunshots rang out behind them, followed by shouting, pounding feet, the crash of a shattered door frame, and then a cascade of gunfire and barking dogs.

CHAPTER 32

"Now what, Captain?" Nidal said, wiping the hard rain out of his eyes. "It won't take the Germans long to find the sheet rope and head this way."

"We could find another vacant building to hide in," Miriam said.

Maduro cocked his head at the sound of barking. "If we run or hide, they have dogs to find us, even in this rain."

"We have to split up," Nidal said.

"No," Rogers said. "You know what Mademoiselle Spy keeps telling me?" They all looked to Miriam for an answer.

"Always have a way out," Miriam said. "But I don't know what it is this time."

"Psalms Number 107. The one about getting help from God is the answer, isn't it, Captain?" Maduro said, somehow managing a grin in the middle of a horrible situation.

"Every sailor and shipowner knows that one. 'They that go down to the sea in ships,'" Rogers said. He led them down the winding streets to the quay, where rows of Pointu boats bounced wildly in the storm. Running from boat to boat, he found what he wanted and called the others over. "Get aboard."

"Captain, the seas are too rough for such a small boat," Nidal said of the vessel, also known as a *barquette marseillaise*, which was some twenty feet long and seven feet wide.

"We don't have a choice," Rogers said. "Miriam, take the tiller. Solomon and Nidal row us out of the harbor entrance while I figure out how to raise the mainsail." As an experienced sailor, Rogers should have done that first before leaving the dock, but there was no time because the barking was getting closer.

As Maduro and Nidal rowed the boat away, Rogers shouted to Miriam, "Turn the bow into the wind as soon as you can! Understand?!"

"Aye, aye!" she yelled over the howling wind, having learned the proper lingo on the *Peggy C.*

The Pointu had one triangular mainsail on a long pole called a "yard," attached to the mast mounted in the bow. Rogers removed the sail ties around the mainsail and let it unfurl. Next, he pulled the halyard, one of the lines, to raise the yard horizontally up the mast. Then he pulled another line that controlled the tack known as a "Cairo" to twist the yard vertically, with one end nearly touching the deck.

Other lines, called "Orças," were used to prevent the yard from swinging in the rough swells. As he dealt not just with all the lines in the rolling boat, but also the high winds and slashing rain, Rogers racked his brain to remember what the local sailors did when he had gone fishing with them years ago.

Shots rang out from the shore, where shadowy figures knelt for balance and barking dogs wove around them like hyenas waiting for bloody scraps. Nidal and Maduro ducked while they pulled and pushed the oars, a job made somewhat easier by the ebbing tide. Miriam had the boat heading for the harbor entrance but lost her grip on the tiller and almost fell overboard before getting her hands back on it.

"Pull to port!" Rogers shouted. "Left! Pull the tiller to the left and hold steady!" With all the lines secured and the mainsail in the proper position, Rogers stumbled to the stern and relieved Miriam at the tiller. "Unship the oars!" he shouted.

Nidal lifted his oar out of the oarlock, but Maduro kept rowing, sending the boat swirling toward a concrete barrier at the entrance. With expert calmness, Nidal leaned over, jerked the oar from Maduro's hands, and tossed it down on the deck.

A bullet smashed into the mast, sending splinters flying all around them. More bullets ricocheted off the barriers at the entrance as the boat passed through into even rougher water. Waves curled over the hull's top edge, which are called gunwales.

Ahead, slightly to the south, Rogers could make out the Château d'If through the shifting fog and rain. There were German batteries on the other islands in the archipelago, so he fought to steer due west along the coast. It was eerily dark because of the wartime blackouts.

Without any lights, any stars, or a compass, and tacking on a churning sea, navigating to Spain would be almost impossible. Barcelona was around 175 nautical miles southwest of Marseille, and Rogers guessed the nearest point anywhere in Spain was a little more than 100 nautical miles as the crow flies. In other words, at least a day, maybe two away, depending on the sea. He glanced at his watch's luminous dial and decided to take his chances.

Even in the gloom, he could feel all eyes upon him. "In case the fog clears, we'll head west along the shore for two hours until we're out of sight of the German batteries!" he shouted. "Then we'll turn to port and hope we can keep a southwest direction for Spain!"

White horses broke over the tiny boat, drenching everyone in freezing water and driving them closer to shore. "Captain," Nidal said, "we can't wait. Head away from shore before we smash into it."

Signaling agreement, Rogers shoved the tiller to incrementally turn into the waves without capsizing and headed toward what he thought might be south. It didn't take long for the thick fog to swallow them up and leave Rogers almost blind, a situation fraught with danger because he couldn't see an errant wave soon enough to steer away from a potentially fatal broadside.

"Listen," Nidal said. "Engines. Must be S-boots searching for us."

"Where does it sound like they're coming from?" Rogers said.

"Seems to me they are coming off the port beam."

"What are you going to do?" Miriam asked Rogers.

"We can't outrun them. But, in this fog, we're smaller than a needle in a haystack. Listen and dodge is all we can do."

Nidal cupped his ears and twisted his head around, trying to zero in on the engines' location over the sound of crashing waves, pounding rain, and howling wind. He perked up, raised his right arm, and chopped to the starboard. Rogers nudged the tiller until Nidal dropped his arm.

The engines sounded closer but coming more from the stern than the beam in the middle of the boat, meaning the S-boots were no longer heading directly toward them. A faint beam of light circled around the fog to their port. *Searchlights!* The Germans were using Aldis messaging lamps in the hunt, but the fog was too thick for the beams to travel far. They also revealed the Germans' position. Rogers, sweating despite the cold and rain, steered the

Pointu back to port and gripped tight to the tiller to hold her steady.

This cat-and-mouse game went on for some time. When the lights finally disappeared, and the sounds faded, Rogers checked his watch. It had been less than an hour. It was going to be a long night sailing in an unknown direction without food for who knows how long. At least there would be water. To catch the rain, Nidal had lashed one of the bailing buckets to the mast. He handed another bucket to Rogers and took over the tiller, both agreeing to two-hour watches. Miriam and her father wouldn't know how to steer the boat to avoid disaster.

After another two hours, the seas calmed and the rain stopped. Squatting close to Miriam in the middle of the boat, Rogers bailed out water for a short while and then held Miriam in his arms, not letting go as they shivered together. Maduro sat huddled up at the bow, head down as if praying.

"How much longer?" Miriam said between chattering teeth.

"If the fog lifts and the sea cooperates, maybe a day," Rogers said. After a long pause, he added, "I'm sorry."

"For what?"

"I should have listened to you about Chantal. If I had, maybe Cookie would ..." Tears welled in his eyes.

Miriam stroked his head. "In the end, she fooled us all," Miriam said. "It does not matter now. All that matters is we are alive for one more minute. That is because we trusted in you. We must not look back. I have stared into my grave, Jake. And your face was the last image in my mind. We must look forward and honor Cookie and those who have given their lives for us to have made it this far."

A gust of wind cleared the fog above, revealing a glorious sky full of stars. "Look, Mr. Nidal, the North Star!" Rogers shouted.

"Which one?" Miriam said.

"See The Big Dipper?" Rogers pointed skyward and drew a line across the stars. "Follow the two stars at the end of the cup down to the next star. That's Polaris, the North Star."

Inspecting the sky, Nidal maneuvered the boat so the North Star was behind his right shoulder and they were heading southwest toward Spain. Rogers kissed Miriam and manned the tiller for his watch. Slowly evaporating fog and mist caressed the boat, and the stiff wind filled the sail, driving the Pointu up the four-foot swells and crashing it down into the troughs and back up again, like a baby rocking in a cradle on the edge of a cliff. They were safe for now but always in danger.

"Oh, no!" Miriam yelled, pointing off the port bow at a silhouette with foamy plumes shooting up from its prow like a snowplow. "U-boat." Rogers and the others moved their heads to track it, waiting with dread for it to open fire or slow down or turn about. Instead, it raced along, oblivious to, or uninterested in, their tiny fishing boat. "Thank goodness," Miriam said. "We are safe,"

"Maybe," Nidal said, drawing a questioning look from Miriam.

"We're too small a fish for a U-boat," Rogers said. "But not for a patrol boat if they radio ahead."

Rogers and Nidal traded places at the tiller for several hours as the fog burned off. Miriam would sit close to Rogers, steer the tiller, gently guided by his calloused hands, and learn the proper technique of tacking over the waves. She told Rogers the monotony of it was joyous. No thoughts, just concentration on the waves. When the sun rose, the vast sea all around was gloriously empty.

"We're safe for a while," Rogers said, letting Miriam handle the tiller on her own. "But I'll feel better when darkness comes."

"How fast are we going?" Maduro said, gripping the gunwales at the bow with both hands.

"Hard to tell," Rogers said. "Mr. Nidal, what do you guess?"

"We have a following sea and are sailing beam reach, so maybe 7 knots," Nidal said.

This time, Miriam turned to Rogers for a translation.

"We are traveling in the same direction as the ocean current, and the wind is coming at us from 90 degrees. Ideal sailing conditions," Rogers said. "If the weather persists and we don't run into any German ships, we might even be able to make Spain before sundown."

At the end of his watch, Rogers curled up on the deck with his head in Miriam's lap and fell immediately to sleep, a sailor's habit. The pattern continued for most of the day: on the tiller for two hours, then off for two. Both

Rogers and Nidal were bleary-eyed, and their hands were rubbed raw and aching from the stress.

Happily, the weather cooperated, and no other ships appeared on the undulating waves of the crystal blue sea. Above, cotton ball clouds scudded across the sky. When Rogers woke up from another nap, Miriam wagged her finger toward the setting sun. "There is a flashing light. See it? It must be a lighthouse. We're almost to land!"

Rogers compared the blinking light to his watch. "Every ten seconds. Must be the Cap de Creus lighthouse. Every lighthouse has its own timing. That means we're less than an hour from shore."

Miriam hugged Rogers in excitement. "We are going to make it."

"No guarantee the Spanish won't send us back or to prison," Rogers said. "Besides—"

"Look at the sky, Captain!" Nidal shouted from the tiller.

Miriam and her father searched the sky for a plane or something else that could have caused Nidal's alarm. Rogers stared up and scanned the horizon. The clouds had vanished. The sky was a radiant blue.

"Too blue," Rogers said. "Prepare for rough seas."

"What?" Miriam and Maduro said in tandem.

"The sky is perfectly clear, and I don't see any waves," Miriam said.

"Feel that cold wind?" Rogers said.

"Yes. What of it?"

"The *Tramontane*," Rogers said. "It's like the Mistral, but with clear, deeper-than-deep blue skies. The wind has blown everything clean out of the air. When that kind of sky comes on suddenly, gale-force winds and monstrous seas can be whipped up in a flash."

Already, the gentle waves were picking up speed, thrashing about with foamy white caps in every direction. A cold wind blasted the boat's starboard gunwale, nearly tipping it over. Each wave felt higher and higher. and they came from every direction.

A towering plume of water shot up into the air a few yards off the bow, and the smell of cordite wafted over the boat. Everyone twisted around to the stern. Another loud explosion several yards behind the pitching boat sent a geyser high into the clear, blue sky. "Germans!" Rogers shouted. "They're bracketing us, trying to find their range! Hold on!"

Pulling on one line after another with one hand and shifting the tiller from side to side with the other, Rogers steered the boat into wild, haphazard turns, trying to zigzag in ten-foot waves to avoid the next shell, knowing he should strike sail in such dangerous weather to prevent capsizing. But he had no choice; he had to maneuver.

Looking over his shoulder, he caught a glimpse on the horizon of what appeared to be a *Vorpostenboot*, a German coastal patrol boat armed with a single 8.8cm deck gun—the type Rogers had seen on U-boats. These V-boots could lob thirty-three-pound shells more than seven miles. Fortunately, most of these vessels were re-purposed merchant ships or yachts that didn't have close to the power of the deadly E-boats, and rarely topped twelve knots. That might provide Rogers time to reach shore before the Germans could hit them. The deck gun was hard to aim in such rough weather.

Ahead, the lighthouse flashed high on a rocky cliff overlooking coves and inlets, some with sandy beaches, others with boat-crushing reefs. No life jackets were on board, and the current would probably suck anyone who fell overboard out to sea or down to the bottom. "Miriam, Solomon, grab ahold of an oar and use it to float in the sea if needed!"

They crawled in the shaking boat to follow orders.

Rogers tried to reassure them. "Don't worry. Mr. Nidal and I are strong swim—"

A shell exploded off the starboard side and hurled the boat high into the air, flipping it over. Rogers watched, in what felt like slow motion, as the others spun through the air and down into the raging sea before he slipped under the waves, his heavy boots dragging him deeper and deeper as if in the ghostly grip of Davey Jones himself.

CHAPTER 33

As she fought to the surface, the last thing Miriam remembered was Rogers' face. He was sinking and fighting to remove his boots when he looked up at her with love and longing but no fear. She wanted to join him, but her lungs were screaming: *Get air, then I can save him, and my father, and Nidal.* Her head broke the surface. Gulping in air, she wrapped her arms around an oar and closed her eyes against the stinging waves.

☆☆☆

Below her, Rogers kicked off his last boot and paddled and kicked his way to the surface, his head popping up just as a wave slapped him, filling his mouth with seawater. He gagged. Nothing was in sight, only the boat's overturned frame. Though he was a strong swimmer, he couldn't seem to make any progress toward the boat because of the stormy waters. Two strokes forward, a wave backward, and repeat. Gradually, he made it and clung to the hull. All around were chunks of the mast and yard.

Nearby, Nidal had a grip on a long piece of the mast and was kicking to reach Rogers. Farther away, toward shore, Miriam and Maduro, on their separate oars, bobbed up and down on the swells.

When Nidal was close enough, Rogers released the hull and swam to join him, holding onto the mast. "We have to swim away from the wreckage. The Germans will be looking for survivors to capture or kill," Rogers said. Nidal nodded, and together they struggled to steer the mast toward land, kicking as hard as they could, and paddling with one hand, all the while trying to catch up with Miriam and Maduro. Rogers twisted his neck to look behind. The German patrol boat loomed larger. "Kick, kick!"

"We're in luck. It's a flood current!" Nidal screamed back, referring to an incoming tide that would help them reach the small cove not too far ahead. He shouted and pointed to Miriam, slipping off her oar and sinking under the waves.

Rogers released the mast and swam with broad strokes toward her, diving under the waves and snatching her by her collar. He hauled her up and towed her back to the mast, where Nidal helped him hold her on it. "Where's Solomon?!"

Nidal kicked to lift himself higher in the water but couldn't see far over the waves. He tried again. "I can't find him." Then a wave lifted them on its crest, and there he was, right in front of them. They kicked over and helped him switch from the oar to the mast and then to hold on for dear life as the three of them kicked, waves crashing all around them. The German patrol boat's engines roared as it closed in for the kill, opening fire with machine guns, ripping holes in the Pointu's hull and scattering shards of wood all around.

"To port, to port!" Rogers shouted. "There's a beach!" With one hand holding up Miriam and the other hand on the mast, Nidal and Rogers fought to steer the unwieldy hunk of wood away from the fast-approaching jagged rocks and, instead, toward the small beach at the back of the cove beneath the flashing lighthouse. Maduro, exhausted and huffing, did his best not to hinder the others and tried to kick.

Out of nowhere, a massive comber lifted them up and sent them tumbling and bouncing toward the beach and then, having carried them closer to shore and salvation, smashed them against the ocean's craggy bottom.

☆☆☆

Miriam coughed up seawater as her eyes fluttered open. She wasn't dead, but she wasn't sure where she was. Her head ached, and her hands were on fire. Flashlights shone all around her as she blinked to focus on the figure leaning over her in the dark. It was a man, and he wore a shiny leather hat and a dark green uniform.

He appeared to be talking to her. His lips were moving, but she couldn't make out what he was saying through the ringing in her ears. Hands lifted her upright and pounded on her back, making her regurgitate even more acrid seawater.

"Breathe slowly. You'll be all right," a vaguely familiar voice said. She turned her head. Nidal and another uniformed man with a shouldered Mauser 1916 Spanish Short Rifle were helping her father sit up. She racked her brain, trying to remember who used that kind of rifle. Spanish Guardia Civil? *But what were they doing in Holland?*

"We're safe for now but under arrest," someone said.

There's that voice again. Miriam craned her neck to get a better view, wiping the blood from her eyes until she found the source of the flashlight's glare: Rogers. Yellow bile and seawater shot up from her empty stomach, splashing onto the beach. Then everything went black again.

☆☆☆

Miriam's eyes flew open and clamped shut as the tiny spot of light drilled a hole into her aching head. When the light clicked off, her eyes half opened. She raised her right hand to cover her eyes, but her arm was stuck to something. Handcuffs bound her wrist to the bed's white metal railing. Someone in a white coat loomed over her with a pinpoint flashlight.

"Water," she said hoarsely in English.

"You are English?" a man's voice said.

She opened her eyes wider as a man in a white coat supported her head so she could sip water from a glass. "Dutch. But I speak English."

"We weren't sure," the man replied in English, using a stethoscope to listen to her heart. "You've been babbling in several languages for the last few days. You took a nasty whack to the head."

"Where am I?"

"Hospital de la Santa Creu in Barcelona. The Guardia Civil brought you here but insisted on the handcuffs and a guard."

She examined the long row of beds on both sides of a brightly lit, cheerful room that more resembled a church than a hospital. It had a vaulted ceiling, tall windows topped by green-tiled arches over gold crowns, and walls covered in exquisite mosaics. Sitting by a door, an armed guard smoked a cigarette and paid no attention to her.

The doctor leaned in close. "Luckily for you, we got your message to your cousin through the British Embassy in Lisbon."

"Cousin?"

"Yes, you were most insistent that we send the telegram. He arrived this morning. Do you feel up for a visit?"

"Certainly," she said, anything but certain what was happening. The doctor waved his hand at someone standing in the doorway.

"Good morning, my dear. Mother sends her love," the man said in a posh British accent.

"Gaylord?" Miriam whispered in shock. "Is that really you, or am I still dreaming?"

"It is I. In the flesh," he said, stroking his pencil mustache with the back of his forefingers. For Miriam, the habit brought back memories of their time on the *Peggy C,* when she had had helped haul him out of the sea after his plane had been shot down. After that, she had patched up his wounded arm. He'd come a long way from waterlogged pilot to member of MI9 and the man who recruited her to work for the SOE in occupied Europe. "It was awfully good to receive your message after such a long silence."

"Where are the others?" Miriam said, her clearing head starting to flood with memories of recent events.

"Oh, I'm afraid there's not much I can do to help the other escapees they found with you. One imagines they are in jail and, I'll warrant, likely on their way soon to the concentration camp at Maranda de Ebro."

"They're not *any* escapees," Miriam said, fighting to sit up. "It's Jake, Mr. Nidal, and my father. You must help them."

"Golly, I'm terribly sorry," Gaylord said. "I will see what I can do. Now you rest. And once this is sorted out and you feel able, we'll take a little trip to Gibraltar."

"Before you leave, would you be a dear and find a toothbrush and bring me the toothpaste from my right jacket pocket?" she said, pointing to her rumpled clothes hanging on a nearby chair.

"What?" Gaylord raised an eyebrow. "Oh, I see," he said, finally catching on. "Right-o." He unbuttoned the jacket pocket and retrieved the tube of toothpaste containing the microfilm Monsieur Segers had given Miriam in Lyon. Checking out the inattentive guard at the door, he slipped the tube into his own pocket. "One can't be too careful when it comes to hygiene, can one?"

☆☆☆

"Where are we going?" Rogers said repeatedly, but the two Guardia Civils didn't seem to understand English or respond to Maduro's questions in Spanish. They led Rogers, Nidal, and Maduro into a waiting train, shoved them down in a second-class compartment, and removed their handcuffs. Shaking their heads in a huff, the officers slammed the compartment door shut, rattling the window. "Guess we're not going to prison after all."

"The train schedule said we're heading to Valencia," Maduro said, luxuriating in the soft seat after days on hard floors and benches in a Spanish jail. "I wonder why?"

The compartment door flung open. "On your way to Gibraltar, chaps," Gaylord said with a grin from ear to ear. He was holding onto Miriam, a large bandage wrapped around her head. Shouts of joy erupted from everyone as they sprang up to hug and kiss and cry.

Rogers and Miriam clung to one another for the entire ride and rarely joined in conversation with the others. "What do we do now?" Rogers said.

"I have to return to England immediately to warn the SOE," Miriam whispered in his ear. "All the agents they're dropping into Holland have been captured, and some have been compromised. They can't trust any messages from them. Otherwise, they'll be sending more agents to their deaths."

"And you can't tell Gaylord that? Can't he take the message back to London?"

"No," she said, snuggling closer. "There is a process. Plus, he is carrying the microfilm I was given in Lyon. I must explain who it came from. No one will believe me until after I've been interrogated for several days. It will not be pleasant, but it is necessary. It is my duty."

"And after that?" Rogers said."

Miriam averted his gaze.

"Please tell me you aren't thinking of going back."

"Let us not think of that right now," she said, burying her head on Rogers' shoulders. "What will you do?"

"I guess Mr. Nidal and I will try to hitch a ride on a Red Duster or a Liberty ship back to the States. They're launching new Liberty ships every day, and they need captains and first mates. I have a duty, too."

At the Valencia train station, a driver loaded them into a four-door French Salmson S4 E for the long drive to the British enclave of Gibraltar, which was not serviced by trains. When they arrived some six hours later, the car pulled up at a military airstrip.

"Afraid we can't dally," Gaylord said. "We must deliver this young lady post-haste to Whitchurch Airfield at Bristol. And then on to London. The Baker Street Irregulars are most anxious to debrief her," he said, referring to officials at the SOE headquarters on Baker Street.

After they all piled out, Rogers took Maduro aside. "I hate doing this, but you need to warn the British that Capt. Griffin was smuggling arms into Ireland for the IRA. I can't have any British deaths on my conscience."

Maduro tilted his head in confusion. "The IRA? What makes you suspect that?"

"An Irishman on an Irish ship loaded with weapons going to Ireland. Who else could they be for?"

"My dear Captain, I assumed you knew," Maduro said with a chuckle. "Capt. Griffin told me he was working for Bob Briscoe. And though he is associated with the IRA, he is not importing weapons for them. He said he is tired of the useless violence."

"Who for then?"

"For our fellow Jews and our mutual friend, Chaim Weizmann."

"So they can kill Brits?"

"No. Briscoe is helping the Jewish Agency gather arms for after the war, when the British will be forced to relinquish control of Mandatory Palestine," Maduro said, referring to the operative wing of the World Zionist Organization headed by Weizmann. "The new Jewish state will need an army. And quickly."

"Well, that's a relief," Rogers said, shaking Maduro's hand. "Stay safe in England."

Miriam hugged Nidal and kissed him on the cheek, making him blush.

"Goodbye, and thank you."

"Shalom ve lehitra'ot," Nidal said.

"I hope I see you again, too," Miriam replied with a sad smile, knowing the odds of that ever happening were slim at best.

Before she said goodbye to Rogers, she whispered something in Dutch to her father, who stared at her, sadness in his eyes, and replied in sharp tones in Dutch.

Rogers scowled. *Why are they behaving like that at a time like this? It's just like that night in Brussels when they argued about something on the couch. Why won't Miriam explain what's wrong?*

Shaking his head in frustration, Maduro waved farewell to the others and headed across the tarmac to a waiting twin-engine de Havilland DH.95 Flamingo.

"What was that all about?" Rogers said to Miriam.

"What I have come to believe is my duty. It must come first, no matter what else is going on in my life. He disagrees because he says you and I may never see each other again. He believes I owe you something."

"You owe me nothing," Rogers said, wrapping his arms around her. "Just remember that I love you. And we will meet again. That I promise." They lingered over their last kiss until Miriam, with tears rolling down her cheeks, pulled away.

"I will love you forever," she said and headed to the plane. When she reached the top of the stairs, she paused, whirled around, and mouthed some words Rogers couldn't hear over the engines' roar, but he could read her lips.

"We have a son."

BACKGROUND

The Hunt for The Peggy C — Capt. Jake Rogers had smuggled Miriam Maduro and her relatives aboard the *Peggy C* in Amsterdam two years ago in the days before America entered World War II. Her father, Solomon Maduro, who couldn't join them, had promised Rogers a huge reward if he delivered them on his neutral American ship to Gibraltar, where they would be safe with family.

But not long after they escaped Amsterdam, a U-boat forced the ship to stop for inspection. Rogers took the four-member boarding party hostage and escaped after tricking the U-boat into shallow water, where it ran aground.

During the nerve-wracking 3,000-mile escape through naval battles, minefields, and horrendous weather, Rogers' ship struggled to outrun a U-boat commanded by *Oberleutnant zur See* Viktor Brauer, an ardent Nazi who believed he was doing God's will. The increasingly unhinged commander knew his shaky career would end in disgrace unless he rescued his kidnapped boarding party from Rogers.

As the journey progressed, Rogers grew close to the family and fell in love with Miriam, who challenged him to change his mercenary ways. Rabbi Levy, Maduro's brother, with his endless stories and parables and affection, became something of the father Rogers never had. Along they way, they rescued RAF Lt. Basil Gaylord, whose plane was shot down over the North Atlantic.

They made it to the British stronghold on the tip of Spain, only to learn that the British had evacuated all the Jews and other civilians. Rogers reluctantly agreed to take the fugitives to Palestine with a stop in Malta to deliver aviation fuel for the British, who promised him a large payment and a pass through the Suez Canal to escape the pursuing U-boat. Most of his crew of misfits were furious. Rogers placated them by lying about the reward being paid them in Palestine. A mission that had started for him as being about money became a mission for love.

Not long after leaving Gibraltar, the *Peggy C* was attacked by "Hitler's Pirates," a German raider disguised as a neutral cargo ship. Rogers was severely wounded but again tricked the attackers into believing his ship was under the control of the German prisoners, who were taking their prize ship to Tripoli. The raiders took away supplies and left the *Peggy C* alone.

Trouble continued when they approached Malta and found themselves in the middle of a minefield. Rogers, who was recovering from his wounds, maneuvered the ship to safety but had to abandon hope of delivering the fuel and getting paid. Instead, he set course for Palestine. That was too much for many of his crew, who freed the German prisoners and mutinied.

The Germans murdered the rabbi as he tried to defend his children, and Obasi was near-fatally wounded in a gun battle after killing two of the Germans. Rogers quashed the mutiny but was captured by the German officer commanding the boarding party. It was then that Miriam proved she was as tough as her rhetoric about Jews fighting back. She shot and killed the German, saving Rogers' life.

There was no time to celebrate. The U-boat, secretly contacted by the mutineers, was closing in on the *Peggy C*. After evacuating almost everyone from the ship, Rogers lured the U-boat in close by dressing some crewmembers in the dead Germans' uniforms and having them pretend they controlled the ship and needed assistance. Once the U-boat was tethered to the *Peggy C*, the last crewmembers abandoned ship.

Rogers, who stayed behind, lit a fuse for a bomb, fought off Brauer, and jumped overboard. The explosion of all the highly flammable aviation fuel in the holds obliterated both ships. Rogers and the others were rescued by a British warship and taken to Haifa, where Rogers recovered from his old and new injuries in a hospital. He told Miriam he loved her but had to return to America to face the music because of a death for which he felt responsible. Miriam said she would wait for him forever.

CHAPTER NOTES

CHAPTER 2

Liberty Ships — Like so many other things in the war, Liberty Ships were invented out of necessity and produced on a scale never seen before. In 1940, Britain was losing ship tonnage to German U-boats more than four times faster than replacement ships could be built, a life-threatening trend for the island nation.

Although America was still neutral in January 1941, President Franklin D. Roosevelt announced an ambitious $350 million plan to build 200 merchant ships by the end of 1942, with 60 going to Britain. There was one problem: No detailed drawings or engineering plans existed for such an "emergency" vessel.

The government settled on a version of a British tramp steamer that had to be modified for oil fuel instead of coal, simplicity of construction, and ease of operation. The new ships—the length of a forty-story building and six stories wide—also had to be equipped with obsolete triple-expansion "up and down" engines; there was too much demand for the more modern turbine and diesel equipment.

Newspapers called the boxy ship an "ugly duckling" because it had been designed to eliminate as many time-intensive curves as possible. Roosevelt, a yachtsman and former undersecretary of the Navy, described it as "a dreadful looking object."

Traditionally, shipyards used the same crew to build a ship from the keel up, a process that averaged 244 days at the beginning of the war—an unacceptable snail's pace in wartime. The solution came from an archetypal American: an ambitious grade-school dropout and son of German immigrants who had never built a ship in his life before 1940.

The "Fabulous Henry J. Kaiser"—as the *Wall Street Journal* crowned him—had worked his way up from being a freelance photographer, to a hardware salesman, to running a small construction company, to manufacturing concrete, to building roads and then ever more giant dams, including the Boulder Dam. Over time, he acquired more than 100 companies.

The relentless entrepreneur got into shipbuilding almost as an after-thought. Over the big steel companies' strong objections, he and a partner were lobbying the federal government for permission to build a steel plant on the West Coast. To overcome those objections and add urgency to the pitch, the partners said they needed the steel to build ships. They got their steel mill—and an order for ships.

By 1942, Kaiser was producing almost a third of all American merchant ships. He did it by adapting others' ideas about pre-fabrication and assembly lines to build the vessels in sections all over the country and then assemble them in one of eighteen new shipyards, employing more than 700,000 work-ers, many of them women and minorities.

Each ship was a Herculean task involving 250,000 parts, forty-three miles of welding, five miles of wiring, and seven miles of piping. The first ship, *Patrick Henry*, was launched on September 27, 1941, along with thirteen others at ports around the country. Roosevelt quoted Patrick Henry's famous line in his dedication remarks: "Give me liberty or give me death." The ugly duckling was now a Liberty ship.

The US Maritime Commission named completed ships after famous Americans and, unlike the US military, manned them with integrated crews and officers. Captain Hugh Mulzac, a native of Saint Vincent and the Grenadines, became the first black captain in 1942 when he accepted command of the *SS Booker T. Washington*, but only after the Merchant Marines agreed it would be manned with an integrated crew and not solely black sailors.

Kaiser's shipyards brought the time for building the ships down to an average of forty-two days and even built one in less than five as a publicity stunt. But building ships so fast and cheap—around $2 million each and with a life expectancy of five years—created unforeseen problems. Riveting hulls to superstructures required too much scarce steel and skill by a four-person crew—one to heat the rivet, one to toss it to another worker to catch and hold it steady while the riveter pounded it into place.

One or two workers with less training could weld Liberty ships. But that left the welds prone to splitting in cold water, which made the steel brittle.

Three of the 2,710 Liberty ships built broke in half without warning, including the SS *John P. Gaines*, which sank in 1943 with the loss of 10 lives.

Corvettes — Like the Liberty ship, the corvette was created out of necessity at the beginning of the war using a British whaling ship as a model. It was smaller and slower than a destroyer but could be constructed in small shipyards in less than half the time with less well-trained workers. Once launched, they could be manned by naval reserves.

British Prime Minister Winston Churchill called corvettes "the cheap and nasties," as in cheap for the English and nasty for the Germans. Sailors called them "buckin' broncos" because they weren't designed for long ocean voyages, bouncing and rolling with such violence that their crews were almost always seasick.

Although the corvette was a deadly ship, it could also be a deathtrap. To speed construction, shipbuilders included few compartments below the waterline, which meant it would sink within seconds of being torpedoed, leaving the eighty-five men crammed aboard it with no time to escape.

Plastic armor — This was another wartime invention born of the necessity to replace expensive and scarce steel. It was created by Edward Terrell, a British barrister and Royal Naval Reserve Officer who wondered why an ancient paddle steamer evacuating troops from Dunkirk suffered so few casualties despite being riddled with bullets and shells. He discovered it had been caulked with multiple layers of an asphalt and cork mixture.

From that discovery, Terrell—an irrepressible inventor with several patents already in his name—came up with the unorthodox idea of covering a thin steel plate with a 2.5-inch-thick layer of stones mixed with asphalt to create a 3-to-4.5-foot barrier that would deflect bullets and not shatter as concrete barriers did. To confuse the Germans, Terrell invented the term "plastic armor."

Leigh Light on Liberators — RAF Wing Commander Humphrey de Verd Leigh had heard from frustrated pilots flying the few long-range B-24 Liberators patrolling the North Atlantic that their new air-to-surface-vessel radar stopped working once they came within a kilometer, or around 1,100 yards, of a U-boat recharging its batteries on the surface at night. Why not put a spotlight on the planes? Leigh wondered. No one would listen.

Churchill and the "Bomber Barons," the top three British and American air commanders, insisted on concentrating air power—particularly the American-built Very-Long-Range (VLR) Liberators—on bombing German cities and not on protecting convoys. So, Leigh secretly worked to develop a prototype on his own and without anyone's permission.

He devised a 1.1-ton carbon arc searchlight with a twenty-four-inch diameter that could be attached to a wing and throw a powerful beam 1,000 yards away. It took him more than a year, until mid-1942, to convince the RAF to begin using the Leigh Light widely. After that, ship tonnage sunk by U-boats dropped from 600,000 to 200,000 tons a month.

CHAPTER 3

Irish Neutrality — The Irish government declared a state of emergency at the beginning of World War II and announced that the country would remain neutral even though it was a member of the British Commonwealth. As a result, British warships had to travel hundreds of additional miles from their bases in Wales and Scotland to reach the North Atlantic.

Although neutrality was popular with the Irish people, "the Emergency," as the government referred to the war, also brought on hardships. The island nation, dependent on imports, had neglected its commercial navy for years, and there were only fifty-six Irish merchant ships at the beginning of the war. None of them was an ocean-going vessel.

In partnership with private companies, the government formed the Irish Shipping Limited company to remedy that dire situation. The company scoured the world in a desperate hunt for ships, regardless of their condition. It managed to round up fifteen ships, which were typically renamed for trees.

CHAPTER 4

Robert Briscoe — Briscoe had a long history with the Irish Republican Army, its political arm *Sinn Féin* (We Ourselves), and Jewish rebel groups in

Palestine. He missed the 1916 Easter Rebellion because he had moved to New York, where he opened a Christmas lights factory.

He sold the factory in 1917 and returned to Ireland, where he set up a clothing business as a front for gun-running. Michael Collins, an IRA leader and later the controversial chairman of the Provisional Government of the Irish Free State, appointed Briscoe to his staff and sent him to buy arms for the IRA in Germany, where Briscoe had studied engineering.

The British Secret Service suspected Briscoe was trouble, so it kept him under observation. Despite that, Briscoe managed to purchase a large cache of rifles, automatic pistols known as Peter the Painters, and ammunition from an underground group of German ex-military officers called *Orgesh*.

He smuggled the contraband out of Hamburg by tricking the British Navy into following an old tramp steamer named *Karl Marx* loaded with cement while a tugboat named *Frieda*, which had towed the *Karl Marx* out to sea, puttered away with the weapons to a cove near Ireland's Waterford Harbor.

Briscoe directed other smuggling trips with all-IRA crews on the rusty 2,000-ton steamer *City of Dortmund*, which he didn't use to import weapons. Instead, he imported innocuous chemicals for a reputable Irish drugstore that so happened to be the ingredients for explosives.

After World War II began, he helped raise funds in America for the Jewish paramilitary group *Irgun* (scout) and even trained its leader, Ze'ev Jabotinsky, in guerrilla war tactics. Briscoe liked to call himself the "Chair of Subversive Activity against England."

CHAPTER 6

Miss 2000 (Jacoba van Tongeren) — Planning a military operation was something she had learned early in life from her father Hermannus van Tongeren Sr., an engineer in the Royal Netherlands East Indies Army in the country local intellectuals thought should be called Indonesia.

Jacoba was born there in 1903 and was reared for the most part by her father and a *baboe*—a nanny—in a mobile home at a remote military camp in the Sumatran jungle, where her father oversaw the construction of railway bridges. There were no schools, so Hermannus taught his daughter himself, emphasizing the military values of discipline and responsibility and devoting several hours every day to studying the science of military codes.

After returning to The Netherlands, Jacoba studied to be a nurse but fell ill and never completed her final exams. Instead, she spent the next seven years recuperating in a health resort and a tuberculosis ward. Once she recovered sufficiently, she became a social worker, traveling the country on behalf of the Central Care for the Unemployed, and continued doing so after the Nazis occupied Holland in May 1940. By then, Hermannus had risen to the rank of major general and was Grand Master of the country's Freemasons, whose beliefs were antithetical to National Socialism.

When a resistance group approached him for help, Hermannus loaned them money to start the underground newspaper *Vrij Nederland* and provided contacts with other Freemasons around the country. Jacoba served as his intermediary, carefully planning her movements in detail and never using real names or addresses, as her father had taught her.

Unfortunately, the Nazis arrested Hermannus for his Freemason work, and he died in a concentration camp in early 1941. Around the same time, the Nazis rounded up more than sixty people connected to *Vrij Nederland* and abolished the Central Care of the Unemployed.

Jacoba avoided arrest by going into hiding for a time and found new work with the Special Family Care, a social work organization run by the nation's churches. Now, with contacts all over the country and traveling without restrictions for her work, Jacoba decided it was time to serve her country.

She formed a national group within the Reformed Church involving more than 100 people from all walks of life and religions to aid people in hiding: Jews, resistance fighters, and young men avoiding forced labor in Germany. It operated with military precision, and everyone used a code name. She became Miss 2000.

The twentieth letter in the alphabet is "T," the beginning letter of her last name. The double zeros meant she was the organization's first member, which became known as Groep 2000. Jacoba and an assistant were the only ones with the key to the code.

Work was divided among several committees and district leaders, who reported only to Jacoba. They had to provide coupons for rationed food, hiding places, false identity papers, support for families of dead or imprisoned resistance members, and even medical care to thousands of people, each of whom was given a code number. Food packages were also sent regularly via the Red Cross to Kamp Westerbork, where Etty Hillesum did her social work.

There was a special assault team that stole coupons from government distribution centers and another unit that provided security for Group 2000's food depots and for the drivers and couriers who delivered the food all around the country.

Jacoba herself was a key smuggler. To conceal as many as 5,000 coupons for transport, she designed a special vest to wear under her clothes, making her appear obese or pregnant and earning her the nickname *De Bonnenkoninging*, the "The Queen of Coupons."

Despite its widespread activities, Group 2000 and Jacoba were almost invisible to the Germans and even other resistance groups. The small number of members who were ever captured couldn't betray others, even under torture, because they only knew their small unit's members and only by numbers, not names.

A deeply religious person, Jacoba often convened a group of pastors to discuss the ethical dilemmas of their resistance work, such as whether they should lie, steal, or even kill. She believed in nonviolence and described her activities as "peace work in wartime." But she also knew violence was often unavoidable.

CHAPTER 8

Churchill and Ireland — Winston Churchill, who so often was prescient and spectacularly right about world affairs, could be just as often shortsighted and spectacularly wrong about the country where his family had a long history.

Ireland was where his famous ancestor, the first Duke of Marlborough, had the first independent command in what was to be one of the greatest military careers in British history. Churchill's grandfather was Lord Lieutenant (viceroy) of Ireland in the late 1800s, and his father, Lord Randolph, served as the viceroy's private secretary.

Churchill's problems with the Irish began in 1918, when he supported a call for conscription in Ireland, which triggered a landslide victory for Sinn Féin, whose members refused to take their seats in the British Parliament and instead created Ireland's first parliament, the *Dáil Éireann*, and declared the independent Irish Republic. It also fueled the IRA's rise and led to the Irish War of Independence in 1919.

Although both sides committed atrocities during the bloody, two-year guerrilla war, Churchill was blamed for many of the worst ones because, as Secretary of State for War, he had sent the notorious "Black and Tans" to crush the rebellion. The paramilitary group, primarily made up of ex-soldiers in mismatched initial uniforms of army khaki and police rifle green pants that could look black from a distance, had a reputation for brutality and wanton destruction, which didn't seem to bother Churchill.

Later, as Secretary of the Colonies, Churchill helped negotiate the harsh Anglo-Irish Treaty that ended the rebellion, led to the partition of Ireland, and replaced the independent Irish Republic with the Irish Free State as a dominion of the British Empire. When opponents of the treaty occupied government buildings in Dublin, Churchill threatened that British troops would take over the country unless Michael Collins and the Provisional Government used force to oust the rebels.

The buildings were cleared with artillery, killing sixty-five and wounding 270, and launching the Irish Civil War that pitted the government against the IRA for nearly a year of more atrocities on both sides. One of the worst was at Ballyseedy in the southwestern County Kerry, where guerrilla fighting was intense.

CHAPTER 9

Asclepius — The symbol was often confused with the *caduceus*, a staff intertwined with two serpents and wings carried by the Greek mythological deity Hermes, a symbol of commerce. The US Army Medical Corps popularized the misuse of the caduceus by adopting the emblem in 1902 at the insistence of a single officer.

Westerbork — Westerbork had been built on a desolate heath in the northeastern province of Drenthe in 1939 to house fewer than 2,000 German Jewish refugees who had fled Nazi Germany. More than 10,000 Jews from all over Holland were jammed into the camp's tiny confines. After the Germans invaded The Netherlands, the camp was converted into a *Polizeiliches Judendurchgangslager* (police transit camp for Jews).

In October 1942, it was commanded by *SS-Obersturmführer* Albert Gemmeker. The son of a poor Düsseldorf stonemason, Gemmeker dropped out of school at fourteen and worked as a policeman before joining the Gestapo.

Unlike previous camp commanders, he did not brutalize the prisoners; he never beat them or shouted at them and didn't tolerate such behavior in his sight. Some even called him a "gentleman commander," who more resembled a handsome English sportsman than a typical Nazi thug.

Gemmeker's goal was to make camp life as normal as possible to keep his desperate inmates calm and distracted from the dreaded weekly whistle of the train that would carry them away to Poland and an uncertain, but no doubt worse, future. Adding to that illusion was the fact that the thousands of prisoners were guarded almost entirely by fellow Dutchmen and Jews; only a dozen SS soldiers, all of them wounded veterans from the Eastern front, reinforced the guards.

Gemmeker, in his thirties, lived in great comfort in a two-story, five-bedroom green house with a cook and maid and his mistress, Elisabeth Helena Hassel-Mullender, Gemmeker's secretary who was recently divorced from his best friend. Inmates called her "she-devil" for her cruel treatment of the inmates. Rather than publicly disobey Gemmeker's orders against abuse, she had prisoners who displeased her shipped off to Poland or locked up in the Punishment Block.

To give the Jews a false sense of hope, Gemmeker allowed them to take educational classes, play in the camp orchestra, engage in sports, and travel outside the camp to purchase groceries or clothing with special camp currency. There even was a hairdresser and a synagogue. Every able-bodied person worked in one of a half-dozen or so of activities: construction, salvaging batteries and valuable metals from wreckage, tailoring, a laundry, bookbinding, manufacturing furniture, and crafting miniature wooden horses and stuffed dolls. More than 120 doctors, dentists, nurses, and 1,000 other employees treated the sick in a well-equipped 1,800-bed hospital, one of the largest in Europe.

Because he loved being entertained, Gemmeker organized a choir and a ballet troupe. He had all the camp's world-class musicians, singers, and comedians put on the *Bunter Abend* (variety show) weekly on a stage built from the ruins of a local synagogue.

He invited local businessmen and farmers to the shows and often entertained high-ranking Nazi officials, including *SS-Obersturmbannführer* Adolf Eichmann, the man in charge of organizing the deportation and extermination of all Jews in German-occupied Europe.

In an insidious twist, confiscated Jewish property funded all the deportations and the camp's construction. Most of the dirty work facilitating Westerbork's real mission was left to the Jews themselves. The Nazis appointed German Jews who had been part of the original refugees as *Kampleiding* (camp leadership).

With typical German efficiency, they created twelve divisions to set camp policy and maintained order in exchange for postponement of their deportation. The most powerful—and dangerous—of them was *Oberdienstleiter* Kurt Schlesinger, the chief administrator with the Hitler mustache known by inmates as "the mayor of Westerbork." The most hated was Arthur Pisk, a former Austrian milliner who commanded the Jewish police. Pisk was known as "the little dictator" because he hit and yelled at his fellow Jews.

CHAPTER 12

Mister 2200 (Gerrit van der Veen) — The sculptor planned and carried out the firebombing of the *bevolkingsregister* (Amsterdam Civil Registry office), where the name, address, and religion of everyone over fifteen had been stored since the invasion. Those names were essential for the Nazis to identify Jews and select gentiles for forced labor. Van der Veen organized a group of artists, medical students, and Jewish and gay resistance members to con its way past armed guards in the former concert hall. They disguised themselves as police.

The medical students sedated the guards with phenobarbital, while others dumped all the personnel files into a pile and doused them with benzene.

Timed explosives were to set off the fire once the unconscious guards and everyone else were out of the building. No one was to be hurt, so their weapons were loaded with blanks.

Walraven (Wally) van Hall   He was a man of many code names: Oom Piet, *Olieman*, and frequently Van Tuyll. But his most important one was *Bankier van het verzet (*Banker of the Resistance). It was a job for which he was ideally suited. As one of ten children born to a well-to-do family of bankers, stockbrokers, and politicians, he seemed destined for a career in finance.

But his love of sailing led him to break with family tradition and enter the Maritime Institute Willem Barentsz. After graduating, he spent the next four years traveling the world as a merchant marine until his career stalled because of bad eyesight. Rather than return home, he joined his brother Gijs, a stockbroker in New York, in 1929. Gijs managed to get him a job at a bank on Wall Street.

In 1931, van Hall returned to The Netherlands and worked as a banker and stockbroker. After the Nazis invaded in 1940, he and his brother helped set up a fund for stranded merchant marines. He also used subterfuge to raise money for underground newspapers and resistance groups to cover the cost of hiding Jews and other fugitives. Wealthy Dutch who donated money received worthless stock certificates that contained coded messages entitling them to a refund after the war, which the Dutch government-in-exile guaranteed.

Van Hall devised other ingenious schemes to raise money for the resistance groups, including stealing bonds from bank deposit boxes, which he replaced with forgeries. The charismatic banker was so well-connected and such a good negotiator that he was often called in to resolve differences among the resistance groups, thus the nickname Olieman (The Greaser).

His life was the subject of the 2018 movie *Bankier ban het verzet*, The Resistance Banker.

Uncle Alexander (Jonkheer Joan Schimmelpenninck) — One of "Uncle Alexander's" first recruits was a twenty-one-year-old midshipman in the Dutch Merchant Navy named **Peter Tazelaar**, whose daring exploits made it possible for the OD to connect with British and Dutch intelligence services in England. He did it by escaping to England as a stoker on a neutral Swiss ship and then returning as part of an audacious plan called "Contact Holland," designed to get resistance fighters in and out of The Netherlands by sea.

On the night of November 23, 1941, Tazelaar was taken by dinghy and dropped offshore near the Palace Hotel, a beachside resort at Scheveningen that the Nazis had seized as their headquarters and party spot. In a wetsuit and armed only with a bottle of brandy, Tazelaar swam ashore, zipped off the specially designed, waterproof wetsuit, and straightened the bone-dry, expensive tux he had worn underneath it.

After pouring the brandy over himself, he stumbled into the hotel swarming with guards, pretending to be a drunken partygoer returning from a stroll on the beach. Although that part of the plan went off without a hitch, the rest didn't, and after a few months, he had to flee back to England, where he trained Dutch troops. (A similar scene was included in the James Bond film *Goldfinger*, although it was not part of Ian Fleming's book.)

SS-Untersturmführer Ernst Knorr — The Gestapo called torture *Verschärfte Vernehmung* (enhanced interrogation), something for which Knorr was infamous. Even some of his superiors were repulsed by his brutality. He was known to gleefully beat prisoners to death or torture them with gruesome methods. Two years before he encountered Miriam, Knorr shoved his baton up the anus of communist resistance fighter Herman Holstege so hard it ripped up his intestines. He howled in agony in his cell for hours before dying of internal injuries. Another resistance fighter, Gerrit Kastein, threw himself out a second-story window while tied to a chair rather than face Knorr's methods.

CHAPTER 16

A. Puls — The dreaded trucks owned by Abraham Puls were one link in the Nazis' insidious chain of looting Jews. It started with requiring Jews to register, which most did voluntarily. Then *Verordnung* (decree) VO189/40 forced all companies owned by Jews or with substantial Jewish shareholders to register. Using that registry, the Nazi Commissariat General for Finance and Economy seized control of more than 20,000 businesses.

In 1941, the Nazis required all Dutch banks to transfer known Jewish accounts to a new institution deceptively named The Lippmann-Rosenthal & Co., a respected Jewish-owned bank seized by the Germans. At the same time, the Nazis required Jews to surrender their money, securities, and even insurance policies to the bank, known officially as the LiRo, but unofficially as the *roofbank* (plunder bank).

They were given itemized receipts and were told they would receive interest payments and could make withdrawals for living expenses. There was even a branch at Westerbork, where clerks assured the inmates the best way to protect their valuables was to deposit them with the LiRo. All proper. All perfectly normal. All cruel lies.

The wholesale looting began in May 1942, when Jews were required to turn over *everything* of value to the LiRo branch at 47-55 Sarphatistraat. A special account called *Sicherungskonto* (Security Account) received part of the proceeds, which the Germans used to cover the cost of the bounties on Jews' heads and for deporting them. By early 1943, the flood of deportations to Westerbork and concentration camps meant that more than 20,000 Jewish homes empty and ripe for plunder by Mr. Puls and company.

CHAPTER 18

Holzbrenner (**wood-burning engine**) — Engineer Ferdinand Porche developed the engine for Volkswagen when oil for civilian vehicles became nearly impossible to find. Thousands of VWs were produced under the label Kdf, which stood for *Kraft durch Freude* (strength through joy), a state-run organization designed to promote the advantages of Nazism through leisure activities.

Drivers had to stop often at special stations to refuel with such hardwoods as birch and oak that had been dried for months and pre-cut into sticks no larger than three inches long and two inches in diameter. Three kilograms (6.6 pounds) of wood produced the same energy as a liter (around a quarter-gallon) of gasoline. The range was 80 kilometers (50 miles), although larger cars could travel up to 170 kilometers (106 miles).

The system used two tanks. One held wood that was heated to the point where it decomposed and produced gasses. That tank was connected through a filtration system to a second tank that held the gasses, which were injected into the cylinders of a standard combustion engine.

Concordat—While some considered the 1933 Concordat a symbol of peace, others thought the accord gave some moral legitimacy to Hitler—a vegetarian, teetotaler, drug addict, and anti-Semite—which damaged the church's reputation. Cardinal Theodor Innitzer, archbishop of Vienna, further muddied the church's reputation when he and other Austrian bishops signed a declaration in March 1938 endorsing Hitler's annexation of his native Austria, a statement Innitzer himself signed with "Heil Hitler."

The following month, the cardinal created even more outrage when he ordered all churches to honor Hitler's birthday by flying the swastika flag and ringing bells. The Vatican repudiated his statements, and Innitzer walked them back, but that was little comfort to Jews.

Associated Press Wirephoto Service — The Associated Press Wirephoto Service started in 1935 and was set up in Europe as AP Gmbh Photo Service. When America entered the war in December 1941, Germany arrested and deported AP's American staff and gave control of the service to *SS*-Obersturmführer Helmut Laux, German Foreign Minister Joachim von Ribbentrop's personal photographer, who often traveled with Hitler.

The Bureau Laux, as the new organization was known, received photos from all over the world using AP's machines and then transmitted them to newspapers throughout occupied Europe, particularly to the network of German-language newspapers like the ones in Brussels and Amsterdam.

The process was fairly simple. The glossy photo was taped to a metal drum spun by a six-volt motor while being scanned by a slowly moving pinpoint light. That light was reflected onto a photoelectric cell, which converted it into electronic signals. Those signals were transmitted over dedicated phone lines to a receiver with its own spinning drum and light to create a negative for printing the original picture. The whole process took less than 15 minutes.

CHAPTER 21

Stalingrad — The city, known for four centuries until 1925 as Tsaritsyn, was in the country's southwestern part between the Don and Volga rivers. It had some strategic value but was not the primary objective of Operation Blue. As operation commander Field Marshall Paul Ludwig Ewald von Kleist put it, "At the start, Stalingrad was no more than a name on the map to us." Their target was the vital oilfields farther south in the Caucasus.

But in August 1942, Hitler diverted the Sixth Army to capture the city at any cost with no option of ever retreating. Stalin responded with a brutal command to the outmanned and outgunned Soviet forces with no air cover: "*Ni shagu nazad*!" ("Not a step backward").

Five months and 900,000 German and 1.2 million Soviet casualties later, the decimated Sixth Army surrendered, and the Nazis were in retreat in Europe for the first time. The Nazi defeat at Stalingrad provided the first glimmer of hope for the occupied countries.

Attack on Gestapo Headquarters in Brussels — It wasn't a crazy British pilot who caused the damage. It was Baron Jean de Selys-Longchamps, a Belgian cavalry officer who escaped capture twice to join the RAF's 609 Squadron. And he wasn't crazy. He was out for revenge. His father had been tortured to death by the SiPo, the German security force comprising the Gestapo and *Kripo* (criminal police).

After a bombing mission in January, de Selys-Longchamps headed without permission to Brussels in his single-engine Hawker Typhoon instead of returning to base in England. Traveling close to the ground, he avoided detection during the thirty-one-mile voyage. Once over Brussels, he buzzed the Gestapo's headquarters with his roaring Napier Sabre engines, drawing dozens of people to the balconies and windows to see what was happening.

On his second pass, he came in low and raked the building with his four 20mm Hispano automatic cannons. The Gestapo publicly acknowledged four deaths, but rumors said he had killed dozens. Before returning to England, he dropped the flags over the Royal Palace and his sister's home. Upon his return, he was demoted for disobeying orders and then awarded the Distinguished Flying Cross.

CHAPTER 22

Capt. Jackson — Prosper Dezitter, also known as Capt. Jackson, was responsible for capturing hundreds of British soldiers left behind after Dunkirk, downed Allied airmen, and other men trying to escape occupied Europe. Born in Belgium in 1893, Dezitter fled to Canada in 1913 after being convicted of rape.

He briefly trained in the Canadian Royal Air Force and worked odd jobs before returning home in 1926 and a life of fraud, embezzlement, and smuggling, for which he served several years in prison. After the German invasion, he infiltrated several organizations helping Allied soldiers and airmen. He changed his name and appearance often, sometimes had a thin black mustache, and frequently wore gloves to disguise the missing little finger he lost in an accident.

He had a fleet of cars at his disposal and always carried a gun and a pass from the Gestapo warning police not to arrest him. He cultivated priests and religious organizations around the country as a way to provide his fake escape line with a steady stream of victims who thought he was a British or Canadian agent or airman on the run.

His accomplice was **Miss Anny**, a native of Barcelona whose real name was Florentine Dings. They were paid from 1,000 to 5,000 French francs for each captured airman or resister. That was a substantial reward, considering the average wage for an industrial worker in Paris was 12.27 francs an hour or around 491 francs a week. Although they worked primarily for the Abwehrstelle and Gestapo, Brosan's fellow GFP officers often provided their protection.

CHAPTER 23

French Rationing — Before the war, a French adult ate, on average, 2,500 calories a day; the average fell to half that during the war. And, with everything being rationed, in short supply, or requisitioned and shipped off to Germany, prices on the black market skyrocketed for such staples as eggs and butter, selling for almost triple the price set by the government. Making things worse, the purchasing power of wages, frozen in 1940, had been falling since the war started.

To survive, the French developed the *"Système de Débrouillage"* or *"Système D,"* meaning a way to get by using a network of friends, family, neighborhood and business contacts, and the black market to beg, barter, or bargain for food. Farmers had difficulty keeping up with demand because their equipment wore out, and spare parts were almost impossible to obtain.

Conditions were worse for city dwellers, who would take trains to the countryside in search of farmers with food to sell, a practice so common trains from Paris were often nicknamed after vegetables, such as the *train des haricots* (green beans) or the *train des pommes de terre* (potatoes).

CHAPTER 24

French Forced Labor — France's Vichy government announced the *Relève* policy in June 1942, under which one of the 1.5 million French prisoners of war would be released by the Germans in return for every three "volunteers" who went to work in German factories.

But the Nazis weren't satisfied with the results, so the Vichy government enacted the *Service du travail obligatoire* (Compulsory Work Service or STO) in February 1943, requiring all men of military age to report for work in Germany.

The law drove thousands of men into hiding as *réfractaires* (draft dodgers) and the underground resistance and, as a result, added one more onerous duty to the stretched-thin French and German security forces.

CHAPTER 26

Monsieur Segers (Johan [Jean] Hendrik Weidner Jr.) — He kept a lot of secrets as the founder of the Dutch-Paris escape line, one of the largest and most successful underground networks. It assisted hundreds of downed Allied pilots, young men fleeing compulsory service, and résistants, as well as Jews and others, persecuted for their faith or race.

A network of more than 300 people helped him lead the desperate men and women to freedom in Switzerland or Spain, with some ferrying military intelligence to London. The escape line was a logistical nightmare, requiring the use of two languages and five currencies to illegally cross over four borders using a plethora of false documents, all requiring up-to-date information about constantly changing policies in six occupation zones.

The time of the ostriches —For years prior to September 1, 1939, when Germany invaded Poland, France had been for years spending more of its GDP on the military than any other country and, together with the rest of the Allies, had vastly more tanks, fighter aircraft, army divisions, and artillery than the Germans.

And it had the Maginot Line, a seven-billion-franc impenetrable line between France and Germany which consisted of futuristic facilities six and seven stories below the surface, concrete bunkers, tank barriers, fortresses, minefields, air-conditioned tunnels, medical facilities, and underground railways that stretched 450 kilometers from Switzerland to Luxemburg.

But none of that mattered much because France had never fully recovered from its "victory" over Germany in the Great War; its population had been bled dry, with nearly 6 million military casualties, including 1.3 million dead, which was about a third of all French males between 18 and 27; with the increase in invalids and widows, the birthrate was cut in half; thousands of veterans suffered from a *crise de tristesse sombre*, an attack of black sorrow, what the British called shell-shock; and France's leaders, military and civilian, were unimaginative old men who prepared for the last war and refused to adapt to modern technology and tactics.

Although many French tanks were larger than the Germans', most had no radios; *all* the German tanks did, and they had mobile units communicating between tank commanders and the Luftwaffe above, giving the Germans an unprecedented ability to coordinate and concentrate their forces with blinding speed, hence the devastating *Blitzkrieg* (lightning war). The command post of Gen. Maurice Gamelin, the 67-year-old World War I veteran commanding the French army, didn't even have a telephone at first.

Gamelin and the other generals also ignored a book by a then-obscure French army officer named Charles de Gaulle advocating the use of speed and concentrated tank formations instead of spreading tanks among separate units across the whole front. The Germans, however, had taken the advice to heart.

And even when the German forces were focusing on Poland, leaving them vulnerable to attack from behind, the overly cautious French leaders did nothing for eight long months, a time dubbed the "Phoney War" or *Sitzkrieg* (the sitting war) by the British press.

When Germany attacked Holland on May 10, 1940, the Allies assumed it was a repeat of the "Schlieffen Plan" from World War I, where the Germans swept through Luxemburg and Belgium, both neutral counties, and then pivoted like a giant scythe into France. So, they concentrated their forces to the north in the Low Countries, confident that the Maginot Line and the densely forested Ardennes would prevent an attack from the east through Luxemburg and the 400-kilometer border with Belgium. Even when French reconnaissance planes reported a 250-kilometer-long traffic jam of German tanks and motorized vehicles in the Ardennes, Gamelin refused to change his plans.

Unfortunately, the Maginot Line turned out to be as effective as a half-open sliding barn door made of steel—impenetrable, but useless at stopping horses from running past it. Defeat was devastatingly quick.

The French prime minister fired Gamelin and replaced him with another, even older, out-of-touch World War I veteran, 73-year-old Maxime Weygand. Within a month, France's government fell, and a new prime minister was appointed: Marshal Philippe Pétain, the 85-year-old French army commander-in-chief during the final years of World War I and hero of the 302-day battle of Verdun, the first battle Pétain had witnessed or commanded. It was one of the longest and deadliest in history. There were more than 700,000 casualties and, like Stalingrad, it was a battle of more symbolic than strategic importance.

Within days of Pétain taking office, France signed a humiliating armistice with Germany. Pétain became a virtual dictator. In his thin, metallic voice—what pundits said sounded like "an old woman" or "a skeleton with a chill"—Pétain, between frequent dry coughs, announced in a radio address "a path of collaboration" with Hitler; he enacted harsh anti-Semitic laws without prompting from the Germans, imposed censorship, and jailed opponents for the "felony of opinion."

Every hour of every day, the French had a sad reminder of their subservience: clocks. The Nazis had ordered them moved forward an hour to synchronize with German time. At first, Germany left a southwestern portion of the country under French control, with its capital in the resort town of Vichy. When the Allies invaded North Africa in November 1942, the Germans occupied the Free Zone as well.

CHAPTER 28

Klaus Barbie — In February 1941, Barbie led a raid on a Jewish tavern in Amsterdam called Koco, where an exploding security device full of ammonia injured a German soldier. In retaliation, Barbie rounded up 425 Jewish men, beat them in full public view, and sent them off to concentration camps. His actions sparked a three-day nationwide strike and marches to protest the mistreatment of Jews.

Three months later, after someone threw a bomb into a German officers' club, Barbie engineered a diabolical reprisal. He tricked the Jewish Council into providing the names of 300 Jewish young men, who he said would be allowed to return to their apprenticeships. Instead, he sent them to the Mauthausen concentration camp as retaliation for the bombing.

CHAPTER 29

Charles de Gaulle - The maddeningly arrogant de Gaulle had always been a polarizing figure, even among fellow French officers. Churchill and Roosevelt despised him; Pétain, his one-time hero and mentor, disowned him as a "very ill-bred" man; the Vichy government rescinded his promotion from colonel to brigadier-general and sentenced him to death for fleeing to England after the armistice; and resistance groups in France paid little attention to him.

And yet...Through his ability to recruit extraordinary men like Jean Moulin to serve as his emissary on the ground in France, an unshakable belief in himself as "*l'homme du destin* (the man of destiny")—as Churchill once described him, and having the BBC broadcast his speeches, de Gaulle gained a prominence that convinced Allied leaders and several resistance groups— united by the tireless efforts of Moulin—to recognize him as head of the free French in exile. It was an uneasy alliance at best.

WHAT HAPPENED TO THEM

Uncle Alexander (Jonkheer Joan Schimmelpenninck)—He was arrested at his home on November 13, 1941, and was imprisoned at the Oranjehotel and several transit camps before being executed on July 29, 1943, at age 55.

Francis André—Nicknamed "*Gueule Tordue*" ("Twisted Face) because of injuries suffered in a car accident, André was sentenced to death by a French court for more than 120 murders and executed on March 9, 1946.

Miss Anny—Florentine Girault, also known as Flore Dings, was captured with Capt. Jackson (Prosper Dezitter) in Germany, and was one of four women sentenced to death in Belgium for wartime activities. She was executed on June 4, 1949.

SS-Hauptsturmführer Klaus Barbie—Nikolaus "Klaus" Barbie, known as "the Butcher of Lyon," is believed responsible for more than 14,000 deaths during his time with the Gestapo. After the war, he worked for American intelligence before fleeing to Bolivia, where he was an arms dealer, worked for West German intelligence, collaborated with Bolivia's authoritarian governments, and did business with Colombian drug lord Pablo Escobar. He was extradited to France in 1983, tried for war crimes, and sentenced to life imprisonment. He died in prison in 1991 at age 77.

Georges Bégué—The French engineer, code-named "Bombproof," was a wireless radio operator and the first of 407 SOE agents infiltrated into France. He was arrested by the French police in October 1941. He escaped from prison in July 1942 and returned to England. After the war, he emigrated to the United States and worked as an electrical engineer. He died on December 18, 1993, at age 82.

Rudolf Breslauer—The German-born photographer of Jewish descent, his wife, two sons, and daughter were deported from Westerbork to Auschwitz in 1944. Only his daughter survived.

Robert Briscoe—The Irish politician, sickened by the violence in his own country, convinced his friend Menachem Begin to turn away from violence with his paramilitary group Irgun and transform the group into an Israeli political party that eventually became Likud. He served in the Irish parliament, Dáil Éireaan, for 38 years and was the first Jewish Lord Mayor of Dublin. He died on May 29, 1969, at age 74.

Johan Brouwer—The Dutch historian and author was captured within a week of participating in the resistance bombing of the Amsterdam Civil Registry Office (*bevolkingsregister*) and was executed along with eleven other participants by the Germans on July 1, 1943. He was 45.

Rudolf Wilhelm Dahmen von Buchholz—The head of the Amsterdam Municipal Police's Bureau of Jewish Affairs was sentenced to life imprisonment after the war. The sentence was commuted to twenty years. He died on August 10, 1967, at age 77.

Tineke Buchter—The Amsterdam medical student, her mother, Marie Schotte, and her grandmother Marie Schotte Abrahams hid more than 100 Jewish refugees in their home for the Dutch resistance during the Nazi occupation. Although the Gestapo raided her house eight times, arrested her nine times, and frequently beat her, Buchter never revealed her secrets.

After the war, she earned her medical degree and immigrated to the United States, where she practiced psychiatry under her married name of Tina Strobos until 2009. In 1989, she and her mother were recognized as Righteous Among the Nations by Yad Vashem, Israel's official memorial to Holocaust victims. Tineke died on February 27, 2012, at age 91. I could not find more information about her mother or grandmother.

Hans Calmeyer—The German lawyer was appointed Director for the Interior Administration, handling Jewish affairs after the German occupation of The Netherlands. He is credited with saving thousands of Jews by accepting fraudulent or ambiguous documentation proving they were not "full-blooded Jews" and not eligible for deportation. He died on September 3, 1972, at age 69. He was recognized in 1992 as Righteous Among the Nations by Yad Vashem, Israel's official memorial to Holocaust victims. However, some historians question his heroism.

Paul Carbone—He was a Corsican criminal who became known as the Emperor of Marseille, a leader of the French Connection, and an inspiration for the film *Borsalino*. He and his partner **François Spirito** joined the Carlingue and worked closely with the Gestapo. He died on December 16, 1943, when the resistance blew up the train he was riding on. He was 49.

Commissioner Fernand David—He was head of the Vichy police's *Brigades Spéciales*, which hunted down resistance members, dissidents, draft dodgers, Jews, and other "internal enemies." He was convicted of treason after the war and executed on May 5, 1945, at the age of 34.

Oberscharführer Ernst Dunker—A military tribunal convicted the Gestapo master sergeant of war crimes on January 21, 1947, and he was executed on June 6, 1950. He was 38.

Dr. Eugène (Dr. Marcel Petiot)—French police raided Petiot's house in March 1944 after neighbors complained about the terrible smell and large amounts of smoke coming from the chimney. They discovered body parts in a coal stove in the basement and all around the house. There were enough bones for at least ten bodies. Petiot went into hiding, adopted a new identity, and became a captain in the French Forces of the Interior (FFI), a resistance group. In October 1944, he was arrested and charged with twenty-seven murders for profit although he was suspected of as many as 200.

He had lured victims with promises of smuggling them to Argentina for a steep fee. But he said the Argentine government insisted that they be inoculated against diseases. Then he injected them with cyanide, stole all their belongings, and disposed of their bodies. Prosecutors said the serial killer made more than 200 million francs from his crimes. Petiot was convicted in May 1946 and beheaded. He was 49.

Capt. Gerald Griffin—The captain of the fictional *Erin Go Bragh* is not a real person. I included him here because he is named for my grandfather, a journalist and son of Thomas Robin Griffin from County Kerry, Ireland, who immigrated to America in 1864, attended Colby College, and graduated from the US Naval Academy in 1869 but resigned his commission to go into engineering. He moved to Somerset, Kentucky, in 1874, where he was a deputy sheriff, mayor, and a feared railroad detective renowned for shooting several would-be bandits to death.

Capt. Jackson (Prosper Dezitter)—He was believed to be responsible for more than 12,000 denunciations of resisters, downed Allied pilots, and Jews, and 1,200-1,800 deaths. Some estimates say the Germans paid him more than $1 million. He was captured in Germany and extradited to Belgium, where he was tried and executed on September 17, 1948, two days before his fifty-fifth birthday.

Henry J. Kaiser—The American industrialist founded dozens of companies before the war. During and after it was over, he created Kaiser Shipbuilding, Kaiser Steel, Kaiser Air, Kaiser Permanente health group, Kaiser Automobiles, Kaiser Aluminum, Kaiser Broadcasting, and the Kaiser Family Foundation, among many others. He died on August 24, 1967, at age 85.

SS-Untersturmführer Ernst Knorr—The man known as "the Doctor" was captured at the end of the war and imprisoned at the Oranjehotel, the very place where he carried out his brutal interrogations. He was found dead in his cell with a rope around his neck on July 7, 1945, but his cause of death could not be determined. He was 45.

Piet Kuijt—He was a beach planter around the Waalsdorpervlakte, where more than 250 people were executed by the Germans and buried in the dunes. Kuijt, who had permission to be in the area to plant beach grass to reinforce the dunes, secretly witnessed several executions while illegally hunting for rabbits.

He would mark the graves with marram grass in unique formations. After the war, he and Reverend Gerrit Bos, pastor of the Oranjehotel, helped Dutch authorities locate the graves. Imprisoned NSB members excavated them. He died around 1971 without ever telling his family about his experience.

SS-Obersturmführer Albert Gemmeker—In the two years he was commandant of the Westerbork transit camp, more than 80,000 (of 107,000 total) Jews, Sinti, and Roma, including Anne Frank and her family, were deported to concentration camps. He was captured in 1945 and put on trial in December 1948. Though claiming he knew nothing about the mass murders of his deported prisoners, he was sentenced to ten years imprisonment, six of which he served. He died on August 30, 1982, at the age of 74.

Elizabeth Helena Hassel-Mullender—Gemmeker's mistress was arrested in 1945 and held to testify at his trial. She was released in 1947. She was arrested again in 1948 and released the following year with no charges ever filed. I could not find anything else about her.

Etty Hillesum—The Dutch diarist who wrote of her spiritual and religious development amid the horrors of the Nazi occupation refused repeated offers to help her go into hiding because she considered it her duty to help those being deported. She voluntarily returned to Westerbork after recovering from an illness in June 1943.

Along with her father, mother, and brother, she was deported the next month to Auschwitz, where all of them were murdered. She was 29. A short version of her diaries, *Het verstoorde leven (An Interrupted Life)*, was published in 1981, followed in 1986 by a complete Dutch edition of her letters and diaries.

Ze'ev (Vladimir) Jabotinsky—The Russian founder of Revisionist Zionist, who also founded Betar and Irgun, died of a heart attack on August 3, 1940, while visiting New York to seek support for a Jewish army to fight the Nazis. He was 59.

Josef Kotalla—He was transferred from the Oranjehotel to become head of administration in Kamp Amersfoort, where his cruelty earned him the nickname "the executioner of Amersfoort." He was sentenced to death after the war, but the sentence was commuted to life in prison. He died there in 1979 at age 71.

Henri Lafont and Pierre Bonny—The two leaders of the Carlingue were captured together in August 1944 and executed alongside each other by a firing squad in December of that year. Lafont's last words to his lawyer were, "I regret nothing, Madame. Four years in the midst of orchids, dahlias, and Bentleys—it pays off!" Lafont was 42 and Bonny was 49.

Pierre Loutrel—The one-time member of the Bonny-Lafont gang, who became known as "Pierrot le fou" (Crazy Pete), joined the resistance in 1944. After the war, he formed his own gang called *Gang des tractions*, named after his favorite car, the Citroën Traction Avant. He was shot during a robbery and died on November 11, 1946. He was 30.

RAF Wing Commander Humphrey de Verd Leigh—The inventor of the Leigh Light was awarded the Order of the British Empire, the Distinguished Flying Cross, and the Air Force Cross. He retired from the military in 1954 and died on June 6, 1980, at age 82.

George Maduro—Nicknamed Joopie, this son of wealthy shipowners from the Dutch colony of Curaçao, as a reserve second lieutenant, won military honors for leading Dutch troops who briefly repelled the Germans outside the Hague. When Holland surrendered, he was taken as a prisoner of war and imprisoned in the Oranjehotel. After he was released three months later, he joined the resistance but was arrested again in May 1941 and returned to the

Oranjehotel. He was released for unknown reasons on December 15, 1941.

Capt. Jackson (a.k.a. Prosper Dezitter) betrayed him in September 1943 during his attempt to flee to England. Maduro had an opportunity to escape when the prison where he was incarcerated was severely damaged by an Allied air attack, but he stayed behind to rescue prisoners trapped under the rubble.

He died at Dachau concentration camp on February 8, 1945, at the age of 29.

After the war, he was awarded the Knight 4th-class of the Military Order of William, Holland's highest and oldest military decoration.

Marcel Marceau—Because of his fluency in English, French, and German, he became a liaison officer with Gen. George Patton's Third Army and later entertained the troops. After the war, the French mime became a much-beloved worldwide star of television, film, and stage, especially for his stage character Bip the Clown. He also wrote several children's books. He died on September 22, 2007. He was 84.

Rut Matthijsen—The university chemistry student and co-founder of the Utrecht Children's Committee with Jan Meulenbelt had to go into hiding in the summer of 1943 after two colleagues were arrested. After the war, he worked for a pharmaceutical company. He was recognized in 1974 as Righteous Among the Nations by Yad Vashem, Israel's official memorial to Holocaust victims. He died in 2019 at the age of 97.

Jean Moulin—The Germans arrested the French civil servant in June 1941 for refusing to sign a false declaration that Senegalese Tirailleurs had murdered civilians actually killed by German bombs. Freed from prison after a suicide attempt, he escaped to London and agreed to help Charles de Gaulle unify the various resistance groups.

He succeeded in getting the three largest groups to form the *Mouvements Unis de la Résistance* (MUR), and then in mid-1943, he united the MUR with other resistance groups, labor groups, journalists, and political parties to form the *Conseil National de la Résistance* (National Resistance Council or CNR). He was captured in June 1943 near Lyon by the Germans, tortured by Klaus

Barbie, and died in July of his injuries while on a train to Germany. He was 44.

Raymonde Pillot—She was 16 when she started working as a secretary for Johan Weidners, head of the Dutch-Paris escape line. According to the Weidner Foundation, she was personally arrested by Klaus Barbie, tortured, and sent to Ravensbrück concentration camp. Allied troops liberated her on May 7, 1945.

Arthur Pisk—The leader of the Ordedienst (OD) police force in Westerbork, known as "chief of the Jewish Gestapo," was arrested in 1945 but released without being charged. He emigrated to Australia and died in 1963.

Abraham Puls—His moving company was responsible for cleaning out many of the 29,000 seized Jewish homes, including the one where Anne Frank and her family were captured. His death sentence was commuted to life in prison and then cut to 24 years. He died in 1975 at age 73.

Reichsminister Alfred Rosenberg—The mastermind of the looting of Jews was captured by Allied soldiers on May 19, 1945, convicted of war crimes at Nuremberg, and executed on October 16, 1946, at age 53.

Audrey Hepburn-Ruston (a.k.a. Edda van Heemstra)—Hepburn moved to London, dropped Ruston from her name, and went on to become one of the few actors to win Academy, Grammy, Emmy, and Tony awards. She died on January 20, 1993, at the age of 63.

Monsieur Segers (Johan (Jean) Hendrik Weidner Jr.)—The leader of the Dutch-Paris escape line was responsible for rescuing more than 1,000 Jews and downed Allied pilots. Though arrested and badly beaten by French police and the Milice, he managed to escape. After the war, he resumed his textile business and emigrated to California, where he and his wife operated a chain of health food stores. He was awarded the US Medal of Freedom with Gold Palm, the French Croix de Guerre, and French Médaille de la Résistance and the French Légion d'honneur, made an Honorary Officer of the Order of the British Empire, an Officer in the Dutch Order of Orange-Nassau, and an Officer of the Belgian Order of Leopold. He was also recognized as Righteous Among the Nations by Yad Vashem, Israel's official memorial to Holocaust victims. He died on May 21, 1994, at age 81.

Baron Jean de Selys-Longchamps—The Belgian RAF captain, who bombed the Gestapo's Brussels headquarters, was killed on August 16, 1943 while attempting to land at an RAF base in a plane with landing gear damaged by German flak. He was 31.

Oberdienstleiter Kurt Schlesinger—As commander of the Jewish security service for Westerbork, Schlesinger oversaw the deportation of more than 100,000 Jews to concentration camps, where almost all of them were murdered. Canadian troops liberated Westerbork on April 12, 1945. Proceedings were started against Schlesinger in 1946, but no charges were ever filed. He testified for the defense in the trial of Westerbork commandant SS-Obersturmführer Albert Gemmeker. He and his wife emigrated to New York. He died in 1964 at age 62.

Pieter Jacob Six—The captain in the Royal Netherlands Army reserves when the war broke out took over the Ordedienst (OD) leadership after the Nazis rounded up the resistance group's top leadership. After the war, he was made a Knight in the Military William Order and received top British and American military honors. He served with various veterans' associations and died in 1986 at age 92.

François Spirito—The Marseille mobster, who was Paul Carbone's partner, fled France at the end of the war and ended up in Toronto, where he organized heroin smuggling into New York as part of the French Connection. He served two years in a New York prison and was extradited to France in 1953. He died on October 9, 1967, at age 69.

Werner Stertzenbach—The German journalist and communist was credited with helping around twenty people escape from Westerbork, sometimes by smuggling them to the crematorium. In 1943, he escaped and spent the rest of the war hiding in Amsterdam. After the war, he returned to West Germany and became editor-in-chief of the weekly *Die Tat*. He died on July 10, 2003, at age 94.

Peter Tazelaar—After escaping from Holland, he trained soldiers in Wales and Canada. He parachuted back into The Netherlands in 1944, where he provided intelligence for England until the end of the war in Europe. He received Holland's highest military award, the Military William Order, and accompanied Queen Wilhelmina on her return to The Netherlands. He also served in Ceylon in 1945 in the fight against the Japanese. After the war, he worked for KLM Airlines and Shell Oil. He died on June 6, 1993, at age 73.

Marie Anne Tellegen—The Dutch lawyer and women's rights activist went into hiding in 1944, the day before the Germans raided her house in Utrecht. In October 1945, she was appointed director of Queen Wilhelmina's cabinet, a position she held until 1959. Her honors included Knight of the Order of The Netherlands Lion, the US Medal of Freedom with the silver palm, Grand Officer of the Order of Orange-Nassau, and commander of the French Légion d'honneur. She died on April 23, 1976, at age 82.

Captain Edward Terrell—After he created "plastic armor," he was appointed to the staff of the First Sea Lord and became head of the Directorate of Miscellaneous Weapons Development, where he continued to create innovative weapons and tactics against U-boats. He returned to his legal practice after the war. He died on November 13, 1979, at age 72.

Ton—Antonius Simeon Marie (Anton) van Schendel, known as "Ton," trained amateur radio operators for the Ordedienst (OD) resistance group. He was arrested while in hiding in Amsterdam on September 4, 1943, and spent the rest of the war in prison. After the war, he returned to his pre-war job at the Dutch Radio Monitoring Service. On June 24, 1954, Dutch Queen Juliana awarded him the Bronze Lion for his bravery during World War II. He died on August 9, 1958, just a week before his 64th birthday.

Jacoba van Tongeren (Miss 2000)—She was the only woman to create and lead a resistance movement during the war. The 150 members of her Group 2000 sheltered more than 4,500 people during the occupation, providing them with food, clothing, ration coupons, and false identity papers. After the war, she was chronically ill and bedridden. She died in obscurity on September 15, 1967, at the age of 63. It wasn't until her memoirs were published in 2015 that her heroics became widely known. She and several other Group 2000 members were recognized as Righteous Among the Nations by Yad Vashem, Israel's official memorial to Holocaust victims.

Walraven (Wally) van Hall—The "Resistance Banker" known as Wally raised more than 50 million guilders for the resistance before being betrayed by a collaborator and executed on February 12, 1945, at the age of 39. The Germans never learned of his role in the resistance. He was awarded the Dutch Cross of Resistance and the American Medal of Freedom and recognized as Righteous Among the Nations by Yad Vashem, Israel's official memorial to Holocaust victims.

Trudel van Reemst-De Vries—"Trude" was released from Westerbork in 1943 after a German decree was issued protecting Jews in mixed marriages. Her husband, **Dr. Theo van Reemst**, was Christian. She worked for the resistance for the rest of the war. After the war, she worked as a German teacher. She and Theo, who was released from Dachau, later divorced. He died on January 14, 1980, at age 71. Trude died on June 7, 2007, at the age of 92. I could not find anything else about her brother-in-law, **Ger van Reemst**, who worked for the Dutch Forestry Commission outside of Westerbork.

Mr. 2200 (Gerrit van der Veen)—The Dutch sculptor and member of Group 2000, who organized the Amsterdam Registry bombing and forged thousands of IDs, tried to free some of his colleagues from prison but was shot and had to flee. He was arrested a couple of weeks later, in May 1944, and executed on June 10, 1944, at the age of 41. He was awarded the Dutch Cross of Resistance and recognized as Righteous Among the Nations by Yad Vashem, Israel's official memorial to Holocaust victims.

Major Gen. Charles C. Walcutt—The Columbus, Ohio native served under Generals Ulysses S. Grant and William Tecumseh Sherman during the American Civil War. He is also my great-great-uncle. He was wounded several times and fought in the battles of Shiloh, Vicksburg, Missionary Ridge, Kennesaw Mountain, Atlanta, and Sherman's March to the Sea. After the war, he was twice elected mayor of Columbus. He died on May 2, 1898, at the age of 60.

Geertruida Wijsmuller-Meijer—The Dutch social worker, also head of Red Cross Services for Group 2000, is credited with saving thousands of Jewish children before and during the war. After the war, she helped displaced Jewish children, served on the Amsterdam City Council, and worked on numerous social projects. She has been honored all over Holland with statues and memorials. Other honors include Knight in the Order of Orange-Nassau, Medal of French Gratitude, and recognition as Righteous Among the Nations by Yad Vashem, Israel's official memorial to Holocaust victims. She died on August 30, 1978, at age 82.

BIBLIOGRAPHY

Adams, Stephen B. 1997. *Mr. Kaiser Goes to Washington.* Chapel Hill & London: The University of North Carolina Press.

Aubrac, Lucie. 2015. *Outwitting the Gestapo.* Lexington, MA: Plunkett Lake Press. Kindle Edition.

Bourneuf Jr., Gus. 1990. *Workhorse of the Fleet.* Spring, TX: American Bureau of Shipping.

Brady, Tim. 2021. *Three Ordinary Girls: The Remarkable Story of Three Dutch Teenagers Who Became Spies, Saboteurs, Nazi Assassins—and WWII Heroes.* New York NY: Citadel Press. Kindle Edition.

Brandt-Carey, Kathleen. 2016. *Knight Without Fear and Beyond Reproach: The Life of George Maduro 1916-1945.* Antwerp: Uitgeverij Unieboek | Het Spectrum bv. KOBO edition.

Briscoe, Robert, and Alden Hatch. 1958. *For the Life of Me.* Borodino Books. Kindle Edition.

Broch, Ludivine. 2016. *Ordinary Workers, Vichy and the Holocaust: (Studies in the Social and Cultural History of Modern Warfare) No. 44.* Cambridge, UK: Cambridge University Press. Kindle Edition.

Bunker, John. 1995. *Heroes in Dungarees.* Annapolis, MD: Naval Institute Press. Kindle Edition.

Cobb, Matthew. 2010. *The Resistance: The French Fight against the Nazis.* London: Pocket Books.

Cowan, Helen I. 1947. "France: Wage Trends and Wage Policies, 1938-47." *JSTOR.* August. Accessed January 09, 2022. https://www.jstor.org/stable/41831305?read-now=1&refreqid=excelsior%3Abcbee1c472f53557ffaca0be7824d98f&seq=6#page_scan_tab_contents.

cryptomuseum.com. n.d. https://cryptomuseum.com/index.htm.

David, Clayton C. 2010. *They Helped Me Escape from Amsterdam to Gibraltar in 1944.* Sunflower University Press.

2021. *Battle Stations: Liberty Convoy- The Primary Weapons in the Battle of the Atlantic.* Broadcast by Documentary HD Channel. Performed by Documentary HD Channel. https://www.youtube.com/watch?v=Zg62b8tOcpc.

dutchparisblog.com. https://dutchparisblog.com/dutch-paris-sites-in-lyon/.encyclopedia.com. n.d. https://www.encyclopedia.com.

Gallery, Daniel V. 2018. *Twenty Million Tons Under the Sea: The Daring Capture of the U-505 .* Laticlave Press. Kindle Edition.

Gardiner, Jonathan. 2021. *One-Way Ticket from Westerbork.* Amsterdam: Amsterdam Publishers. Kindle Edition.

Geroux, William (2016). *The Mathews Men: Seven Brothers and the War Against Hitler's U-boats.* Penguin Publishing Group. Kindle Edition.

Gildea, Robert. 2015. *Fighters in the Shadows.* Cambridge, MA: Harvard University Press. Kindle Edition. 2004. *Marianne in Chains: Daily Life in the Heart of France During the German Occupation.* London: Picador. Kindle Edition.

Gunn, George. 1999. *Tramp Steamers at War.* Llandysul, Ceredigion, Wales: Gomer Press.

Helgason, Gudmundur. n.d. *Uboat.net.* Accessed 2022. uboat.net.

Herbert, Brian. 2005. *The Forgotten Heroes: The Heroic Story of the United States Merchant Marine.* New York: Tom Doherty Associates. Kindle Edition.

HolocaustResearchProject.org. n.d. www.HolocaustResearchProject.org.

InternetArchive.org. n.d. https://web.archive.org/.

JSTOR. n.d. *Digital Library.* JSTOR.org.

King, David. 2011. *Death in the City of Light.* New York, NY: Crown. Kindle Edition.

Kix, Paul. 2017. *The Saboteur.* New York: HarperCollins. Kindle Edition.

Koreman, Megan. 2018. *The Escape Line.* New York: Oxford University Press. Kindle Edition.

Lee, Christopher. 2012. *Eight Bells and Top Masts: Diaries from a Tramp Steamer.* London: Faber & Faber, Kindle Edition.

Liempt, Ad van. 2005. *Hitler's Bounty Hunters: The Betrayal of the Jews.* Oxford, UK: Berg.

Major Delaforce, S.O.E. 1945. "The Case of Prosper de Zitter." *The National Archives UK.* British Intelligence Agencies. Accessed November 2021. https://discovery.nationalarchives.gov.uk/details/r/C11235019.

The Battle of the Rails. Directed by René Clément. Performed by Jean Clarieux and Jean Daurand Marcel Barnault.

McFarren, Peter, and Fadrique Iglesias. 2013. *The Devil's Agent: Life, Times and Crimes of Nazi Klaus Barbie.* Xlibris US. Kindle Edition.

Mumford, J. Gordon. 2000. *The Black Pit...and Beyond.* Renfrew, Ontario, Canada: General Store Pub. House.

Museum, Nederlands Filmmuseum (Dutch Film. n.d. *Westerbork Film (complete version).* https://www.youtube.com/watch?v=8E-IWGjbGZM.

Museum, United States Holocaust Memorial. n.d. https://collections.ushmm.org/search/.

Network Warfare History. https://warfarehistorynetwork.com/.

Ogilvie, Bruce Campbell. 2020. Kindle Edition. *Dead Reckoning: Ten Months Aboard Liberty Ships 1943-1944.* Frankfort, MI: The Chanticleer Press.

openarchives.sncf.com. http://openarchives.sncf.com/archive/e-7051.

Othen, Christopher. 2020. *The King of Nazi Paris.* London: Biteback Publishing. Kindle Edition.

Ousby, Ian. 2000. *Occupation: The Ordeal of France, 1940-1944.* New York: Cooper Square Press. Kindle Edition.

PDXScholar.library.pdx.edu. n.d. https://pdxscholar.library.pdx.edu/.

Rosenberg, Justus. 2020. *The Art of Resistance: My Four Years in the French Underground.* New York: HarperCollins. Kindle Edition.

Ross, Stew. 2021. *Where Did They Put the Gestapo Headquarters? Vol. 1.* Punta Gorda, FL: Yooper Publications.

Scharrer, Jos. 2018. *The Dutch Resistance Revealed: The Inside Story of Courage and Betrayal.* South Yorkshire, UK: Pen & Sword Books. Kindle Edition.

Scheck, Raffael. 2005. "'They Are Just Savages': German Massacres of Black Soldiers from the French Army in 1940." *The Journal of Modern History* (JSTOR) 77 (No. 2): 325—44. https://doi.org/10.1086/431817.

Smith, Meredith. 2010. "The Civilian Experience in German Occupied France, 1940-1944." *digitalcommons.conncoll.edu.* Accessed January 8, 2022. https://digitalcommons.conncoll.edu/cgi/viewcontent.cgi?article=1005&context=histhp.

Sternhell, Charles M., and Alan M. Thorndike. 1946. *Antisubmarine Warfare in World War II, OEG Report No. 51.* Operations Evaluation Group, Office of the Chief of Naval Operations, Navy Department, Washington D.C.: Columbia University Press.

tracesofwar.com. n.d. https://www.tracesofwar.com.

trouw.nl. https://www.trouw.nl/.

Unsworth, Tim. 2017. *Neighbours, Guards, Residents & Controversial Traces.* Pamphlet translated into English by Tim Unsworth, Camp Westerbork Memorial Centre, The University of Amsterdam.

van Reemst, Trudel, interview by Netherlands Documentation Project. 2004. *Netherlands Documentation Project* United States Holocaust Memorial Museum, (June 18).

Walters, Anne-Marie. 2009. *Moondrop to Gascony.* Edited by David, Introduction and notes Hewson. Wiltshire, Great Britain: Moho Books.

War, American Merchant Marine at. 2007. *US Merchant Marine in World War II.* Accessed 2022. http://www.usmm.org/ww2.html#anchor261637.

warhistoryonline.com. n.d. https://www.warhistoryonline.com/.

Whitehead, Edward "Ted" Jones. 2018. *Down Below: Reminiscences of a World War II Engine Room Merchant Seaman.* Self. Kindle Edition.

Woodhouse, Patrick. 2013. *Etty Hillesum: A Life Transformed.* London: Bloomsbury Publishing. Kindle Edition.

Woodman, Richard. 2011. *The Real Cruel Sea: The Merchant Navy in the Battle of the Atlantic, 1939—1943.* Barnsley, South Yorkshire, United Kingdom: Pen & Sword Books. Kindle Edition.

Workman, Charlie. 2010. *From Hardships to Steamships: Memoirs of a Merchant Seaman During World War II.* Ailsa, Castle Gate, Penzance, Cornwall, United Kingdom: United Writers Publications Ltd. Kindle Edition.

wwii-netherlands-escape-lines.com. https://wwii-netherlands-escape-lines.com/evasion-of-tom-applewhite/tom-got-to-freedom-the-hard-way/.youtube.com. n.d. www.youtube.com.

ACKNOWLEDGMENTS

First, I'd like to thank my publisher, Bruce Bortz, for encouraging me to keep writing when I turned in the final draft of *The Hunt for the Peggy C*. Until then, I hadn't planned on writing a sequel. Nor was I sure what my characters could do for an encore. Then, I stumbled on a book about Dutch bounty hunters chasing Jews. OK, but how would any of my characters get back into Holland and out again? And why would they want to do so? I stumbled upon another book about the British Special Operations Executive, other books about European resistance movements, and several about Liberty ships.

Out of all that, I dreamed up the first and last scenes of the book, but only a few highlights in between. What to do? Fortunately, a whole bunch of people came to my rescue with ideas, information, translations, and editing. So here are the people I'd like to thank:

My Dutch friend Marc Coolen helped me immensely with translations, historical information, and even research.

Novelist and former Random House editor Chris Evans worked with me as a development editor, helping me with suggestions on plotting, character development, and how to weave in historical background without interfering with the action.

Fellow author Matt Zullo, a retired US Navy master chief officer who served on submarines, made sure I got all the nautical lingo and descriptions right.

Several friends were kind enough to read my early drafts and offer suggestions. These include Ron Mitchell, my first editor at the University of Kentucky student newspaper and current tennis partner, and Jonathan Miller, my cousin and a non-fiction author.

And I'm always amazed at how helpful perfect strangers can be in answering my pesky questions. These include Diane Jerbi, Project Liberty Ship Inc.; Brian Boyce, Rosslare Maritime Enthusiasts; Vincent Delomenie,

SNCF public information; Marijke Nagtegaal, De Bezige Bij rights manager; Rudi van der Sluis, Stichting NDSM-Herleeft; Jane Thynne (journalist and author of *Queen High*); Ann Sebba *(Ethel Rosenberg: An American Tragedy)*; and Jehan Ashmore (*Afloat Magazine*).

Finally, I want to thank my lovely and patient wife Margo for editing everything I write and not laughing out loud.

ABOUT THE AUTHOR

John Winn Miller is an award-winning investigative reporter, foreign correspondent, editor, newspaper publisher, screenwriter, movie producer, and now a novelist.

As a foreign correspondent for The Associated Press, Miller covered wars in Beirut, Chad, and Eritrea. He traveled with Pope John Paul II, and covered such varied stories as the hijacking of the *Achille Lauro*, Mafia busts, and terrorist attacks around the Mediterranean. He briefly served as Rome bureau chief of the Wall Street Journal/Europe before returning to his hometown to work for the Lexington (Ky.) Herald-Leader.

In Lexington, Miller was part of a team of reporters that wrote a series that helped trigger educational reform in Kentucky. The series won the 1990 public service award from the Society of Professional Journalists, top honors from Investigative Reporters and Editors, the $25,000 Selden Ring award, and was a Pulitzer Prize finalist.

He was named executive editor of the Centre Daily Times (State College, Pa.) in 1996 and executive editor of the Tallahassee Democrat (a Knight Ridder newspaper like the Herald-Leader and the Centre Daily Times) in 1999. When Knight-Ridder traded papers with Gannett in 2005, Miller was named publisher of one of the newly acquired papers, The Olympian in Olympia, Wa.

After McClatchy acquired Knight Ridder, Miller helped merge most of his paper's operations with The Tacoma News-Tribune and then took early retirement in 2009.

He returned to Lexington, where he wrote screenplays and TV shows and partnered in a social media marking startup called Friends2Follow.

Miller also helped produce four independent feature films: *Hitting the Cycle* with Bruce Dern; *Armed Response*, starring Ethan Evans and Michael Gladis and three generations of Arkins—Adam, Alan, and Ayote; *Band of Robbers*, written and directed by Adam and Aaron Nee, and *Ghost in the Family*.

In September 2010, Miller was hired as publisher of the Concord (N.H.) Monitor. Two years later, he was elected to The Associated Press board of directors and selected as a juror for the Pulitzer Prizes for the second year in a row.

He retired again the next year to return home to Lexington, where he taught journalism at The University of Kentucky and Transylvania University.

Born and raised in Lexington KY, he attended Emory University in Atlanta before graduating from The University of Kentucky.

He lives in Lexington with his wife Margo, a potter and former college English teacher. Their daughter Allison Miller is an actress-screenwriter-director who most recently starred on the ABC series *A Million Little Things*.

RESCUE RUN: Capt. Jake Rogers' Daring Return to Occupied Europe is Volume Two of *The Peggy C Saga* (the first was *The Hunt for the Peggy C*).

CAN I ASK A SMALL FAVOR?

As you close the final chapter of this tale, I hope it has left you with a sense of wonder and fulfillment. If so, could you please take a moment to share your experience by leaving a review on Amazon? Your words hold immense power, not just for me as the author, but for potential readers seeking their next literary escape.

Your honest feedback fuels the momentum of this book's journey, helping new readers discover this story. With each review, you pave the path for more stories to be written and shared with others.

Thank you for your time, your support,
and for being a part of this adventure.

John Winn Miller